AT PASSION'S MERCY

"If you think I would share a bed with a common criminal, you're wrong," she said defiantly.

"I'm a most uncommon criminal, I assure you." He looked her up and down, his eyes mocking her.

Her rising indignation swept aside her fear of the highwayman. "No doubt you are considered quite a prize by your trollops back in Whitefriars," she said. "But to me, you are no better than Jem and his gang of ruffians."

The mockery left his face, and his eyes were cold now. Striding to her side, he pulled her against him. He bent her back, molding his body to hers until she could feel the strength of his long, lean thighs, the pressure of his chest against hers. "No, oh, please . . . no—"

"Since you think me no better than Jem and his men, you should know it is useless for you to beg for mercy."

His mouth covered hers . . .

HISTORICAL ROMANCE FROM PINNACLE BOOKS

LOVE'S RAGING TIDE   (381, $4.50)
by Patricia Matthews

Melissa stood on the veranda and looked over the sweeping acres of Great Oaks that had been her family's home for two generations, and her eyes burned with anger and humiliation. Today her home would go beneath the auctioneer's hammer and be lost to her forever. Two men eagerly awaited the auction: Simon Crouse and Luke Devereaux. Both would try to have her, but they would have to contend with the anger and pride of girl turned woman . . .

CASTLE OF DREAMS   (334, $4.50)
by Flora M. Speer

Meredith would never forget the moment she first saw the baron of Afoncaer, with his armor glistening and blue eyes shining honest and true. Though she knew she should hate this Norman intruder, she could only admire the lean strength of his body, the golden hue of his face. And the innocent Welsh maiden realized that she had lost her heart to one she could only call enemy.

LOVE'S DARING DREAM   (372, $4.50)
by Patricia Matthews

Maggie's escape from the poverty of her family's bleak existence gives fire to her dream of happiness in the arms of a true, loving man. But the men she encounters on her tempestuous journey are men of wealth, greed, and lust. To survive in their world she must control her newly awakened desires, as her beautiful body threatens to betray her at every turn.

EMBRACE THE FLAME

DIANA HAVILAND

PINNACLE BOOKS
WINDSOR PUBLISHING CORP.

PINNACLE BOOKS

are published by

Windsor Publishing Corp.
475 Park Avenue South
New York, NY 10016

Copyright © 1991 by Florence Hershman

First printing: May, 1991

Printed in the United States of America

Chapter One

Desire Guilford glanced quickly about her as she hurried along the dark London streets. Although night had fallen hours ago, the shadows could not hide the ugliness and squalor of the city's notorious Whitefriars district. When a scrawny cat brushed against her threadbare skirt, the dark-haired young girl started violently. Then she reminded herself that she had far more to fear than the touch of a stray cat.

Soon, perhaps within the hour, she would enter upon a new and dangerous way of life, one that might lead her to a cell in Newgate Prison, to the whipping post, or even the hangman's noose. The laws against theft in England in 1665 were brutal, and judges made little distinction between the hardened criminal and a frightened seventeen-year-old girl who had to steal to survive.

Desire could hear Old Sally's cracked voice as if the fat, greasy-haired hag were standing right beside her now.

"Ye must make a choice, my fine miss. Go lie with the men t' earn yer keep . . . or steal. Ye've been livin' off my charity long enough, girl."

"Charity, indeed!" Desire had thought indignantly. Sally didn't know the meaning of the word. When she had first found Desire wandering through Whitefriars, soon after the girl's parents had died, Sally had offered her a home. It had not taken Desire long, however, to find out what the crone had planned for her newest "boarder."

Yes, Sally had been only too happy to give the small attic room to Desire Guilford, with her long, lustrous black hair and sea-green eyes. She had questioned the girl and learned that she was still a virgin — a real prize, with high, pointed breasts, a slender waist, and long, shapely legs.

Desire, like the other girls who lived in Sally's dirty narrow house in a Whitefriars alley, was expected to sell her body to any man who paid a few shillings. When Desire refused, and proved more stubborn than Sally expected, the old woman had beaten her; but even the stinging blows of the cane had not forced her to give in.

"Ye'll pay yer board one way or another," Sally told her. "If ye won't spread them pretty legs for a man, ye'll have t' learn t'steal. And ye'd best make up yer mind fast, or ye'll be beddin' down in the nearest alley." The old woman had cackled maliciously. "And ye'll lose yer precious maidenhead fast enough out there."

Now Desire quickened her steps, shivering as the chill February wind caught at her torn skirt. She had already passed a few men who looked like good prospects for a skilled pickpocket, but she hesitated each time; even with Sally's lessons, she was still terrified of being caught stealing.

What would her parents have felt had they known that their adored, gently reared daughter would find herself faced with such a terrible prospect? Desire's father had been a respected wine merchant, her mother pretty and ladylike. But Desire reminded herself sternly that she must not think of her parents. She had to put aside all thoughts of the past, and especially of the agonies her parents had suffered during the plague that had swept through London last summer.

It was no use. She shivered, hearing again in her mind the rumbling of the carts on the cobblestone streets, the cries of "Bring out your dead!"

One of those carts had carried off her parents, two more bodies in the pile of victims. And while Desire was still dazed with grief, the creditors had descended, telling her that her house, its furnishings, the very clothes in her closets, no longer belonged to her.

Because so many of her family's friends had either fled the city or had died in the plague, Desire had no one to advise her and no way of knowing which debts were genuine and which invented. Her father had never discussed his business affairs with her; it was enough that she should know how to read and write, to embroider, and to help her mother oversee the maids in their household chores.

And so, threatened with debtors' prison by her father's creditors, Desire had fled one night shortly after her parents' deaths and had lost herself in the winding alleys and narrow streets of the city. She had been close to starvation when Old Sally had found her and had showered her with feigned sympathy.

Desire's thoughts returned to the present as she heard the pounding of hooves close behind her. She flung herself aside in time to keep from being trampled by a big grey stallion, but she lost her balance. She fell to her knees and landed in a filthy puddle. Cold slimy water splashed over her face and arms.

A moment later the rider, a tall cloaked man, swung himself down and raised her to her feet. The moon, which had emerged from behind a rack of heavy clouds, revealed his strong, arresting face beneath his wide-brimmed, plumed hat. Even now, dazed as she was by her fall, Desire caught her breath at the sight of his features, etched in the silver moonlight. She saw his dark eyes under their straight black brows, the strong line of his jaw, his jutting chin and high, angular cheekbones. Power and virility were set off by a unmistakable appearance of breeding. Desire allowed herself to rest her weight against the man's chest, and she felt the iron-hard muscles under his his flowing cloak.

"Are you hurt?" he asked.

"Only a bit shaken," she replied. But even though she was stirred by the closeness of this handsome stranger, grateful for his solicitude, she could not forget her purpose. He was well-dressed, his cloak made of fine, heavy wool and collared with thick beaver. His tall-crowned hat was in the height of fashion, and the hand that supported her arm was encased in a cuffed glove of the finest leather.

Although Desire was beginning to recover from her fall she remained leaning against him. Then, after a moment's hesi-

7

tation, she slid her hand under his cloak and found the pocket inside. Her fingers closed over a leather pouch. But although she knew well enough what her next move should be she was held back by her upbringing.

"Are you sure you're unhurt?" the man was asking. She heard the concern in his deep voice and was filled with guilt over what she was about to do.

"Yes, thank you, sir."

"Then you'd best be on your way. It's too late for a beautiful young girl to be abroad in these streets unless—" He gave her a speculative glance.

"I'm on an errand for my mistress." Even as she spoke, keeping her eyes fixed on his, her fingers drew the pouch from the inside pocket of his cloak. "I'll be going home now, sir."

With a swift movement she turned her back and then pushed the pouch down into her bodice between her breasts. A moment later she was darting off into the nearest alley. Her feet sped over the slippery cobblestones. She heard the man calling after her.

"Stop, girl! Stop, I say!"

But she only quickened her pace, losing herself in the maze of winding streets and evil-smelling courtyards. She was forced to pause at last in a narrow alley to catch her breath. She took refuge in a doorway where a lantern shed a dim light from overhead.

She had done it. She was a thief. Right now, however, she could feel only an overwhelming relief at having eluded her pursuer. She retrieved the leather pouch from her bodice and opened the strings. Her green eyes widened under her thick, black lashes as she examined her haul.

A gold watch—no, there were two watches, and each had been engraved with a different name. That was curious, Desire thought. A pair of glittering shoe buckles. Could those stones be real diamonds? Some of the king's courtiers wore such luxurious ornaments, her mother had told her. Now she drew out a magnificent necklace, an elaborate creation of large sapphires and gleaming gold.

8

She lifted the necklace up toward the dim lantern light to get a better look. What on earth would a gentleman be thinking of, to go riding about Whitefriars late at night with such a collection of valuable objects?

Why should he be there at all? she asked herself, unable to forget the tall, well-dressed stranger. Surely a gentleman in search of female companionship would go to one of the better brothels, where the girls were carefully chosen for their beauty and accomplishments. Such a thought would not have occurred to Desire a short time ago, but having heard the endless bawdy talk at Old Sally's house, she had learned something of such matters.

A moment later Desire went rigid with fear as the door of the tall, narrow tenement creaked open. A huge, shaggy-haired man in a leather jerkin stepped out of the shadowy hallway to confront her. His hand closed around her wrist in a brutal grip.

"What ye got here, my lovely? Been out shoppin' in Goldsmiths Row this time o' night, have ye?"

When Desire did not answer, he twisted her wrist. She cried out as a sharp pain shot up her arm. The man jerked the pouch out of her hand, took the necklace from her, and stuffed it back inside with the rest of the valuables. Now a man with light, unkempt hair emerged from the doorway, and following him, a barrel-chested ruffian with a scar that ran down the side of his face from cheek to jaw. Desire gagged at the overpowering stench of raw spirits, unwashed male bodies, and dirt-encrusted clothes.

"We're in luck tonight," said the man who had taken the pouch. He stuffed it into his leather jerkin. "Found ourselves a real windfall without doin' a bit of work."

"This wench looks to be a windfall all by herself, Jem," said the light-haired man. He had a narrow face and eyes like slits.

"A rare tasty morsel," the scarred man agreed.

"So she is," said the man who still grasped her wrist. His grin showed jagged yellow teeth. "Come along, girl, and we'll talk business."

9

"I have no business with you. Let me go."

"Why, a pretty creature like yerself, who can lift a pouch full of fine trinkets, could be useful to us. We'll buy ye a dram t' warm yer insides and then we'll have a chat."

The light-haired man gave a short, ugly laugh. "We could warm her up right here, Jem," he said. He licked his lips in anticipation, his tongue darting like a lizard's. Desire stiffened with revulsion. She knew that Whitefriars was a sanctuary of thieves and murderers, where criminals were left to their own devices. Even a constable would not dare to invade this dangerous area.

Jem pushed her up against the wall of the narrow building. It would be useless to cry out for help, for no one was likely to come to her aid. In desperation, she kicked out and caught Jem on the shin. He swore but he did not let her go. Instead, he pulled her against him. She smelled his foul breath and felt the hard bulge of his engorged organ against her thigh.

"Behave yerself and we might let ye keep one o' them trinkets. If ye can pleasure us here and now—"

"Oh, she'll pleasure us right enough," said the scar-faced man.

"No! I've never lain with a man, I swear it! I've never—"

Jem and his companions whooped with obscene laughter. "A virgin, are ye? I'll teach ye all ye need t' know," said Jem, "an' have ye beggin' for more. Rare fine teacher, I am, when the girl's so young an'—get a look at these tits!" Jem grasped one of Desire's breasts in his free hand. She felt a mounting terror at the pressure of his hot fingers as they dug into her flesh through her worn bodice.

Again she kicked, but this time Jem was ready for her. He grasped her ankle and she fell to the wet, dirty stones of the alley. The moonlight scarcely penetrated the narrow space between the two rows of crumbling houses. She felt engulfed, smothered by the darkness around her.

"I want a go at her too," she heard one of the others say.

"When I've had my fill," Jem retorted. He was kneeling over her now, fumbling with his breeches, setting free his huge member. Even though she knew it was useless, Desire heard herself screaming again and again. Jem struck her a hard, backhanded blow that caught her on the side of the head. A glittering shower of sparks danced before her eyes, but her screams went on and on, fueled by some primitive instinct.

Jem forced her legs apart and knelt between them. His hand moved swiftly to explore her rounded thighs. He tore at the worn dress, and she felt the chill damp air against the smooth flesh of her belly. He found her soft triangle, with its dark, downy covering, and now his hard, probing fingers explored her most private parts. She writhed, sickened and horrified at this cruel invasion.

She heard Jem's harsh breathing, and then another, more distant sound — the pounding of a horse's hooves, moving at a gallop. The hoofbeats were growing louder now.

Raising her head, she looked over Jem's shoulder, past his crouching body, and saw the cloaked rider who spurred his mount down the alley. He was heading directly for her and Jem. Then Jem's weight lifted off her, and he raised himself to his feet.

His voice was hoarse as he buttoned his breeches. "What the devil do ye want here?" he demanded. When the rider made no answer, Jem went on, "This don't concern ye. Get about yer business."

But the cloaked rider had reined to a stop a few feet away, and he remained motionless, looking down at Desire and her captors. In the dull lantern light, Desire recognized the hard jaw, high cheekbones, and dark eyes; the fur-collared cloak and wide-brimmed hat left no doubt as to the intruder's identity. The man's eyes narrowed, moving from her to the three men who surrounded her.

"I'll not warn ye again," Jem said. "Mind yer business or ye'll wish ye had."

"This *is* my business. The wench there stole my property. Toss me my pouch, if you please, and I'll be on my way." He spoke quietly, with the accents of a gentleman, but Desire heard the clash of steel in his tone.

"I don't know about any pouch," Jem said. "This here's a

11

common trollop. We paid 'er fer our pleasure an' now she's turned skittish. Got t' be taught a lesson."

The mounted man drew a flintlock pistol from his belt. "I want the pouch. Now."

"If ye fire on us ye can't be sure of not hittin' the wench," said Jem. He pulled Desire to her feet and thrust her against the light-haired man. "Hold 'er, Bert."

Bert's arm shot out, closing around Desire's throat in a stranglehold. She struggled, fighting for breath.

"Unless ye want t' take a chance on killin' such a good lookin' little—"

"To hell with her. Toss me the pouch. I won't ask again."

Jem hesitated, his eyes fixed on the unwavering hand that held the pistol.

"Take it, then, and be damned!" Jem snarled. He reached into his jerkin and threw the leather pouch to the mounted man, who caught it deftly in his free hand.

"Don't leave me here with these men—" Desire could scarcely force out the words because of Bert's iron grip against her throat.

Even as she made her frantic plea, the cloaked man was turning his horse, a difficult maneuver in the alley, where two rows of house had been built so close together they appeared to meet overhead. Only the most skilled rider could have managed such a feat of horsemanship. Now he cantered off, apparently satisfied with the return of his property.

He's going to leave me here . . . Desire was swept by a wave of despair. *He believes what Jem said. He thinks I'm a common trollop—*

Now that Jem and the others had been deprived of the valuable loot, they would surely treat her with even greater brutality than she might otherwise have expected. She sagged against Bert's arm, hoping that she might lose consciousness and be spared the full awareness of what was about to happen to her.

Suddenly she heard an outraged protest from Jem. She raised her head and her eyes widened. The rider, having reached the open space beyond the mouth of the alley, wheeled his powerful stallion about and was now galloping back at full speed. She heard him shout, "Let her go!"

Bert's grip loosened as he dodged aside.

"Over here, girl," the rider commanded. Desire stumbled forward on unsteady legs. She reached up to catch his proffered arm, and an instant later he swung her up into the saddle in front of him.

The narrow alley, the crumbling buildings on either side, whirled and danced in her blurred sight. Too dazed to do more than clutch at the pommel of the saddle, Desire let herself lean back against the man's powerfully muscled, ironhard chest. She breathed the odors of leather, brandy, and another more intimate, masculine scent that she found strangely unsettling. The pounding of the stallion's hooves rang in her ears as they left the alley.

To her surprise the man appeared to have no difficulty in finding his way through the maze of Whitefriars streets. How could a gentleman be so familiar with this notorious district, this squalid enclave that served as a refuge for debtors, forgers, sneak thieves, and highwaymen? No peace officer dared enter these precincts, and even the warrant of the chief justice of England could not be carried out here without the aid of a company of well-armed dragoons. Yet Desire's rescuer, with his fine clothes, his well-bred speech, and aristocratic air, was obviously untroubled by his surroundings.

For the first time since he had lifted her into his saddle, she felt a stirring of uneasiness. But she was still too shaken to examine the cause of her misgivings.

Having left Jem and his companions far behind, the rider slowed his mount to a trot. Desire still trembled with her reaction to all that had happened within the past few hours. Her rescuer, feeling the quivering of her body against his, spoke softly. "Don't be afraid. They won't follow us."

She relaxed slightly. Then, remembering what Jem had said about her, she spoke unsteadily. "I want you to know, I'm not a trollop."

"Only a common pickpocket."

Desire stiffened, angered by the amusement in the man's

voice.

"That's a lie! I've never robbed anyone before!"

The man laughed softly. She turned her head to look at him and saw that his dark eyes were regarding her with sardonic humor. "I can well believe that," he said. "You're obviously unskilled at your chosen profession."

Looking up at him she was stirred, in spite of herself, by the virile power of his moon-silvered features. His strong, sensual lips were parted in a teasing smile. She fought against her growing attraction, for his words had aroused her hot temper. But it would be useless to try to convince him that she had turned thief only out of desperation. Why should he believe her when he knew nothing about her?

Then she thought again of the terrible punishments meted out to thieves, and she went taut with fear. "You have your property back," she said. "Let me go now."

He did not answer but spurred his horse to a faster gait. They rode on in silence, Desire's fears mounting with every beat of the horse's hooves. Now she realized that they were only a few streets away from Old Sally's house. The shabby little shops were closed, but the taverns were filled, their doors swinging open as drunken men and their doxies went in or came stumbling out.

He drew rein before a shop where some of Old Sally's boarders bought their bedraggled, second-hand finery. Drawing out the pouch, he swiftly examined its contents. "All here."

"Then you won't turn me over to the constables, sir? Please, let me down. I'll go straight home. You'll never see me again."

"Home?" One dark brow shot up. "And where might that be?"

Desire could not frame the answer. If she went back to Old Sally's house empty-handed, the hag would toss her into the streets again. But where else could she go?

"Speak up, girl. I've wasted too much time already." But his eyes narrowed in a long, appraising look and his arms tightened around her waist. "Under other circumstances, the

14

prospect of dallying with you would be tempting, but at the moment I have more urgent business."

He released his hold on her and dismounted. "I won't be long," he said. "I'd advise you to stay where you are."

Remembering Jem and his men, panic shot through her. "Don't leave me."

He made an impatient gesture, then pulled his pistol from his belt and cocked it. "Do you know how to use this?"

"I've never even held one."

He thrust the weapon into her hand. "If anyone tries to molest you — or to steal the horse — let him get a look at this. You probably won't have to shoot it."

Before she could protest he left her. Although the front of the shop was shuttered, he went around to the side door and knocked with the handle of his whip. The door opened and he disappeared inside.

Desire clutched the heavy pistol with one hand, keeping the other on the pommel. What sort of business did the man have in such a place at this hour? Then she remembered that one of Old Sally's girls had said the used clothes shop carried on another trade, a far more lucrative one; the proprietor was a receiver of stolen goods.

Desire's eyes widened. Since her first meeting with the stranger she had wondered at his presence here. Now she wondered no longer. The peculiar contents of his pouch, his ease with a pistol . . . all was plain to her.

She gave a start as she saw him emerging from the shop. His "business" had not taken long. No doubt the owner knew him well, and perhaps also knew it would be useless to dicker over prices with such a man.

He reached her in a few swift strides, retrieved his pistol, and mounted again. "Now tell me where you want to go. Or shall I leave you to wander around here alone?"

"I have no home — not really. Old Sally gave me shelter after my parents died in the plague. She forced me to choose between whoring or thieving. If I go back now without means to pay my board, she'll turn me away."

For a moment the man was silent, his dark eyes thought-

15

ful. Then he said, "It looks as if I've taken on more than I bargained for when I came after my loot."

"Then it is true! You are no better than I am."

"Not in the moral sense. But I'm certainly more practiced at my trade." His strong, sensual lips curved in a slight smile, and his black eyes glinted.

"Then you can't turn me over to the law."

"Under the circumstances, that would be somewhat impractical, Mistress—"

"Guilford. Desire Guilford."

She felt the motion of his powerful chest as he drew a long breath. "Desire." His voice was deep and husky now. "That suits you." His eyes moved over her slowly, caressingly, lingering on her delicate features before going to the long line of her throat, the fullness of her high, pointed breasts.

She spoke quickly. "You know my name but you haven't told me yours."

"Morgan Trenchard at your service, Mistress Desire."

Never had anyone spoken her name in that deep, compelling tone. She heard the passion in it, the hunger. The man was dangerous, she knew, but although she felt uneasy, she was aware of another, stronger sensation—a swift, tingling that began in the pit of her stomach, that moved along her thighs and spread to every nerve of her body.

Morgan Trenchard was a stranger, a criminal, and she knew that every moment she spent with him increased her peril. How could she allow herself to give way to these unfamiliar feelings that threatened to overwhelm her good sense?

A moment later two brawling drunks stumbled out of the doorway of the nearest tavern, followed by a shouting crowd, urging them on. The uproar broke the spell, and Morgan Trenchard spurred his horse to a gallop. Desire felt an instant's relief, but it disappeared as she thought that he probably planned to take her to a more deserted spot and then . . . What would he do with her? Had he rescued her from Jem and the others only to take his pleasure with her himself?

Then all thought was swept away, for Desire had to concentrate on keeping her balance, steadying herself against

16

him as they sped through the night.

She was free from Old Sally, but now she was a captive of this ruthless man. She kept her eyes fixed straight ahead, as if she could pierce the shadows and glimpse her own future, but all she could see were the dark clouds, wind-driven across the sky, the occasional fugitive rays of moonlight dappling the road that stretched on and on before her.

Chapter Two

They rode through the city gates, and soon London was far behind them. Morgan spurred the horse at a steady gallop, slackening the pace only when they reached a tree-lined high road that bisected the main thoroughfare of a small outlying town.

"Where are we?" Desire asked.

"This is Stepney," he told her.

She looked about and could not see the gleam of a single light in any of the small shops that lined the street. Even so, she knew what she must do.

"You've got to let me go now," she began.

"Go where? It's past midnight."

"I don't care." Her voice shook slightly with the desperation she felt. "I'll seek a deserted barn, a haystack—anywhere I can rest until morning."

"And what will you do then?"

"I'll find employment. Surely in a small town like this one—"

"What skills do you have? I'm afraid your training as a pickpocket leaves much to be desired."

"I was speaking of respectable employment." Her voice was tight with anger. No matter what the circumstances of their meeting, surely Morgan Trenchard must have sensed that she was no common thief. "I can—"

But indeed, what *had* she been trained to do? Her father had taught her to read and write, and although she had found needlework boring, she had tried to please her mother by learning to embroider. She could play a few tunes on the

18

harpsicord and the dulcimer. A dancing master had taught her the intricate steps of the saraband, the gavotte and the minuet.

Would those accomplishments help her to get a post as a governess? Probably not, for she was too young for such responsibilities, and she had no letters of reference. What father would entrust his daughters to the care of an unknown girl who appeared at his door wearing a torn, soiled dress?

"There are shops here," she said, trying to sound more confident than she felt. "Surely they are in need of workers—"

"This isn't London," Morgan told her. "In these small country towns, a shopkeeper's wife and children help him. Or he can take his choice of the local girls."

"I'll be a servant if I must."

"Scrubbing floors and emptying chamberpots? Fighting off all those amorous footmen—and perhaps the master himself?"

"That's no concern of yours. Once you let me go—"

"You might run to the nearest constable and inform on me."

"I wouldn't. I promise . . ."

Morgan did not reply, but instead he spurred his horse to a gallop once more.

She thought of screaming for help, but she knew it would be useless. If she roused the town, what good would it do her? Morgan was a criminal, and even now the king's dragoons might be searching for him. Who would believe that she was his captive, and not his doxy? Perhaps she would be accused of aiding him in his recent robbery.

Morgan Trenchard's doxy. Such a thought, frightening though it was, intrigued her too. All at once she was keenly aware of the man's closeness, the strength of his powerful arms holding her steady in the saddle. She remembered how easily he had lifted her from her feet back there in the Whitefriars alley, while he had controlled the huge stallion with his muscular thighs. At the memory, she felt an unfamiliar warmth stirring deep within her.

She heard the tremor in her voice as she asked him:

19

"Where are you taking me now?"

"You'll find out soon enough," he replied. "I can promise you a meal, when we reach our destination. And a warm bed for the rest of the night."

Morgan's talk of a meal was most welcome, for Desire's healthy appetite had not been satisfied by the meager portion of bread and cheese grudgingly provided by Old Sally hours ago. But his mention of a warm bed filled her with misgivings, for she was sure that he intended to share the bed with her.

They left Stepney behind, and now they were riding down a narrow dirt road with branches of towering oaks interlaced overhead, shutting out the night sky. Desire heard a rippling of a nearby stream, the movement of small, nocturnal animals in the underbrush. Because she had grown up in London, she found this isolation frightening.

Her body ached with the strain of the long ride, and her taut muscles were beginning to throb when, at last, they reached a clearing in the woods. She could make out the dark, irregular shape of a large farmhouse, with a few outbuildings nearby. Surely there would be people here, and perhaps one of them might be persuaded to help her get away from Morgan.

But as they drew closer her heart sank, for even at this hour of the night she could see the unmistakable signs of long neglect. When the wind-driven clouds parted, the moonlight revealed the fields, overgrown with a tangle of weeds, and the broken chimneys and smashed windows of the house. Part of the roof was missing, and the remaining portion sagged dangerously.

"No one lives here," she said.

"I do—for now," Morgan told her. "It is a convenient hiding place."

"But suppose the rightful owner should return—"

Morgan drew rein so abruptly that Desire was jolted forward. He swung himself down and stood looking up at her. She saw that his strong, sensuous lips were set, and that his dark eyes held an icy anger. "The rightful owner, and his

20

family, won't be coming back. They were slaughtered by Cromwell's soldiers. The farmer's wife and daughters were ravished first, while the man was forced to look on. That's what is said in these parts, at any rate."

Desire caught her breath in horror and revulsion. Although she had led a sheltered life, even she had overheard servants' gossip about the terrible depredations of the Puritan forces.

"That sort of violence was not uncommon during the war," said Morgan, his voice carefully expressionless. "But the villagers hereabouts give this place wide berth, for they believe it is haunted."

"No doubt that's all to the good, so far as you are concerned," Desire said sharply.

Morgan did not answer. He lifted her from the saddle and for a moment she swayed, her legs too cramped to support her. He put his arm around her, while using his free hand to grasp the reins and lead the stallion to a nearby stable. Desire leaned against a splintery wall and watched as he rubbed the animal down and gave it oats and water.

"The beast has earned his keep," he said over his shoulder. "He served me well tonight."

Then, having finished seeing to the horse's needs, he led Desire from the stable, across the high, damp grass and up to the door of the farmhouse. She hesitated before entering, for she could not forget what Morgan had told her about the fate of the former inhabitants.

How many families had been slaughtered, their homes left in ruins, during the Civil War? After the capture and execution of Charles I by Cromwell's Puritan forces, the tide of battle had swept across England. The handsome young heir to the Stuart throne, along with a party of his Royalist supporters, had been forced to flee the country and had taken refuge on the Continent, but the war had raged on, with Roundheads and Cavaliers locked in combat.

In 1653, Oliver Cromwell, scorning to take the royal title, had accepted the title "Lord Protector" instead, and had proceeded to change the face of England. Desire had spent her childhood in a country in which the most harmless pleasures were forbidden by law. The traditional Maypole dance, the festivities marking Christmas, even the yule log and the mistletoe were banished. Theaters were closed, for the Puritans had seen them as headquarters of the devil and his minions.

It had been a grim and dreary time for the English, and they had welcomed the restoration of the monarchy in 1660. Desire remembered the enthusiastic crowds that had filled the London streets to celebrate the coronation of Charles II. How excited she had been on that sunlit May afternoon as she had watched the dashing Charles Stuart enter the city after his fifteen years of exile. She had thrilled to the pealing of the bells, the booming of the great cannons.

The city's fountains ran with wine that day, and Desire glowed with pride, knowing that her father had provided his share from his great warehouses near the river. "Fine for business," her father had remarked, but Desire knew that the coronation of the new king meant far more to him. Both her parents had always been loyal to the Stuarts, and she had often heard her mother warning her father to guard his speech and hide his true feelings during Cromwell's reign.

"Come inside." Morgan's voice brought Desire back to the present with a start. "Unless you believe the house to be haunted."

Desire followed him inside, and the scarred oak door creaked shut behind them. Morgan lit a candle and led the way down a hall to the rear of the house. Desire caught a glimpse of a room that must have served as the parlor, with its high-backed chairs and mildewed window curtains. A tall cupboard that had once been the pride of the farmer's wife, no doubt, now stood empty and festooned with cobwebs. She shuddered, remembering what Morgan had told her about the women who had lived here. No, she did not believe in ghosts, but an icy chill enveloped her nonetheless.

As if sensing her feelings, Morgan pressed her hand and said, "The kitchen's this way. I'll build a fire and have you warm soon enough."

Desire was surprised and moved by his concern. Once inside the large kitchen with its beamed ceiling, she watched while he got the fire started in the wide stone hearth. The flames soon leaped up, and she moved closer, taking comfort from the warmth. Realizing how badly her dress had been torn during her struggle with Jem and his men, she tugged at the bodice to try to cover her shoulders. She could do nothing about the long jagged tear that ran halfway up her skirt.

Fortunately, Morgan was too busy to look at her closely. He took a loaf of bread and part of a ham from one of the cupboards, then got down a large bottle from another. Obviously familiar with his surroundings, he had no difficulty in finding a couple of pewter tankards, a long knife and two-pronged fork.

He used a corner of his cloak to dust a space on one of the long benches flanking the heavy table. Then, giving Desire a half-mocking bow, he said, "Will you be seated, my lady?"

She sank wearily onto the bench, while Morgan, having tossed his cloak and plumed hat onto a nearby settle, took a seat opposite her. She needed all her willpower to remember her manners, for she was famished. Although she was thirsty, too, she hesitated before tasting the contents of her tankard.

"It's the best French brandy," Morgan told her. "Drink it down and it will soon take the chill from your bones."

Although Desire's father, as a wine merchant, had sold brandy, he had never allowed her more than a single glass of sweet sherry. "A suitable drink for a young lady," he had called it.

But now she heard Morgan urging, "Drink up," and she obeyed. She coughed and her eyes watered, but the powerful brandy sent a welcome warmth to her insides and then to the tips of her chilled fingers and toes. She felt relaxed all at once—even a little lightheaded.

"Such brandy should be served in fine glasses," Morgan said, "to do justice to the bouquet."

"My father dealt in wines," Desire retorted.

"And no doubt you emptied many a bottle over dinner," he said, his dark eyes teasing her.

"Certainly not. Papa never permitted me to—" All at once

Desire was seized with sadness, remembering the care with which her parents had raised her, their loving plans for her future. She turned her face away to hide her grief. A moment later Morgan's hand closed around hers.

"Don't," he said. "It doesn't do to look back, Desire. Here we are, with a warm fire and the finest brandy money can buy—"

Desire jerked her hand away from his.

"Did you buy it?" The drink had loosened her tongue so that she blurted out her thoughts without hesitation. "More likely you stole it from the home of a gentleman."

"I bought it with the gold I . . . acquired . . . from a fat-bellied lout who was traveling to London by coach. Since he was carrying so much excess weight of his own, I thought it a kindness to relieve him of his heavy purse." Morgan's white teeth flashed as he laughed.

"You *are* a highwayman." He might be more skilled at thievery than she was, but he was a common criminal all the same.

Only a few months before, Desire would have made no distinctions between the various kinds of criminals who infested London's teeming underworld; but now she remembered how Belle, one of Old Sally's girls, had described the hanging of "Gentleman Johnny Burke," one of that notorious breed.

"Ye should've seen 'm," Belle had said with undisguised admiration in her eyes. "There 'e was, Gentleman Johnny, 'imself, ridin' from Newgate to Tyburn lookin' like a bridegroom on 'is way to church. I was lucky. Found myself a place right close to the scaffold. Such a fine speech 'e made, smilin' an' blowin' kisses to the ladies, brave as ye please."

The rest of the girls had murmured approvingly, and even Old Sally had cackled, her broken teeth showing in a grin. " 'E was a game one, like all his breed," she had said.

In Whitefriars, a highwayman was a commanding figure, feared by the men and sought after by the women. But although Desire had been stirred by Morgan's touch, she knew that she was in danger here with him.

I must get away — and quickly . . .

She stood up, her small, slender body poised for flight. What was wrong? She felt the floor shifting under her feet, felt her head reel. She should never have drunk all that brandy. She drew a deep breath to steady herself. The heat of the fire only increased her dizziness. She fixed her eyes on a heavy door at one end of the room, and then she made a dash for it. She tugged it open, but instead of finding herself outdoors, she realized that she was in another passageway.

In desperation she plunged forward into the darkness until she stumbled over a loose board. Before she could regain her balance, Morgan was at her side, his steely fingers gripping her arm.

"Where the devil do you think you're off to?"

"Outside this house, anywhere, so long as I'm away from you, Morgan Trenchard!"

His eyes narrowed to onyx slits. "You'll go nowhere until I'm ready to set you free." He lifted her into his arms. She struggled fiercely, and even when his grasp tightened, cutting off her breath, she went on twisting, kicking, trying to claw at his face.

He swore softly, then threw her over his shoulder. Her head spun dizzily as he carried her back to the kitchen. When he set her down, she had to grasp at the edge of the table to keep her balance.

A moment later she saw that he was pulling a wide pallet out of one of the cupboards. He threw it down in front of the fire and unrolled it. "We'll sleep warm tonight, as I promised you," he said. "My cloak's wide enough to serve as a coverlet for both of us."

"If you think I would share a bed with a common criminal, you're wrong."

"I'm a most uncommon criminal, I assure you." He looked her up and down, his eyes mocking her. "I suspect you have never shared a bed with any man, Mistress Desire."

"I have not —"

He laughed softly. "Then how can you be sure you won't enjoy the experience? It all depends on the man, of course."

25

Her rising indignation swept aside her fear of the highwayman. "No doubt you are considered quite a prize by your trollops back in Whitefriars," she said. "But to me, you are no better than Jem and his gang of ruffians."

The mockery left his face, and his eyes were cold now. Striding to her side, he pulled her against him. He bent her back, molding his body to hers until she could feel the strength of his long, lean thighs, the pressure of his chest crushing her breasts. "No, oh, please . . . no—"

"Since you think me no better than Jem and his men, you should know it is useless for you to beg for mercy."

His mouth covered hers and she stiffened, bracing herself to endure the violence she was sure he would inflict on her. Then his warm lips brushed hers lightly, leaving her surprised and bewildered. His fingers slid into the shining ebony waves of her hair, stroking softly.

His tenderness aroused a swift response, and she knew that her hands were moving, as if with a will of their own. She felt a new excitement as she clutched at the hard muscles of his back. "Morgan, please . . ." But she was no longer certain what she was asking of him.

"My sweet Desire," he whispered, his voice deep, husky. His tongue parted her lips, and then slowly, lingeringly, he began to explore the warm moist velvet within. Her own tongue came up to meet his, as if in a primitive dance. She breathed deeply, inhaling the scent of brandy and leather and another—clean, masculine, and all his own.

He drew her down on the pallet, then pushed her torn bodice from her shoulders. His hand cupped her breast, and she sank back, lulled by the heat of the fire. But a more powerful blaze stirred to life within her. She felt its sparks whirling along every nerve of her slender young body.

Morgan bent his dark head and his mouth touched the pointed nipple. She gave a little, wordless cry of protest as he drew the silken peak between his lips. Feeling as if she were lying at the edge of a high and unknown precipice, she tried to turn her body away.

When she moved, the rip in her skirt revealed one of her

legs, as far up as the thigh. A moment later Morgan's hand touched the long, delicate curve. Instinctively she drew her legs together.

"Are you afraid, my love?"

She tried to speak, but the words would not come.

"You must not fear me," he said tenderly. "I won't force you to yield against your will."

His fingers, light and caressing, went on with their exploration. Now he was parting her thighs, and she did not try to stop him.

But all at once his muscles tightened. He lifted himself from her with one swift movement. His head turned as if listening to a faraway sound.

"Morgan, what is it?"

"Be quiet."

He got to his feet, and now she could hear it too: the pounding of horses' hooves coming toward the farmhouse at a gallop.

Desire's awakening ecstasy gave way to a surge of icy terror. She was sure that, in a few moments she and Morgan would be confronted by the king's dragoons. What would she do? Even if she pleaded that she had not accompanied Morgan here of her own free will, why should the soldiers believe her?

Terrifying visions rose up in her mind. A filthy cell in Newgate. A judge whose eyes showed no spark of pity or understanding. Then the scaffold on Tyburn Hill.

"Morgan —"

He silenced her with a gesture. Pistol in hand, he moved across the room with the light, noiseless tread of a jungle cat. She watched as he disappeared into the hallway leading to the front of the house. Crouching on the pallet, she drew her bodice around her, trying to do up the buttons.

Then she heard Morgan's voice. "Niall. Enoch. You made good speed."

These were not the dragoons she had feared, and she was able to draw a deep breath again. The men came tramping into the kitchen. She leaned forward to hear what they were saying.

". . . we made a good haul . . ."

". . . rode like the devil was after us . . ."

". . . that damn mare of mine nearly stumbled coming across the bridge . . ."

Morgan came in first, followed by two others. One was a stocky fellow, his unfashionably short brown hair touched with grey. His round, placid face belied his desperate calling, Desire thought; he might have been an ordinary farmer. The other, tall and thin, had light grey eyes. He turned them on Desire with such a fierce look that she shrank back instinctively.

Morgan held out his hand and helped her to rise. "Mistress Guilford, may I present my associates." He gestured toward the stocky, round-faced man. "This is Enoch Hodges." Then he indicated the tall, thin one, saying: "And he is Niall Forret." He might have been performing the introductions at a court ball.

"Have you lost your wits, Trenchard?" Niall Forret demanded. "What right had you to bring your trollop to this place?"

"Guard your tongue. Mistress Guilford is a lady."

"Call her what you will. She should not be here."

"Are you questioning my right to make the decisions for all of us?" Although Morgan did not raise his voice, Desire heard the unmistakable ring of authority.

"Easy, Morgan," said Enoch Hodges. "You give the orders, we understand that. But was it wise to reveal our hiding place to an outsider?"

"Mistress Guilford and I met under unusual circumstances," Morgan said. "She was embarking on a new profession, and her daring exceeded her skill. I could not leave her where I found her, so I was obliged to bring her along."

He gave Desire a mocking half-smile before turning to Niall Forret. "You both must be hungry. Sit yourselves down and we will see if Mistress Guilford is capable of making herself useful. From what I understand, she has been trained in the womanly arts."

Desire stared at him in bewilderment. "Get plates for these gentlemen," he ordered.

"This matter's not been settled yet," Forret said. "You've a right to indulge yourself with these wenches back in London, but where you bring one of them here, that's different, *Squire* Trenchard."

Morgan's voice was hard, his eyes burning with barely controlled violence. "You're not to call me that, Forret. Not ever. As for Mistress Guilford, she stays as long as I choose to keep her here."

"And when you're finished with her?" Forret persisted.

Morgan shrugged. "I'll dispose of her in my own time and in my own way."

Desire's temper flared. What kind of man was Morgan Trenchard, to kiss a woman, embrace her, and then to speak as if she were a possession, with no control over her own future? Her anger gave way to self-hatred when she remembered that she had been ready to offer herself to him willingly.

Enoch sat down at the table, and after a moment's hesitation, Niall joined him. Desire went about setting their places, but even as she put down two tankards and poured the brandy she could scarcely manage to keep her hands steady.

Her other emotions gave way before an icy tide of fear. How did a highwayman like Morgan Trenchard dispose of a woman when he was finished with her?

Chapter Three

"We ride out tonight," Morgan said.

Desire's body tensed in rising panic. During the two nights she had spent in the farmhouse she had tried to make herself as inconspicuous as possible, all the while waiting for a chance to escape. But now, with Morgan's unexpected announcement, she knew she could wait no longer.

She glanced at the men, who were seated around the table. Then, putting down a heavy iron pot she had been cleaning with a mixture of sand and fuller's earth, she began to move toward the kitchen door. Her heart pounded in her chest.

If only she could slip out through the back door without drawing attention to herself, she would have a chance. Once outside, she would make a dash for the wooded stretch beyond the meadow.

Now, while Niall and Enoch listened to Morgan's orders, surely they would not notice her. In any case, she had to take the risk.

"There'll be a private coach crossing the heath after dark," Morgan was saying. "Sir Hugh Bodine and his guests are bound for London. They'll want to reach the city before dark, no doubt. But unfortunately for them, one of His Lordship's footmen will discover a break in a wheel. The man will go off in search of the nearest wheelwright, but he won't return until dusk."

"If the footman keeps his part of the bargain," Niall interrupted.

"He will," Morgan said. "If he knows what's good for him. It will be near on midnight when the coach reaches the stretch of road below Blackthorn Bluff."

"What if Sir Hugh and his friends decide to spend the night at the inn?" Niall asked. Desire sensed that the man was doing all he could to find fault with Morgan's carefully laid plan.

"Bodine is to attend a court ball tomorrow night. He and his friends won't want to offend His Majesty by their absence," Morgan said calmly.

Desire was surprised by the extent of Morgan's information. She had assumed that a highwayman need only wait in the darkness to pounce on his prey. Obviously, there was far more to the infamous trade than she had thought.

"His Lordship's one of the king's friends, then?" Enoch put in.

Morgan's lips tightened. "So I was told." Desire heard the bitterness behind his casual words. Had Morgan favored Cromwell and the Puritan cause during the recent war?

She reminded herself sternly that this was no time to brood about Morgan Trenchard's political sympathies. With any luck, she'd soon be far away. She would never see the tall, dark-eyed highwayman again.

Carefully, she continued her progress toward the door. Once she was free of Morgan and his men, she would head for Stepney, where someone would surely be willing to offer her honest work. Better to be a serving wench in a tavern than a prisoner of these lawless creatures.

"We'll leave here at moonrise," Morgan was saying.

Niall interrupted again. "And what do we do with her?" He jerked his head in Desire's direction.

She had all she could do to keep back a cry of despair. Only a few more feet and she'd have reached the door. Now, turning her back on the men, she opened one of the cupboards, and pretended to be going over the supplies.

"Leave her to me," Morgan told him.

Niall's thin lips tightened. "We have, these past two nights. And no doubt you've had good sport with her. But when you propose to let her stay here, unguarded, you're risking my neck and Enoch's as well. What if your fancy piece waits until

31

we're gone and goes running to turn us over to the law?"

Desire's face burned at Niall's words. He was wrong in his assumption that she was Morgan's mistress, but he could not know that. Since the arrival of the other two men, Morgan had only made use of her services as a skivvy, preparing meals and cleaning up afterward.

Although Niall and Enoch had bedded down in the passageway, leaving the kitchen to Morgan and Desire at night, he had found himself another pallet. He had slept apart from her, with the whole width of the huge fireplace separating them, and although he could have pounced on her in the night and taken her by force, he had not chosen to do so.

All the same, she could scarcely blame Niall for believing that she was Morgan's doxy. Both Enoch and Niall treated her as if she were Morgan's property, and neither man had shown the slightest inclination to make advances to her.

When Morgan had ridden out alone to gather information about Sir Hugh Bodine and his party, he had placed her in Enoch's care, with the warning that she was not to be left unguarded even for a moment. To her surprise, the stocky, sandy-haired fellow had been unexpectedly decent, even when he had accompanied her on her necessary trips to the privy behind the house. He had waited outside the ramshackle wooden structure, and when she emerged, there he was, leaning against the nearby oak tree, whittling a stick and humming tunelessly to himself.

He always took her arm to escort her back along the overgrown path leading to the kitchen, but his touch was respectful. Sometimes he talked about the probability of an early spring, or said what a shame it was that such good farmland should be so neglected.

She knew that he was trying to ease her embarassment at having a man go with her on so personal an errand, and she was grateful. Somehow, she sensed that she had little to fear from Enoch Hodges.

Niall, however, frightened her. He did not eye her with lust—she would have hated that, but it would not have surprised her. Instead, he watched her with cold resentment. 'He looks as if he'd like to strangle me with his bare hands," she thought. But what reason did he have for feeling that way?

Now, unable to keep up her pretense of examining the cupboard any longer, she turned around. Niall was leaning forward, gripping the handle of his tall pewter tankard, his eyes narrow with tension.

"Don't be a fool, Morgan," he was saying. "If we leave the wench behind tonight, what's to stop her from running off to the nearest magistrate to give evidence against us?"

"I've told you before, Mistress Desire's my concern."

"The devil she is! A word from her could put a noose around my neck."

"I'll make sure she doesn't betray us." Morgan's cold, expressionless tone sent a shiver of apprehension through Desire's body.

"You never should've brought her here in the first place," Niall said, his eyes raking her with contempt. "There are enough whores in London to slake any man's lust."

Morgan said nothing, and the other man went on recklessly. "But they're not good enough for you, are they? A fine gentleman like you wants this delicate morsel, with her airs and graces."

Desire wished she could make herself invisible. If only she'd attempted to escape sooner.

"Now you've had your way with her, you're ordering Enoch and me to ride out and leave her unguarded here. Maybe you think she's so besotted with passion for you that she'll keep our secrets. The hell she will! A man can't trust any female, whether she be a whore or a duchess."

"When I want your opinion about women, I'll ask for it." Morgan said.

"Why not tie her up and leave her in the cellar while we're gone?" Enoch suggested.

"And after tonight, what then?" Niall turned on Enoch. "Are we to keep guard over her every moment?"

"After tonight," Morgan said, "we'll have nothing to fear

33

from Mistress Guilford."

"Why not?" Niall demanded.

Morgan turned and looked at Desire, his black eyes glinting with sardonic amusement. "When we ride out tonight, she goes with us."

Desire made a strangled, wordless sound of protest.

Morgan's lips curved in a teasing smile, as if he were planning a boyish prank.

"That first night we met, it was plain you had no knack for picking pockets," he reminded her. "Maybe you'll do better riding out on the king's highway with us."

"Morgan, no! Oh, please don't force me to—"

He went on as if she had not spoken. "If you make yourself helpful to us, you'll get your share of the loot. That's fair enough, isn't it?"

"I'd be of no use to you," Desire began, turning cold inside. She could already feel the rough hands of the Newgate jailer laying her back bare for the first cut of the lash, the hempen noose being fastened around her neck.

"Maybe the lass don't ride," Enoch said.

"I ride well enough," Desire blurted out. "But—" Oh, why hadn't she kept quiet? She fought back tears of despair.

"There we are, then," said Morgan. "Enoch'll go and find you a horse."

"With a lady's saddle?" Enoch asked calmly. No doubt this would not be his first experience as a horse thief, Desire thought.

Morgan shook his head.

"She'll ride astride. There are those old trunks packed away in the attic. No doubt she'll find suitable garments in one of them."

"I won't do it!" Desire's voice rose shrilly.

"Hear that?" Niall said. "You haven't tamed the bitch as well as you thought. That's what comes of treating her like a lady. Sharing the kitchen with her, all snug and warm in front of the fireplace, while Enoch and me were sleeping out there in the passage. I suppose your duchess of Whitefriars is too modest to open her legs when there're others in the

34

room."

"Another word and *you'll* be in no condition to ride out with us tonight," Morgan warned him.

"Easy, now." Enoch put a restraining hand on Morgan's arm. "We've still got plans to make before nightfall, remember."

Desire half expected Morgan to turn his anger on Enoch, but instead he nodded.

"You're right," he conceded. "Now go find a horse." He grinned. "There's no one like you for finding whatever's needed at short notice."

When Enoch had gone out the kitchen door, Morgan turned to Desire. "We'll go up to the attic and look for a suitable outfit for you."

"Please don't force me to ride with you tonight," she begged. "Tie me up if you must. Lock me in the store-room—"

"That's enough," he told her. "You'll do as I say. After you've helped us loot His Lordship's coach, you won't be tempted to turn us in."

He turned to Niall. "Even you should find no fault with the plan."

"I suppose not," Niall muttered grudgingly.

"You've done well for yourself by following my orders so far," Morgan's dark eyes flashed a challenge, but the other man remained silent. "Think of all those fat purses waiting for us tonight. And the ladies' jewel cases. That ought to stiffen your spine for this night's venture."

Although a part of the roof was a charred ruin, the rest remained, shielding several attic chambers from the rains and snows of the years that had passed since the war. Cromwell's troopers had raped and killed without pity, no doubt, and perhaps had made off with horses and livestock, but it was plain that they had given no thought to the chests stored up here.

"Find yourself a suit of boy's clothing," Morgan ordered

impatiently as he opened the heavy, iron-bound lid of the nearest chest. "A man's breeches would be far too large for you."

She went hot all over, remembering how he had begun making love to her in the firelit kitchen, only to be interrupted by the arrival of Niall and Enoch. That had been two night ago, but it was as if she could still feel the sensuous movements of his hands cupping her breasts, stroking her hips, curving around her small, rounded buttocks. Yes, he knew her size and shape well enough.

"Get on with it," he told her. "We don't have all day." Quickly she knelt beside the chest and reached out, then drew her hand back.

"Afraid of finding a spider or a black beetle?"

She shook her head, stung by his words. "You wouldn't understand."

"Try me."

"See how carefully these clothes were put away." She fingered the garments, her touch hesitant. "Here's a child's frock . . . and a girl's shawl." Her full, soft lips quivered as she went on. "You said the troopers had . . . raped the farmer's womenfolk . . . that they forced him to watch while his wife and daughters . . ." Her voice had begun to shake at the thought of such cruelty. How could a man as ruthless as Morgan be expected to share her feelings?

"Forget that!" His voice was harsh, but a moment later his hand dropped to her shoulder. To her surprise, his touch was gentle, comforting. "You've gone through enough grief of your own, Desire. Don't tear yourself apart dwelling on the sufferings of those you never even knew."

He was right, she told herself, but she still hesitated to go on with her task. Morgan got down beside her and rummaged through the clothing. "Women's stuff—that's of no use to us."

He tossed the garments on the dusty floor, ignoring Desire's wordless sound of protest. Then he held up a pair of boy's breeches and shook them out. "These'll serve the purpose."

36

"I can't wear breeches. It's indecent. And as for riding astride, only a shameless trollop would let herself be seen in such a disgraceful position."

Morgan's laughter interrupted her indignant protest. He threw back his head, his dark eyes gleaming with merriment. "You are the damnedest female," he told her. "You're going to ride out on the highway to commit a hanging offense, and you're concerned with preserving your modesty. I'm starting to suspect your parents were Puritans after all."

Desire's temper flared at his words. "You know nothing about my parents. My mother had all she could do to keep Papa from speaking out for the Stuart cause." She glared at him, her eyes narrowing to jade green slits. "Any young girl of good family — Puritan or Royalist — was taught to be a gentlewoman. But I suppose you wouldn't understand what that means."

"Perhaps I do." He did not raise his voice, but there was something in his tone that silenced her. "The war changed all our lives, Desire. Even now, with Charles Stuart back on the throne, nothing can ever be the same. If you want to survive, you'd do well to remember that."

"If I thought as you do, I'd have given in to Old Sally's persuasions and sold myself in the streets," she lashed back.

"What stopped you?"

"To lie with a man for money? I would never do that!"

"Would you yield to a man for your own pleasure, then?"

"Certainly not. I mean, not until after marriage."

"You're sure of that?"

She heard the teasing note in his voice. Was he remembering how she had lain in his arms, dazed by his caresses, not making the slightest attempt to hold him off? She had been on the brink of willing surrender. But he had plied her with brandy that night until she had lost all sense of right and wrong. That would never happen again.

He tossed the breeches to her. "Put these on," he ordered. And find yourself a shirt, boots, whatever else you'll be needing."

She put a hand on his arm and looked up at him, her eyes

37

pleading. "Morgan, don't force me to go through with this. You can't! Highway robbery's a hanging offense."

"I'm glad you realize it," he told her dryly. "And since you're about to join us in our lawless adventure tonight, you won't be tempted to turn informer. Even Niall sees the sense in my plan."

"Niall is . . . he's evil," she protested. "The way he looks at me, the cruelty in his face . . . It's as if he hates all women. But you—"

"Are you going flatter me, Desire? To tell me you believe I'm somehow better than he is? Kinder, perhaps? More chivalrous?"

"Hardly," she lashed out at him. "But Niall said you were a gentleman. He called you Squire Trenchard. What made him say that?"

His dark eyes went bleak, and his face set in grim, harsh lines.

"We've wasted enough time up here," he told her. "Go look in that cabinet over in the corner. You'll need a stout pair of boots. See what you can find."

Night had fallen when Desire, mounted on a handsome bay gelding, prepared to ride out with Morgan and the others. Her horse was mettlesome, tossing its head restively. After Morgan had helped her to mount, she knew it would take all her skill to manage the animal. Almost immediately she put aside her misgivings about this new and immodest way of riding. Ladylike or not, she would have to make the best of it.

Bending forward in the saddle, she patted the horse's neck. She spoke softly to gentle her mount, as her riding master had taught her.

Morgan raised a gloved hand in a commanding gesture, and the small group rode forward into the deep shadows cast by the elms, down the weed-grown path and out onto the road. Her heart lurched and she could feel its quick beating under the coarse shirt and woolen coat she wore. Surely no one would guess at her sex, not in these garments. She would be shielded, too, by the darkness of the night. Stars glittered in an ebony sky, and the only other light came from the thin, silver-crescent moon.

Like the men, she had concealed the lower half of her face with a large handkerchief. She wore a wide-brimmed hat pulled low to shade the upper half of her face. Her long dark hair was fastened atop her head, the sable waves hidden under the hat's high crown.

Following Morgan's lead, Niall and Enoch spurred their mounts to a brisk canter. Desire's thighs tightened as she urged the gelding to move faster. They had entered a heavily wooded stretch where the road was so narrow they had to ride in single file.

Here the starlight scarcely penetrated and the moon was lost from sight. An owl swooped low on silent wings in search of its prey.

What if she were to turn the horse now? Desire asked herself. Suppose she spurred the beast around and plunged into the blackness of the wood?

Even as the frail hope crossed her mind, she dismissed it. With three men on her trail she'd have no chance of escape. And although Morgan had never turned on her in anger, he could be dangerous. He was a criminal, in spite of his sometimes gentlemanly behavior.

Her muscles were starting to ache from this unfamiliar style of riding. Morgan did not slacken his pace, and she had all she could do to keep up with the men. Now they left the woods behind and thundered across a wooden bridge. After that, the trees were fewer and the heath stretched out on either side. Her horse shied as a small animal — a rabbit, perhaps, or a badger — ran across their path and into a thicket on the other side.

She drew a sigh of relief when Morgan gave the signal to halt in a grove of trees crowning a high bluff. Down below, she saw the wide highway. She looked around, but could not catch a glimpse of a farmhouse, an inn, or even a shepherd's hut. Morgan had chosen this place with care.

"We should be seeing Bodine's coach in a few minutes," he said.

"Unless your informer has decided to play you false," said Niall.

"His Lordship and his guests will be on time, never fear." Morgan said.

"Don't you have any qualms about preying on the gentry?" Niall mocked him. "Some day you may be recognized by one of your former friends."

Before Morgan could reply, Enoch spoke quickly. "Not likely. Morgan's own mother, rest her soul, wouldn't know him with his face covered and —"

"Let's go over our plans," Morgan interrupted. Desire shivered, for though he spoke calmly enough, she heard the edge to his voice and saw the hard glint in his eyes. Once more Niall's gibe had touched a raw nerve.

"We wait until the coach reaches that outcropping of rocks below. Then we ride down and surround them."

"The girl's not going to find it easy, managing that mettlesome beast on a steep slope," Enoch observed.

"Mistress Desire will stay up here in the shadow of these trees and act as lookout," Morgan said. "It's unlikely we'll be interrupted, but in case she catches sight of an intruder —" He drew a spare pistol from his cloak and handed it to her. "You will fire one shot, straight up."

"So you're protecting your doxy, after all!" Niall did not bother to curb his outrage. "She'll be safe up here, hidden from sight. We'll be taking the risks while she skulks in the shadows!"

"Listen!" Enoch interrupted. He gestured with a sweep of his arm. "That should be Bodine's coach now."

The night wind carried the rumbling of wheels, the thud of hooves, the sharp crack of a coachman's whip. His Lordship was eager, no doubt, to cross the heath and reach the relative safety of London as quickly as possible.

Desire's body tensed in the saddle. In spite of herself, she felt grateful to Morgan. She'd be far safer up here. Niall was right about that.

She saw Morgan's gloved hand raised in a brief, commanding gesture. A moment later he was over the edge of the bluff, descending the steep slope with the easy skill of one bred to the saddle. Enoch followed, his sturdy mount moving swiftly. Only Niall remained motionless. Desire stared at him in bewilderment. This was not the first time he'd ridden with Morgan and Enoch on such a dangerous venture. Why should he lose his nerve now?

Morgan had reached the coach, with Enoch close behind. She heard his shout of "Stand and deliver!" The coachman was pulling the team to an abrupt halt, while the two footmen sat frozen in their places atop the vehicle.

Out of the corner of her eye, Desire caught a glimpse of movement. Niall gathered his reins into one hand. With the other, he tore the concealing handkerchief from her face.

She bit her lip to stifle a cry of protest. An instant later, Niall raised his whip and brought it down on her gelding's flank with brutal force.

The beast whinnied and reared, pawing at the air with his front legs. Desire fought to control him, gripping his sides with all the strength in her slender thighs. It was useless. Niall went galloping down the slope and her own horse carried her after him. Pain shot up along her legs. Her arms felt as if they were being torn from their sockets. She bent forward as she struggled to keep from being thrown.

Without the protection of the trees, she caught the full force of the night wind as it came gusting across the heath. She felt her hat being lifted from her head. The wind carried it away. Her hair tumbled down around her face and over her shoulders.

The horse, on level ground now, did not slacken its pace. Desire went cold with terror when she saw the glow of a lamp through the darkness. Her mount was thundering forward at full gallop, heading directly for the side of the large, heavy coach, and she was powerless to stop it.

41

Chapter Four

Desire was so close to the coach that she could see the gilded crest emblazoned on its door. She tried to cry out but no sound would come. She braced for the collision, then, a moment later, she saw Morgan wheeling his stallion around.

Controlling his mount with only the powerful grip of his booted legs, he tore Desire's reins from her hands. Her frightened bay gelding whinnied and reared, but Morgan did not release his grasp. Then her horse plunged to a shuddering halt so abruptly that Desire was nearly flung from the saddle.

She caught a glimpse of Morgan's face. A ridge of hard muscle stood out along his jaw as he held fast to her reins a moment longer, positioning his stallion between Desire's horse and the coach.

Desire drew a deep breath as she tried to steady herself. Cold perspiration sprang out all over her, and she felt a trickle of moisture trace a line down between her breasts. She tried not to think how close she had come to being smashed against the side of the coach.

Now her lips parted and she filled her lungs with the cool night air. Regaining a measure of calm, she heard a man's voice from inside the vehicle.

"Devil take me if that's not a girl! Riding out for plunder on the highway, no less!"

The speaker leaned from the window and stared at Desire with mingled surprise and admiration. In the glow from the carriage lamp, her eyes blazed like emeralds and her long

42

black hair framed her face, offering a vivid contrast with the ivory white pallor of her skin. Under the tight-fitting boy's coat, her breasts rose and fell, while her breeches revealed the lines of her long, shapely thighs.

"She's a beauty, I'll say that for her." She heard another man's voice coming from within the coach.

"Shameless creature! Dressed in male attire and riding astride—" a woman cried out indignantly.

"Hand over your money and your jewels."

Morgan's steely tone silenced the passengers. Now he turned his attention upward to the box, where the coachman was fumbling inside his cloak.

"Throw down your weapon!" Morgan ordered.

The coachman hesitated a moment, then tossed his pistol to the ground. He was plainly unwilling to forfeit his life in defense of his master's property.

Desire gripped her horse's reins and prayed silently that no one would be foolhardy enough to put up a fight. Robbery was bad enough, but murder . . . Her insides knotted with fear at the thought.

She caught the swift glance that passed between Morgan and the tall young footman in splendid blue and gold livery seated on the box beside the coachman. The young man did not look either surprised or frightened.

He is the informer, Desire thought. For a share of the loot, he had betrayed his master's trust.

Her eyes moved to the second footman, who was perched on the boot at the rear of the coach. This one shifted uneasily, his eyes wide with apprehension.

"Your pistol!" Morgan ordered.

"I don't . . . I'm not armed, sir. I swear—"

He lapsed into terrified silence. Niall gave a contemptuous shrug, then reached down and opened the coach door. "Get out, all of you."

The man nearest the window was first to obey. He was probably in his late thirties, thought Desire, and a gentleman, to judge by his long, carefully curled wig, dark velvet

43

suit, and plumed hat.

"Damn it all, Sinclair," the second man rumbled from inside the coach. "The arrogance of these devils—"

"Best do as we're told, Sir Hugh."

Desire watched the portly, middle-aged nobleman struggling to get out of the coach. The younger man reached up a hand to assist his traveling companion.

Enoch swung down from his horse. With calm, deliberate movements, he set about his work, stripping Sir Hugh Bodine and his friend of their leather purses, ordering them to remove their gloves, then taking a couple of gold rings from His Lordship's pudgy fingers.

"Now for the women," Niall said. "Let's see what trinkets they have to offer us."

He dismounted. "Down with you, and be quick about it," he told them. As they hesitated, his eyes narrowed with cold ferocity. "Move your tails. Or would you rather I dragged you out?"

Desire leaned forward in her saddle. She peered into the coach and saw a girl of about her own age, swathed in a garnet-colored velvet cloak, lavishly trimmed with beaver. Soft blonde curls framed her delicate features.

"Get down here!" Niall snarled. With a squeal of fright, the girl buried her face against the broad bosom of the plump lady beside her.

The third woman, who sat opposite the other two, wore the unadorned, serviceable garments of a lady's maid. The starched white ruffle of her linen cap peeped from beneath her grey woolen hood. She held herself erect, her thin lips pressed together in a tight line.

Niall mounted the coach step and wrenched the blonde girl away from the older woman, his hand gripping her slim shoulder with cruel force. He lifted her to the ground, then pulled aside her fur-trimmed cloak. His narrow lips twisted in a mirthless smile as he caught sight of an ornate ruby and diamond brooch.

He gave the girl no chance to unfasten the valuable ornament. His hand shot out and he tore it from her silk bodice, ripping the delicate fabric, baring the curves of her white breasts.

"You *would* wear your brooch, you vain, silly girl!" The older woman's voice shook with indignation.

"I never thought . . . Oh, Mama, I'm so sorry—" The girl was sobbing now.

"Enough of your cackle," Niall said. "You fat old sow—hand over your own jewels."

The older woman bristled. She opened her lips, but something in Niall's face silenced her. She pulled off her gloves, removed a plain gold wedding ring, and handed it to him quickly.

"You're bringing your finest ornaments to London, I'll be bound. Let's see them, fast! If I have to search you, I promise you'll regret it. I'll strip you naked and leave you out here on the heath."

Desire was sure Niall meant what he said. He had never bothered to hide his contempt for women, and he had a streak of cold cruelty in his nature.

What could she do to spare these members of her own sex from humiliation, and perhaps worse?

"The maid is probably carrying the jewel case," she told Niall.

"Give him what he wants. Hurry!" she urged the stern-faced maid. The woman glared up at Desire, then reached behind her and pulled out a large leather case; but even now, she could not bring herself to give it up.

Driven by fear for the other woman, Desire reached down and seized the large leather case. Quickly she thrust it at Niall, and saw it disappear into his saddlebag.

"Took you long enough," Niall said to the maid. "I've got a mind to make you pay for that."

"You'll do nothing unless I give the order," Morgan said. His eyes locked with Niall's. Desire felt the tension crackling between the two, like heat lightning before a storm. It was Niall who gave way.

45

"To hell with them," he muttered.

But Desire knew now that the clash between Morgan and Niall was inevitable, and she dreaded the outcome.

"Have I your permission to assist the young lady back into the coach?" Sinclair asked Morgan with a faint touch of irony.

Morgan nodded. "We have what we came for," he said.

Sinclair helped the girl inside, then offered his hand to Sir Hugh before getting in after them. Enoch, at a gesture from Morgan, unbuckled the harnesses holding the handsome four-horse team to the coach. "Away with you, my beauties!" he shouted. The horses went galloping off into the darkness.

Even if the coachman could recover the team, Enoch's action would delay Lord Bodine and his companions, Desire thought. But as soon as His Lordship did reach London, he would lose no time in seeking vengeance.

He was a nobleman. More than that, he was bound for the court festivities—at His Majesty's invitation. That was what Morgan had said only a few hours ago. Desire felt a surge of despair, for she knew that the authorities would move heaven and earth to hunt down those who had robbed Sir Hugh and his companions.

Niall and Enoch swung up into their saddles, and with Morgan in the lead, they turned and rode off in the direction of the bluff. Desire urged her mount to a canter and followed close behind.

"You'll pay for this, all of you!" Sir Hugh's angry shout came to them from the darkness. "I'll see you swinging on Tyburn Hill . . ." Now as Morgan and the others went charging up the side of the bluff, the pounding of their horses' hooves drowned out whatever other threats Sir Hugh might still be hurling after them.

Morgan set a swift pace, but although Desire strained every nerve to keep up with the others, she could not dismiss her fears.

How long would they be able to evade the law? And when

they were captured, what chance would she have of convincing a judge that she had been forced to take part in the robbery?

She had helped to spare the ladies from Niall's brutality by pointing out the maid and taking the jewel case from her. But this would not save her when she stood in the courtroom, chained hand and foot. No doubt Sir Hugh and his companions would testify that she had seized the jewels out of greed for her share of the loot.

Visions of Newgate Prison rose up to torment her. Behind those stone walls, women were treated as mercilessly as men. She might be flogged or branded on the cheek . . . Desire flinched as if she could already feel the cut of the whip, the searing heat of the iron.

Morgan and the others were slowing down now, and she realized that they were nearing the farmhouse. Desire rode after them up the weed-grown drive to the front door. They reined to a halt, and Enoch helped her to dismount while Morgan led the way inside.

She followed the men through the dilapidated parlor and down the passageway to the kitchen. Gratefully, she sank down in a chair beside the hearth. Enoch piled more wood on the fire, but for all its warmth, she could not get rid of the chill deep inside her.

The men put down their loot on the long table. Watching them, Desire saw the hard anger in Morgan's dark eyes, the deeply etched line between his straight, black brows.

When he turned away to light two tallow candles on the table, her gaze rested on the taut muscles clearly visible under his white linen shirt.

Even now, shaken as she was by the crackling tension in the room, she was stirred by the look of him. What a magnificent body he had: wide, powerful shoulders tapering to a lean waist; long, muscular legs in their high black boots. It did not help to remind herself that Morgan Trenchard was an outlaw, a predator who roamed the night like a wolf in search of his prey. His overpowering masculinity aroused her, so that she felt a sweet-hot stir in the deepest part of her being.

But he appeared unaware of her presence as he turned his look on Niall. The silence between the two men grew until she could not bear it. She dug her nails into her palms and forced herself to remain silent.

"We made a good haul tonight," Niall said at last.

Morgan stood across the table from Niall, his booted legs planted apart, his body as motionless as if carved in granite.

"We haven't had a look inside the jewel case," Niall went on, his eyes shifting uneasily. "I'll wager those high-born trulls were carrying a fortune in gems, to deck themselves out for His Majesty's ball—"

Morgan turned and strode over to confront Desire. His dark eyes held hers. "Why didn't you stay up on the bluff, as you were told?"

Her mouth went dry. She swallowed, but the words would not come. She remembered that Morgan and Enoch had not seen Niall's treacherous action.

"Can't blame the wench for losing control of her mount," Enoch intervened. "If I'd been able to get her a less mettlesome beast, she might have managed him better."

Desire forced herself to looked at Niall. She flinched before the loathing in the man's face, the threat in his grey eyes. She understood his silent warning, but she knew she could not give way. Her spine stiffened and her chin went up.

"I didn't lose control until Niall cut my horse across the flank with his whip."

She did not know if Morgan believed her. He had no reason to take her word against Niall's.

"Do you think I wanted to come galloping down the bluff—to risk a broken neck?" she demanded. "Maybe you believe I tore the handkerchief from my face, too—so that they could get a good look at me?"

"I knew that bitch would make trouble," Niall interrupted. "You said she was coming with us tonight so she would not be able to inform on us later. Then you turned soft and left her out of sight on the bluff."

"You disobeyed my orders, Forret" Morgan said.

He does believe me, then, Desire thought with a sigh of relief.

"I only did what had to be done—to keep my neck out of the noose—yours and Enoch's, too."

"It was not for you to make the decision," Morgan went on, ignoring the other man's excuses. "And to pay for your mistake, you will get no share of tonight's loot."

Niall glared at Morgan. "You've no right—"

"Do you wish to dispute my rights as leader?"

Niall took a step forward, and Desire drew in her breath. Morgan hooked his thumbs in his belt and waited, unmoving. She saw Niall's hands curve as if he longed to spring for Morgan's throat.

But he could not bring himself to attack. Instead, he backed off. He even managed a slight shrug, but there was no mistaking the barely controlled fury inside his tall, thin body.

"You haven't answered me," Morgan reminded him.

"It's your right," Niall muttered sullenly. He turned away, and started toward the door. "I'll water the horses now."

"Not so fast." Morgan's eyes swept the table. "I don't see that fine brooch you took."

Niall reached inside his doublet, pulled out the brooch, and dropped it on the table, where it blazed in the candle-light. Then he went slouching off down the passageway. Moments later, Desire heard the heavy front door slam shut behind him.

Now Morgan opened the jewel case. "Those ladies were carrying a king's ransom," Enoch observed.

Desire, moved by curiosity, got to her feet. Morgan led her to the table and her eyes widened, dazzled by the glow of gold, the soft shimmer of ropes of pearls, the sparkle of emeralds, and the deep, violet fire of amethysts. "I said you might earn your share of the loot," he reminded her. "And you have." He picked up a pair of emerald earrings. "Do

49

you fancy these?"

Her voice shook with outrage. "If you think I'd deck myself out in stolen goods . . . You forced me to take part in the robbery tonight, but I'm not one of your kind."

Morgan laughed softly. "Perhaps you've already forgotten the circumstances of our first meeting. You were not so troubled by scruples when you made off with my pouch back in Whitefriars."

"But that wasn't the same. I didn't—"

"As you please," Morgan said. "It'll be more practical to fence the jewels, no doubt. Brooches and earrings can be easily identified, but when they're exchanged for a heap of gold coins, no one will know their source."

"I'll take no pay—not in jewels *or* coins. You may believe what you wish about me, Morgan Trenchard, but we are not alike. I stole from you to save myself from starving or turning whore. While you—"

"Don't stop now." His lips curved slightly.

"You have the manners of a gentleman. Niall called you *Squire* Trenchard. But whatever you were once, you are a common thief now, a highwayman. And you'll end like the others, making a bold speech as you ride in a cart to Tyburn—"

Morgan's lips clamped together, and two hard lines bracketed his mouth. Although Desire sensed the danger, she could not stop herself. She was not sure why this man had the power to arouse such anger in her, why she felt a driving need to strike out at him.

"You'll win the admiration of every trollop in Whitefriars on the day of the hanging. They'll weep for you, or toss flowers when the noose drops around your neck—"

Morgan's hand closed on her arm, his fingers biting into her flesh so that she had to force back a cry of pain. Her breath came quickly, and she looked up at him in fear.

"You will have your share, in gold," he told her, his voice level, without emotion. "It should cover the cost of your journey."

50

"My journey?"

He released his grip and pushed her away, then turned to Enoch. "As soon as we've fenced the jewels and fitted Mistress Desire with suitable clothes, you're to take her to Cornwall. You will leave her at Ravenscliff."

"Ravenscliff," Enoch repeated. Then he nodded slowly. "She'll be no trouble to us there. No one will come seeking her in such a place."

Desire looked first at Enoch, then at Morgan, in stunned disbelief. Cornwall! From what little she'd heard, it was a wild, desolate place. And this Ravenscliff—what might it be? The haunt of wreckers, perhaps, or smugglers, who roved the rocky coast. Outlaws even more dangerous than Morgan.

"I won't go! You can't force me—"

But the words trailed away, for as she looked up into his face and met his hard, implacable stare, she knew how helpless she was. He could send her where he chose, turn her over to the worst sort of criminals. He would be rid of her for good, and there was nothing she could do about it.

Chapter Five

Desire threw Enoch a look of mute appeal, hoping that he might take her side. He had treated her with a certain degree of consideration, and perhaps even now, if he protested against escorting her to Cornwall, Morgan would reconsider his decision.

But her hopes were dashed when Enoch nodded. "Ravenscliff — yes, that's the best place for the wench. I'll take her there, soon as you give the word."

He yawned, stretched his thick, muscular arms over his head, and started for the door.

"I'll get a fire going in the parlor," he said. "Niall and I can bed down there. It'll be less drafty than the passageway."

Desire's heart sank as she watched Enoch close the heavy door behind him. She threw an uneasy look at Morgan, who stood resting his arms on the oaken mantelpiece, his eyes fixed on the blazing fire.

She and Morgan had exchanged sharp words before, she reminded herself, but this time she feared that she had gone too far. What a reckless fool she had been to use her tongue like a whip, cutting him to the quick. She should not be surprised that he wanted to rid himself of her forever.

What inner demons had driven her to lash out at him that way? Now she sought to understand the feelings she had been hiding not only from him but from herself as well.

Since their first meeting that night in Whitefriars, she had been bewildered and frightened by her feelings toward Morgan. She had tried to convince herself that she despised him for his violent, lawless ways, that she wanted nothing more than to get as far away from him as possible.

But gradually, inexorably, she found herself drawn to him against her will. Perhaps it was her need to quell her unwanted emotions that had driven her to turn on him with such fury tonight, to speak of Newgate and Tyburn Hill. No doubt she had been trying to convince herself she did not, *could* not love such a man. To love Morgan would be to share his lawless life—to follow him to the gallows. But no matter what had caused her to strike out at him, she had not expected such a swift, harsh reprisal.

She tried to imagine her future in faraway Cornwall. Ravenscliff—that was her destination. Once Enoch had left her there, she would have no one to defend her. The prospect was a terrifying one.

For a moment she felt despair sweep over her, but she fought it back. She raised her chin, stiffened her spine, and took a deep, steadying breath. Summoning all her courage, she forced herself to go to Morgan's side.

When she put a hand on his arm, she felt the muscles go iron-hard beneath her fingers. He did not even look at her, but kept his gaze fixed on the leaping red and gold flames.

"Surely there's no need to send me as far as Cornwall," she began. "Halfway across England—"

"I should think you'd be only too pleased to see the last of me." He turned to look at her. A corner of his mouth lifted in mockery. "Since you think me such a deep-dyed villain, surely you want nothing more than to be free of my company." At least, she told herself, he was willing to speak to her.

"I'm sorry for saying those terrible things. My nerves were stretched to the breaking point by all that happened tonight, but I had no right to lash out at you—"

"Are you trying to say that you've had a change of heart about me? Rather sudden, isn't it?"

Damn the man for his cool sarcasm! Quickly she reminded herself that she must not let her temper override her common sense a second time. Not if she hoped to talk

Morgan out of shipping her off to Cornwall.

"You must not let your maidenly modesty keep you from declaring your feelings, my dear." He spoke lightly, but his dark eyes were fixed on hers, as if trying to fathom her innermost thoughts.

Quickly she shifted to a new tack. "Since Lord Bodine and his friends could identify me as one of your followers, I would be a fool to inform on you—even if I wanted to."

"I've always known that women are unpredictable creatures," he said. "But you . . . first you berate me like a fishwife. Yet now, if I did not know better, I might be vain enough to believe you have a certain fondness for me."

She looked away, afraid her eyes would betray her. "Not that, but I *am* grateful to you, Morgan."

"And what have I done to win your gratitude?"

"You saved my life. When I lost control of my horse out there on the heath, I might have been battered against the side of the coach. If you had not risked your own safety—"

"I acted on impulse," he interrupted, his white teeth flashing in a careless grin. "No man in his right senses would have wished to see such beauty as yours destroyed." Was it the reflection of the leaping flames that stirred those dancing sparks in his eyes?

Her cheeks burned with embarrassment, as she went on. "These past two nights we have slept in the same room. You might have used me as you wished. But you left me unmolested."

"Are you saying that you feel safe with me, Desire? You see me as a chivalrous gentleman?"

"I'd rather trust myself to you than to a . . . a band of lawless cutthroats in Cornwall."

"Better the devil you know, is that it?"

"I've never thought you a devil!"

The words came unbidden from her lips, and she felt a swift surge of warmth deep within her as she looked at him in the firelight. She could not take her eyes from his face, with its high, angular cheekbones, its hard jaw, and jutting

54

...in now touched with a rich, copper glow.

Moved by an instinct too strong to resist, she forgot her pride. Her hand closed on his arm, and she heard the harp, swift intake of his breath. But when he spoke, his voice was hard, his face set.

"The sooner I'm rid of you, the better," he told her. "You've made trouble for me ever since our paths first crossed back there in Whitefriars."

"How can I be a source of danger to you now?" she demanded.

"A girl like you means danger for any man, one way or nother." But his voice was deep and caressing. His hands went to her shoulders. "Desire — they named you well. Sweet, green-eyed sorceress . . ."

Although he held her gently, she felt a hot current coursing through her body at his touch. His fingers burned through the thin fabric of her well-worn shirt.

She might be a witch, indeed, he thought as he drew her into his arms. He breathed the scent of her blue-black hair, framing the whiteness of her face. Her eyes, slightly tilted, glowed with emerald fires under thick, curving lashes. His body molded itself against hers, and her soft red lips parted. Swiftly he darted his tongue between them.

Desire knew she should draw back, and quickly, but she could not. She pressed herself to him and felt the hard muscles of his chest against her breasts. Her nipples tingled at the contact, then peaked into small buds as she moved against him.

Now he was bending her backward, supporting her with his arm. She made a sound of protest as one of his legs parted her thighs. No petticoats, no billowing skirts shielded her body. Through the tightly fitting breeches she wore, she was shockingly, almost painfully aware of the taut pressure of his manhood, thrusting against her. Virgin though she was, she had brought him to this state. A fierce pride coursed through her as she sensed her own power.

Her body spoke for her, making its hunger known. Her

55

hands went to his shoulders, and she ached with need at the feel of his hard, taut muscles, the clean male scent of him

His strong fingers traveled down along her back, caressing, exploring, lingering briefly at her narrow waist, then went lower still to cup her small, round buttocks, so tantalizingly outlined by her breeches. He was moving his loins against her, and now she too began to move, as if in a dance for which there was no name — a ritual as old as time itself

She longed to be free of the garments that covered her, for her whole being cried out to know the touch of his flesh on hers. And as if her need communicated itself, one of his hands went quickly to the buckle of her belt and opened it

Now she felt the heat of his strong, skilled fingers against the satin flesh of her taut belly. A shock ran along her nerves and she began to tremble.

She told herself she must stop him, but the only sound she could make were wordless little moans deep in her throat. Slowly his questing fingertips traced a line downward until they touched the soft triangle of dark curls below

Her head fell back, and his tongue moved along her throat. She opened her shirt, her fingers trembling, and bared the softness of her breasts to him. He took one hard peak between his lips, drawing it into his mouth, flicking at it, then sucking hungrily.

She gasped, feeling the warm moisture that laved her secret places, untouched until now. A moment later his fingers parted her virginal cleft and slid smoothly inside.

She moved against his fingertips, arching her loins . . .

The spell was shattered for an instant by a sound like pistol shot. Only a log, cracking in the heat of the flames, but it brought her back to reality. Drawing on every ounce of willpower, she put her hands against his chest and tried to push him away.

"Morgan — no!"

But his arms only tightened about her. "I won't hurt you, my sweet," he whispered urgently. He tried to draw her down on his pallet, but she went on struggling, her body twisting in his embrace.

"If you take me, it must be by force!" she cried out. "And I'll go on fighting you as long as I can—"

He stared at her, his dark face set in harsh lines. Then he released her so suddenly that she swayed, her legs trembling under her. Her whole body ached with its thwarted need. The room spun around her, and she heard him speak again as if from far away.

"I'll not force you." His voice shook with anger. "Or keep you with me an hour longer than I must."

"You'll send me to Cornwall?"

"Damn right, I will!" He balled his hands into fists and rammed them into his pockets. "You won't have the chance to play your little games at Ravenscliff," he told her.

Was that what he thought? That she had led him on, then stopped him before the moment of fulfillment, only to amuse herself? He was wrong, so wrong . . . Even now, her whole body ached with frustration, and she longed to tell him so.

But it was safer to keep silent, for although she had had little experience with men, she sensed that he was in no mood to listen to explanations. His lips were pressed together tightly, and the muscles stood out along the line of his jaw. It came to her then that Morgan Trenchard was a dangerous man, and that she was not safe from the leashed violence within him.

She had made the only possible choice, she assured herself. If she had offered up her virginity to the highwayman, she would have joined herself to him with unbreakable bonds. There would have been no need for a marriage contract or a parson's blessing. Had she allowed Morgan Trenchard to possess her completely, she would have belonged to him from that moment on. And she would follow him wherever he led her, she knew that, too. Even if their shared path ended, as it surely would, at the gallows.

And yet, even knowing this, how could she face the separation from him? She felt her throat constrict at the thought. Never to feel his hands on her, or the fire of his mouth as it claimed hers.

"I won't go away. Not now . . ."

The words came from her unbidden. Better to face his fury than his icy silence.

"Has it never occurred to you that I'm sending you to Cornwall for your own safety?" he demanded.

"My safety!?" She stared at him in disbelief. "You must think me a fool indeed if you'd have me believe that, Morgan Trenchard. There'll be no safety for me once Enoch turns me over to a band of thieves and ruffians at Ravenscliff."

"You know nothing of Ravenscliff," he reminded her.

"I know of Cornwall, and more than you suppose," she told him.

"How can you, when you were born and bred in London? That's what you told me, isn't it? Your father was a wine merchant in the city."

"Papa often entertained other merchants, and sea captains, as well. They spoke of the far-off places they'd visited. I was supposed to be abed, but sometimes I'd slip down to the staircase landing to listen."

"You surprise me, Desire. No well-behaved young miss would have left her room and sat eavesdropping." He was taunting her now, but she did not allow him to distract her.

"My father and his guests spoke of the men of Cornwall, who smuggled in fine brandy, silks, and laces across the Channel from France," she went on. "And I heard about others far worse. Men not satisfied to profit by evading the government's lawful taxes."

"And what did they do, those others?"

"I think you know perfectly well," she told him. "They were the wreckers, who showed false lights along the Cornish coast to lure innocent seamen to their deaths. Then they swarmed down to loot the ships."

She shivered, remembering those tales she had overheard, crouched on the landing in her nightdress.

"Sometimes a sailor survived the destruction of his ship, only to be murdered by those . . . those creatures. Those are your Cornishmen! And you'd make me believe you are sending me to them for my own safety."

"You naturally assume that Ravenscliff is a hiding place for such men?"

"Surely you don't expect me to believe you have friends among the gentry. Supposing there are any in Cornwall worthy of the name."

He made an impatient gesture. "Think what you please," he told her. "Now lie down and get your sleep. There's many a long mile between here and Ravenscliff. You'll need to be well rested."

Slowly, reluctantly, Desire sank down on her straw-filled pallet, her eyes stinging with unshed tears. She gave Morgan an uneasy look.

"You needn't worry," he told her in chipped tones. "You'll be quite safe, Mistress Guilford."

She lay back, but she went on watching him through half-closed lids. She saw him gather together the loot spread on the long table. He knelt on the far side of the hearth, pushed his pallet aside, then pried up a few large, heavy bricks from the floor. There he put the jewel case and the leather pouches he had taken from Lord Bodine and the other gentleman — all the booty from the night's adventure. Carefully he replaced the bricks and positioned his pallet so that it covered them.

Only then did he stretch himself out. He turned his back on Desire and pulled his blanket over him. It was as if he had renounced all further contact with her, and the knowledge made her ache inside.

She felt tears on her cheeks, but pride kept her from making a sound. Morgan had told her to sleep, but how could she, tormented as she was by her dread of the future?

Gradually, however, her eyelids began to close. Her taut muscle relaxed, her tears dried, and she drifted down into the velvety darkness . . .

Now it seemed to her that she stood alone, surrounded by high, jagged rocks. Overhead, the icy stars glittered in a night sky. White-crested waves reared up, then broke with terrible fury against a towering cliff. A fierce wind whipped at her hair and tore at her skirts.

And then she heard a voice. Papa's voice from somewhere among the rocks. She looked about her. Why couldn't she see him?

"A strange, savage breed, the men of Cornwall . . ." The wind carried her father's words to her.

"Papa, where are you?" Desire cried out. Surely he would come to her now. She would be safe with him. But his voice was lost in the roar of the waves. And another sound, even more frightening.

The thunder of a horse's hooves. She whirled and saw the beast bearing down on her, eyes glowing red in the darkness. She fought to get out of its path, but somehow her muscles were frozen, immobile.

She cried out in terror and woke with her heart hammering against her ribs, her body bathed in icy perspiration.

"Desire! What's wrong?"

The fire had burned low in the hearth and only a few coals still glowed red. The first faint light of dawn slanted through the tall, narrow windows.

Morgan came to her and dropped down beside her pallet. She felt the tension in her body begin to ease as his warm fingers touched her shoulder.

"A horse — bigger than any I'd ever seen — riding down on me."

"A nightmare —"

"But I heard hoofbeats. They were *real*, I tell you!"

He stroked her hair lightly. "No doubt they seemed so. But you're awake now. And your phantom horse is gone."

Comforted by his nearness, she did not mind the teasing note in his voice. She wanted him to remain beside her, but

60

he was getting up now, returning to his own pallet. Was it possible that he did not trust himself to touch her and do no more?

Before she could pursue the thought, the door to the passageway creaked and swung open. Enoch stood in the doorway.

"Niall's gone," he told Morgan. "I was on my way back from the privy when I saw him sneaking into the stables. I followed him, and a good thing, too. He might have driven off our horses. As it was, he went galloping away like the hammers of hell."

Morgan's dark eyes narrowed, but he said nothing.

"We've seen the last of him, I'll warrant," Enoch went on.

When Morgan remained silent, Enoch looked uneasy. "You've kept the loot safe, no doubt."

"Under the bricks beneath my pallet."

"Good enough. We'll be better off with the bastard gone, then."

Although Desire would not have expressed herself in those words, she was in complete agreement with Enoch. But Morgan stared at the brick floor, his black brows drawn together in a frown.

"What's troubling you, Morgan? We managed well enough before we joined forces with Niall Forret. Let him go to the devil."

"It's not that simple, Enoch. He could be a threat to us, even now. Remember, I held back his share of the loot."

"He'll not go running to the nearest constable to lodge a complaint about that," Enoch said.

"It's possible that he'll devise a way to turn informer without implicating himself."

"I don't see how."

"He grew up in the gutters of Whitefriars," Morgan reminded Enoch. "No doubt he knows others of his kind who could be persuaded—or bribed—to inform on us. If he can strike at us without risking his own neck, he'll do it."

Even as he spoke, Morgan thrust his pistol into his belt

61

and reached for his cloak. "We'd do well to be out of here—and soon."

"What about Mistress Desire?" Enoch asked.

"We've no choice for the present," Morgan said. "When we leave, we'll take her with us."

Chapter Six

It was late afternoon when Desire, Morgan, and Enoch guided their horses through the narrow, rocky pass and into the clearing beyond. Enoch pointed. "There's the blacksmith's hut, up ahead."

They had left the farmhouse at dawn of the previous day, and with hard riding they had reached the first rolling foothills of the South Downs. Now, as Desire caught sight of their new hiding place, she felt a sinking sensation.

No smoke rose from the chimney, and the path leading to the hut was choked with dead leaves and encroaching vines. Tall beech trees raised their leafless branches against the sky.

"We should be safe enough here," Enoch said. "It was deserted when I came upon it last summer. We had to split up after we robbed the Sussex coach."

"I remember," Morgan said tersely. He drew rein, swung down from his tall stallion, then helped Desire to dismount. She remained for a moment, resting her hands against his shoulders to steady herself. Standing so close to him, she felt a swift physical response.

Enoch's voice broke the spell. "There's no stable. We'll tether the horses in the shed there."

After tying the horses' reins securely to the shed's posts, Morgan and Enoch lifted down the saddlebags, then made their way to the hut, with Desire following.

The door to the forge hung on one rusted hinge. It creaked shrilly when Morgan pushed it open. Desire's first glimpse of the inside of their new quarters did little to reassure her.

A blacksmith's forge should have been a bustling place, with the husky smith and his apprentices hard at work shoeing horses and repairing farm tools. Even passers-by, who had no work for the smith, often stopped to warm themselves at the roaring fire, which was kept going day and night. The farmers discussed the local gossip and travelers supplied information from farther afield, while the hammers rang and sparks shot in all directions.

But this forge was silent now, and the air felt damp and chilly. Although Desire still wore her woolen coat, breeches, and boots, she shivered slightly. At least, she thought, trying to console herself, they would be safe in this long-deserted hut on the Sussex Downs.

A moment later her lips tightened, as she caught sight of the thick grey cobwebs that covered the disused anvil and heavy hammers. A smith's leather apron, covered with greenish mildew, hung on a peg, and a collection of files, once used for smoothing off new horseshoes, now lay rusting in a corner. How many years had passed since the forge had been used, since farmers, waggoners and packhorse drivers had congregated here?

"That door leads to the living quarters," Enoch said. "And there's a little shed attached. Probably the apprentices bedded down there. No doubt the smith had a decent trade here before the war."

"We're not close to a main thoroughfare," said Morgan. He had to duck his head as he went through the low door leading to the adjoining room. He set down his saddlebags, then removed his heavy cloak. "But perhaps the smith did well enough with the trade he got from the farms hereabouts."

"That was before Cromwell and his Roundheads went on the march," Enoch said. "Destroyed every farm in their path, they did. Unless the farmer was on their side, or claimed to be." He shook his head ruefully. "Shepherds' huts, thriving farms, manor houses, too. When I think of Pendarren, with its fields lying fallow, the cattle slaughtered, and all the purebred horses confiscated—fancy word for stealing . . ." He bent to open his saddlebags. "And the house, itself, standing deserted."

"It's not deserted now." Desire heard the icy resentment in Morgan's voice.

"But he that calls himself master. He's got no right to be there," Enoch interrupted. "Sir Arthur Wyndham. And him not even a Cornishman." He gave a snort of contempt. "I'll warrant His Majesty hadn't settled his arse on the throne before Wyndham came hurrying to London, smiling and fawning and greasing every palm along the way to buy an audience with the king."

Desire saw Morgan's body go taut, his powerful shoulders tightening under his fine linen shirt. He rammed his fists into his breeches pockets. His eyes glinted dangerously under his dark, heavy brows. But Enoch, bending over his saddlebags, did not notice these storm warnings.

"No doubt Wyndham begged a reward for his service to the Stuart cause. And he got Pendarren."

"That's enough!" Morgan's voice shook with fury. "Never speak to me of Pendarren again!"

Although he did not turn his anger against Desire—indeed, he appeared to have forgotten she was there—she shrank back instinctively There was no mistaking the violence that possessed Morgan at the very mention of Pendarren.

But Enoch only sighed and shook his head.

"Sorry, Morgan," he said. He picked up a couple of wooden buckets from a sagging shelf. "I didn't mean to let my tongue run away with me." He started for the door. "We'll be needing water. There's a stream out back."

Morgan clapped Enoch on the shoulder. "Always the practical one," he said, forcing a smile. Desire could see that he was making an effort to regain his self-control.

Enoch went off for the water, leaving Desire possessed by curiosity. What demons had driven Morgan into such an outburst of rage against his friend? And why had he turned

65

on Niall Forret that night in the farmhouse, when the man had called him squire?

But Desire knew that this was not the time to satisfy her curiosity. Instead, she looked around the room that probably had served the blacksmith and his family as both kitchen and bedchamber. The rays of the setting sun slanted in through the small, square opening cut in the wall. No ordinary country smith could have afforded the luxury of a pane of glass. The sunlight revealed all the signs of long neglect.

"The hearth's filthy," she said. "And that iron pot—ugh! As for plates and cups, if I can find any—"

"We didn't come here on a pleasure trip," Morgan reminded her brusquely. "Be thankful that Enoch remembered this place." Then he smiled with genuine warmth. "I can always count on Enoch. He's gotten me out of many a tight place."

"That didn't stop you from turning on him a few minutes ago, as if he were your worst enemy. Why did you, Morgan?"

"That's no concern of yours," he told her. And before she could protest he went on, "You'd better start unpacking those saddlebags. The food we were able to carry should serve for a day or two."

"And after that?"

"Enoch's handy at setting snares. With any luck, you'll be able cook us a rabbit stew."

"You expect me to cook in that fireplace? Look at it. It's full of leaves and rubbish. Maybe even a dead mouse . . ."

"I'll clean the hearth."

"And that cooking pot?"

"That's your task, my lady. Or shall I rig a spit over the fire for you to cook the meat on?"

"I don't know how to work a spit," she told him indignantly. "I've never had to—"

"Sorry I couldn't pick up a jack and cage along the way. And a turnspit dog." Morgan said through clenched teeth.

66

She saw that he was making an effort to control his temper. "No doubt your mother kept a few of the bandy-legged animals in your kitchen at home."

"No, she did not!" she told him. "Mama couldn't bear to watch one of those poor little dogs running round and round in a cage for hours at a time to turn the roast."

"I trust your mother was equally thoughtful of her kitchen maids." She glared at him, her green eyes narrowing with resentment as she caught the irony in his tone.

"I've known many a fine lady to treat her overfed pet spaniels far better than her servants," he went on, unperturbed by her look.

"Mama was not like that," Desire told him.

Not that she herself had gained firsthand experience with the endless, complicated chores that had kept their London house running smoothly. Her mother had urged her, instead, to devote herself to her dancing lessons, to acquiring skill in playing the harpsicord and the dulcimer, and in making witty but proper conversation with their guests.

Desire, with her emerald eyes, her shining black hair and white skin, her exquisitely molded features and slender, graceful body, showed early promise of a rare beauty.

"She will have many admirers," said the French dressmaker who had come to the house to design her fashionable gowns. "See her bosom, how it is rounding out now. Her waist — so small and tapering. And her movements, so graceful. Ah, yes, Madame Guilford, it will not be long before your drawing room is filled with fine young gentlemen, all seeking her hand."

Although Mama protested that such flattery would make Desire conceited, she was proud of her daughter's beauty. She ordered concoctions of cucumber and rose water, or lemon juice, pulverized eggshells, and white wine, to enhance Desire's complexion, and almond milk to rub on her hands every night. She gladly paid for the services of the best music and dancing masters, the most sought-after riding instructor.

The matter of a dowry would present no problem, for Desire was an only child, and her father's business was flourishing. Although Puritan farmers and rural shop-keepers might frown on the consumption of wines in England during Cromwell's reign, many a fine London gentleman would not allow his male guests to rise from the table before they had emptied half a dozen bottles of Port, Rhenish, or brandy.

Wine had remarkable curative powers, too, and every wise housewife, like her mother before her, kept an ample supply in the stillroom for medicinal purposes. She used a mixture of wine, treacle, and pepper as an emetic. She baked eels dry, crushed them fine, then mixed the powder with Canary or Malaga wine, to cure those stricken with consumption. Poppy syrup, in a glass of sweet Burgundy, brought swift and healing sleep.

Desire's father was on his way to becoming a wealthy man, highly respected in the City's business community; Mama had great hopes for her daughter's marriage prospects.

"Your future husband will surely provide you with a competent housekeeper," Mama had assured her. "There's no need for you to spend your time in the kitchen or the stillroom. Go along, my dear, and practice that pretty new ballad."

Mama had been so sure that nothing could come along to upset her plans. Desire would be safe, cared-for and cherished by an adoring husband. A staff of hard-working, well-trained servants would attend to her every need.

All at once Desire was jolted back to reality. Morgan was speaking to her, his voice brusque.

"Since we brought you along, the least you can do is stop complaining and make yourself useful."

"I didn't ask to come with you."

"And how long do you suppose you'd have escaped the law if we'd left you on your own?"

"If not for you, I wouldn't be wanted by the law," she retorted. She could not forget Lord Bodine's angry threats of revenge, carried after them on the night wind as they had ridden away across Hampstead Heath. Fear clawed at her now. "His Lordship's already sent the dragoons after us— I'm sure of it!"

"No doubt he has," Morgan agreed as he hooked his thumbs into his belt with a careless gesture. "Don't look so alarmed, my sweet—you'll be safe enough in Cornwall. Even the king's dragoons won't carry their search that far."

As he spoke he took off his waistcoat and tossed it on the bench along with his cloak. She watched uneasily as he began to unbutton his shirt.

He gave her a teasing smile. "It'll be a filthy job, cleaning out the hearth. And I'm sure you would not enjoy scrubbing my shirt clean. I'm particular about the whiteness of my linen, you know."

Wash his shirt, indeed! She tried to think of a scathing retort. Then all at once, her anger was swept aside. Seeing him standing before her, stripped to the waist, she was stirred by another, more urgent emotion.

The light of the setting sun, streaming in through the window opening, turned his deeply-tanned skin to glowing bronze, reminding her of the statues of pagan gods in her father's high-walled garden. But Morgan's body was alive, virile with male urgency. Remembering the feel of of him the last time he had held her, she was caught up in a tumult of sensations.

She could not look away from those wide, powerful shoulders, those muscular arms and that broad chest. Her eyes rested on the flat, male nipples, the mat of dark, curling hair tapering down to a narrow line like the shaft of an arrow. Her gaze traced that line to the place where it disappeared beneath a belt of fine Spanish leather circling his lean waist.

All at once she caught the knowing glint in his dark eyes and saw his teasing smile. She went crimson and looked down at the floor, cursing him silently. Damn the man! It was as if he could read her most intimate feelings at a glance.

"I'd best see if I can find a few plates somewhere about here. Or at least a trencher or two" she said quickly.

In the poorer households a trencher—a block of wood hollowed down into a rough bowl in the middle—would hold porridge, meat, and vegetables, to be shared by two or more diners. Although such humble articles had never appeared on her table at home, she had seen them in the Whitefriars' market stalls.

By early twilight a fire burned on the hearth. Morgan had sent Desire to gather up what dry wood she could find close to the hut. Then he had started the fire by flashing a bit of powder in the pan of his pistol to make a spark.

Desire managed to reheat the scrag-end of ham they had carried away from the farmhouse, and although the meat proved to be tough and fatty, they were all far too ravenous to complain. The one trencher she managed to find served the three of them.

Morgan and Enoch drank sparingly from a bottle of brandy they had brought along. "We mustn't get you tipsy again," Morgan told her as he diluted a little of the fiery liquor with spring water before passing it to her.

It was his way of reminding her of that first night at the farmhouse. Although she had tried over and over again to convince herself that she had yielded to his caresses because her senses had been addled with brandy, she knew better now. And so, she suspected, did Morgan.

She rose abruptly and began to clear away the remains of the meal. As she went about her task she listened to Morgan and Enoch, who were making plans for the night ahead. They would take turns standing watch.

"There's not likely to be a hue and cry this far from London," said Enoch. "Not yet, at any rate."

"Maybe not," Morgan said, "but I'll stand watch from

70

now until midnight. You get a few hours sleep, and then take over until dawn."

Desire, not wanting to hear any more talk of possible pursuit and capture, went outside to the stream to scrub the pot and trencher. She was guided by the sound of the water, rippling over the stones.

Catching sight of a small, deep pool, shielded by beeches, juniper scrub and thorn, she longed to strip off her clothes and bathe herself, but it was too cold for that. Only clusters of snowdrops, the first wildflowers of the season, were in bloom, their petals gleaming against the carpet of bracken.

By the time spring arrived, with crocuses and daffodils lending their beauty to the woodlands, she would be far away from here. And from Morgan.

Maybe she would never get as far as Cornwall, she thought, as she rose and started back to the hut. What if, in spite of all their precautions, they were captured and carried off to prison?

She quickened her step, stumbling a little on the unfamiliar path, in her eagerness to get back to the warmth and light of the kitchen. She found Enoch and Morgan deep in conversation.

"The narrow trails and thick woodlands up here should hamper the best-trained troop of dragoons from London," Enoch was saying. "They don't know their way about the Downs."

"We've more to look out for than the dragoons," Morgan reminded him. "If there's a hue and cry after us, we'll have to be on the move again soon enough."

"Plenty of farmhouses around here are standing empty," Enoch said.

"But not all." Morgan rose as he spoke and thrust his pistol into his belt.

No doubt he was right, Desire thought dismally. There would be many sturdy farmers hereabouts, along with their sons and their laborers, ready to join in the pursuit, willingly or not. It was the duty of every able-bodied subject of

71

His Majesty to take part in the hue and cry after a hunted criminal. No law-abiding Englishman—farmer, weaver, shepherd, or shopkeeper—might refuse without facing immediate and brutal punishment.

Desire stood looking at Morgan as he went outside to take the first watch. How could he bear to live like a hunted animal? He was no product of the Whitefriars' slums, she was sure of it. Neither was he the son of a dispossessed laborer, who had seen his family turned out of a hut to beg on the roads or take charity in a workhouse. His features, his bearing, his speech, and above all, his manner of authority proclaimed his gentle birth and breeding.

What, then, had driven him to commit robbery on the king's highways? She was possessed by a driving curiosity to know more about him. As she began making preparations for sleep, her thoughts were not on the blanket she was unrolling and setting down near the fire. She looked over at Enoch.

"How long have you known him?" She tried to keep her voice casual.

"Morgan? Known him since the day he was born."

"You are no relation to him, are you?"

"Me, kin to the Trenchards?" He smiled broadly, then he shook his head. "Served the old squire—Morgan's father. Started by tending the geese, feeding the hogs. Then I helped Silas, the gamekeeper, hunt for poachers. When he got too old for the work, the squire made me gamekeeper on the estate."

"That was . . . Pendarren?"

Enoch nodded.

"And Morgan's mother? Was she married to his father?" Perhaps Morgan was illegitimate. A bastard son, shamed by the stigma of his birth, embittered at having no claim on his father's property, might turn to highway robbery to show his defiance of society.

But Enoch lost no time in assuring her otherwise. "Morgan's mother was a young lady of good family, and lawful wife to Squire Trenchard. And Morgan was born in the great oaken bed in the master's chamber, and christened in Truro church like all the Trenchards before him."

"Then he is the lawful heir to Pendarren," Desire began indignantly.

"He would have been. And worthy of his heritage, too. But there was Master Roderick, ye see." Enoch's usually placid features hardened. "The squire's son by his first wife. He was ten years older than Morgan, and rightful heir in the eyes of the law."

"And Morgan took to the highways because he couldn't inherit his father's estate?"

Enoch shook his head. "Morgan had the devil's own pride. If he'd been old enough at the start of the Great Rebellion, he'd not have stayed on the estate, taking second place to Master Roderick. He'd have gone off to fight for the Stuarts like his father did."

He fell silent, but Desire knew that she could not rest before she knew more about Morgan.

"And after the squire went off to war, what happened then?"

"Killed early on, he was, in the fighting at Stratton. And that same year, Morgan lost his mother, too. She caught a fever nursing one of the tenants, and it killed her. Fourteen, Morgan was then. And he had no one to turn to for consolation."

"What about Roderick? Surely Morgan might have turned to him at such a time."

Enoch shook his head. "Morgan and his half brother never got along. And when the war started, Master Roderick took sides with the Parliamentarians. Not that he dared speak out for Cromwell, not while old Squire Trenchard was there at Pendarren. But once he rode off to fight for the Stuarts, Roderick didn't have to guard his tongue any longer. And then, when word came of the squire's death and Roderick took his place as master of Pendarren, all hell broke loose. Many's the quarrel he had with Mistress Tren-

73

chard, I can tell you."

"She sided with the Royalists too?" Desire asked.

"That she did. She wouldn't allow Roderick's Roundhead friends in the hall. A gentle lady, she was, and frail, but she stood up to her stepson all the same."

"And what about Morgan?"

"He sided with his mother. But what could he do, a boy of fourteen?" Enoch's eyes went bleak, and he looked past Desire, caught up in his memories. "Mistress Trenchard had been laid to rest in Truro churchyard less than a month when Roderick invited his Roundhead friends to dine with him at Pendarren."

Desire leaned forward, taking in every word Enoch spoke. She tried to picture what Morgan had been like as a boy; to see him as he had looked that night.

He had sat at the long, polished dining table, not touching a morsel of food. His dark eyes were fixed on Roderick, and his body was tense with repressed fury, but he kept silent. Until the moment when Roderick raised a toast to Cromwell and the forces of Parliament. Then Morgan had leaped up and knocked the glass from his half brother's hand.

"Big for his age, he was, and strong—but no match for his elder brother. Even so, it took more than one of Roderick's friends to pull the lad off. Then they had to hold him while Roderick beat him senseless."

Desire went white with indignation, but she said nothing, for she did not want to distract Enoch until she had heard the rest.

Following Roderick's orders, two footmen carried Morgan into the woods and left him there to die. But Enoch, who was making his usual rounds that night, looking for poachers, found the boy, battered and bleeding, and carried him to his own cottage.

"Next day I got us a ride on a wagon bound for Falmouth. Morgan had two cracked ribs and he looked like he'd been kicked in the head by a carthorse. Out of his wits with fever, too. But he was young and strong. When he was healed, I got us aboard a ship, and we worked our passage to the West Indies."

"What did you do there? How did you live?"

Enoch grinned. "Mighty interested in Morgan's past, aren't you?"

"I want to know something about the man who's been holding me prisoner all this time. There's nothing so odd about that, is there?"

"And that's the only reason for all your questions?" Enoch gave her a long, searching look. "Couldn't be you're fallin' in love with Morgan, could it?"

"Falling in love with Morgan! As if I—as if any respectable woman could love such a man! He forced me to help him rob a coach. And now he can scarcely wait to ship me off to his thieving friends in Cornwall."

Enoch gave her a placid smile. "Easy now," he said softly, as if he were gentling a fractious mare. "No need to flare up so. You wouldn't be the first to lose your heart to Morgan. He's always had a way with a female. Tavern wenches and high-born ladies—more than willing, they were. Why, when we were living in the Indies, planters' wives ran after him something shameless. And him not yet twenty—"

"They must have been a lot of silly fools." Desire fought to stifle a swift surge of jealousy. "I could never love a man like Morgan. Never!"

"If that's true, it'll be all the better for you." Enoch spoke quietly, and she saw the concern in his face. "Morgan wasn't bred to be a highwayman, but if he's caught, he'll hang, same as any thief."

Desire knew that Enoch's blunt words were meant to warn her away from a love that could only destroy her. Although she had done her best to convince him that she could feel nothing but contempt for Morgan, obviously she had not succeeded.

"If he hangs, it will be no more than he deserves. He knew well enough the risk he was taking."

"As I did," Enoch said quietly.

Desire stared at him, stricken with remorse. Enoch had always treated her with consideration, and she had not intended to include him in her diatribe against Morgan. She was sure that it had only been his loyalty to Morgan that had made him take to the highways.

But before she could find a way of telling him so, he said, "I'd best get some sleep now. But first I'll bring you a bucket of water from the spring. No doubt you'll want to tidy yourself after our long ride."

After he brought the water and set it down beside the hearth, he went to bed down in the adjoining forge. "A good night to you, Mistress Desire," he said, before closing the door behind him.

She tore a few pieces of cloth from the already-tattered dress she had carried along with her. Stripping off her boots, shirt and breeches, she washed as thoroughly as she could. Then, kneeling by the bucket, she pushed her long hair forward into the water and scrubbed vigorously. She used another strip of cloth on her hair, rubbing it until it shone with blue-black highlights. It was good to feel clean again, she thought, as she dried her hair before the fire.

A delicious languor began to steal over her. She pulled on her breeches and shirt, then stretched out and wrapped herself in her blanket. The floor was hard, and she thought wistfully of the straw-filled pallets they had been forced to leave behind at the farmhouse. Shifting her body, she tried to find a comfortable position.

But although she was tired, sleep did not come at once. She lay wide-eyed, watching the shadows flickering on the beams overhead, remembering all Enoch had told her about Morgan tonight. But she still was troubled by so many questions about the dark, enigmatic highwayman who had come riding into her life to change it forever.

Even though Morgan had been forced to flee from England, he had returned after Charles II had ascended the Stuart throne. Why then had he taken to the highways, instead of claiming his father's estate?

Roderick, the squire's first born son, had supported Cromwell openly. As a traitor to the Stuarts, he could have no claim on Pendarren any longer. Although Charles II was not a vengeful man, he would scarcely have rewarded one of his father's enemies.

What was it that Enoch had said earlier that day? He'd spoken of a certain Sir Arthur—Wyndham, who was now master of Pendarren. "And him not even a Cornishman."

Why had King Charles given Pendarren to Sir Arthur Wyndham, instead of to Morgan? She would find a way of getting Enoch to explain it all tomorrow, she thought. Then her heavy lids closed and she sank into a deep, dreamless sleep.

When Desire awoke, she felt the cold and dampness. Raising her head, she saw that the fire was flickering out. She got up and found the poker. She was stirring at the heap of twigs, trying to revive the blaze, when Morgan came in.

"That won't do any good," Morgan said, taking the poker out of her hand. "The wood's nearly burned away. Tomorrow, you'll have to gather more—and dried moss, too."

"But I'm cold now," she protested. "Even with the window shuttered, the wind's coming through the cracks in the walls."

"I apologize for the accommodations, milady," he said with a mocking bow.

"It was foolish of me to think you to care if I froze to death in this dreadful hovel." Her green eyes glinted like those of an angry cat.

"You wrong me, Desire," he said. "Have no fear, I'll see that you sleep warm for the rest of the night."

Before she could protest, he got his blanket roll and spread it out next to hers. Back in the farmhouse kitchen, he had left the width of the great hearth between their two pallets. Tonight, she realized, they would sleep side by side.

He took off his heavy cloak. "I can't offer you a satin comforter," he said. "But you'll find this good enough."

"There's no need . . ."

But he was already seated on his blanket, pulling off his boots. When he stretched out close beside her, her breath caught in her throat. A moment later she felt herself enveloped, not only by his cloak but by the heat of his body.

His voice was deep and husky, his lips pressed against her throat. "We will warm each other tonight, Desire." His arm went around her and he drew her to him. Now she shivered with anticipation as the length of his body molded itself against hers.

With Enoch's warning still echoing in her thoughts, she tried to draw away, but her newly awakened senses betrayed her. She lay still, even as Morgan's fingers moved deftly, removing her coat, unbuttoning her shirt. Her breasts already ached for his touch, and when he cupped one of them, she made a wordless sound of satisfaction.

Somewhere, far back in her mind, a memory stirred. She felt as she had on that first night when he had lifted her onto his horse and ridden away with her. Then he had been carrying her away from her past, toward an unknown destination.

Now she knew all too well where he meant to lead her, and for a moment, her body tightened, resisting his invasion. He took his hand from her breast, and his dark eyes held hers. Even now it was not too late to stop him.

But she could make no sound, as his lips claimed her breast, and he began to suckle there. She felt all tension flow from her, replaced with a sweet-hot languor that moved from the taut rosy peak, spreading outward until it engulfed her completely.

Chapter Seven

Desire lay back, her green eyes half closed, her dark hair fanning out around her face, as Morgan went on undressing her. After removing her shirt, he unfastened her belt. Possessed by her awakening need, she raised her hips so that he could draw down her breeches.

He paused briefly to stroke the silken skin bared to his touch. The feather-light caress of his fingers sent a long, delicious shiver down along her limbs. And now, as he took his hand away and bent his head, pressing his warm mouth to the slight curve of her belly, the exquisite sensation grew and spread. His lips moved against her flesh, and she felt the heat of his breath as he spoke softly.

"You looked well enough in your male attire, but I like you better this way."

"Perhaps you were forgetting I was a female."

"Desire, my sweet, I could never forget that, not for a moment."

He slid his hands under her bottom and lifted her off the blanket so that he could complete the task of removing her breeches. Then he tossed them aside and a moment later she heard him catch his breath. His dark eyes glowed in the firelight, paying homage to her body.

"Beautiful," she heard him saying. "So beautiful—"

His words sent a warm glow of pride surging through her. How wonderful to know that the sight of her body could stir him so deeply.

Even as Morgan forced himself to leave her side for a moment to take off his own clothes, he could not look away.

His breathing quickened, and he felt a hard, tightening sensation in his loins as his eyes drank in the soft white curves and the delicately shadowed hollows of her body.

He must possess her now. He had waited long enough. Too long. A primitive need surged up in him as he stood above her, looking down at her rounded breasts, her rosy nipples firm and pointed. A fierce hunger shook him as his eyes moved over the flatness of her belly and came to rest on the dark patch of soft curling hair concealing the untouched core of her womanhood.

Then he heard her small, wordless protest, and saw the flicker of fear in her eyes. He could feel the latent passion within her, but he thought he understood her reluctance, her instinctive dread of his invading manhood.

Lowering himself down beside her once more, he made a silent promise that he would hold back until she was ready. No matter how urgent his need, he would lead her slowly, gently, to the moment when all trace of her fear was gone — when she could give herself willingly, joyously.

He turned her on her side so that she faced him, and began to stroke the length of her back, his fingers light against her smooth white skin. His hand moved lower to caress the sensitive place at the base of her spine, just above the curve of her buttocks, and he felt the shiver that ran through her. He stopped then, his gaze locked with hers. He felt that he was losing himself in the sea-green depths of her eyes.

How long could a man hold out against his need for complete possession? His hands cupped her hips, his fingers pressing deep into the soft, rounded flesh. He moved her against him, his tumescent maleness creating a sweet-hot friction with her soft mound.

She put her palms against his chest. Was she trying to hold him off? Surely she realized that her small gesture of reluctance could not stop him for a moment.

Or did she trust him enough to believe that he wouldn't use his strength to overcome her hesitation? That he would understand and wait until she was ready for him?

"You will have all the time you want, love," he said gently, moved by her sweet vulnerability.

She started to take her hands away, but he covered them with his own, holding them firmly against his chest. "You can pleasure me with your touch, if you will," he told her.

"I'm not sure I know how . . ."

But her fingers began a delicate exploration of the crisp curling hair that covered the hard muscles of his chest. She saw his lips part in a smile. Encouraged, she went on to touch his flat, brown nipples, and was surprised to feel them harden. She had so much to discover about a man's needs.

She bent her head forward, her hair veiling the sides of her face. The tip of her tongue darted out and flicked with a delicate motion.

"You learn quickly, my love," she heard him saying. He lay back looking up at her, his eyes dazed with sensuous delight. "Don't stop . . ." His voice was deep and a little unsteady.

Emboldened by his words, she let her tongue linger at his nipples, tracing warm, moist circles. He began to stroke her hair, his fingers entwined in the thick, blue-black waves.

Desire allowed Morgan to guide her now, wanting to know more of his body yet still unsure of herself. But her lingering reluctance was slipping away . . .

She rested her face against the hard arc of his ribs for a moment. Then, growing bolder, she yielded to her own needs. Her tongue began to trace a path down along the narrow, sharply defined line of dark hair — there was no belt now, no breeches to conceal his masculinity.

Morgan's hands gripped the sides of her head more firmly, and although she sensed the growing urgency of his touch, she did not understand at first what he wanted. Then, with scalding clarity, she knew. And drew back swiftly.

"Oh, no, Morgan I can't—"

For a moment she feared that his frustration might lead him to lose control, to force her to satisfy him as he wished.

Then she heard his soft, rueful laughter. He raised himself, and with one swift movement he rolled her over onto her back.

"Since you're not yet ready to pleasure me that way . . ."

He shifted, his hands moving with a slow, sensuous touch. His fingers cupped her warm mound, stroking her, parting her, finding the moist peak of her passion.

Fiery ripples moved through her, and she raised herself to savor this new sensation to the fullest. She was opening herself more and more, driven by the inexorable demands of her whole being.

"Morgan, please . . ."

Although she wasn't sure what she was asking, nay, demanding of him, she knew that only he could fulfill her. He raised himself and moved up to straddle her with his legs. Once more he was kissing her, lingering over her nipples, encircling first one, then the other, with his tongue.

He took her hand and guided her fingers down over the hard muscles of his abdomen, then closed them around his hard shaft. She gave a gasp of surprise as she discovered how hot and smooth that part of him felt to her touch. When he took his hand away she began to stroke him, until a groan from deep in his throat made her stop.

She looked up questioningly to see that his eyes were half closed. He was smiling with unconcealed satisfaction. Reassured, she continued her stroking motion until, with startling swiftness, he took her hand away.

Now he was kneeling over her, parting her legs, positioning himself between them. She reached out and put her arms around him, clinging to him with all her strength. But he did not enter her at once. Instead, he stroked himself against her satiny moistness, his movements slow and tantalizing.

It was not enough. She wanted him deep inside her. *Now.*

At the first thrust, she cried out, startled by the swift, searing pain. He stopped, and now he was soothing her with his whispered endearments. "My love, my sweet love . . ."

The pain was ebbing away, and she began moving again as her need came upon her once more, stronger than before. There was an aching void deep in her loins, demanding to be filled.

Her arms tightened around him, drawing him closer and still closer. Her whole body arched upward, pleading wordlessly for release. Morgan began to move inside her, his strokes slow and sensuous at first. Now her long, slender legs closed around him. He quickened the pace, moving deeper, faster.

Her body was pulsating with a burning, all-consuming need until she felt she could bear it no long. Morgan was carrying her up, higher and still higher, on wave after wave of ecstasy. Together they touched the heights, and locked in each other's arms, they went spinning out into the gold-sparked darkness.

Morgan was holding her against him as the waves ebbed gradually. Even when her heart had slowed to a steady beat, and she could breath evenly once more, he kept his arm around her. She reached up to brush back a stray lock of his hair from his damp forehead. He caught her fingers in his and kissed them.

Then he turned over on his back and drew her head against his chest. "I didn't know . . ." she murmured.

"Know what, love?"

She had not known, nor could she have imagined, the beauty and wonder to be shared by a man and woman. Nothing she had heard during her stay in Whitefriars had prepared her for this. The girls at Old Sally's house had spoken of men's needs with contempt or revulsion.

Even when she knew how much she wanted Morgan, she still had feared the moment when he would take her. His tenderness, his understanding, had changed all that. Now she wished only to belong to him, to share the rest of her life with him.

Raising herself slightly, she saw that he was looking at her and she heard him saying, "If only we could stay like this forever."

His words filled her with joy. He wanted her, not only for tonight but for all the days and nights that lay ahead. She moved closer to him as she thought of the years to come.

Hazy pictures began to take shape behind her half-closed lids. Although she had never seen Pendarren, she imagined herself walking beside Morgan in a garden overlooking the sea. A great stone house loomed behind them, its walls bathed in sunlight. "Mistress Trenchard of Pendarren," she thought drowsily.

She was jolted back to reality as she felt Morgan drawing away from her. He sat up abruptly, and she saw that he was looking past her at the window. The rosy light of dawn was glowing through the cracks around the closed shutter. From a tree outside came the first tentative call of a lark, and now other birds were joining in.

"We'd better get up," Morgan said. "Enoch'll be returning from his watch soon."

She tensed, for his words reminded her why Enoch had been standing guarded outside. Her fingers closed around Morgan's arm, and she looked up at him, her eyes asking him not to put so abrupt an end to the glory they had shared.

"Desire, my sweet," he said softly, "there'll be other nights."

"Will there?" Her voice was sharp with fear. "How can you say that when you know the dragoons could be combing the Downs, searching for us right now. If Niall has turned informer—you said he might—"

"Easy, love." He stroked her hair, but his touch could not dispel her mounting terror.

"If Niall's informed on us, the troopers could have picked up our trail at the farmhouse. That would make it all the easier for them to find us."

"I've managed to avoid capture so far," he reminded her.

"But your luck can't hold forever." She raised herself, her legs drawn up under her, and she gripped him more tightly. "How can you live this way? Running, hiding, without a home to call your own?"

"I had a home . . . once."

"And you can again. You should be master of Pendarren, like your father and his father—"

He wrenched himself free from her clinging hand.

"Enoch's been talking out of turn."

"Don't blame Enoch. I bedeviled him with my questions. But there's still so much I don't understand."

Morgan stood up and pulled on his breeches. His face was dark with anger, but Desire refused to take refuge in silence. "Why didn't you claim the estate after you returned from the Indies?" she demanded. "Roderick was one of Cromwell's supporters. Surely His Majesty would never have given Pendarren back to him."

"Roderick's dead. He was killed in the fighting at Naseby," Morgan told her.

"Then you have the only legitimate claim to the estate. Not Sir Arthur Wyndham. Why is he master there?"

"That doesn't concern you."

She drew back as if he had slammed a door in her face. How could he shut her out like this? Only moments ago they had been locked in each other's arms, as close as two people could be.

Now he tossed her clothes to her. "Get dressed," he ordered harshly. She obeyed him, but her fingers were clumsy with the buttons.

Morgan hadn't meant what he said. He must know, deep down, that everything about him concerned her. Why, he was a part of her now, and he always would be. He had lashed out at her, driven by self-hatred—she was sure of it. But she could change all that.

He opened the shutter, and the cool freshness of the morning filled the room. Desire went to him and put her

85

hand on his shoulder. When he turned to face her, his eyes were still remote and unyielding.

"Your father was a gentleman," she began, speaking quickly, before she lost her courage. "He fought and died honorably for the Stuart cause."

His straight, dark brows drew together, his body rigid with barely leashed violence.

But Desire stood her ground. "You were no more than a boy when Roderick used you so cruelly. You had no power to defend yourself, not then. But since he's dead now, surely it's not too late to return to Pendarren, to live the life you were bred for."

"There's no going back, not ever. Those years in the West Indies changed me. I got by any way I could. And I learned not to waste time brooding over the past. As you will learn, if you are to survive."

"I don't understand," she faltered.

"Don't you?" He gave a mirthless laugh. "Surely your mother didn't mean for you to become a common cutpurse, roaming the alleys of Whitefriars. But that's what you were up to the night we met. Because you didn't want to become a whore, and you weren't willing to starve."

She tried to turn away so that Morgan would not see the swift tears evoked by his words, but he caught her by the shoulders and held her immobile.

"Tears won't change anything. Forget what you might have been."

"I'll never do that!"

Even as she brushed the tears away, her head went up and her words rang out with defiant pride. "I won't steal again, ever. And I won't go on running away." She threw her arms around him and held him with all the strength in her slender body. "I love you, Morgan Trenchard. And I want to spend the rest of my life with you. But not like this."

"I never asked you to share my life, Desire. I never will. That's why I'm sending you to Cornwall as soon as I can." He freed himself from her clinging arms and pushed her

86

away.

Her vision of their future together had disappeared, swept away by the cold finality of his words. She had given him her love—all the tenderness and passion within her. But he had never loved her, not for a moment.

"Damn you!" she cried. "You've had your pleasure and now you mean to ship me off to that awful place—Ravenscliff. You're going to pass me along to your cutthroat friends, to use as they wish."

Morgan threw back his head, and she realized that he was laughing at her.

No! It wasn't possible. How could he shame her so?

Why, he was worse than Niall Forret, who had never bothered to disguise his contempt for her. As Morgan's laughter echoed through the small room, her hands closed into fists. She lunged forward to strike at him. He stopped laughing.

Grasping her wrists, he held her away. She writhed and kicked out at him. Beginning to feel weak and giddy, she heard his voice, as if from far away.

"You little fool. Ravenscliff's a lonely place, far from any town, but it's respectable enough. It is the home of my great-aunt, Mistress Arathusa Tregannon. She's a widow, well into her nineties." He released his grip, and she swayed slightly.

"How was I to know that?"

"You might have trusted me a little." He shrugged. "No matter. Now that you do know, I'm sure you can't wait to start your journey."

"That's right." But she knew she was lying, and she turned away quickly. She should be thankful for the prospect of a safe refuge, since Morgan had made it plain she could have no place in his life. Whatever last night had meant to her, it had been only a pleasurable interlude for him.

She remembered what Enoch had told her about all those other women Morgan had dallied with. Some had been more beautiful than she, no doubt. And many would have been far more experienced in satisfying a man's needs.

Because she had fallen in love with him, she had been sure that he felt the same about her. But she knew so little about men. How was it was possible for a man to feel passion, even tenderness for a woman, without wanting to make her a part of his life? She drew on her pride to sustain her. If Morgan did not love her, at least he must respect her.

"How am I to get to Cornwall?" She managed to keep her voice steady.

"You'll travel by public coach, with Enoch," he told her.

"But Lord Bodine and his guests saw my face," she protested.

"They saw a hoyden in breeches, riding astride, her hair flying." He grinned at her. "When you board the coach for Cornwall you'll be dressed as a proper young lady in a suitable traveling costume."

"And where do you mean to conjure up these fine clothes?" she asked.

"In London. I'll be leaving later today to fence the jewels."

"London! No, Morgan, you can't!"

"While I'm there, I'll buy whatever you need to turn you from a highwayman's cull into a genteel miss."

"It's far too dangerous. You'll be caught—"

"Would you be sorry?"

"Why, I—"

"Only moments ago you were ready to pounce on me like a wildcat, and now you're worried about my safety." He laughed softly. "Don't fret over me, my sweet. My luck's held out so far."

"But if Niall's found a way to inform on you, without risk to himself, the king's dragoons could be lying in wait for you in Whitefriars."

"I've considered the possibility," he said calmly. He cupped her chin in his hands and smiled down at her. "Now tell me, what sort of traveling costume would you prefer? Garnet silk, perhaps, or dark green velvet."

"How can you talk about dresses when . . . Oh, Morgan,

you could be riding into a trap. Don't go to London, not yet."

In another moment, Desire might have tossed away her pride, and thrown herself into Morgan's arms, pleading with him not to risk his life in this foolhardy plan. But the door creaked open and Enoch came into the kitchen, carrying a load of dry wood.

"There's no need for Morgan to go," he told Desire. He set down his burden. "I'll take the jewels to London. It'll be easy enough for me to hire on for a few hours' work driving a string of mules. Or helping a waggoner load his goods. Once I'm inside the City, I'll head straight for Whitefriars."

Morgan shook his head. "Not Whitefriars. We can't risk taking the loot to the usual shop this time."

"There's Moll Fisher's den," Enoch suggested.

"That's no better. If Niall's peached on us, Moll's place may be watched too."

"Then where—" Enoch began.

"I'll go straight to the Royal Exchange." Morgan spoke with quiet confidence. "I know a milliner there who deals in our sort of merchandise—for a chosen few. She'll be able to chose a suitable traveling costume for Desire. Everything from bonnet to slippers."

How had Morgan come to know the woman? Jealousy clawed at Desire, only to be swept aside by her fear for his safety.

"No doubt you'll draw less attention at the 'Change than I would," Enoch agreed reluctantly.

The Royal Exchange, in the high-vaulted arcade between Cornhill and Threadneedle street, served as an elegant meeting place for fashionable ladies and satin-clad, beribboned gentlemen, who lingered to share the latest court gossip and to shop for the most sought-after luxury goods in London. Chinese silks and French laces, rubies from India, diamond-buckled satin slippers and ostrich plume fans were all on display in the stalls.

Enoch, who looked and spoke like a bluff country fellow,

would be too conspicuous, but Morgan, with his fine cloak and plumed hat, would blend in easily with the crowd at the Exchange.

"Besides, the lady I spoke of has known me a long time," Morgan was saying. "When it comes to receiving stolen goods, she can't risk dealing with strangers."

At last Enoch gave way, partly because Morgan's arguments made sense. And also, perhaps, because he could not overcome his lifelong habit of obedience to the Trenchards.

But he looked at Morgan uneasily. "You've had the devil's own luck so far. Let's hope it holds for you once more."

Chapter Eight

Desire set her bucket down beside the stream and leaned against the trunk of a tree. The sun was warm on her face, and a mild breeze stirred the strands of her dark hair. The twigs of the elms and beeches were thick with buds, and the banks of the stream were bright with the yellow blossoms of the coltsfoot.

Shading her eyes against the bright slant of early morning sunlight, she gazed wistfully at the tall, grey boulders that marked the entrance to the ravine. Still no sign of Morgan, she thought, with a long sigh.

Four days had passed since he had ridden off to London, and this morning she had awakened feeling that she could bear the waiting no longer. He had promised to return in three days, and she had tried to keep busy, to make the time pass more quickly. She had cleaned the hut and carried in enough wood shavings and dried twigs to keep the fire going for a month. When Enoch had found a rabbit in one of his snares, she had managed to prepare a tasty meal for him. As for herself, she had little appetite.

The nights were the worst. She slept lightly, waking every few hours, listening for the approach of Morgan's stallion. But she heard only the hooting of an owl or the sharp yelping of a fox.

Why couldn't Morgan have waited a few weeks at least, before heading for London to sell his loot? By then the constables would have slackened their search so that he would have stood a better chance of returning safely. But no, he had been determined to lose no time in selling the jewels, and buying a suitable traveling costume for her.

"He can't wait to get rid of me," she told herself. If only she could make herself hate him, she would stop fearing for him. But it was no use at all. Even if Morgan didn't love her, she could not change the way she felt about him.

Suppose he'd already been captured? She cringed inwardly before the dreadful pictures taking shape in her mind. Morgan, locked in a filthy cell in Newgate, lying on a damp stone floor. Or standing, his hands chained behind him, his broad, tanned back bared for the stroke of the jailer's whip.

She picked up the bucket and walked along the bank of the stream to the place where it was widening to form a pool, set in a half circle of rocks. Then she drew in a long breath of sweet fresh air, and for a moment her spirits lifted. Morgan would come back to her.

She bent to fill her bucket.

"No need for you to do that." She had been too lost in her thoughts to hear Enoch coming out of the woods behind her. "You only had to ask me."

"I needed to get out, away from the hut."

He took the bucket from her and set it down on a flat rock. "You'll get away soon enough," Enoch said. "And it won't be an easy journey, jolting along in a coach from here to Cornwall. You'd do well to get all the rest you can before Morgan returns."

"But why isn't he back yet?" Then, with a pang of self-reproach, she went on. "If only I could have stopped him from leaving so soon. I should have found a way to keep him here until—"

"Nobody stops Morgan once he's made up his mind to take action," Enoch told her. "Now don't you fret yourself into a spell of the vapors. Not over Morgan's safety. He knows what he's about. Who else would have thought of strolling into the Royal Exchange, bold as you please, his pockets filled with jewels stolen from Lord Bodine? What other highwayman would've had a chance of carrying through such a plan?"

"But you can't be sure he *has* carried it through. Oh, Enoch, why didn't he go to that fencing shop in Whitefriars, as he did before? Old Sally used to say that few constables would dare risk their lives poking about the courts and alleys there."

"And Old Sally, whoever she might be, spoke true. But when Morgan chose Lord Bodine for his prey, he made a dangerous enemy."

"His Lordship wouldn't go chasing after the jewels himself. And with the constables afraid to go into Whitefriars—"

But Enoch shook his head. "Like as not, Bodine was able to get a royal warrant, right from the chief justice." Then, seeing her puzzled expression, he went on, "Such a warrant's backed up by a company of musketeers, or dragoons. Seasoned fighting men, they are, armed with muskets and bayonets. They won't be driven off by a mob of Whitefriars bullies."

He gave her a reassuring grin. "That's why Morgan went to the 'Change, instead. No doubt he's already completed his business there and is on his way back."

"Don't, Enoch," she protested. "I'm no child, to be comforted so easily."

"No, you're no child. More's the pity." His smile disappeared. "You're a woman, afraid for the man she loves."

"That's not true!"

Enoch's level look told her that she had not convinced him. She could not keep her feelings locked inside any longer. "I do love him, I always will," she whispered.

"I tried to warn you," Enoch said. "But what good's a warning when a young maid like you meets such a man?"

"He's your friend," Desire reminded him. "You're fond of him."

"And of you, too. I knew from the first that you were no common Whitefriars trull. I could see that you'd been bred a lady."

93

"But Morgan's a squire's son."

"That doesn't change anything. He's not for you, Desire. He never can be."

"I don't believe that. He's the heir to Pendarren, now that his brother's dead."

Enoch's shaggy eyebrows shot up. "Told you about that, did he?"

"Yes, but he didn't say why this man, this Lord Wyndham, is master of the estate now. Surely when His Majesty returned from his exile on the continent, Morgan might have petitioned for the return of his property. Why didn't he go straight to the king and—"

"We were off in the West Indies when King Charles took back his father's throne. It was more than a year before we heard the news and found ourselves the means to return. The king had already given Pendarren to Lord Wyndham."

"But surely, if Morgan had demanded an audience, even then the king would not have refused to see him."

"Good Lord, girl, do you know how many Royalist supporters were besieging the king, demanding the return of their lands? Men who'd fought at Marston Moor or been wounded at Naseby? And those others, who'd risked their necks back in '51 helping His Majesty escape from Cromwell's men, and get across to France?"

"Even so," Desire persisted stubbornly, "I can't believe Morgan would have let go of his property without a fight."

Enoch shook his head. "A man can't fight his way into the king's audience chamber with his sword or pistol. It takes gold, and plenty of it, to grease the palms of the court."

"And Morgan returned from the Indies without money?"

"We landed at Falmouth with the clothes on our backs and enough coin for a few nights' lodgings. The landlord at the Mermaid warned Morgan away from Pendarren—and a lucky thing for him, too."

"But why?" Desire asked.

"This Lord Wyndham had taken possession of the estate months before. He served as magistrate for the district. A hard man, he is, and without scruples. That's what the landlord said. The fellow had been a friend to Morgan's father, and he warned Morgan to get as far from Pendarren as he could—and to stay away."

Desire felt her throat tightened with pity as she thought of Morgan, returning from the Indies, only to be met with such overwhelming obstacles.

"Roderick fought against the Stuarts," Enoch went on.

"But Morgan didn't."

"And you think Wyndham would have given him a chance to prove that? With a prize like Pendarren at stake? He'd have had Morgan hung as a traitor to the Crown—or transported. And me along with him. Wyndham was the law in that part of Cornwall—he still is, no doubt."

All those years in exile, Desire thought. And then to return to England only to discover that Pendarren was lost to him forever. How angry Morgan must have been, how bitter at the injustice that had taken away all his hopes.

"And so he turned to highway robbery," Desire said slowly.

Enoch nodded. "And now it's too late. He can't hope for a pardon, let alone the return of his property."

But even now, Desire could not accept defeat. There had to be a way for her to be with Morgan. "We could leave England," she said. "We could go to one of those islands in the Indies, or to France—"

"Hush, girl! Enoch cut in. "Down there in the ravine . . ."

She caught the sound of hoofbeats, and her hand went to her throat. Heedless of danger, she was racing toward the mouth of the ravine. But Enoch quickly caught up with her and seized her arm. "Keep down. No telling who it might be."

She froze, her heart hammering against her ribs. The seconds dragged by. Her fingernails cut into her palms as she forced herself to remain still.

Then she went weak with relief at the first glimpse of

Morgan, spurring his tall grey stallion forward. He drew rein and dismounted. In that moment, she forgot about the harsh words they had exchanged before he had left her. She only cared that he was alive, free — and standing here.

She ran to him, then stopped for a moment, uncertain of her welcome. But he opened his arms and now he was holding her against him. She lifted her face and his mouth came down on hers. *He's back, back here with me, and nothing will ever part us again,* she thought.

"I chose the busiest time of afternoon to visit the Royal Exchange," Morgan was saying. He paced back and forth before the hearth. "The arcade was crowded with shoppers and idlers — all decked out so they looked as bright as those parrots from the Indies. And made more noise than a whole flock of them."

"And your milliner friend's still at the same shop?" Enoch asked as he set down Morgan's saddle-bags, along with a few large parcels and a small valise of brocaded cloth.

Morgan nodded. "She offered me a fair price for the jewels, and passed them along to a highly skilled goldsmith. He'll reset those stones so that even the original owners wouldn't recognize them."

"No doubt she helped you choose Mistress Desire's finery, too," Enoch put in. "That stallion was loaded down like a pack mule."

"He's not used to carrying such burdens," Morgan said. "But my milliner assured me that all these fripperies would be absolutely necessary for my purpose." He turned to Desire. "Spread out a blanket and open your parcels. I think you'll approve of your traveling costume."

His words sent her spirits plummeting. In her fierce joy over his safe return she had not allowed herself to believe that he was still bent on sending her away.

"Get on with it," he said, and now his voice held an edge of impatience. "We haven't much time."

She obeyed, her fingers dealing mechanically with the knotted strings and carefully folded wrappings. But her eyes were fixed on Morgan, who was talking to Enoch.

"I want you to set off as soon as possible. There's an inn with a coaching stop about six miles to the north of here. I'll give you the exact directions before you go. Find out when the next stage leaves. I doubt there's any direct route between here and Cornwall.

"Try to work out a route with the fewest changes along the way," Morgan said. "The sooner you get Desire away, the better."

Desire looked up from her task and saw the tension that had come into Morgan's face. Enoch must have sensed his mood too.

"Niall Forret?" Enoch spoke the name with disgust.

"I knew he'd make trouble for us if he could. And he hasn't lost any time."

"He's informed already?"

"It's likely enough."

Desire lifted a dark green silk traveling dress from its wrappings and shook it out. At any other time, she would have stopped to admire the elegant garment. Now it could have been a skivvy's rags, for all she cared. She kept her eyes fixed on Morgan, taking in his every word.

"I'd have returned sooner, but since I was in London, I took time to make the rounds of the better bordellos off Drury Lane. I found what I was seeking at Kate Claffley's place."

"Many a man has," Enoch said. "Fine female, Kate is, and her girls are as choice a nosegay as—"

"No denying that. But I was on a different errand this time."

This time. Desire's full, red lips tightened as she caught the implication.

"Kate said that Niall'd been to her place only a few nights before. He came swaggering in, calling for the best wine and one of her girls to share it with him, upstairs. When

Kate asked after me, he laughed. Said she'd see me soon enough—dancing on the air at a rope's end."

"I wonder she'd put up with such talk," Enoch said. "Always liked you, she has."

"She's a loyal friend," said Morgan. "She took Niall into her private parlor and gave him all the wine he wanted. Kate knows how to get what she wants from a man. It didn't take her too long to get at the truth."

Morgan's dark eyes narrowed with contempt. "Our Master Forret has had enough of riding the highways. He's turned informer. Earned his own pardon, and a pocketful of gold, peaching on us."

"Treacherous bastard," Enoch said. "I'd like to get my hands on him, here and now."

"We'll deal with Forret, never fear. But right now, we've more urgent matters to attend to."

"I'll get Mistress Desire out of here by nightfall," Enoch assured him. "And you can trust me to guard her well."

But Desire could contain herself no longer. The silk dress slid from her fingers and she came running to Morgan's side. Clutching at his arm, she stared up at him, her green eyes wide with fright. Morgan patted her shoulder reassuringly. "Don't worry, my love, Enoch means what he says. He'll see you safely to Ravenscliff."

"And what about you? Lord Bodine and his friends never got a glimpse of your face the night of the robbery. A tall man in a cloak, that's all they saw. But if Niall gives your description to the magistrates, you'll be fair game! Oh, Morgan, come with us—"

He shook his head. "It'll be safer for all of us if we split up now—today."

Belatedly, she suffered a pang of remorse. "If that's true, then I should travel to Cornwall alone while you and Enoch go your separate ways."

"A generous notion," Morgan said, giving her a smile. "But foolish and impulsive, as *you* are, my sweet. A young girl can't travel on coaches and stop overnight at inns alone

Unless she wants to be taken for a common strumpet — and treated like one."

"I hadn't thought of that," she began.

"That's why you must do exactly as I say." He put his arm around her and she felt the reassuring warmth of his body, pressed against hers. "Don't worry about me. I've no intention of remaining here once you and Enoch are gone."

"Where will you go?"

"That's no concern of yours. Enoch and I have had to go to ground before. Once he's left you at Ravenscliff, he'll know where to join me."

"But when will I see you again?"

He did not answer, but released her with a light pat on the bottom. "Finish unwrapping those parcels. We've only a few hours to complete your transformation into a young lady of quality." He looked her up and down, his eyes glinting with the familiar touch of mockery she had learned to know so well. "That'll take a bit of doing," he added.

He reached into one of his saddlebags and tossed her a small parcel. "Castile soap," he said. "It's favored by the ladies at court, so my milliner friend told me."

How could he speak so casually when he was preparing to send her away?

"I'll fetch you another bucket of water," he went on.

"Don't trouble yourself." She could scarcely get the words past the tightness in her throat. "Now it's turned warm, I'd rather bathe in the pool." Clutching the soap, she ran from the hut.

Desire gasped as she lowered her naked body into the pool. Even with the noon sun slanting through the branches overhead, she felt a chill at her first contact with the cool water. But she clenched her teeth and immersed herself up to her shoulders. The soap, made of Spanish olive oil, was a great luxury, much in demand by those who could afford it.

Swiftly she bathed her face and neck with the rich, soft

foam. Then she turned her attention to her breasts, her arms, and all the rest of her. After she had lathered her hair, she set the soap on a flat rock and, taking a deep breath, ducked down under the water.

"I think I'll join you."

Startled, she surfaced, shook back her hair, and looked up to see Morgan on the bank. He was already stripping off his clothes and piling them beside hers.

She wanted to protest, but she could not make a sound. She could only fill her eyes with the sight of him. Her gaze lingered shamelessly on his massive shoulders and deep chest, his lean hips and long, muscular legs.

He swung himself over the edge of the pool, and then he was beside her, his arms around her, drawing her against him. At the first touch of this body, she tried to pull away. "I've nearly finished," she was saying.

"But I have not yet begun," he told her with a teasing smile.

His meaning was plain in the look he gave her, his dark eyes glinting. The arrogance of the man! What gave him the right to think he could take her at his pleasure then send her away?

"Let me go!"

He lifted her feet from the sandy bottom of the pool, then released her so swiftly that she slipped backward, arms and legs thrashing. She had never learned to swim, and now she went under, choking and gasping.

Morgan's hands circled her waist, bringing her to the surface again. He lifted her higher, so that the rivulets of water ran from her rounded breasts, down over her firm, pink nipples.

She went on struggling, determined not to yield to him — not this time. But his hands tightened, and he raised her higher still, until his face was on a level with those round, wet globes. His tongue flicked at one sparkling drop of water, then another.

"Let me go!"

100

"Not before I've slaked my thirst," he said. His tongue went on teasing her moist flesh, and her nipples hardened into firm peaks. She drew in her breath sharply, feeling a quiver run down her body, setting every nerve atingle.

She would not give in! She would not—

His hands moved lower to cup her buttocks, his knowing fingers teasing her, exploring her most intimate crevices until she could no longer resist the sweet torment that surged up inside her. Her long legs parted to encircle his hard flanks. She threw back her head. Her long hair drifted on the surface of the water. His mouth caressed her throat, the curve of her shoulder.

As he raised her up still higher, her legs tightened around him. He supported her shoulders with his arm, and she rested her head against his chest, feeling the wet roughness of the matted hair against her cheek, hearing the steady beating of his heart.

The water ran from her limbs as they emerged from the pool. He was carrying her up the steeply sloping bank. There he lowered himself to the thick carpet of bracken, drawing her down on top of him.

Then somehow she found that she was kneeling above him, her thighs apart. She moved a little, positioning herself over his narrow hips to receive the first swift, hard thrust of his entry.

Instead, he began to move slowly, sensuously, stroking his hard length against the small, rosy bud of her womanhood. Tension coiled deep in her loins, building until she could bear it no longer. His hands filled with the white roundness of her buttocks. "Morgan . . . I want you inside me . . . now . . ."

He looked up at her through half-closed lids, his dark eyes glinting. "You must take what you want, love."

Her need left no room for hesitation. Swiftly her fingers closed around him to guide him to her moist cleft. And now she was lowering her hips, taking him deep inside her,

She gave a soft cry of sheer pleasure as he filled her,

pressing against her moist inner softness. Her hands gripped his shoulders, her body descending, rising, and then slipping down once more in an ever-quickening rhythm.

Only now did he answer her movements with his own, thrusting, withdrawing, deeper, harder. Her head went back and she cried out as he drew her with him, plunging on to the moment of fulfillment.

Desire held up the hand mirror, one of the small luxuries Morgan had brought with him from London. She scarcely recognized the girl who looked back at her.

It had been no easy task to fasten her fine silk gown, and she had found it even more difficult to arrange her hair in an elaborate coiffure. Even with the tortoise shell pins—Morgan had thought of everything—it had taken nearly half an hour to fasten the flat chignon at the back of her head and to get every one of her long ringlets to fall properly so that they framed her cheeks. She dipped her finger into the tiny silver pomade pot and was arranging a few feathery curls about her forehead when she heard Morgan calling to her.

"Aren't you ready yet?"

Before she could answer, she saw him coming through the door. He stopped on the threshold, his lips parting slightly as he stared at her.

She felt uneasy. It had been so long since she had dressed as a proper young lady, and then she'd had her maid to help her. "I did the best I could," she began.

He went on looking at her, silent, unmoving. Although he wanted to reassure her, he was too deeply stirred by the sight of her to speak. From their first meeting back in Whitefriars he had seen the beauty in her, despite the ragged dress, the tangled hair and smudged face. Even when she'd been dressed in boy's clothing, she had stirred his senses with her lush femininity. But the girl who faced him

102

now was a stranger, cool and lovely, with a gentle dignity about her.

If he had ever doubted what she had told him of her parents and her upbringing, every trace of uncertainty fell away. This was no Whitefriars cutpurse, no highwayman's doxy. This was a lady, a lady like those who used to come calling at Pendarren, when his mother had been mistress of the great house.

For the first since he had turned his back on his home and taken to the highways, he was shaken with an overpowering sense of loss, of longing for what might have been.

He wanted to sit at the head of the long, polished table in the dining hall at Pendarren, to see Desire's face, serene and infinitely lovely as she smiled at him over the ornate silver candelabra, her face glowing in the soft, golden light. He felt a swift, overpowering need to lie beside her in the great canopied bed upstairs in the master's chamber.

Even now, he could see how it would be, holding her to him, their limbs intertwined. And from their joining children would come, to carry on the name of Trenchard.

He couldn't let her go. He couldn't watch her ride off, knowing he would never see her again.

Casting aside all reason, he held out his arms and she came to him, her silken skirts rustling, her green eyes aglow. He drew her against him, breathing deeply, drinking in the delicate scent of her hair. "Morgan—my love," she cried softly. And now her face was upturned to his, her warm, red lips parted to receive his kiss.

Chapter Nine

When they drew apart, Desire looked up at him, her green eyes filled with a warm glow. "You won't send me away, will you, Morgan?"

Although he was moved by the soft urgency in her voice, he knew he must not betray his own feelings by word or gesture.

"You don't want me to go—you know you don't."

She was right, but nothing she could say would force him to admit it. If only he had not allowed himself to dream, even for a moment, of what might have been.

Inwardly, he cursed himself for a fool. How often had he warned her not to look back, not to waste her time grieving for a way of life that was forever out of reach?

With one swift movement he freed himself from her clinging embrace. His eyes raked over her. "You've done quite well," he said, with cool approval. "You will surely be able to pass yourself off as a lady, dressed as you are. And your hair—" He gave a brusque nod of satisfaction. "The height of fashion, so far as a mere male can tell."

He saw the uncertainty in her face, the quiver of her full red lips. But a moment later she put a hand on his arm.

"Don't send me away. We belong together—you must know that now."

It wasn't easy for him to ignore the naked longing in her face. Lord, how lovely she was, looking up at him that way, with her whole passionate being reflected in her eyes. How long could he go on denying his own overwhelming need for her?

"A touch of that lip rouge I brought you," he heard himself saying, "and perhaps one of those beauty marks, beside your eyebrow."

104

She pressed her lips together and he could see that she was struggling not to let him know how his words were hurting her.

"And remember, it won't be enough to alter your appearance," he went on, speaking like a dedicated schoolmaster. "You'll have to learn to think differently, too. You must remember what's at stake here. One slip of the tongue, however trivial, can give the game away long before you reach Cornwall."

"Come with us," she pleaded. "I've had so little experience at this sort of thing. I'll never be able to carry it off unless you're with me."

"Keep reminding yourself that your neck's at stake, and Enoch's, too. That should help you to keep your wits about you." He heard her draw in her breath sharply and saw the shadow of fear deep within her green eyes. Setting his jaw, he reminded himself that she'd be far more terrified if she found herself in a prison cell.

"I'll be careful," she told him. Then a faint hope lit her face. "But later on, you could come to me in Cornwall, couldn't you? They won't go on hunting us forever," she persisted.

"Desire, for the love of heaven—"

"I don't care how long I have to wait," she went on, "if only I can think about how it will be when we're together again. We can leave England, sail from Falmouth to . . . There are so many places we could go."

He did not answer, and she went on speaking quickly, driven by her desperate need. "Oh, Morgan, you'd find a way for us to get along, I know you would. Why couldn't we sail for the islands of the West Indies? Surely they must need men to work the sugar plantations there. And maybe one day we could have a plantation of our own."

When he did not respond she moved closer, her hands gripping his arms. "I'd work beside you in the fields. I'd wash your clothes and cook for you—"

"A most tempting offer," he said. "But it would scarcely be fair to you."

"Why not?"

"Because when I'd had enough of you I'd walk out on you."

He steeled himself against her cry of pain and humiliation.

He turned his back on her and picked up the brocaded valise he had brought from London. He opened the buckle and pulled out a length of heavy dark green velvet.

It was a moment before she realized that he was holding a cloak, cut in the latest fashion.

"Cost me a pretty penny," she heard him saying. She stood like a porcelain doll as he came back and draped the garment over her shoulders. "Let's see how it looks with the hood in place," he went on.

Obediently, she pulled the hood, with its black fox trimming, over her hair. The thick fur would help to shade her face from view.

"You've thought of everything," she told him. "I'll be sure to keep the cloak wrapped about me so that none of my fellow passengers can get a good look at me."

"But only if it's cool," he warned. "Otherwise you might arouse their curiosity." Once more his manner was brisk and impersonal. "You'll have to travel north for awhile, since there are no direct coach routes between here and Cornwall. The weather could be damp, even a bit chilly. But once you're heading into Devon, and then on to Cornwall, it should be warmer. The climate down there is mild, different from any other part of England. There'll be a sea mist in the hollows early in the mornings . . ."

And even now, he thought, the celandines would be spreading their golden carpet in the gardens at Pendarren, and the soft air would carry the fragrance of bluebells.

Then he realized that Desire was looking at him intently, her delicate, slanting brows drawn together in a puzzled frown.

Celandines and bluebells . . . Lucky for him she couldn't read his thoughts.

"Whatever you do, you must not attract attention to yourself," he went on quickly. "Try to avoid conversation with other passengers on the coach. If one of them tries to draw you out with questions about where you've come from and where you're going, pretend to fall asleep. Can you remember that?"

"I'm not a fool," she began.

"But you've had little experience with this sort of thing," he reminded her. "So listen, and remember. Public coaches usually don't travel by night. That means you'll have to spend a few nights at inns along the route. Enoch will bespeak a room for you—the best in the house."

"I shouldn't wish to put you to unnecessary expense—"

"You're traveling as a young lady of quality," he reminded her. "It's natural that you would demand the finest accommodations and the choicest dishes the inn has to offer."

"And what about Enoch's lodgings?"

"Enoch'll bed down in an attic or stable loft. He's your servant, remember."

"It's hardly customary for a young lady to travel without a female companion," Desire remarked. "If not a relative, then surely a maidservant."

"You had a maid of your own when you were living at home?"

"Why, certainly I did."

"And what became of her?"

"She ran off as she soon as discovered that Mama had been stricken with the plague. The other servants did, too—all except for old Prudence, our cook. And she paid for her loyalty with her life . . ." Desire's voice trembled, remembering the terrors that had followed.

"The plague wiped out whole households," Morgan was saying. "Surely there were other young women left as you were. It'll be awhile before the old social order is completely restored. If you're careful, no one will question your traveling with only a manservant to protect you."

"I hope you're right," Desire began.

"Now, as for Aunt Arathusa." He reached into his coat pocket and handed her an envelope. Like most gentlemen, Morgan wore a signet ring, and Desire saw that he had made use of it to impress his initials into the blob of dark blue sealing wax. "The letter inside will serve as your introduction. Naturally, I've spared my great-aunt the reasons for your unexpected arrival. As far as she'll know, you are a young lady in reduced circumstances, eager to serve as her companion."

"You've thought of everything." There was a sharp edge to her voice.

"Unfortunately, that's impossible. There's always the element of risk." His eyes held hers, and she saw the urgent warning there. "Never let down your guard, not for a moment. If there's unforeseen trouble, you'll have to do your own thinking—and be quick about it."

"But Enoch will be there to help me."

"And you can trust him, as I've always done. But sooner or later, you must learn to take care of yourself."

It was late afternoon when they left the hut. Morgan stood holding the reins of her horse.

"How did Enoch get hold of a lady's sidesaddle?" she asked.

"He can be relied on to get hold of whatever's needed," Morgan told her. "One way or another."

Because she could not bring herself to look at Morgan when their parting was so near, she kept her eyes fixed on Enoch, who was already mounted on his horse. The sun was low in the western sky now, and long shadows rose along the rocks at the mouth of the ravine.

"You'll probably have to spend tonight at the coaching inn," Morgan was saying. "It'll be best if you dine in your room. If one of the servants tries to draw you into conversation—"

"I'll pretend to be exhausted and I'll go to bed as early as possible."

"You're learning." He gave her an approving nod. "There's no direct coach service between here and Cornwall. That means you'll have to travel north until you reach the Golden Anchor, where you'll change for the Cornwall coach."

"We'd best be starting," Enoch called.

Desire caught her breath, realizing how little time remained before she would leave Morgan. But this couldn't be their final parting, she told herself desperately. Somehow they would find one another again.

Morgan put his hand into the pocket of his cloak, and drew out a small box. "These are for you," he said.

"Morgan . . . what . . ?"

"Open it."

She obeyed, and her eyes widened at the sight of the emerald earrings, part of the booty from Lord Bodine's coach.

"I had planned to fence these, along with the rest of the jewels, but their color reminded me of—" He broke off and looked away for a moment. "I promised you a share of the loot."

"And I told you I would not accept stolen goods." Her voice shook with indignation.

He closed her hand firmly around the box. "Take them. You won't be able to wear them on the journey, in case they should be seen and recognized, but one day . . ."

She felt a swift warmth course through her. He would come to her, she told herself. And when he did, she would put on the emerald earrings.

"One day you'll be be glad you took them. And if you should meet a Cornish gentleman—a prosperous farmer or a shipowner, perhaps—why, they'll serve you as a dowry."

She drew back, stunned by his words. Enoch had been right to pity her for loving Morgan, for Morgan didn't love her. How could he, when he spoke so casually of her marriage to another man? He was able to feel passion, even a brief tenderness, perhaps, but not love.

She took the box, and put it in her bodice. "I'm most grateful for your advice," she told him. "No doubt it will serve me well."

He lifted her into the saddle and handed her the reins. She spurred the horse forward. "A safe journey to you both," Morgan called.

She wouldn't turn to look at him again. She didn't dare.

Morgan stood unmoving in the crimson and gold glow of sunset, looking after Desire and Enoch as they disappeared between the grey rocks that marked the entrance to the ravine. He would wait until dark, then ride out himself.

He'd make straight for Lena Yarrow's lodginghouse in Southwark, where he had stayed before. Mistress Yarrow was always ready to provide decent lodgings and good food to any man wanted by the law, so long as he could pay her price. Once he had gone to ground in her house, he would feel reasonably safe. And when Enoch had delivered Desire to Cornwall, he'd join Morgan there.

It was best to leave here as soon as possible and to travel under cover of darkness. His mouth twisted in a self-mocking smile. Why the devil should he try to deceive himself? He didn't want to spend tonight alone in the hut where he and Desire had made love. How could he hope to sleep beside the hearth, tormented by the memory of her body, white and gleaming, her long limbs, her hair lying across his chest like a dark, sweet-scented cascade?

He had made the only rational decision when he'd sent her away. She would be safe with Aunt Arathusa, and in time, she would forget him. Even without a dowry, she would have little difficulty in finding herself a good husband, a decent, respectable gentleman who would be proud to claim her for his wife, who would provide her with a comfortable home and servants to help with the daily chores. There would be no more running and hiding for her, but a familiar routine, day following day in an orderly pattern.

But what of the nights? Morgan's hands clenched into hard fists. Another man would lie beside Desire, and she would yield up her body, as a dutiful wife should. Perhaps, if the man was kind and decent, in time she would come to care for him, to give herself willingly, even, her white arms outstretched, a welcoming smile on her soft red lips.

Morgan muttered a curse, turned on his heel, and strode to the shed where his stallion stood, saddled and ready. He mounted and spurred the beast to a canter. Soon he was plunging into the shadowy depths of the ravine, leaving the forge behind, setting his face toward London.

Chapter Ten

The public coach creaked and rattled as it went lumbering over the rutted road. Although a few of the newest and most luxurious coaches were now equipped with springs, this was one of the older kind: a square, heavy, boxlike vehicle that jolted each time it struck a deep hole left by last winter's rains. Desire sat next to a dusty window, trying to ignore the discomforts of the ride and the conversation of her fellow passengers.

After spending the first night of the journey at a small, but comfortable inn a few miles away from the forge, she had boarded the coach early the following day. She had not allowed herself to forget Morgan's advice for a moment. Drawing reassurance from her fine new clothes, she had acted the part of a highborn young lady, polite but distant with the three travelers with whom she shared the swaying vehicle. For the past hour she had kept her eyes closed, feigning sleep.

"We'll reach the Golden Anchor well before dark," said the plump gentleman in dark, sober garb. He was a prosperous silk mercer with a business in Cheapside, which, in spite of its name, was the most expensive shopping street in the City.

"I've stayed here before many times," the mercer was saying. "The food's cooked to a turn and the landlord's most amiable."

Desire opened her eyes and sat up straighter, smoothing the folds of her green velvet cloak. She hoped that there would not be too many more nights to spend at inns along the way, for she would not be able to breathe easy until she was safe at Ravenscliff. Thank heavens for Enoch, stolid and reliable, riding on top of the coach. Last night he had proved his usefulness when he got down to bespeak the best chamber for his mistress. He had treated her with exactly the right mixture of protectiveness and respect, playing the part of the well-trained manservant to the hilt.

Now she found herself listening as the mercer, a garrulous man, went on about the accommodations at the Golden Anchor. "We'll find a hearty welcome there, a good fire in the parlor, and a well-cooked dinner."

The stout, middle-aged lady in brown who sat beside Desire gave a sigh of relief so deep that her ample bosom threatened to burst the laces of her bodice.

"For my part, I'll be thankful to see the inside of the place, no matter the quality of the food," she said. "I feared we might be delayed on the road until nightfall. The terrible tales one hears of innocent travelers set upon in by highway robbers under cover of darkness."

"Lawless miscreants," said the mercer. "They lie in wait to strip honest men of their hard-earned money. And they'll not hesitate to shoot the coachman dead if he dares to resist." He glanced over at Desire. "But we must not frighten the young lady with such talk." Desire acknowledged his thoughtfulness with a forced smile, but remained silent.

"Ah, 'tis the helpless females who have most to fear from the highwaymen," lamented the stout lady. "They are not content with stealing our gold or jewels. Shameless brutes, they are, without respect for a virtuous maid or a respectable widow like myself."

"I fear you are right," the mercer agreed. "But Providence is just, madam. Such men are punished as they deserve." Warming to his subject, he went on, "Why, scarcely a month passes but some highway robber goes to meet his maker at Tyburn."

"And a fine sight it is," said a young fop, who sat beside the mercer. "As amusing as any performance to be seen on the stage at the king's theatre."

Desire glanced at the fop with distaste. He wore a sky-blue coat with gold embroidery, immensely wide knee breeches, yellow silk stockings with beribboned garters, and high-heeled shoes. His own hair was covered by an elaborate periwig of glossy black curls. One ringlet, known as a lovelock, fell over his shoulder, and was tied with a ribbon bow. His face was powered and rouged.

"I make it a point never to miss a hanging when I'm in London," he rattled on. "I remember one, last year, it was, where the fellow took a long time dying. The hangman was unskilled at his work, no doubt. After they drove the cart out from under the prisoner's feet, he hung there, kicking at the air like one of those rope dancers at Spring Gardens. He made a fine sight until two of his friends came and pulled on his legs to put him out of his misery. His face had turned the most striking shade of puce, I do declare."

Desire felt her body go tense, and a shudder ran through her. Her teeth sank into her lower lip. "Dear God," she thought, "suppose Morgan's taken prisoner." She went icy cold as if she could already see him standing in a cart, his arms and legs chained, with only moments to live.

"Hold your tongue, sir, if you please!" The mercer spoke sternly. "I'm sure these ladies find such talk most unseemly."

"It's been my experience that members of the fair sex enjoy the entertainment as much as the gentlemen." He turned a languishing look on Desire. "Have you never attended a hanging, madam?"

She swallowed, trying to control her revulsion. "No, I have not," she managed to say.

"Then I should deem it a privilege if you would allow me to escort you to—"

"The purpose of a public hanging is not to entertain light-minded young fools," the mercer interrupted. His outraged glare silenced the fop. "It is intended as a warning to those who might be tempted into a life of corruption. I always give my apprentices the day off so that they may attend a hanging at Tyburn."

The stout lady nodded her approval. "And I don't doubt the young fellows profit by such a lesson."

The coach was slowing down now. The driver turned off the road and drove through the stone archway into the yard of the Golden Anchor.

"Here we are, and well before dark," the mercer exclaimed with a look of satisfaction. "And there'll be a fine dinner waiting, mark my words. I could relish a pigeon pie, to start with." The coach drew to a halt. "A saddle of lamb, a fat capon, perhaps . . ."

He stared out the window, a puzzled frown on his round face. "Why, what's amiss here? The yard's usually busy this time of day. Pack trains laden with fish, wagons carrying bales of wool or leather to London . . ." He shook his head in bewilderment. "And where's the landlord? He's always on hand to greet the passengers."

"There is not even a hostler in sight to unhitch the horses," the fop remarked.

Desire leaned forward to get a better look from her window. The innyard was empty except for a handsome black and white stallion, whose rider was glancing about impatiently as if he, too, was annoyed by the lack of service.

"Look there!" the stout lady cried out. "Redcoats, a whole company of them!"

Desire started violently, possessed by fear. The redcoats, His Majesty's dragoons, were everywhere. Some were on foot, running out of the inn door or from inside the stables, others came pounding down from the rise behind the inn. The yard of the Golden Anchor exploded into a turmoil.

Confused images began to swirl before Desire's wide-eyed gaze: sunlight glinting on the gold buttons of the dragoons' scarlet coats, heavy muskets, raised and held at the ready, the glitter of a saber brandished by their captain, a giant of a man, his face brick red under his white peruke.

A moment later Desire's view was blocked; a man came leaping down from the top of the coach, then stopped for an instant outside her window. She saw Enoch's ruddy face, and as their eyes met, she caught his intense, urgent expression. He was trying to tell her something, but what was it?

A moment later musket fire exploded from all sides, and Enoch was running, dodging, while the bullets ploughed up clouds of dust around him. He was only a few feet from the black and white stallion when a stray bullet struck the beast.

It reared up into the air, throwing back its head, whinnying with pain. The rider, his cloak flaring about him, fought to control the terrified animal, only to be hurled to the ground.

Enoch came into view again, running under the flailing hooves of the stallion, making for the gate. Desire's hands clenched in her lap. *He's got to get away! He mustn't be taken!*

But the dragoons had seen him too. The officer shouted, "Halt! In the king's name!" And to his troopers: "Stop him! Shoot to kill!"

The horse, thrown off balance, fell over sideways, its legs kicking at the air.

Enoch kept going. Now another volley rang out, and Desire saw that he was clutching at his shoulder, dropping to his knees. One of the musket balls had found its mark.

The officer half rose in his saddle, pointing with his saber, shouting orders. But his men were blocked by the huge body of the stallion. Somehow, Enoch was rising to his feet; he swayed unsteadily for a moment. Desire sat still, every muscle taut, watching him, as he went plunging through the stone archway out of the innyard and was lost to view.

"After him!" the officer shouted. One of the troopers spurred his own mount over the prostrate stallion, the others following his example.

At first Desire could feel only intense relief for Enoch's sake. But now she became aware of her own predicament. Did he believe she could make her escape on foot? He must have known how little chance she would have, hampered by her skirt and cloak, her dainty, high-heeled slippers.

Then she understood.

Enoch was taking the only possible course, leading the dragoons away from her, giving her a chance to escape. And with her understanding came a determination she had not known she possessed.

She could not let him sacrifice himself to no purpose. Somehow she must make use of the time he had given her to get away. She wrenched at the door handle beside her.

"Stop, you mustn't —" the mercer protested, seizing her arm. "You're safer in here, young lady."

But she heard the captain of the dragoons ordering a couple of his troopers to stay behind. She saw them closing in around the coach.

115

She gathered her strength, then, somehow, she broke free from the mercer's grip and twisted the handle so that the coach door opened. Lifting her skirts, she jumped to the ground.

It would be foolhardy to run. Such an action would be sure to arouse the suspicions of the dragoons. Her eyes darted about the innyard and came to rest on the black and white stallion.

The bullet must have done no more than graze his flank, for he was back on his feet now, and a couple of hostlers came running from the stable to care for him.

His rider, a man in a plum-colored velvet cloak, lay motionless, his face masked with blood. The innkeeper, a tall, balding man, was hurrying across the yard in his direction. But Desire moved even faster.

Acting with a swiftness born of desperation, she threw herself to her knees beside the young man, clutched at his hand and cried out, "Oh, my brother, my dear brother! He must have help—quickly—"

The captain of the dragoons strode over to her. "Allow me to offer my assistance," he began.

But he was the last one Desire wanted near her. Turning on him, her green eyes blazing, she cried out, "You, sir, keep your distance. You are to blame for this dreadful accident."

The captain flushed. "You wrong me, mistress. We were dispatched to the inn to lay in wait for a gang of cutthroats—"

Ignoring his explanation, she turned to the landlord, who stood there with a small group of servants clustered near at hand.

"Have my brother carried inside at once," she ordered. "Take him to your best chamber. Send for a physician." The landlord stood staring for a moment.

"Do as I tell you, and waste no time about it," Desire went on, gaining confidence as she sensed the effect she was having on the man. No doubt her fashionable and expensive clothing and her imperious manner impressed the landlord, for he turned to a sturdy manservant. "You, there, Colin. Carry the gentleman upstairs to the front bedchamber. Nan, don't stand there gawking! Go along and see that all is in order. Make up a good fire, bring extra blankets."

Desire stood at the window of the spacious chamber on the second floor of the inn, looking down at the red-coated captain and his two men as they mounted and rode out of the yard. No doubt they would join in the pursuit of Enoch. How far could he get, wounded and on foot? She fought down a wave of despair that threatened to engulf her.

Morgan had put his trust in Enoch. She had no choice but to do the same.

Turning from the window, she went to the large bed where the injured man lay. For the first time since she had rushed to his side, she was aware of him, not as a means of her own deliverance, but as someone who needed her help.

She lifted the heavy ewer of water from the top of the commode, filled the basin, wet a clean cloth, and began to sponge the blood from man's face. He was young, perhaps in his early twenties. She winced as she saw the deep cut on his temple. She folded a towel into a compress and held it to the wound.

Had he struck his head on a sharp stone, or had he been cut by one of the stallion's flailing hooves? Perhaps he was suffering from other injuries she could not see. If only the landlord could bring a physician quickly, she thought.

She took one of his hands in hers and felt its icy coldness. Instinctively, she chafed his hand to warm it. She noticed that he wore a signet ring, not unlike the one Morgan had used on the waxen seal of the letter he had written to his great-aunt.

She looked at the ring more closely. The initials G and W stood out against the gold surface, carved in an ornate script, surrounded by a intricate design of leaves. The young man's eyelids fluttered slightly. Perhaps he would soon regain consciousness.

It was foolish of her to wait here, she told herself. Enoch had given her this brief time, and she should be making use of it. But how could she leave the young man injured and helpless? At least she must stay with him and do what little she could until the physician arrived.

Quickly she unfastened his plum-colored velvet cloak. As she did so, her fingers came into contact with a hard, square object in one of the pockets. A purse, she thought. She remembered Morgan's mocking smile as he had assured her that she had no skill as a pickpocket. But it took no skill to steal from an unconscious man. She felt a surge of revulsion. Had she begun to think like a criminal?

She reminded herself that if she succeeded in making her break for freedom, she must have money to pay her way. Dressed as she was, she could scarcely go roaming about the roads on foot without arousing suspicion.

She reached into the cloak pocket and found herself staring, not at a purse but at a leather-bound book. Useless to her, she thought, dropping it on the blanket.

It fell open and she saw the inscription on the flyleaf. *Sir Geoffrey Warrington.* And beneath it, in smaller script: *An account of a Tour through the Scotland and Wales along with Observations on the Flora and Fauna indigenous to these Regions* . . .

She closed the book and went on unfastening his cloak. Her fingers worked with quick, light movements as she undid the fine lace ruffle at his throat and opened the top buttons of his shirt.

Smoothing his blond hair back from his face, she got a closer look at his features: the lean, longish face, now drained of color, the thin, cleanly defined lips, the patrician look of him.

She rose to her feet and smoothed the blankets over him. The coal fire blazing on the hearth should keep him warm enough, she assured herself.

Turning away from the bed, she started for the door, but before she reached it she heard the landlord's voice and heard his heavy footsteps.

The landlord came bustling in and cast an anxious glance at the bed. "How is the poor young man faring now?" he asked.

"He hasn't yet regained consciousness. I fear for his life," said Desire. There was no need for her to feign distress as she glanced at the young man's pale, still face.

A small, thin chambermaid stood behind the landlord, holding Desire's valise, her only piece of baggage. She set it down with a curtsy. "Your own chamber's being made up now ma'am. It's right next to this one."

"As if I'll be able to rest, with my brother in such a condition," Desire said.

The landlord shook his head. "Nothing like this has ever happened at the Golden Anchor before. My establishment is most respectable, I assure you, and I only regret that you — that your brother —"

So long as she could keep the landlord on the defensive, Desire knew that he would not start to wonder why a young lady of breeding should have been traveling alone on a public coach.

"Respectable, indeed! To think that I came here to meet my brother, only to find the place taken over by a company of bloodthirsty dragoons." She wrung her hands. "Oh, if only dear Geoffrey had not been so adventurous. But he *would* go traveling all the way to Scotland, on horseback, without a single servant to attend him."

She stopped short as she saw the landlord's eyes, alert and frankly curious.

"My brother is Sir Geoffrey Warrington," she told the landlord.

"Ah, yes, yes." He bowed. Desire saw that her words had made a deep impression on the man, as she had intended they should. "I am honored, madam, to be of service to His Lordship. And to you, my lady."

"Indeed," she said, with a haughty lift of her chin. "And how is my brother to recover in a place like this one, filled with rampaging soldiers?"

"The dragoons are gone now," the landlord hastened to assure her. "And good riddance to them. A hard-drinking lot who can empty an honest landlord's cellar and go riding off without paying the reckoning —"

"And do they also make a practice of attacking innocent travelers?"

"No, my lady, I do assure you, such was not their intent. They were ordered here, to lie in wait for a gang of robbers — Knights of the High Toby. Your pardon, my lady. That's what common folk call the highwaymen who plague our roads."

"That fellow who rode atop the coach, was he one of those they were seeking?"

"I don't doubt it," the landlord told her. "Else, why would he have run the moment he caught sight of the redcoats? Honest travelers don't behave in such a fashion."

Although she knew she was treading on dangerous ground, Desire was anxious to find out what had happened to Enoch.

"Do you think they'll catch him?"

"He's not likely to get away, wounded as he is. But the rascal may lead them quite a chase, even so. Fear of the hangman's enough to keep him moving as long as he has the breath left in him."

The landlord gave her what was no doubt meant to be a reassuring smile. "You must not concern yourself with such creatures, mistress."

"My only concern is for my brother," she told him. "And he is in a most desperate state."

"I've sent one of my servants in search of a physician," the landlord told her quickly. "Meanwhile, you must try to compose yourself."

The little maid spoke timidly. "Perhaps if my lady would take some refreshments. Strong tea or a little blackberry cordial."

"Just so, Nan," the landlord said, relieved at being able to offer tangible help to the young lady. "A morsel of that capon, right off the spit, done to a turn."

"I couldn't possibly swallow a morsel," Desire began.

"But you must try," the landlord urged. "After your journey, you have need of sustenance."

And as Desire made no objection, he sent the maid scurrying off to the kitchen. He followed, but paused at the door. "The moment the physician arrives, I'll bring him up here to you."

Desire sat alone, sipping her dish of tea. The strong, hot brew revived her, and then, remembering that she had not eaten since early that morning, she took a bite of golden-brown capon. It was hot and tasty, and she finished it quickly, along with the newly baked bread.

The stout woman who had traveled with Desire on the coach had sent a message with the maid. She would be only too happy to keep the young lady company until the physician arrived

Desire had refused the offer, with thanks.

It was enough of a strain keeping up the masquerade for the benefit of the landlord and the maid, Desire thought. And how much longer could she hope to deceive them? If the young man were to regain consciousness, she was lost.

She wiped her fingers on her napkin, and pushing aside the tray, got to her feet. Since she would not have need of food and drink for awhile, this was the time to get away.

But she could scarcely try to make the journey to Cornwall on foot, trudging along the roads in her green silk gown and fur-trimmed cloak. No doubt the thin soles of her slippers would be worn through before she'd gone a mile.

Desire's purse held only a few coins, for Morgan had handed over the leather pouch with most of the travel money to Enoch for safekeeping. She thought, briefly, of the emerald earrings, still tucked into her bodice. Valuable, no doubt, but where could she hope to sell them without arousing suspicion?

She turned toward the bed. Since she'd found no purse in Geoffrey Warrington's cloak, perhaps he carried his cash in a money belt. Setting her jaw, she moved toward the unconscious young man.

"His Lordship's here, in my front chamber."

Desire started, hearing the landlord's voice in the hall outside. A moment later he came bustling into the room, followed by a tall, thin gentleman who carried a square leather satchel. He bowed and introduced himself as Lucas Munroe, physician.

She forced a smile, knowing that she must carry on her masquerade as best she could.

Chapter Eleven

The doctor leaned over the bed and pulled back the blankets. After he had completed his examination of the patient, he shook his head, gave a deep sigh, and turned to Desire.

"Your brother's injuries are grave indeed," he said. "Besides the blow to the head, inflicted by a kick from his horse, he suffers from a severe shock to the constitution. The disturbance in balance of the bodily humors has been most severe."

"Can you do nothing for him?" Desire interrupted.

"I shall exercise all my skills, and these are considerable, but you must not get your hopes up, my lady. In a case such as this one, the outcome is unpredictable. I recall a gentleman in London who was in a similar state after having been run down by a coach and four—"

"We are speaking of my brother," she reminded the doctor impatiently. "What can you do for him?"

Dr. Munroe drew himself up, his sense of self-importance offended. How dare this slender young girl question him in such a fashion, her cool green eyes challenging him with their level gaze? Then he reminded himself that the girl was sister to Sir Geoffrey Warrington.

He turned to the landlord and began rapping out orders. "Fetch hot bricks, at once. And as many stone hot water bottles as you can lay your hands on." He opened the straps on his black bag and drew out a lancet. "I shall require a basin and all strips of clean linen you can find. I shall bleed His Lordship, to begin with."

"Hasn't he lost enough blood already?" asked Desire.

"You must trust my judgment, my lady. Fortunately for

122

your brother, I am no country practitioner. I make my home in London, where my skills have earned me a great following among the gentry. Indeed, I would not be in these parts but that I was called to the estate of Sir Richard Carstairs, whose lady was stricken with an inflammation of the lungs. He would have none of the local physicians."

Desire suspected that Dr. Munroe was more concerned with impressing her with his skills, and earning a fat fee, than in devoting himself to the healing art. But he was the only doctor at hand, and the young man needed immediate aid.

Although Dr. Munroe tried to bustle her out of the room, she insisted on staying. When he had finished bleeding Sir Geoffrey, the young man's face looked paler than ever, but the doctor nodded with satisfaction.

He buttoned the lace-trimmed cuffs of his cambric shirt, adjusted his coat, and gave further orders to the harassed-looking landlord.

"Prepare a hot wine caudle, and be sure it includes figs, rue, and Venice treacle."

"We have dried rue in the pantry, and a few figs, but as for Venice treacle, I have never had a request for it."

"That's your concern," the doctor told him coldly. "Next, a compress soaked in a mixture of vinegar, and dried, powdered snails. A dozen snails, no less. This should be applied to His Lordship's forehead and changed each time it becomes dry. Keep the windows tightly sealed at all time—fresh air is poisonous to one in His Lordship's state." He reached into his bag and took out a small metal box. "Fortunately, I happen to have this with me—a most rare and costly powder combining powdered unicorn's horn, Mithridate, and Bezoar stone. You will place the entire contents in a pot of boiling water and keep it steaming by the patient's bedside, so that he may inhale its curative vapors."

He gave Desire a deep bow. "I can do no more for His Lordship now, but be assured, I will wait upon him tomorrow. Perhaps a merciful Providence will see fit to spare him."

Scarcely had he taken himself off when the chamber, the hall, the stairs were all astir with servants, dashing about to carry out his orders. It was after midnight when Desire was left alone with Sir Geoffrey, to wait out the rest of the night.

She longed to open a window, for the room was stifling and the steaming "curative vapors" gave off a sickening stench. Although the adjoining chamber had been prepared for her own use, and she would have welcomed a few hours of sleep, she was unwilling to leave Geoffrey Warrington in his present state.

It was close onto dawn when the young man woke her by calling out. He appeared to be delirious, mumbling words she could not understand. Quickly she went to the bed and leaned over him.

She saw his eyelids flutter and then realized that he was looking directly up at her. His hand moved over the blankets and she took it in her own. "My head . . ." he groaned.

"You had a bad fall," she reassured him gently. "Lie quietly and don't try to speak."

His fingers tightened around hers and she felt an enormous sense of relief. He was coming around, either because of the doctor's ministrations or his own sturdy constitution. Probably the latter, she thought, trying not to gag at the stench from the "curative vapors."

"Thirsty," he muttered. "So thirsty . . ."

She poured a cup of the wine caudle, and he took a swallow, then pushed it away. "Water, please . . ."

After a moment's hesitation she emptied the exotic mixture into the chamberpot and offered him a cup of clear spring water. "You must sip it slowly," she told him, putting her arm around his shoulders to raise him slightly.

When he had finished drinking, she tried to draw away, but he made a sound of protest and pressed closer to her, as if for reassurance. "I can't remember. How did I get here?"

"Hush," she told him softly. "You'll remember in good time. Now you must close your eyes and rest."

"Don't leave me—"

"I will be right here as long as you need me," she promised. His lips curved in a faint smile, and he rested back against the pillows. She dipped the compress in the mixture of vinegar

124

and powdered snails—why snails rather than oysters? she wondered—and applied it to his forehead.

After smoothing his blankets, Desire began to nod, lulled by the overpowering heat and the heavy, medicinal odors that filled the air. No matter what chance of fate had brought her to Sir Geoffrey Warrington, she realized, with a faint surprise, that she felt a growing responsibility toward him. *As if I really were his sister,* she thought. A moment later she dropped off to sleep with his fingers still closed around hers.

It was early morning when she awoke. She heard the sound of horses, stamping and jingling their bridles in the yard below. A moment later, she heard the crack of a coachman's whip and the sound of wheels receding into the distance. She tried to free her hand from Geoffrey's so that she might rise and stretch, after sleeping in the chair. But her movement brought a moan of protest from him, and a moment later she saw that he was looking at her.

"Hot . . . it's so hot . . ."

The revolting stench from the vapor pot would have been enough to make even a healthy man gag, she thought.

"The window . . ." he was muttering now. Dr. Munroe had forbidden her to open the windows, she reminded herself sternly. Geoffrey began to toss about on the bed, his eyes entreating.

Unable to refuse, she rose and raised one of the windows a few inches. The sweet scents of spring filled the room, and she took a deep breath. Surely the mild, spring air could do him no great harm, covered as he was with heavy blankets. She compromised by drawing the shades once more, so that the light would not trouble his eyes.

He rewarded her with a grateful smile. She offered him fresh water, and he drank again.

When the landlord came in a few moments later, he was relieved and gratified to find his illustrious young guest conscious. He bustled and bowed his way over to the bed. "Providence be thanked," he said fervently. "Dr. Munroe is a most

125

excellent physician. And Your Lordship is most fortunate to have had your sister here at your side through this dreadful ordeal."

Desire drew in her breath sharply and braced herself. In a moment Sir Geoffrey would deny her claim that she was his sister. She would be dragged off in disgrace by the outraged landlord and turned over to the nearest magistrate.

But the young man remained silent, his brow furrowing slightly. Desire seized the opportunity to get the landlord out of the room. "My brother needs some nourishment," she said. "And so do I. Strong tea, I think. And two boiled eggs. Then tell your cook to prepare a strong meat broth. Beef or fowl, not mutton."

The landlord smiled, mentally adding these additional items to the reckoning. "Perhaps a pot of marmalade, made of the finest Seville oranges. I happen to have one left in the larder."

As soon as he was safely out of the room, Desire turned to Geoffrey Warrington, who was looking at her closely. "That man you were speaking to," he began.

"He's the landlord of this inn. The Golden Anchor."

"He mentioned my sister. But you're not —"

"Please, do not excite yourself," Desire said. "After you have had your tea we will speak of these matters."

He tried to sit up, then dropped back against the pillows. "My head," he groaned.

"You were thrown by your horse. The doctor said the beast must have kicked you as well."

"Good Lord!"

"You must keep perfectly still until the doctor returns," she told him. "Otherwise, you may do yourself further harm."

"You are not my sister." He gave her a searching look. "Who are you?"

There was still time to make a run for safety, Desire told herself. If her luck held, she could be down the back stairs and out of the yard before the landlord returned. But how far would she get once Sir Geoffrey had a chance to tell the landlord the truth?

126

She chose her words carefully. "You were badly injured yesterday. I was nearby and offered my help. I have had some experience caring for the sick."

"I remember your face in the candlelight," he said slowly. "Each time I woke, you were there. Your voice was so gentle, and the touch of your hands . . . cool and light . . ." His blue eyes were warm with gratitude. "To show such kindness to a complete stranger—I owe you more than I can ever hope to repay . . ."

"Then if I were to ask a small favor of you?"

"Only name it."

"Don't betray my harmless deception to the landlord, to anyone, I beseech you."

"You have my word on it." He clasped her hand, as if to seal the promise. His gaze lingered on her dark, luxuriant hair, her delicate features, and tilted emerald eyes. "I'm glad you're not my sister," he told her.

". . . so you see, I was forced to travel in a public coach, and all alone. A young lady in such a position must guard her reputation. If I had not claimed to be your sister, how could I have accompanied you into the inn, and spent the night here in your chamber, without being taken for a common . . . you do understand, surely?"

"Indeed, I do," Geoffrey assured her. He had finished his tea and a bit of toast, and now he rested against the propped up pillows. "But why were you traveling alone?"

Desire went on, speaking the truth when she could, but weaving in half-truths and blatant lies when nothing else would serve.

"I was on my way to Cornwall, to stay with my great-aunt. I have no other relatives, since my parents were taken in the plague, and those of our servants who did not die had fled long ago. I did hire a new maid, who presented me with the most impressive references." Desire sighed and shook her head. "She took my money and my jewels, even my trunks, and slipped away from the inn where we were staying on the first night of the journey. She left only that small valise over there, and the coins I carried on my person."

"A common thief, a creature without a conscience—she must have been—to go preying upon a helpless, trusting young lady like you," he said indignantly.

"Don't excite yourself," Desire soothed him. "If only I am able to reach my great-aunt's home in Cornwall, I will be safe enough."

Perhaps Geoffrey Warrington might be moved to show his gratitude by offering her enough money to see her on her way.

"Is it necessary for you to go on to Cornwall at once?"

"Why, where else am I to go?"

"That's easy enough," he said with calm assurance. "You must come with me to Warrington House in London."

She drew back, thrown off guard by his unexpected offer. Until this moment she had thought only of getting as far as possible from London, and hiding away in Ravenscliff.

"I could not possibly accept such an invitation, my lord," she began.

To her surprise, the young man looked slightly embarrassed. "I mean you no harm, I swear it. My mother and sister are both in residence at the townhouse. Your reputation would not suffer the slightest blemish while you are under our roof."

Desire looked away. Geoffrey had completely misunderstood the reason for her refusal. What if he knew that she was no innocent virgin, fearful of her reputation, but a highwayman's mistress? But he would never know, for she must ask him, outright, for enough money to get her to Cornwall. Such a loan would mean little enough to a young man in his fortunate position.

"You are most kind," she said demurely. "But my great-aunt will take good care of me." She paused and gave him an appealing look. "If I can find the means of continuing my journey, I will find a respectable home with her. I will earn my keep by serving as her companion," she added.

"Jesú, what dreary prospect for a lovely young lady!" he exclaimed. "Companion to an elderly aunt in Cornwall. No, it's all settled. As soon as I am able to travel you must come home with me."

"But Aunt Arathusa—"

"Later, if you still feel you must go off to Cornwall . . . but perhaps you will have changed your plans."

Although under ordinary conditions it would be prudent to get as far from London as she could, Geoffrey's offer opened up new possibilities. Surely as a guest of Geoffrey Warrington she would be safe from the slightest trace of suspicion.

"His Majesty's returned to London, and his court is the only place to be this spring. You must sample at least a few of the city's pleasures. Mother would never forgive me if I allowed you to ride away before she met you and thanked you properly. And as for me, only say you will honor me with your company, for a little while, at least."

Her mind moved swiftly. Once in Cornwall, what chance would she have of seeing Morgan ever again? She would not even be able to learn what had happened to him, whether he had escaped or been captured. But in London . . .

She looked down, her long lashes shading her green eyes. "I will come with you, my lord."

"My name's Geoffrey. And you are—"

"Mistress Desire Guilford."

"Desire," he said softly. "A most unusual name—but one that suits you well."

Chapter Twelve

"You must stay here with us for as long as you wish, my dear," Lady Mirabelle Warrington told Desire. "I do hope this bedchamber is to your liking. It's not one of the largest, but you do have a fine view of the gardens, and the river, as well." She led Desire to one of the tall windows and drew aside the cream-colored velvet drapes. "The tulips are coming into bloom now, you see. And there is the lime walk — most romantic in spring, I always think. It was designed by Mr. Inigo Jones, himself."

Although Desire had met Geoffrey's mother only a short time ago, she had already discovered that the small blonde woman chattered incessantly, skipping from one subject to another with scarcely a break. She emphasized her chatter with little birdlike nods of her head, so that her high-piled curls were set aquiver.

Desire and Geoffrey had arrived at his imposing townhouse on the Strand only half an hour ago. As soon as he had introduced Desire and explained how she had cared for him during the four days they had spent at the Golden Anchor, Lady Mirabelle had showered her unexpected guest with gratitude.

"Certainly dear Mistress Guilford must stay here as long as she wishes," said Geoffrey's mother, after which she had immediately begun making plans for Desire's entertainment.

As soon as Geoffrey had retired to his own room to change his travel-stained clothes, his mother had led Desire through the vast entrance hall and upstairs to one of the many bedrooms reserved for visitors.

Now, turning away from the tall window, Desire looked

about the room itself. Her gaze moved from the wide, canopied bed with its cream-colored satin curtains, embroidered
in silver threads, to the small chairs, with their gilded frames
and brocaded upholstery. The gleaming parquet floor, with its
alternating squares of light and dark wood, was polished to a
high luster. In one corner stood a taffeta-draped dressing table
with a large silver-framed mirror.

"I've never seen so fine a chamber," Desire said.

"You deserve the best we have to offer," Lady Mirabelle assured her, putting a dainty hand on her arm. "When Geoffrey
told me how you cared for him with such skill and kindness
. . . To think of my poor boy, so terribly injured, alone and
helpless. And then you appeared, like a guardian angel."

Desire felt a pang of guilt, remembering that it had been
her instinct for self-preservation that had sent her running to
Geoffrey's side when he had lain unconscious in the yard at
the Golden Anchor. It was only later, as she sat watching beside his bed, that she was moved by a genuine concern for the
young man.

"Indeed, madam, there was little enough I could do for
your son. It was his own strong constitution that helped him to
recover so quickly."

"You are far too modest," her hostess assured her. "No matter, for now that you are here, we shall keep you with us until
summer, at the least."

"Nothing would please me more," said Desire, "but I cannot
delay my journey to Cornwall for anything like that long. My
great-aunt will be expecting me."

"I shall write to her," said Lady Mirabelle, dismissing the
problem with an airy wave of her hand. "I'm sure she will understand your wish to prolong your visit until you have tasted
all the pleasures we have planned for you. Geoffrey and I, and
dear Rowena, of course, will do all we can to make your stay
an enjoyable one."

What on earth would Morgan's great-aunt make of such a
message? Desire was about to protest that if a letter were to be
written, she herself should attend to the matter, but Lady
Mirabelle had already gone off on another tangent.

131

"Now that His Majesty has returned to London, there'll be no end of festivities. Perhaps we'll catch a glimpse of him on the deck of the royal barge next week. There's to be a splendid fete on the river, and you know how fond the king is of that particular entertainment." Lady Mirabelle obviously assumed that Desire knew all about the doings of the king and his court. Nothing could have been further from the truth, for Desire's family had never moved in such exalted company. Her father's friends had been solid, prosperous merchants like himself.

"We'll take our own barge out on the Thames, of course," she went on. "I have ordered a new, gold-fringed canopy for the occasion. I do hope you enjoy the fireworks as much as I do."

"I'm sure I will, my lady," Desire managed to say before Geoffrey's mother went on chattering in her high, girlish voice. Although she was probably in her late forties, Lady Mirabelle had the speech and manners of a young miss, recently out of the schoolroom. She dressed the part as well, for her pink taffeta gown was ornamented with many satin rosettes and ribbons, while her stays were were so tightly laced that her ample breasts were pushed upward into reasonable youthful contours. Desire was sure that although Her Ladyship's hair had once been the same shining blonde shade as Geoffrey's, she kept it that way with rinses of chamomile and marigolds, as so many fashionable ladies did. She wore a star-shaped beauty patch beside her eyebrow, and her cheeks had been rouged to a soft shade of pink.

"We will attend the theater often, now that they've been permitted to open again," she was saying. "And we'll have an evening at the Spring Gardens."

During the plague, and for several months after, all public places of entertainment had been shut down by royal edict, but now London was returning to its usual hectic pace. From what Lady Mirabelle was saying, Desire could only suppose that His Majesty and the members of the court were throwing themselves into a round of pleasure with renewed vigor, as if they were determined to put the whole dreadful calamity behind them.

Until her arrival here at Warrington House, Desire had not given much thought to Geoffrey's social position, except for her her fervent hope that while she was under his roof she would be safe from pursuit by the law. His name and rank would surely shield her from suspicion long enough for her to plan her next move.

But now, as his mother went on describing the many festivities to be crowded into the next few weeks, Desire realized that the Warringtons were well known at court. So long as she remained here, she too would be accepted into the charmed circle surrounding His Majesty himself.

"I suppose that Lady Castlemaine will be sharing the royal barge at the fete," Geoffrey's mother was saying. "Such a striking creature, don't you agree? That auburn hair and magnificent shape. And her jewels! The king has been most lavish with her, hasn't he? Although they do say that His Majesty is beginning to grow a little weary of her outbursts of temper."

Lady Mirabelle looked at Desire, as if expecting confirmation of this bit of gossip. "Indeed, Madam?" was all Desire could say.

"My dear, I've heard that she can outswear any common fishwife, when her temper's roused. And with so many other lovely ladies for the king to choose from, there is no reason why he should put up with Lady Castlemaine's ill-humor. Do you think it's true what they are saying, that her youngest baby was fathered not by the king but by the Duke of Buckingham?"

Although Desire, like everyone else in London, had heard of the king's long liason with Lady Castlemaine, she knew none of the intimate details. She was completely at a loss, therefore, as to how to answer her hostess's question. But fortunately, Geoffrey's mother did not wait for a reply.

"It's quite remarkable when one remembers that, when His Majesty was restored to the throne, Lady Castlemaine was only plain Barbara Palmer, the wife of Roger Palmer—no more than an ordinary lawyer. How fortunate for her that she caught His Majesty's eye, directly he had returned from his years of exile." Lady Mirabelle gave a tinkling little laugh. "Of course, he is no more faithful to Her Ladyship than he is to the queen herself. He has a roving eye—that's because of his French heritage. And Italian, too. Little wonder His Majesty can be captivated for a night by a pretty little orange seller at the theater. And as for these actresses—a shameless lot, but most fetching, some of them."

Geoffrey's mother paused for breath and gave Desire an apologetic look. "You are so quiet, my dear. I trust I have not shocked you."

"No, Madam," Desire said politely. "It's only that I am a little fatigued by the journey."

"And all those nights when you sat up caring for my son. Dear me, you must think I am most thoughtless. I'll send Tilda to unpack for you and help you to disrobe. Then you must lie down and rest until dinner."

Although the bed was comfortable, and Desire, stripped down to her chemise, was soothed by the delicious sensation of the silk sheets against her skin, some half-formed thought kept nagging at the back of her mind so that she could not drop off to sleep. What was it Lady Mirabelle had said? She closed her eyes, her body tense as she went on trying to remember. Her hostess had been rattling on about the king . . .

Then Desire sat up in bed, the satin comforter sliding away from her body. Her green eyes were aglow with excitement, and her mind began to move swiftly.

The king and Lady Castlemaine . . . the king and all those other women—orange sellers, actresses . . .

Even when she had lived at home with her parents she had not been completely ignorant of the gossip about the king. She knew, as every Londoner did, how King Charles would go haring off in pursuit of a pretty female.

Next week she would get a glimpse of the king aboard his barge, but that would not serve her purpose. However, if she remained here at Warrington House as long as her hostess expected her to, surely she would have a chance to get nearer to

His Majesty. Accompanied by Geoffrey and his mother, it might even be possible to speak to the king.

And then . . . and then . . .

What was it Enoch had said that day, back there at the forge?

"A man can't fight his way into the king's audience chamber with his sword or pistol."

But a pretty young girl who made use of her opportunities might be able to arrange for a private audience.

Surely such a course of action would be dangerous. Desire reminded herself of all she had heard about the formidable — and jealous — Lady Castlemaine. No doubt the lady would look with disfavor on any possible rival for the king's attention. And what about all the other ladies of the court, who fluttered about the king like so many brightly colored butterflies?

"And suppose I did manage to catch his eye. What if he were to agree to give me a private audience?" Desire asked herself. "What could I hope to gain from such a meeting?"

A royal pardon for Morgan.

She felt a surge of excitement, mingled with uneasiness. If she asked the king for a favor, what might he demand of her in return?

She would not even allow herself to consider that, not yet. The whole scheme was so unlikely. It was scarcely possible to imagine herself, a girl who had taken part, however unwillingly, in the robbery of a nobleman's coach, confronting His Majesty and asking him to pardon the highwayman who was her lover. She must be mad to consider taking such an action.

And yet she knew with absolute certainty that even if there were only the slightest chance of success, she would make the attempt. It didn't matter that Morgan had sent her away, that he had given her the emerald earrings to use as a dowry. He did not care if she married another man. He did not love her, and perhaps he never would.

There was no reason she should lift a finger to try to help him. Let him save himself if he could, and if not . . . he had always known that he might end his career on the gallows. He had taken to the highway of his own free will.

But it was no use trying to reason with herself, not where Morgan was concerned. For she knew that whatever he was, she would move heaven and earth to protect him. In their brief time together she had given him not only her body but her complete devotion.

That evening at dinner, Desire met Rowena Warrington, a tall, thin woman, whose gown of pale tan silk did nothing to disguise her angular figure or enhance her coloring. Even before Geoffrey introduced his sister, Desire saw the resemblance between them. Rowena, however, had none of her brother's striking good looks. Geoffrey's blond hair was bright and lustrous, while hers was dull, mouse-brown; her eyelashes were so pale and sparse that were nearly invisible. But Desire quickly discovered that there was a quick mind at work behind her faded blue eyes.

"How very fortunate that you were on hand in the yard when my brother was thrown from his horse," Rowena said.

"Fortunate, indeed." Lady Mirabelle smiled warmly at Desire. "And we must do all we can to show our gratitude. I have already been telling Desire—I may call you that, may I not, my dear?—I've been describing my plans for her entertainment while she is staying here with us."

"I believe Geoffrey said you were traveling by public coach, isn't that so?" Rowena asked, unwilling to be sidetracked by her mother's chatter.

"I was on my way to Cornwall—"

"You were going to visit your aunt."

Desire hesitated slightly and took a sip of the Canary wine before her.

"My great-aunt. She is in her nineties and has little contact with the outside world."

"And you were kind enough to undertake such a long journey to cheer an elderly recluse."

"She has offered to provide me with a home," Desire began.

"And she is, no doubt, looking forward eagerly to your arrival." Rowena spoke politely enough, but Desire felt uneasy under her relentless questioning.

"I had planned to be at her home by now," said Desire.

"But you did not hesitate to change your plans, to interrupt your journey so that you might offer your assistance to my brother — a complete stranger?"

"Desire is blessed with a most generous disposition," said Geoffrey's mother.

"So it would appear," Rowena agreed, without the slightest trace of warmth in her pale, sparsely lashed eyes. "Tell me, Mistress Guilford, why did you offer your help to my brother? Couldn't the landlord have taken charge of Geoffrey's care, at least until a physician had been found?"

"I have had some experience in caring for the sick," Desire said. She took another sip of her wine, then started on her soup, a rich, well-seasoned blend of leeks and cream.

Geoffrey and his mother had accepted her presence without question, but it was becoming plain that Rowena would be more difficult to convince.

"And what was the nature of this . . . experience, Mistress Guilford?"

"I cared for my parents when they were stricken by the plague."

"You had no servants to assist you?"

"The servants ran away as soon as they saw the first signs — except for our old housekeeper. She was stricken too, and I had to care for her as well."

Desire shrank from the memories of those terrible days when she had bathed fevered bodies, changed soiled linens, held basins of blood-streaked vomit, and tried to force useless medicines between cracked lips, only to be defeated in the end.

Now, seated here at the candlelit table in the high-ceiled diningroom of Warrington House, she felt herself being drawn back, swiftly, inexorably, to those shuttered chambers, rank with the nauseating stench of sickness. She remembered her mother's scream of agony when she had tried to lance the horribly-swollen bubo in her groin. She heard, again, her father mumbling in delirium, calling for his wife over and over again, while Desire sat beside him in the stifling hot bedcham-

137

ber. The front door of their house already had been marked with a red cross, a warning that none should leave — and that anyone rash enough to enter would do so at his own peril.

Desire set down her soup spoon with a clatter and pushed away her bowl. She tried to draw a deep breath, but felt her throat constricted as if by a metal band.

"You must forgive my sister's questions," Geoffrey said quickly. "None of us would willingly remind you of so cruel an experience."

"How perfectly dreadful to think of one so young, left alone to deal with such horrors," Lady Mirabelle said. "Fortunately, we were not in London at the time. We stayed at Northcote, our home in Yorkshire."

Before she could go on, Rowena threw another question at Desire. "Had you no relatives here in London who might have offered you shelter?"

"No, I did not." Desire had managed to regain a measure of her self-control. She must not allow Geoffrey's sister to throw her off balance again. "I consider myself fortunate to have been offered a home by my great-aunt."

"Scarcely an inviting prospect for a girl as young and attractive as you are, my dear," said Lady Mirabelle.

"I hope she may grow fond of me, in time — and I of her."

"You have never met this aunt of yours?" Rowena asked.

"My father's business kept him here in London. We did little traveling."

"Your father was a tradesman?" Rowena's pale eyebrows shot up, and she gave Desire a look of distaste.

"He was a wine merchant, highly respected by others in his trade," said Desire with quiet dignity.

"No doubt," said Rowena. "But do tell us, Mistress Guilford, how did you manage to get on all these months after your parents were taken from you?"

Desire kept her eyes on one of the polished silver bowls filled with pink and white roses while she searched frantically for an acceptable answer. Suppose she told them the truth? What if she described those wretched weeks in Old Sally's crumbling Whitefriars den, filled with the lowest kind of streetwalkers?

She tried to imagine the horror in Lady Mirabelle's eyes if she were to tell about the night she had tried to pick Morgan Trenchard's pocket, only to be set upon by Jem and his men. What would Geoffrey say if she described how she had been thrown down on her back on the slimy wet stones of the alley, and how only Morgan's unexpected arrival had saved her from being raped?

Morgan.

The table, the huge dining room with its ornate molding of plaster fruit and flowers, took on an air of unreality. Rowena was speaking again, but at that moment her words were unimportant, meaningless . . .

Where was Morgan now? Had he reached the place of safety he'd spoken of, or was he still on the run? If only she could be sure that he was alive, free. She had managed to use her wits to save herself for the time being. But how was she to go on unless she could hope to see Morgan again? To feel his arms around her, the warmth and strength of him enveloping her?

"Mistress Guilford?"

By a tremendous effort of will, Desire forced herself to listen to Rowena. "I fear I may have distressed you again," Geoffrey's sister was saying. "Do forgive me. I only wondered how you managed all alone since the death of your parents. You are young to make your own way in London, with the city in such a state of upheaval."

"I was not alone," Desire said carefully. "I stayed at the home of one of my father's clerks. But as he has not yet been able to find another position, and can scarcely provide for his own family, I did not want to burden him any longer than necessary."

If Desire hoped that her explanation would satisfy the indefatigable Rowena, she quickly discovered her mistake. "This person, this clerk you speak of. In what part of London does he live?"

"For the love of heaven, Rowena!" Geoffrey turned on his sister, his voice tight with anger. "Surely you know better than to trouble Mistress Guilford with your impertinent questions.

She is here at my invitation, and so long as she choses to accept my hospitality, you will treat her with respect. Is that understood?"

Rowena caught her breath, and two spots of color burned high on her sallow cheeks. She had cared for her brother, loved and pampered him, since infancy. Because of the difference in their ages, she had sometimes felt more like a mother than a sister to him. Now, all at once, it came to her with stunning clarity that he was no longer a petted baby brother but a handsome and self-assured young man.

Cold fury rose up in her, but it was not directed against her brother. Desire Guilford, this beautiful, green-eyed young girl — *she* was to blame. A scheming little nobody who had met Geoffrey purely by chance and had used her wiles to insinuate herself into their home.

No, not "our home," Rowena reminded herself. Geoffrey had not only inherited their father's title but his property . . . and his complete power over his sister. He was nine years younger than she, but in the eyes of the law, he was master here.

"It would give us the greatest pleasure to provide you with suitable diversions so long as you are with us, Mistress Guilford," Rowena said, forcing her thin lips into the semblance of a smile. "And since your trunks have been lost —"

"Not lost," Geoffrey put in. "Stolen."

"Ah, yes, stolen by your maid. Most distressing for you. In any case, I should be pleased if you would borrow a few of my own dresses. Tilda, my maid, could make the necessary alterations. She is a skilled needlewoman."

"Nonsense, my dear," said Lady Mirabelle. "Desire must choose a new wardrobe. I shall send for my own dressmaker in the morning."

"You are most kind," said Desire quickly, "but I could not possibly accept —"

"My dear, you must. Rowena's gowns would be most unsuitable for one so young as you." Lady Mirabelle clasped her hands together, her eyes sparkling. "Clothes are my passion, and it will give me such pleasure to see you fitted out properly."

Desire could only smile and accept her hostess's offer. If she were to carry through her plan, she would first have to catch the king's eye and persuade him to give her a private audience. The proper wardrobe help her to make the most of her appearance.

Since fate had offered her this chance, she must make the most of it. She would use every weapon at her command to try to win a royal pardon for the man she loved.

Chapter Thirteen

Morgan paced the length of the small, dingy chamber on the top floor of Lena Yarrow's lodginghouse in Ram Alley. He had made his way here nearly three weeks ago, lying low by day and traveling by night. But now, although safely hidden from the law, he felt a growing uneasiness as he waited for Enoch to join him.

He knew one way to ease the tension. His full, sensuous mouth curved upward in a brief, ironic smile. There was Polly, Mistress Yarrow's younger sister, a ripe, flaxen-haired girl, with large, firm breasts that pushed against her worn bodice and a well-rounded rump that swung in a most enticing way when she walked.

The wench had given Morgan many a meaningful glance since he had arrived here. Each time she had brought his food, she had lingered as long as possible; she also came upstairs with fresh bed linen far more often than was customary in such an establishment, and always she perched herself at the foot of the bed, smiling enticingly at him, her full lips parted to reveal her even white teeth. She had brushed against him even when there was plenty of room to get by. Indeed, she had done everything but to tell him in so many words that she was ready to lie with him, eager to pleasure him in whatever way he chose.

And he knew from experience that Polly had mastered every trick in the book. Like most of the girls in this part of Southwark, she had lost her maidenhead before her fourteenth year.

The wenches of Ram Alley were not famous for their virtue, any more than the men were for their honesty. Cutpurses and pimps, forgers and burglars, counterfeiters and dealers in stolen goods, all congregated here, giving the district its reputation as one of the most heavily populated centers of criminal activity in London's teeming suburbs. Ram Alley, Pickering Court, and Fetter Lane were lined with dilapidated houses and were connected by unlit passageways and rat-infested courtyards. Men who were on the run from the law could find a haven in Mrs. Yarrow's lodgings, or one of a dozen like it, so long as they could pay her outrageous prices.

Constables or watchmen foolish enough to come into the district to hunt for a wanted man had little chance of success, even if, by great good luck, they escaped a ferocious beating by the armed ruffians who made these courts and alleys their refuge. Few outsiders found their way to Mrs. Yarrow's domain in any case; for it was a "blind house," its entrances and exits were concealed behind a maze of other broken-down buildings.

But even as Morgan reminded himself how fortunate he was to have found such a haven in which to wait for Enoch to join him, he was far from easy. Enoch should have arrived in London from Cornwall days ago, and come here straight away as they had agreed.

He stopped his pacing to stand at the dirt-streaked window and stare down moodily at the filthy stretch of alley below. Enoch could take care of himself in a tight place; he'd proved that often enough.

And in the meantime, there was Polly. Next time she came up to his room, why shouldn't he tumble her on the sagging bed? If nothing else, she could ease his male needs and provide him with an hour or two of casual distraction. No doubt the ripe, good-natured wench was bewildered, even a little offended, by his standoffish behavior.

On other occasions when he had taken cover here, he had not hesitated to pleasure himself with Polly. For a few moments he lingered over the fleeting images of her naked

143

body stretched out beneath his: the large, deep pink nipples of her ample breasts, the fullness of her thighs and the pale flaxen triangle that both concealed and enhanced her lush womanhood. The way she had of sliding down, her eyes half closed, her lips parted to encircle him, to take in his hard masculinity.

But it wasn't Polly he wanted, not now. And the realization made him curse himself for ten kinds of fool.

There was only one woman he needed, and he himself had placed her forever out of his reach. He had been right to send Desire away. No question of that. What other course could he have taken? She was not suited for the sort of life he led. Hadn't she told him so herself?

He flinched inwardly, remembering the look in her green eyes when he had said good-bye to her that afternoon at the forge. When he had handed her the emerald earrings and told her to use them for a dowry, he had wounded her to the core, exactly as he had intended to do.

Every time she thought of him she would be filled with bitter humiliation. She would hate him for having taken her and then abandoned her. And that was all for the best, Morgan assured himself. It would be easier for her to turn to another man when the time was right.

A moment later, Morgan's hand closed into a fist, and before he realized what he was doing, a jarring pain went shooting from his knuckles up his arm. He shook his hand ruefully. Damn good thing he had struck the rotting wooden frame instead of the glass, or he would have put his fist through one of the panes. And no doubt Lena Yarrow would have added the cost of the damage to her fee.

"Master Trenchard, sir . . ." He turned swiftly, recognizing young Barney Yarrow's shrill voice. Barney was Lena's son, a dirty, sharp-witted brat who had somehow managed to survive to the age of twelve, thriving in these dangerous, disease-infested surroundings.

"Yer friend's here, sir."

Morgan opened the door and felt an overwhelming sense

144

of relief at the sight of Enoch standing on the threshold. He tossed Barney a small coin, and the boy disappeared down the narrow, unlit stairs.

"The roads between the Downs and Cornwall must have been in worse repair than usual, to keep you traveling for so long."

Enoch sank down on a rickety chair, but he did not speak, nor did he give Morgan a smile. His usually ruddy face looked somewhat drawn.

"Nothing's amiss at Ravenscliff, is it?" Morgan demanded. "I've always thought of my great-aunt as being indestructible, but at her age—"

"We never made it as far as Cornwall, Morgan. Mistress Desire and I got no farther than the Golden Anchor together when—"

Morgan grasped Enoch by the shoulder, his powerful fingers closing in a brutal grip. "Where is she now?"

Enoch drew in his breath, and Morgan saw the flicker of pain in his friend's eyes.

"What the devil's wrong with you?"

Enoch managed a shamefaced grin. "I stopped a dragoon's musket ball with my shoulder," he said.

"And Desire?"

"I only wish I knew." Enoch shook his head.

"Lena can get hold of an apothecary," Morgan said.

"No need. I'll do well enough, now I can rest here. Get me a tot of brandy, if you've got it."

Morgan complied quickly, and as Enoch drank he explained what had happened at the innyard. "That slimy bastard, Forret, must have given out our descriptions far and wide," he finished. "No way I could've fought them off—"

"So you led the hunt away from Desire," Morgan said quietly. "Wounded as you were."

"I gave you my word to take care of Mistress Desire," Enoch reminded him. "Since I wasn't able to get her to Ravenscliff, I took the course I thought best."

Morgan turned away quickly, his jaw tightening with the

145

effort to conceal his feelings, for he knew that any expression of gratitude would only have embarrassed his friend.

"But how could you manage to get away from the redcoats with a musket ball in your shoulder?" Morgan asked.

"I carried the purse of coins with me, as you told me to," Enoch reminded him. "A golden sovereign or two, placed in the right palm, can work wonders." Now he managed a smile. "I'll tell you all about it one day—"

"And Desire?" Morgan demanded. "How did you expect her to escape from such a trap?"

"As to that, I had no choice. But the lass is quick-witted, and she doesn't lack for courage, Morgan."

"What good will her wits and courage do when she's had no experience in fleeing from the law?" Morgan demanded. His eyes darkened with self-reproach. "She didn't want to ride out with us that night when we robbed Lord Bodine's coach. She begged to stay behind at the farmhouse. But I forced her to go along, and now she's been taken. How can she hope to persuade any damned magistrate of her innocence?"

"Steady on, Morgan. You don't know that the girl's been caught."

"And there's no way I can find out," Morgan said, beginning to pace again.

"Maybe there is." Enoch drained his glass of brandy and set it down, his pale blue eyes thoughtful. "Last I saw of her, she was safe inside the coach at the Golden Anchor. So we've got to try to find out what happened to her after that."

"And that should be easy enough. All I have to do is ride out to the inn and ask the landlord what became of a girl in a green velvet cloak."

"The way you've been taking on, nothing you might do would surprise me overmuch," Enoch said. "You're plain daft over the girl, and no mistake."

"That's got nothing to do with it," Morgan began.

"As you please. But if you can hold your temper long enough to hear me out, I'll tell you how we might get word of Mistress Desire's whereabouts without your putting your neck in the noose."

"Go on."

"There's Barney — Lena's brat. He could steal a ride on a wagon. He'd reach the Golden Anchor and get back in a day or two."

"And how would he go about finding out what's become of Desire?"

"Leave that to him, Morgan. He's Lena's spawn, isn't he? I'll warrant he'll know how to handle the task. Clever little weasel, he is."

Morgan was silent for a moment as he weighed Enoch's suggestion carefully. A boy who had grown up in Ram Alley, tutored by the scum of Southwark, was a likely choice for a job such as this.

"Make it worth his while," Enoch said. "And young Barney'll find out what's become of Mistress Desire, if anyone can."

Chapter Fourteen

"Desire, my dear, your new gown is most fetching," Lady Mirabelle said. "Madame Lisette has positively outdone herself. But the whole effect will be spoiled unless you agree to wear the pearls."

Her Ladyship opened the velvet jewelbox, and Desire's eyes widened as she saw the pearls glowing with soft radiance against the blue satin lining.

"They are magnificent, but I cannot possible wear them," Desire protested. "How can I accept such a valuable heirloom, even for one night?"

"But you must have some jewels to set off your gown."

"Perhaps I might tie a length of silver ribbon about my neck, with a flower fastened to the side. One of those white roses from the garden."

"We are not going to a country fair or a harvest festival," said Lady Mirabelle reproachfully. The sunlight, slanting through the tall windows of Desire's bedchamber, gleamed on Her Ladyship's curls, which quivered with her agitated movements. Her hair was a brighter shade of gold than it had been yesterday, before a visit from her hairdresser.

"At least you must try on the pearls." Lady Mirabelle gestured to Tilda. "Come and assist Mistress Guilford."

The maid set down the white and gold box that held an ostrich-feather fan and hurried to obey. Her fingers were quick and deft as she placed the necklace around Desire's long white throat and fastened the intricate clasp.

"Now do you see?" Lady Mirabelle gave Desire a triumphant smile. "I was right, was I not?"

There was no question that the necklace, with its intricate loops, and the teardrop-shaped earrings, provided the perfect finishing touches. The gown was a triumph of the French dressmaker's art, with its clinging sea-green satin bodice, full sleeves and wide skirt, and its transparent overskirt of silver lace. The deep, round neckline was cut fashionably low, so that Desire's firm young breasts, forced higher by her tightly laced busk, revealed their enticing curves with only a bit of silver lace ruching to cover her nipples, the delicate glow of the pearls enhanced the silken whiteness of her skin and the highlights of her midnight-dark hair.

"Lord Sedgewick's ball will be one of the most important events of the season, I do assure you," said Lady Mirabelle. "They say that His Majesty may put in an appearance, and so you can be sure that every lady will be wearing her finest jewels."

She paused and cocked her head to one side. "See how becoming the pearls are, as I knew they would be. My maid has concocted a most wonderful lotion for whitening the skin, but at your age . . ." Her ladyship sighed, her blue eyes a trifle pensive. "And as for dear Rowena, I simply cannot persuade her to make use of any lotion. She will not apply even a touch of rouge or lip salve. I confess, although she is my own daughter, I have never understood her."

Although Desire made the appropriate responses whenever Her Ladyship paused for breath, her thoughts were far away.

It was not true that she had no jewels of her own, for although she dared not put on the emerald earrings, she had hidden them away in a tiny pocket in the lining of her green velvet cloak. How moved she had been by Morgan's gift . . . until he had told her to use the earrings as a dowry. Even now she flinched inward at the memory of his cool indifference which he had spoken of her marrying another man.

Why couldn't she stop loving him? Remembering their

149

nights together, the hard strength of his body, the touch of his mouth, and the teasing caresses of his tongue, she felt a compelling need for him. To lie in his arms once more . . . to know the fulfillment of their joining . . .

But this was the worst kind of folly, she warned herself. Unless she kept her wits about her, she might lose her only chance to save Morgan from the hangman.

If King Charles *did* come to the Sedgewick ball tonight, she must make an immediate and unforgettable impression on the womanizing monarch. She might not get another opportunity. Tonight was all-important to Morgan's future, and her own.

"I will wear the pearls," she said. "If I hesitate it's only because you have done so much for me already Your Ladyship."

That was no more than the simple truth, for in the weeks she had been a guest in Geoffrey's home, his mother had devoted herself to making the visit a memorable one. Desire had attended the water fete with Geoffrey and his mother, and had marveled at the sparkling showers of multicolored fireworks that had blazed in the night sky above the Thames. A few evenings later, Geoffrey had escorted her and Lady Mirabelle on an excursion to Spring Gardens, where they had shared a light supper of jellies, syllabubs, and blackberry tarts. They had taken her to the theater several times, and she had enjoyed herself thoroughly, although she was somewhat startled by the risqué dialogue and the appearance of women in the female roles, instead of boys.

In the afternoons, she had accompanied Lady Mirabelle to the Royal Exchange to shop for feather fans, embroidered silk stockings, ruffled garters, perfumed gloves, high-heeled satin slippers, and beribboned chemises. And Her Ladyship had insisted that Desire must be outfitted by her own dressmaker, Madame Lisette.

Desire's closet was filled with her new clothes: walking dresses of silk, trimmed with French lace and velvet; taffeta afternoon gowns in deep rose, azure, and saffron. Now, having deftly removed the pearls and returned them to the jewelcase, Tilda helped Desire off with the ballgown and went to hang it away with the rest.

It wasn't right to take advantage of Lady Mirabelle's trusting nature, Desire told herself with a pang of guilt. She had entered this house under false pretenses; had deceived her ladyship and Geoffrey, too. But how could she reveal the truth, even now?

I helped rob a coach, and I was running from the dragoons when I first saw Geoffrey. I pretended to be his sister so that I could remain with him until the hunt moved away from the inn.

No—it was unthinkable.

But with luck she need not keep up her masquerade much longer. If only the king did appear at the Sedgewick ball tonight—and if he agreed to grant her an audience—she would find a way to obtain a royal pardon for Morgan and herself. Surely she could explain that she had not taken to the highway of her own free will, and that Morgan had only turned highwayman because he had been deprived of his lawful inheritance. The king was a man of wide experience; she would make him understand. She must!

And then? She would leave Warrington House and go on to Ravenscliff. And maybe one day Morgan would come seeking her there and . . . No, she must not even allow herself to think of that.

"Geoffrey, don't turn away. You must listen to me." Rowena's pale eyes glittered with a resentment so fierce and consuming that it swept aside her customary self-possession. Her brother shifted uncomfortably and wished he had gone straight out for his morning walk in the garden instead of allowing her to sidetrack him here in the library.

"You've already said enough, Rowena." He glanced impatiently toward the closed oaken doors. "Let us put an end to this conversation before we both have cause to regret it."

"You can say that when I've told you Mother means to

151

lend the pearls to Mistress Desire? Those pearls were a gift from Queen Elizabeth to the first Lady Warrington, on the occasion of her marriage to Sir Lionel—"

"I know our family's history quite as well as you do," Geoffrey told his sister coldly. "And I see no reason why Desire should not wear the pearls at the Sedgewick ball tonight. Since Mother offered to lend them to her, why should she refuse—"

"She *did* refuse, at first," said Rowena. "She's a clever one, your Mistress Guilford. Indeed, she put on a most polished performance before she agreed to wear the pearls. They were much too valuable, she protested. She said she would rather wear a ribbon and a posy from our garden . . ." Something in Geoffrey's face silenced her.

"You overheard the conversation?"

"Certainly not. But Tilda did. She was helping Mistress Desire into her new ball gown."

"And she lost no time in giving you a full account of all that she had heard."

"Tilda has been my personal maid for many years. No doubt she felt it her duty to warn me of what has been going on in this house, since the arrival of Mistress Guilford."

"How kind of you to offer Desire the services of your own maid. But rather unnecessary since we have so many others who might have been sent to wait upon her."

"Why, I—"

"Have you so little decency that you would set your servant to spying on any guest of mine?"

Rowena's sallow face flushed, for Geoffrey's remark had struck uncomfortably close to the truth. But she rallied quickly and went on.

"Mistress Guilford is a most unusual guest—a young lady with no maid or female companion of her own. What respectable girl of seventeen goes roving about the country alone, traveling on a public coach and staying the night at an inn?"

"She explained how she happened to be in such an unfortunate predicament."

"Ah, yes. Her own maid ran off with her luggage and her money. Most touching. And Mother was generous enough to buy her a costly new wardrobe to replace the one she lost. So why should you take me to task for offering her the service of my maid?" Her pale eyes glittered with resentment. "Mama positively fawns over that brazen little creature."

"That is enough!" Rowena caught the warning in her brother's voice, but she was too carried away with indignation to stop herself.

"I can't help it if I'm the only member of the family who refuses to accept this little upstart at face value. Mother has always been silly and sentimental."

"And do you consider me equally gullible?"

"You, brother dear, are a foolish boy with no experience of the world. How else could you be so deceived by a pretty, scheming creature who flaunts herself before you like any Drury Lane trollop?"

"Hold your tongue! If you say another word against Desire Guilford you'll have cause to regret it."

Rowena trembled with outrage as she fought to keep silent. She stared at her brother as if she had never really seen him before. Geoffrey was no longer an easygoing boy, to be petted and fussed over and sometimes scolded, for his own good.

And now, all at once, he had turned from her to Desire Guilford, a green-eyed young upstart.

A dull ache gripped her shoulders and moved upward into her neck and then her head. It was as if an iron band encircled her skull.

"I will not permit anyone to speak of Desire as you have, Rowena."

"Can it be that she means more to you than your own sister?"

"I never imagined that anyone could mean as much to me as she does. That is why you must say nothing you'll have cause to regret later on."

153

No — it wasn't possible! Until now, she had wondered if her brother meant to make Desire his mistress. A young man in Geoffrey's position must be allowed such follies, no doubt. But what if he was so completely besotted with the girl that he was thinking of marrying her?

The pain in her head was becoming unbearable, and it took all her willpower to keep her standing erect and composed before him.

For the first time, Rowena fully understood what it meant be a spinster, and she cringed under the bitter humiliation of that knowledge. Geoffrey had always been kind and indulgent toward her. Because of their mother's flighty ways, he had allowed his sister to control the running of the household, but she had only as much authority as he chose to give her. He provided her with a generous allowance, but at word from him it could be taken away. Should she displease the future Lady Warrington, she might find herself sent off to enforced exile on the Yorkshire estates.

But she would not allow that to happen. She needed time to recover from the blow he had dealt her, to gather her resources and regain her power over him.

"I am sorry I displeased you, Geoffrey," she said carefully. "I fear I am not myself. One of my headaches. I must go and lie down."

In spite of their angry exchange, she still had a faint hope that he might express concern. She waited for him to take her arm and offer to help her upstairs.

But he only said, "Let's hope you will have recovered before it is time to leave for Sedgewick's ball." He bowed and stood aside, and she moved past him in frozen silence.

"Rowena, surely you won't allow a slight indisposition to keep you from going out tonight?" Lady Mirabelle regarded her daughter with a mixture of concern and irritation. Really, the girl had always been a great trial to her. "I was looking forward to the ball. And Desire will be so disappointed if she cannot wear her new gown—such a magnificent creation."

"I see no reason why my headache should prevent anyone else from attending the ball," Rowena said without raising her head from her pillows.

"But I want you to come. We all do. Tilda, you must bring your mistress a dose of hartshorn."

"I won't swallow it."

"Now you are being too provoking. Indeed you are. I should think you would be eager to show off your new gown—all those yards of brocade. And Madame Lisette assures me that russet is the most fashionable color in Paris this year. Although I did think that perhaps a more delicate shade would have been more flattering. I did mention pale primrose, if you recall. But since you expressed no preference—"

"Mother, please! Russet or primrose, what does it matter?"

Lady Mirabelle threw up her hands in a gesture of despair.

"I do not understand you, Rowena. I never have. How is it possible for you to care so little about your appearance? Why, it is positively unnatural."

"Am I to blame if I am not the daughter you would have wanted? If I were to walk into the ballroom decked out like Lady Castlemaine it would make no difference. I think I must have been born to be a spinster, for no man has ever loved me, and none ever will."

"Rowena! That isn't true."

"I've had offers of marriage, but only from those who were enamored of my dowry. Penniless young wastrels or aging lechers who had squandered their own fortunes on their whores. And how even those few suitors must have shrunk from the thought of bedding me." Her voice shook with self-loathing.

For a moment Lady Mirabelle was at a loss for words. But she recovered herself quickly. "Indeed, you are quite beside yourself or you would not speak this way. Tilda, will you get the hartshorn, or must I ring for one of the other servants?"

"The hartshorn won't help," said Rowena dully. "It never has. Nor have any of your other remedies."

"Perhaps if we were to summon the apothecary, he could apply leeches to your forehead."

"I won't have allow him near me. I cannot bear the thought of those dreadful, wriggling leeches. Nor his live pigeons, cut in two and applied to the soles of my feet. The mere memory of it sickens me."

"Very well, we won't have him. But there must be someone . . ." She pursed her pink lips for a moment. "I have it. The physician who cared for dear Geoffrey after his accident. What was the man's name?"

"If you please, madam, I believe Mistress Guilford mentioned a Dr. Munroe," said Tilda.

"Munroe . . . Yes, that was it. How clever of you to remember. And he lives right here in London. How fortunate. We must summon him at once."

Desire left her bedchamber and walked along the hallway. She would go out into the garden and seek the seclusion of the marble bench in the lime walk where she would have a quiet half hour to make her plans for tonight.

She paused when she caught sight of Tilda, who was preceding a soberly dressed gentleman up the wide staircase. Her hand went to her throat and her green eyes filled with dismay as she recognized Dr. Lucas Munroe.

For a moment Desire stood frozen, then instinct took over and she turned swiftly, hoping to get back to her room before the doctor caught sight of her. It was already too late, however, for Lady Mirabelle, emerged from Rowena's room, blocked off that line of retreat.

Desire pressed herself against the wall. Perhaps in his haste to reach his patient, Dr. Monroe might not notice her.

156

But a moment later he was standing before her.

"It is a great privilege to see you again so soon," he said, with a deep bow and a fawning smile. He was interrupted by Lady Mirabelle, who came bearing down on him, her elaborate pink skirt billowing around her.

"How fortunate that we were able to find you so quickly, Dr. Munroe. And that you were not away attending on another patient. My daughter is in desperate need of your care."

The doctor cast a brief look at Desire before turning back to Lady Mirabelle. "I am honored that you called upon me, Your Ladyship, but I doubt you need fear for your daughter. She looks positively blooming, if I may make so bold."

Her ladyship's brow furrowed briefly in a puzzled frown. "My daughter? But you have not yet seen her." Then she gave a tinkling little laugh. "This lady is not your patient. No, indeed. She is Mistress Guilford, who is visiting with us. My daughter is prostrate in her chamber with a most dreadful headache. And she could scarcely have chosen a more unfortunate time."

The doctor, who was thoroughly bewildered now, waited for Her Ladyship to explain.

"The ball at Lord Sedgewick's home—it would be such a pity if Rowena were unable to attend. Do come along, Doctor."

For once, Desire was thankful that her hostess was unable to concentrate on any one subject more than a few moments. Perhaps Lady Mirabelle would forget the doctor's supposed mistake. But Tilda had stopped for a moment, and was giving her a long, speculative stare. Desire felt a sinking sensation as she turned and went on down the stairs to the garden.

"A few drops of this cordial, taken with a cup of fresh cream, containing a well-beaten egg and a sprinkling of cinnamon. I am sure it will prove most effective."

157

Dr. Munroe, having completed his examination, decided that his patient suffered from nothing more than a headache brought on by the strain of preparing for the ball. Nevertheless, he was anxious to find favor with both the lady and her mother, a flighty female whose chatter would be enough to give a marble statue an attack of the vapors.

If he could win Lady Mirabelle's trust, and her daughter's approval, he would gain a prestigious connection and a most welcome addition to his already considerable income. What a fortunate chance that he had been called upon to attend His Lordship at the Golden Anchor.

"Then my daughter *will* be well enough to attend the ball tonight?"

"I am confident that she will. I should not advise her to take too many refreshments at the banquet table. She should avoid the more highly seasoned dishes and eat sparingly of the marchpane. Also, it might be better if she doesn't stay too late. A young lady with so delicate a constitution must exercise caution at all times." He had deliberately called her "young," although Rowena Warrington was surely over thirty. A little well-timed flattery never failed to please.

"There now, you see, my dear? A dose of the cordial — it sounds most palatable, does it not? — and a nap, and I am sure you will soon recover from your headache. How fortunate that I thought to send for you, Doctor."

Lady Mirabelle now remembered that, she, too would require a few hours of rest in order to look her best tonight. She was halfway out the door when she turned and said: "Now that you know my daughter, you won't make the same mistake you did today, will you, Doctor? Such a mix-up, wasn't it. When I think of the look on dear Desire's face . . . Ah, well, no matter —"

"Mistake?" Rowena raised her head from the piled-up pillows. At the mention of Desire's name, she was like a hound on the scent.

Lady Mirabelle was already gone, and Rowena turned to

her maid. "Tilda, do you know what Her Ladyship was speaking about?"

"A small matter, my lady," the doctor said quickly. Although his curiosity had been piqued by the curious encounter in the hallway, he did not care to pursue the matter just now. If the green-eyed little beauty had been passing herself off at the inn as his lordship's sister, that was none of his affair.

"The doctor thought he recognized Mistress Guilford," said Tilda, eager to supply whatever information she could. "He supposed that *she* was His Lordship's sister."

Rowena was sitting up now in bed now, her eyes fixed on Dr. Munroe's face. "Please take a chair, Doctor. I should like to know more of this."

"Another time, surely—when you are feeling stronger."

"Now," said Rowena Warrington. Her voice had the ring of a tempered blade.

Perhaps Dr. Munroe could provide her with a weapon to use against the scheming little adventuress. Scarcely aware of her headache any longer, she confronted the doctor, her pale eyes narrow, her lean body taut with determination. She would stop at nothing to discredit Desire Guilford, to drive her out of this house while there was still time.

Chapter Fifteen

"The hostlers at the Golden Anchor remembered the lady," Barney told Morgan with a grin. "Said she was a real choice bit o' sweetmeat."

"Guard your tongue, brat. I sent you to find out what became of her."

"I'm gettin' to that," said Barney Yarrow. "Them hostlers always know everything that's going on around the place, working in the stables like they do. I lent them a hand shoveling out the stalls. Told them I was a poor orphan, ready to work for a bed and—"

"Was the lady taken by the dragoons?" Morgan thundered. Barney jumped at the sound and moved cautiously toward the door.

"The dragoons didn't go nowhere near her. They went chasin' after Master Hodges here—raised a hue an' cry all over the countryside, they did. An' all the time, your pretty little cull—your lady, I mean—was snug and warm in the best chamber of the Golden Anchor."

"I said she could take care of herself."

"So you did." Desire had not been taken. She wasn't languishing in a cell in Newgate, after all. Morgan felt an overwhelming sense of relief. But a moment later, his brows drew together in a puzzled frown.

"How do you suppose she managed to pay for such lodgings, Enoch? You were carrying most of the money. She had only a few spare shillings for herself."

160

"Your lady had no need of ready money. She was sharing her chambers with a real fine gentleman. Sir somethin' or other, no less."

"You lying imp of Satan!" Morgan seized Barney by his soiled collar, twisting it so tightly that the boy began to turn brick-red.

"The brat can't talk with you choking him," Enoch intervened.

Morgan slackened his hold, and Barney retreated with a reproachful look. "I'm only tellin' you what them hostlers said. I ain't to blame."

"Who was the man she went with?"

"His name was Waringham—no, Warrington. That's it. Sir Geoffrey Warrington. Him and the lady stayed at the inn for nearly a week and then they left in a private coach. Bound for London, they was. The coachman told the hostler when they were hitchin' up the horses. An' that's all I know. An' . . . you promised me a gold sovereign."

Although Barney was afraid of the highwayman, he stood his ground, determined to exact full payment for his services. But Morgan Trenchard was staring past him, his jaw set, his eyes dark with anger.

"This Warrington might have been old enough to be Desire's grandfather. Desire's a well-spoken lass with a way about her. He may have offered her shelter out of kindness," Enoch said.

"He weren't no old gaffer," the boy interrupted. "Young and comely, he was. He came ridin' into the innyard on a fine great stallion that reared up an' threw him—"

"Shut your mouth!" Morgan reached into his pocket and tossed the boy a coin. "Now get out, damn you!"

Barney caught his money and ran from the room, pounding down the rickety stairs as if the fiends of hell were after him.

"At least she's not in prison," Enoch said. "I told you she was quick-witted."

161

Morgan glared at him in angry silence.

"Now don't judge the lass too harshly. She did what she had to do."

"Damn right she did. She lost no time in finding a wealthy gentleman to provide for her. Young and good-looking, too."

"It was you she wanted," Enoch reminded him. "She pleaded with you to let her stay, no matter the risk. But you sent her off to Cornwall."

"And wouldn't she have been better off there than with me?"

"Of course she would. But since we couldn't get to Ravenscliff as we planned, she had to find another way to escape capture."

"No doubt." Morgan strode to the row of pegs set along the wall. He took down his cloak and put it on.

"Where are you off to?" Enoch demanded.

"I've been cooped up in this damn hole too long."

"It might be prudent to lie low awhile longer."

"I need to get out." Morgan thrust his pistol into his belt.

"There's no sense risking your neck just because Mistress Desire's found herself another man."

"That's got nothing to do with it—"

"She may not even be with Warrington now," Enoch went on, undeterred by his friend's anger. "She may have given him the slip and gone off alone."

"That's no concern of mine." His mouth twisted in an ironic smile. "A girl as beautiful and clever as she is—she'll do well enough for herself now she's rid of me. No more hiding in ruined farmhouses, sleeping on straw. She'll not lack for a soft bed, or a gentleman to share it with."

"And that's what's driving you daft." Enoch sighed and shook his head. "I told her you weren't the sort to fall in love with any female, but I was wrong. You love Desire, any fool can see that."

162

"Don't you ever speak her name again to me."

Morgan headed for the door.

"I'll go with you," his friend said calmly.

"Stay here. I don't need company tonight."

"You're in no fit state to go wandering about on your own," Enoch told him, following him out of the room.

Kate Claffey's bordello stood in one of the narrow streets off Drury Lane. In spite of its unimpressive facade, it was one of the best of its kind in all of London.

The doorkeeper, a muscular giant in a shining white periwig and scarlet satin livery, recognized Morgan and Enoch at once. He bowed, took their cloaks, and led them through the entrance hall into a luxurious reception room, ablaze with candles. Kate had prospered greatly since the Puritan government had been overthrown, and obviously she had put a large portion of her profits back into her business.

The room was impressive, with frescoes on the high ceiling and heavy red velvet drapes, embroidered and fringed with gold. Kate's girls and their gentlemen visitors were seated on gilded chairs and couches of burgundy satin or rose damask. The enormous pink marble fireplace was flanked on either side by long glittering mirrors.

Now Kate came forward to greet the new arrivals; but Morgan noticed that she looked a little uneasy. Although she embraced him as she always did, and gave Enoch a wide smile, her eyes were guarded.

Kate Claffey had been a beauty in her time, but now she had grown stout. Her large bosom billowed over the low-cut bodice of her yellow satin gown, with its sheer black tiffany overskirt and train. She flourished a huge fan of black and yellow ostrich plumes.

"That's a splendid rigout, Kate, my love," said Morgan. "It's good to see you flourishing."

163

"I do well enough, now Cromwell's gone and his psalm-singing lot are out of favor." Her gaze moved uneasily to the stairway that led upstairs to the chambers of pleasure above.

"*We're* no Puritans," said Enoch. "Let's see what you have to show us tonight, Kate."

"I have a couple of new ones, fresh from the country. You are partial to yellow-haired girls, are you not, Enoch?"

She led him to one of the velvet couches and left him there in the company of a pink-cheeked blonde.

"And for you, Morgan, there's a lovely little thing with as fine a pair of tits as you've ever seen. She's got black hair and a genteel way about her."

"Not tonight, Kate."

She stared up at him, taken aback by his abrupt refusal.

He managed a smile. "My tastes have changed. That redheaded wench over there. She'll do well enough."

"Always rains harder over new scenery," Kate agreed, and led him to the girl he had indicated. "Corinna, this gentleman has asked to join you. You'll be wanting to share a bottle of wine while you're getting acquainted. What shall it be, Morgan? Rhenish? Burgundy?"

"A bottle of each," he said. "And we'll have them upstairs." Kate's painted eyebrows went up. Morgan Trenchard usually sat in the reception room and drank a glass or two with the girl of his choice before he went up to her room.

But Corinna, who was new to Kate's establishment and saw nothing odd about Morgan's request, rose with one graceful movement and took his arm. He was overpowered by the scent of Neroli unguent.

She was a tall girl with full breasts tipped with large round nipples, a small trim waist, and lushy curving hips; her splendid body was scarcely concealed by her robe of sheer, sky-blue tiffany trimmed with matching plumes. As

164

she moved close beside him, the skirt of her garment parted to reveal her long, well-shaped legs in their embroidered silk stockings. Like all Kate's girls, she wore satin slippers with four-inch heels, studded with glittering stones.

Corinna led Morgan up the staircase, with its delicate pierced panels of gilded wood. At the top stood a pair of tall, slender newels, each carved with a nymph and a faun, cavorting in naked abandon.

The red-haired girl's breast brushed against his arm. "I was hoping you would choose me," she said with an enticing smile. "I swear you are the handsomest gentlemen I've seen since I came to London."

"No doubt my friend would have pleased you as well — or any other man who could pay for your services."

The words were scarcely said when he reproached himself inwardly. Why inflict his private anger on the girl?

"I'm sorry," he said. "I'm out of temper tonight." He put his arm around her and drew her to him. "No doubt a few glasses of wine and your own charming self are all I need to —"

He stopped short, silenced by a girl's shrill cry of pain.

"That's right, you slut." It was a man's voice, brutal and unexpectedly familiar. "Scream yourself hoarse, but stay down there. Before this night's over you'll be whimpering like a whipped bitch."

Morgan's body went rigid.

"It's poor little Letty in there," Corinna said. "Kate didn't want that brute to have her, but he can be dangerous when he's crossed. And him being an informer —"

He didn't hear the rest, for he had already pushed Corinna aside and grasped the doorknob. When the door would not open, he stepped back and kicked his booted foot through one of the painted panels.

He saw a naked girl, her hair falling around her face, the candlelight flickering along her slender white back and small curving buttocks.

"What the hell—" Niall Forret looked up and his eyes met Morgan's. The informer was dressed in breeches and boots, his ruffled shirt open at the throat. In one hand he held a riding crop.

Morgan's stomach lurched as he saw the fresh cuts on the girl's back. A red mist of rage enveloped his brain, and he was scarcely aware that he was reaching for his pistol. It was in his hand now, pointed straight at Niall Forret's head.

The girl scurried into a corner, her body trembling.

"If I needed one more reason to kill you, you've given it to me," Morgan said softly.

He saw the fear in Niall's eyes. It pleased him.

"Get out of here," he told the girl without looking at her. She ran past him into the hall. Morgan heard the sound of her hysterical sobbing.

"Wait," Niall said quickly. "I have no pistol."

"Neither did the girl."

"But you would not shoot down an unarmed man." Morgan kept the pistol steady; his black eyes did not waver for an instant. "You call yourself a gentleman, don't you, Squire Trenchard?"

Morgan shrugged. "Suit yourself, Forret. It will give me satisfaction to break you in half with my bare hands." He set down his pistol on a lacquered table.

From the hallway came the babble of voices, but Morgan was scarcely aware of the hubbub as he advanced on Niall. His usual caution had been swept away by the sight of man who had betrayed him.

He swung at Niall, throwing all the force of his powerful body behind the blow. It caught the man on the jaw so that he swayed and staggered back.

But a moment later, Niall recovered his balance and struck out. Girls in the hallway were screaming shrilly, the men cursing. Niall caught Morgan a punishing blow over the left eye, opening his flesh. Blood came pouring down his face, blinding him momentarily.

Morgan shook his head to clear his sight, then threw himself on his adversary with the speed and fury of a jungle beast. He felt the savage satisfaction of striking out and catching Niall full in the throat with his closed fist.

Niall went down and Morgan moved in for the final blow. He stood for a moment hands linked above his head, poised to bring them down full force on the back of Niall's neck.

"Morgan—no!"

He was distracted by Kate's shrill cry. Niall's hand went to his boot, and Morgan saw the candlelight glittering on the blade of a knife. The blind fury that had engulfed his senses gave way to caution. Moving warily, Morgan began to retreat toward the hallway. Niall, using his advantage, came after him.

Morgan stepped out into the hallway. With girls and men milling about, someone had knocked over a statuette, and he stumbled over it. He lost his footing for a moment. Niall raised his knife, but Morgan managed to regain his balance. He felt a line of fire ripping along the flesh of his chest as Niall struck. Shifting his weight from side to side, Morgan went on moving until he stood with his back to the top of the long stairway.

Niall dropped into a crouch as he moved in for the kill. But Morgan raised his arm and sprang to one side. Thrown off balance, Niall clutched at the gilded finial atop the newelpost.

Morgan brought the side of his hand down in a swift, chopping blow that caught Niall on the side of the neck. Niall cried out hoarsely as the finial broke off in his grasp.

A girl in the room below began to shriek as she saw the man smash through the railing. He struck the floor, fifteen feet below, and lay face downward, motionless.

Morgan raced down the stairs, but Enoch was already

turning Niall over. The impact of the man's fall had driven the knife blade deep into his chest. He lay there with open, unseeing eyes. His lifeless hand still clutched the gilded finial, with its carving of the nymph and faun.

Chapter Sixteen

The Sedgewick mansion, a short distance up the river from Warrington House, was built in the elegant and symmetrical Tudor style. Although Julian Bainbridge, the present earl of Sedgewick had imported rare plants and shrubs from the New World, he had kept the elaborate maze of yew and holly planted in the days of Queen Elizabeth. Marble benches stood in the more secluded spots, where amorous couples could find a measure of privacy.

It was still early in the evening when Geoffrey and Desire, having paid their respects to their host and his lady, left the already-crowded ballroom and strolled across the terrace and down into the garden to enjoy the mild evening breeze. The moonlight sent a rippling silver path across the waters of the Thames, where skiffs, wherries, and barges went moving by. The spring air was sweet with the scents of early roses and lavender. Although the dancing had not yet begun, the strains of the lute and the viol drifted out from the musicians' gallery overlooking the ballroom.

Geoffrey, who knew his way around the garden, led Desire into the maze and drew her down beside him on a bench.

"This is a charming spot," she said, "but I had hoped to get a view of the river so that I might see the king's barge arriving."

"Never fear," said Geoffrey with a smile. "The moment he enters the ballroom, we will know it."

"He *is* coming tonight?" she asked anxiously. All her hopes were centered on meeting the king, so that she might persuade him to give her a private audience.

"No doubt he will try to put in an appearance, though there is no telling how long he will stay." She looked at Geoffrey with dismay. "His Majesty has more than one engagement nearly every evening," he explained.

He reached over and took her hand, and she stirred uneasily under the warmth of his touch.

"Perhaps we might walk to the river steps," she said. "Although the maze is fascinating."

"Fascinating beyond words," he told her, his dark blue eyes fixed on her face. Although she had expected this moment to come, she had hoped that Geoffrey would wait longer before declaring his feelings for her. They had met only a little over a month ago, after all.

But his eyes were moving now, from her face to the curve of her long, slender throat, and then to her breasts, which were only half concealed by her low neckline.

She must say something to distract him, and quickly. "How fortunate that Rowena recovered from her headache in time to come with us. She looks in excellent spirits tonight."

"A little overwrought, I should say. But I didn't bring you out here so that we might speak of Rowena." Geoffrey put his arm around her and drew her closer. "You are enchanting tonight, Desire. In that green and silver, you remind me of a sea goddess out of an ancient legend."

"Thanks to the skill of Madame Lisette," Desire said lightly. "She has excellent taste. And her ladyship was most kind to lend me these pearls."

"I want you to have the Warrington pearls, not only for tonight, but always. It's as if they were meant for you. Desire, surely you must know that there is nothing I would not offer you if you would do me the honor to—"

"Don't say any more." She tried to draw away, but his arm tightened around her waist.

From somewhere in the depths of the maze she heard a girl's breathless laughter and a man's voice, soft and urgent. The maze was a lovers' retreat, Desire thought with dismay.

She should not have lingered here with Geoffrey.

"Listen," she said. "Do you hear the guitar? The dancing must have started. Let us go and join the others." He made no move to rise, and she went on: "That is the saraband, one of my favorite dances."

"We will dance together often, my love, but not yet—" He leaned closer and his lips brushed her cheek. Although his mouth touched her lightly, she felt the urgency in him. Her slender body tightened as she tried to draw away.

"Don't be afraid, Desire. I swear I'd never do anything to harm you. Since that night at the inn when I awoke and saw you leaning over me—you looked so lovely by candlelight, your eyes so caring, and your hands so cool and gentle—I think I knew even then that I wanted you for my own."

"You were not yourself that night, Geoffrey."

"I am entirely myself tonight," he said, his voice deep with ardor. "And I am more in love with you than ever."

"You are confusing gratitude with love."

"What do you know of love, young and innocent as you are?" He caught her in a close embrace, bending her backward on the bench. She was startled by the hard male strength in his tall, slender body, the passionate urgency of his hot, searching kiss.

When she did not respond, he released her. She did not meet his eyes, but dropped her gaze to the plumed fan in her lap.

Geoffrey wondered if she, like Rowena, thought he was no more than a foolish, headstrong boy who did not understand his own feelings. But he could not accept such a blow to his pride. He cast about for another reason, and he found it.

He had frightened Desire with the force of his passion. Yes, that must be it.

"Forgive me, my sweet," he said. "I should have been less impetuous, perhaps. But you keep saying you must leave for Cornwall soon, and I can't let you go."

"Geoffrey, you must. We can have no future together. I could never become your mistress—"

"I would not dream of dishonoring you with such an offer," he told her. His dark blue eyes shone with the intensity of his feelings. "I want you for my wife."

"That can't be." She put her hand on his. "I've never tried to hide my family background from you." And that was the only thing she hadn't lied about, she thought ruefully. "What would people say if Lord Warrington were to marry the daughter of a merchant?"

"I need answer to no one for my choice of a bride," he told her. "I am my own master."

"But your family — surely you must want their approval?"

"Mother is already deeply fond of you."

"And Rowena?"

"You need not concern yourself over Rowena. She will treat you with the greatest respect, I can promise you that. As for my friends, they will envy me for my good fortune in finding so beautiful and virtuous a wife. You will be admired, sought-after. You will be Lady Warrington."

Desire was deeply moved. She was far too fond of him to hurt him. She must not allow him to go on hoping, but she must be tactful, even as she refused his proposal. Her mind was in turmoil as she cast about for the right words.

He spoke gently. "Is it your fear of marriage and its duties that makes you hesitate? His smile was boyish, a little shy. "I will be gentle. I'll wait until you are ready to be my bride. Only don't refuse me."

Why shouldn't I marry him?

In the midst of her confusion, the question came to her with startling clarity, and her mind began to move in a cool, practical way. As Geoffrey Warrington's wife, she would share his title and estates. She would take her place at court and enjoy the endless round of pleasures there.

And what of their private moments together? Would she be able to give herself to Geoffrey, to share his bed and bear his children?

He was young and ardent, undeniably handsome, with his tall, slender body, his fine-boned features, and aristocratic bearing. He would respect and cherish her, she was sure of that.

If she became his wife, she would have nothing more to fear. She could put her past behind her forever.

She was jolted back to reality by the thought. She could not turn away from the past, because Morgan Trenchard was a part of that past — a part of herself. She could never consent to marry Geoffrey, for if Morgan were to come to her on the eve of her marriage, if he held out his hand, no power in heaven or hell would keep her from following him.

She got to her feet. "Please take me inside."

"Desire, wait —"

But before he could go on they heard the sound of footsteps close by. A couple hurried past them toward the house, then another followed.

"His Majesty has arrived," she heard a lady saying to her companion. "I told you that was the royal barge I saw, docking at the river stairs."

"His Majesty . . ."

"He must be in the ballroom now . . ."

"Lady Castlemaine's with him . . ."

Geoffrey took Desire's arm, and they joined the stream of guests who were moving in the direction of the great ballroom at the rear of the house. Her green eyes glowed as she caught sight of King Charles and his mistress, Lady Castlemaine, who were being received by the earl of Sedgewick and his countess.

Desire's heart began to thud against her ribs. As Geoffrey escorted her into the room she was filled with a mixture of fear and anticipation. She tried to steady herself by drawing in a deep breath of warm, heavily scented air, and wished that Tilda had not laced her busk so tightly. She was beginning to feel a bit lightheaded.

Even now it was not too late to abandon her dangerous plan. When she was presented to the king, all she had to do was to curtsy, smile sweetly, and move on.

And give up what might be her only chance to help Morgan.

"Don't be afraid," Geoffrey whispered, pressing her hand. "I'll be right beside you." He gave her a brief, boyish smile.

173

"His Majesty is only a man, after all."

King Charles bowed and Desire curtseyed as they joined hands and moved into the first figure of the saraband together. She decided that although His Majesty was not a handsome man in a conventional sense, he was undeniably striking, with his dark hair and eyes, sensual mouth, and long, straight nose. He towered over her, for he was at least six feet tall, and his coat of purple velvet, vest tunic of silver cloth, and black velvet breeches, showed off his athletic body to advantage.

He had inherited all the Stuart charm, and since he had been exiled from England and forced to live on the Continent from his sixteenth to his thirtieth year, he had learned the best of courtly French manners. He could flatter a lady with a glance from his smouldering black eyes, and set her pulses racing with a touch. His queen, Catherine of Braganza, loved him enough to overlook his many indiscretions.

He smiled down at Desire. "It was heartless of Lady Warrington to keep so lovely a guest from court," he said as he led her with practiced ease through the elaborate figures of the dance.

"Your Majesty is most gracious." She looked up at him from under her dark lashes, her emerald eyes glowing, her soft red lips slightly parted in a demure smile. "I arrived in London only a few weeks ago."

They turned back to back now, arms raised, and then pivoted around again. His Majesty's arm encircled her narrow waist as they moved into the next steps of the saraband.

"Now that we have met, you must give us the pleasure of your company, and often." She felt the hard muscles of his arm tighten slightly. "There's to be a costume ball at Whitehall next week. You will grace the affair with your presence, Mistress Guilford."

When she did not answer at once, his dark eyes probed hers. "Are you affianced to young Warrington?"

"Oh, no, sire," she assured him.

His eyes grew warmer, and he made no effort to disguise his satisfaction. "Naturally, Sir Geoffrey, his sister, and Lady Warrington will also attend. But it is you I wish to know better, Mistress Guilford."

Once more they were parted by the elaborate measures of the dance, and once more they came together again. "You have not yet promised to attend the ball," he reminded her with a smile.

"I am most honored that you should ask me, sire." She drew a quick breath as she realized that this was the final figure of the dance. It was time to speak up, and quickly. "But I had hoped . . . If I might meet with Your Majesty under more private circumstances, I should be most grateful."

"Nothing would give me greater pleasure," he said.

Desire could not mistake the frank male sensuality in his look. Had she given him the wrong idea? She had no experience with the sort of banter that went on at court, but Lady Mirabelle had spoken often of the scandalous behavior of the ladies who frequented the palace at Whitehall. Dear heaven, surely he did not think she would be bold enough to ask for an invitation to the royal bedchamber! She was so dismayed at the mere thought that she could not go on.

From the corner of her eye she caught a glimpse of Lady Barbara Castlemaine, the king's voluptuous mistress, who had detached herself from a circle of hangers-on and was moving in the direction of her lover.

Before Desire could summon up the courage to go on, the dance was over. Lady Castlemaine was standing beside them now, staring at Desire with resentment and perhaps a touch of fear. Although the red-haired beauty was Charles's most-favored mistress, and had held him longer than any of the others, she was taking no chances. As Barbara Villiers, she had dazzled all of London with her beauty. At eighteen she had married Roger Palmer. A year later, she had displayed her magnificent body and her amorous skills in the royal bed so successfully that she had held sway over the king ever since.

Other beauties had come and gone, but Barbara kept her hold over the king. She had her own magnificent apartment at Whitehall. Charles squandered enormous sums of money upon her, and allowed her to sell political appointments. He even overlooked her violent outbursts of temper. But she knew enough about men—her royal protector, in particular—to realize that they were easily attracted by the charm of novelty.

She had watched the king dancing with the dark-haired young beauty, his eyes roving over the lush, creamy curves of her half-bared breasts, the tapering line of her waist.

His Majesty introduced Desire to Lady Castlemaine. Desire smiled and acknowledged the introduction, then turned away quickly to speak to the king once more. Time was slipping by and she could not let him get away before she had secured the favor she wanted so desperately.

"If Your Majesty might grant me a audience, a few moments only, on a matter concerning an—an acquaintance of mine. It is not entirely a private matter, sire. It concerns the justice and order of the realm." There was surely some truth in what she said, since robbery upon the king's highway was a most serious offense against the laws of the land.

Her face was upturned to his, her green eyes burning with the urgency of her emotions. He smiled indulgently. "As grave as all that, is it?"

"Indeed it is, sire."

"We have been overwhelmed by such requests, Mistress Guilford. Since our return to England, so many of our subjects have flocked to court, demanding to be heard. And each insists that his case should have precedence over all the rest."

She felt her hopes wavering, but she could not give up. She gave him a repentant smile. "Forgive me, sire. No doubt I have been too presumptuous."

"Beauty has its own privilege, Mistress Guilford," he said. "Since this matter is of such great importance, we must hear more. We shall speak to Sir Roger Darwent, who is in charge of arranging private audiences. He shall find a suitable time for our meeting. And soon."

"Oh, thank you, sire." Desire curtseyed low before him, her eyes glowing with heartfelt gratitude.

Lady Castlemaine shot an icy sidelong glance at Desire, then put a gloved hand on her lover's arm. "I think it is time we were taking our leave, Your Majesty. You did say that you might look in on Lord Buckminster's banquet."

Charles nodded. "We have not forgotten, madam."

But before he walked away, he gave Desire a reassuring smile. "Never fear, Mistress Guilford. We do not forget our promises."

Although Desire no longer felt any need to remain at the ball, she knew that she must go on dancing, smiling, making polite chatter until the Warringtons were ready to leave. She had no lack of partners, and she moved gracefully through the complicated figures of two more sarabands. Then a lively gavotte, full of kissing and kicking up of heels, left her breathless.

When Lady Mirabelle came over with yet another gentleman in tow, Desire was about to suggest that she and her new partner might seat themselves and watch the other dancers, but before she could speak, she noticed something disturbingly familiar about the man, with his long, carefully curled periwig of light brown. Where had she heard that deep, pleasant voice before?

". . . Phillip Sinclair . . . a most accomplished dancer . . . longs for you to partner him in the next dance . . ."

She searched her mind with growing uneasiness even as the gentleman was bowing low before her. Then, as he straightened, she knew where she had met him—he had been a passenger on Sir Hugh's coach the night of the robbery . . .

The crowded, candlelit ballroom began to spin before her frightened eyes. She had to stop herself from running head-

177

long across the polished floor to make a dash for the garden, to hide herself in the twists and turns of the maze.

Dear God! First Dr. Munroe, and now Phillip Sinclair. Although her legs began to tremble under the sea-green satin of her skirt, she managed to curtsy, while at the same time raising her fan to conceal her face.

"If you would do me the honor, Mistress Guilford," Phillip Sinclair was saying. "It is a pavane, is it not?"

Desire's dancing master had taught her the pavane, which had been brought from Spain to the French court, and thence to England. More like a procession than a dance, it was made up of several stately movements in which the partners moved side by side. She took his arm and allowed him to lead her onto the floor. Somehow she managed to get through the endless variations of the stately dance, accompanied by the rhythm of the guitars from the musicians' gallery overhead.

When Phillip Sinclair mentioned that he had first seen the dance performed in Spain, she smiled and said she longed to visit that country one day. Yes, she had heard that the climate of Seville was most delightful. And he had visited Italy, too? Were there really canals instead of streets in Venice, and did one get about in boats there? How fascinating.

Even as she forced herself to listen to his answers, she saw that he was looking at her closely, his light brows drawn together in a puzzled frown. The guitars went twanging on and on until she thought her nerves would snap. She tried to keep her attention fixed on the other dancers in their splendid costumes of yellow, emerald, carnation, violet, and silver, until the colors began to weave fantastic patterns before her eyes. By the time the final strains of the music had died away, she could scarcely make a pretense of conversation.

She breathed a heartfelt sigh of relief as she saw that the footmen were opening the tall paneled doors to the adjoining room. She caught a glimpse of the banquet table. It stretched along the full length of the far wall, and was hung with loops of glossy green leaves intertwined with violets and white roses. A moment later, Geoffrey came to her side, bowed, and offered his arm. At the same time, Lady Mirabelle fixed her eye on Phillip Sinclair and led Rowena in his direction.

Rowena and Sinclair were seated together at one of the small black lacquered tables set about the room. Because His Majesty enjoyed the new way of serving a banquet in the buffet style, the practice had spread quickly to the more fashionable houses in London.

The great banquet table held an imposing array of dishes: a magnificent roasted swan flanked with suckling pigs, golden-brown ducklings surrounded with sliced oranges and lemons, pheasants braised in wine, wafer cakes, preserved fruits, and elaborate towers of brightly colored sweet marchpane. But Rowena showed little interest in the assortment of delicacies before her.

"Mistress Guilford is a great success tonight," Rowena said. She stabbed at a morsel of pheasant, then set down her fork. "Her first appearance in London society has been a triumph."

Lady Mirabelle had maneuvered Sinclair into taking her daughter to supper, and he was determined to make the best of it. On other occasions he had felt only pity for Rowena Warrington, whose drab looks and utter lack of feminine charm had surely condemned her to spinsterhood. A good-natured gentleman, he had gone out of his way to be attentive to her. But tonight he felt distinctly uneasy in her company, for although her conversation was conventional enough, he could not help noticing the hectic flush on her sallow cheeks. Her pale, sparsely lashed eyes glittered with peculiar intensity.

"His Majesty certainly has taken a fancy to your house-guest," he said. "Young Geoffrey had better declare his intentions quickly."

"I have no reason to believe that my brother has any serious intentions where Desire Guilford is concerned." Rowena gave a shrill laugh that set Sinclair's teeth on edge. "And His Majesty has never considered marriage an obstacle when a lady takes his fancy. Lady Castlemaine's husband was more than willing to exchange his wife in return for an earl's title and estates."

"Not every husband is as complaisant as Roger Palmer. If I were married to Mistress Guilford, I should take her away from court as quickly as possible."

"I do believe you, too, have been captivated by our dear little Desire. Perhaps that is why you were trying to find out about my brother's intentions toward her." She tapped him lightly on the arm with her fan.

"She is surely a beauty," he agreed, "but I am a confirmed bachelor."

"Even a confirmed bachelor has been known to change his ways. When you were dancing with Mistress Desire you could not take your eyes from her face."

"If I stared at Mistress Guilford, I had another reason."

"And what might that have been?"

Rowena leaned forward, her eyes alert.

He did not answer her question. Instead, he glanced at her untouched food. "The pheasant is not to your taste, I see. Perhaps there is some other delicacy you would prefer."

Rowena was not to be distracted so easily. "Do tell me why you were looking at Desire that way."

"If I told you, I fear I might give offense. It was only a passing notion, and a foolish one—"

"Now you *have* aroused my interest, sir. If you don't explain I shall certainly be offended."

He hesitated briefly, then decided that it might be best to satisfy Rowena's curiosity. She was not herself tonight, and he did not wish to provoke her. "Very well, then. A few months ago, when I was traveling to London in Lord Bodine's private coach, we were attacked by a band of highwaymen."

"I believe I heard something about it. Lord Bodine was outraged over the incident. But what has that to do with

Desire Guilford?"

"For a moment, I thought she looked like the girl — a green-eyed little hellion who was one of their band." He gave an embarrassed laugh. "An unlikely notion, was it not? Now perhaps you can understand why I did not wish to—"

"Our little Mistress Desire, riding about the countryside in such company?" Once more she gave that shrill laugh he found so disturbing. "You do have an odd turn of mind, sir, to imagine that any guest of ours—"

"I did not mean to give offense. And to be honest, there was little enough resemblance between that bold young creature, riding astride in breeches and shirt, and your charming houseguest. Only the color of her eyes, that brilliant shade of green." He stopped himself. "But you must promise not to speak of my fanciful ideas to anyone else, madam. Otherwise I might run the risk of being sent off to Bedlam."

"Hardly, sir. You have always struck me as being a gentleman of uncommon good sense. But I give you my word, I will not repeat what you have said. Indeed, I dare not. Dear Mama would be laid low with an attack of the vapors at the very thought of having shared her home with such a shameless baggage." Rowena's shrill laughter caused a few of the guests to glance briefly in her direction. "What an idea! Mistress Desire riding out with a band of common robbers!"

"Their leader was rather an uncommon sort," Sinclair said thoughtfully.

"Uncommon? In what way?" Rowena spoke lightly but her thin body was tense under the heavy folds of russet brocade.

"He was armed, but he did not use his pistol, as so many of his kind do. And he took no liberties with the ladies in our party. Although perhaps some ladies would not be offended by his attentions."

"Was he so handsome, then?" Rowena said.

"He was tall and strongly built, with the speech and manners of a gentleman."

181

"And his face?"

"As to that, I couldn't say. His features were concealed by a large handkerchief, as were those of his men."

"And the girl? You only saw her eyes?"

He shook his head. "She wore no handkerchief or mask of any sort. A daring little thing, she was."

"Any female who takes to the king's highway to rob coaches must be reckless," she said.

"Rowena, my dear." Lady Mirabelle had approached the alcove unnoticed. "It is time we were leaving."

"But it is only a little after midnight," Rowena protested.

"Nevertheless, you look quite flushed. A bit feverish, I should say. You remember Dr. Munroe's instructions."

Rowena could have strangled her mother without a qualm. Silly, meddlesome woman. But Phillip Sinclair was already on his feet.

"If you are indisposed, it would not do to flout your doctor's orders," he said. He held out his hand and helped her to rise. No doubt she was suffering from some sort of nervous malady, he thought. What else would account for her burning eyes, the tension in every line of her long, pale face?

He gave a deep sigh of relief as Rowena departed with her mother. Then he strolled back to the banquet table to sample the wine posset and seek out more agreeable company.

Chapter Seventeen

"Be off, you little beggar, or you'll feel the weight of my fist!" The Warringtons' footman, a tall, powerfully built man in grey and gold livery, glared at the shabby boy who hovered near the iron gates.

Rowena, returning from her round of morning calls, stopped on the wide brick path to the front door.

"What is the trouble, Jennings?"

Barney Yarrow dodged under the footman's upraised arm and ran over to the tall, thin lady in her gown of striped brown and cream-colored taffeta. "Please, ma'am. Are you Mistress Guilford? I got a letter for—"

The footman quickly overtook Barney. "Begging your pardon, my lady, this young ruffian's been lurking about the gate for near on a hour. I drove him off a couple of times." He seized Barney by one skinny shoulder and aimed a blow at his head.

"Stop!" Rowena ordered. "Let him go." She dismissed the footman with a gesture, and he went back to his post at the gate. He stood there, his heavy shoulders bulging under his satin coat, his baleful eyes fixed on the intruder.

"I will take the letter, boy." Rowena said to Barney.

He looked at her doubtfully. "Beggin' your pardon, ma'am, I was told to give it to no one except Mistress Guilford. You ain't her, are you?"

"The letter," Rowena repeated, holding out her hand. "Give it to me at once. Otherwise I shall turn you over to my footman. He knows how to deal with thieving little beggars."

"I ain't no thief, nor no beggar, neither," he protested. He reached into his coat and pulled out a square, sealed envelope. "Here's the letter, see?"

Her gloved hand darted out, swift as a striking snake, and she snatched it from him.

"If you please, ma'am, the man what sent me said I was to give it to Mistress Guilford."

"She is not at home now. I shall see that she gets it as soon as she returns."

Barney hesitated. It would be easy enough to grab the letter back from the skinny bitch, but he didn't want to tangle with the footman, still standing guard at the gate and eager to give him a sound beating, no doubt.

This was a fine fix, Barney told himself with chagrin. He should have known at a glance that this horse-faced female could not be Trenchard's doxy. Not Morgan Trenchard, with his handsome face and elegant manners. He could take his choice of all the best-looking girls in Whitefriars. But he had lost his head over that one little bit of sweetmeat. No doubt she was a rare fine piece, Barney thought. Why, even the hostlers at the Golden Anchor had vied with one another in praising the beauty of Mistress Desire Guilford.

The boy cursed himself silently for his blunder. Then he sought consolation in the thought that Trenchard need never know of his mistake. That was a mercy, for the highwayman had been in a evil humor since he had arrived at the lodginghouse. There'd been talk that he'd done in Niall Forret at Kate Claffey's place for informing on him. Barney didn't want to feel the weight of his anger, that was sure.

He started down the path, but the lady called out to him. "Wait, boy. I've not finished with you."

Eyeing her warily, he stopped and scuffed his torn shoe against the brick path. "Let me go, please, Your Ladyship," he begged. "You got the letter, ain't you?"

"Who gave it to you?"

"Don't know his name. Never seen him before. I run errands for them that pays me, that's all. My mum and dad are dead and I got two little sisters to care for—an' one's

184

cripple." Perhaps the lady might be moved by his pathetic tale and give him farthing or two.

"Describe the man." He heard no trace of pity in her voice.

"Don't rightly remember what he looked like," Barney said cautiously.

"How unfortunate . . . for you." She took out a silk purse, embroidered with gold threads, and moved it slowly back and forth.

Barney fixed his close-set eyes on the purse. Trenchard had already paid him a shilling to deliver the letter, but the boy was always on the lookout for a way of making an extra bit. "He had on a blue coat and white stockings. An' he was tall—"

"How tall?"

The lady was a sharp 'un, Barney decided. Rich as she was, she would demand value for her money. The boy remained silent, weighing the risk. He did not want to meet the same fate as Niall Forret.

"I ain't sure. 'Bout as big as that ugly brute of a footman, maybe."

"And well built?"

"Strong as a bull, an' no mistake."

"A gentleman?"

"There's some says he used to be a real toff before he took to the road—" The lady pounced on his words like a starved cur leaping at a bone.

"You did not meet him for the first time today, did you?"

"Guess I might've seen him before."

Rowena's eyes were flinty. "You do know I can have you taken in charge by the magistrates, don't you, boy?"

"What for? I ain't done nothin'."

"My footman will say he caught you trying to slip into the house to steal."

"That ain't true, Your Ladyship. You know it ain't."

But Barney Yarrow had enough experience of the world to be certain that no magistrate would take the word of a Southwark guttersnipe against that of a fine lady's footman.

185

Especially if the lady herself were to back up the complaint. Before the day's end, he might find himself lodged in Newgate Prison, and left to rot there.

"On the other hand," the lady said with a tight smile, "if you will cease your foolish games and tell me all I want to know, I shall give you six gold sovereigns. A fair price for a little information, is it not?"

Barney stared at her, temporarily robbed of the power of speech. Six gold sovereigns. For such a sum he would sell his mother to the heathen Turks, and throw in Polly for good measure.

"What kind of information would you be after, ma'am?"

"Tell me all you know of Desire Guilford."

It was late afternoon when Desire, having returned from a shopping expedition at the Exchange with Lady Mirabelle, went upstairs to her room to put away her purchases.

"This letter came for you while you were away," said Tilda, presenting it to her on a silver tray. At the sight of the seal, Desire's hand flew to her lips. She had all she could do to remain outwardly calm while the maid helped her to change for dinner.

Rowena, having listened to Barney's description of his trip to the Golden Anchor, had paid him off and sent him about his business. Then she had lost no time in opening the envelope and reading the letter. She had resealed it so carefully that Desire saw no sign of tampering. If the set into the wax was a trifle blurred, she scarcely noticed. Her hands shook slightly as she read the message.

I am in London, but I shall not remain here long. I need to see you, to speak to you. Meet me at noon, a week from this day, at the perfume shop of Mrs. Latimer, in Paternoster Row. I will reserve one of the private rooms on the second floor. Enoch has told me how you parted from him at the Golden Anchor, but I wish to hear, from your own lips, what happened to you after that.

If you do not come to meet me, I shall be able to guess the reason. We will go our separate ways, and you need never fear that I will try to see you again.

How had Morgan managed to find out that she was at Warrington House, she wondered. But it didn't matter. He was safe, and he wanted to see her.

It would not be easy for her to leave the house alone; Lady Mirabelle or Geoffrey surely would ask where she was going. She made and discarded several plans before devising one that might serve her purpose. But she did not speak of it until dinner was nearly over.

Geoffrey opened the way for her. "You have been unusually quiet, my dear. I trust you do not find this unseasonable heat oppressive," he said.

She shook her head. "Not at all. I was thinking of a chance encounter at the Exchange this afternoon," she said. "It happened while you were being fitted for your shoes, Lady Mirabelle."

"I confess it took me a great while to decide upon a pair of new slippers. The blue pair with the rosettes were most fetching, but the ones with the diamond buckles caught my eye."

"Pray, do allow Desire to tell us of this meeting of hers," Rowena interrupted. Her eyes fixed on Desire's face with a peculiar intensity.

"Why, it was of no great moment. I'd gone off to look at some fans, and I chanced to catch sight of someone I knew, a sempstress who used to come to the house to help with the fine sewing. She is in reduced circumstances now, and I promised I would call upon her at her lodgings."

"A kind thought, my dear," said Lady Mirabelle. "Shall I go with you?"

"I fear she would be embarrassed at having to receive Your Ladyship in such humble surroundings."

"I should be pleased to escort you," Geoffrey began.

"Desire is quite capable of looking after herself," said Rowena. "We must not make her feel that she cannot go about

187

freely on her own errands," said Rowena. "And she'll be perfectly safe since she will be in the carriage, with one of the footmen to watch out for her."

Although Rowena had treated her with unusual friendliness since the evening of the Sedgewick ball, Desire was not easy in her company. Several times she had caught Geoffrey's sister looking at her like a hungry cat, preparing to pounce on a mouse.

"Perhaps I might hire a sedan chair," Desire said. "I don't know how long I'll be."

Geoffrey laughed indulgently. "My dear, you must learn not to concern yourself with such matters. Our carriage is at your service any time you want it."

The sky was overcast, and grey clouds scudded over the city when Desire drove up to the perfume shop on Paternoster Row. She had put on her green silk dress, the one Morgan had given her; and had thrown the velvet cloak over her shoulders. The emerald earrings were still concealed in one of the pockets. Perhaps when she and Morgan were together she would wear them for him.

He had said he would be leaving London soon. If only she could persuade him to wait, at least until she had her audience with His Majesty. Should she tell Morgan about that, she wondered?

Desire realized, with a start, that the Warringtons' coach had drawn to a halt before a tall, narrow building. A blue and gilt sign, in the shape of a perfume flask, swung over the door. The breeze was growing stronger, so that the chains holding the sign made a creaking sound. The clouds were thickening overhead, promising a spring downpour, but Desire was indifferent to the weather. Soon she would be with Morgan, he would hold her in his arms, and she would feel the hard strength of him pressed against her once more.

"Begging your pardon, Mistress Guilford. You're sure this is the right place?" The carriage had drawn to a stop, and the footman had leaped down from the box to help her to alight, but there was a puzzled frown on his face.

MRS. LATIMER
PERFUMES AND LOTIONS

The gilt lettering on the bow window was plain enough. "This is the place," said Desire impatiently. "Please hand me the basket." Because she could not have refused without arousing Lady Mirabelle's suspicions, Desire had allowed the cook to fill a large basket with an assortment of delicacies suitable for a lady in reduced circumstances.

The footman continued to hesitate, all the while he exchanged a long look with the coachman, and Desire felt her nerves stretch to the breaking point.

During the week since she had received Morgan's letter she had not been able to think of anything else. No doubt he had tried to forget her, but he hadn't been able to. He loved her, as she loved him. He was leaving London—he had said so in his letter—and wanted her to go with him.

"Your basket, Mistress Guilford." Although his tone was correct enough, she thought for a moment that she caught a knowing look in his eyes, a slight smirk on his lips. She rebuked herself for her overactive imagination. She refused his offer to carry it for her, took it on her arm, and hurried inside.

The shop was heavy with the mingled scents of perfumed unguents, creams, and lotions for smoothing the complexion and whitening the hands. There were clove-scented pomanders, tiny inlaid beauty patch boxes, and an assortment of gloves that gave off the fragrance of violets or Neroli. Mrs. Latimer, a small woman in neat black silk, rose and curtseyed at the sight of the elegant young lady who had descended from the crested carriage.

"How may I serve you, my lady?"

"I have an appointment . . ." Desire hesitated, not sure how to proceed. But Mrs. Latimer looked her over and nodded. "Perhaps you would like to leave your basket down here." She relieved Desire of her burden and led her to a door at the rear of the shop. "One flight up, my lady," she said with a smile. "Second room on the left."

Lady Mirabelle had spoken of fashionable shops that rented rooms to highborn ladies who wished to meet their lovers in discreet seclusion. More than likely, Mrs. Latimer's establishment was one of these. But Desire did not care. In a moment she would be with Morgan.

Her heart was hammering as she reached the second floor hallway and found the door she was seeking. She knocked and a moment later Morgan stood on the threshold, looking down at her. He took her hand, drew her inside, and turned the key in the lock.

His dark eyes moved over her, but where was the warmth, the tenderness she had expected?

"I seem to recognize your costume," he said.

"You should. It is the one you bought for me."

Desire was somewhat taken aback by his greeting. She had expected that after their long separation he would sweep her into his arms, kiss her, and tell her how eagerly he had awaited this meeting.

"I'd have thought a clever girl like you would have managed to get a whole new wardrobe from Lord Warrington by now."

She flinched at the mockery in his dark eyes, and now she felt uneasy.

"Or are you playing him as a skillful angler plays a fish?" he went on.

"I don't know what you're talking about."

"I think you do." His voice was harsh with anger. "The mistress of such a wealthy gentleman should already have persuaded him to give her new gowns, jewels, her own fine carriage and pair. But perhaps you are bold enough to play for higher stakes."

"Higher stakes?" she said, her cheeks growing warm.

"A wedding ring, my sweet Desire. But take my advice, don't overreach yourself or you may end up back in Whitefriars. And you know you lack the skill to be a really first-rate cutpurse."

Every night for the past week she had dreamed of this

190

reunion, and now she felt the sting of disappointment. Surely Morgan had not sent for her only to insult and humiliate her this way.

"If you must know, Geoffrey—Lord Warrington—has already asked me to be his wife."

She heard the sharp intake of his breath and saw him stiffen slightly. But he recovered himself and made her a brief, formal bow. "My congratulations, Desire. Obviously you need no one's advice, least of all mine. You are headed not for the gutters of Whitefriars but for the ballrooms at Whitehall Palace." She caught the raw pain beneath his words. "Perhaps when you are dancing with His Majesty, you may spare a thought for Enoch and me, out riding the highways."

"I have already had the honor of dancing with the king," she said quietly. Should she tell him now about her expected audience with King Charles? Perhaps not, so long as he was in this strange, unpredictable mood. Instead she shifted to safer ground.

"Was Enoch badly wounded?"

"Not so badly that he did not risk his life to draw the soldiers away from you. Apparently no man is safe from your charms, not even Enoch."

Her eyes flashed green fire. "How can you possibly suspect that Enoch and I—"

"You and Enoch!" He threw back his head, his white teeth flashing as he laughed. "Lord, no! I only meant that you managed to convince him of your innate goodness. No matter that a few hours after you met Lord Warrington you had already found your way into his bed."

She drew back her arm, but before she could strike out at his face, he seized her wrist. His fingers dug into her flesh, and she bit back a cry of pain. "You wished to see me, and you have," she panted. "Now turn me loose and let me leave."

But she could not free herself. "Let me go, damn you!"

"Not until I'm ready." He stood looking down at her, his dark eyes searching her face. "Tell me, when is the wedding

191

to be?"

"That doesn't concern you."

"When are you going to marry your precious Geoffrey Warrington?"

"I refused his proposal."

"Why?"

She glared at him defiantly, her lips set in a stubborn line. He shifted his grasp, his hands closing on her upper arms.

"Tell me. I have a right to know."

"You have no rights, where I am concerned. Damn you, Morgan Trenchard! Why did you send for me? Ever since that letter came I dreamed of seeing you again because I thought. . . I hoped . . ." Her voice began to tremble so that she could not go on.

He pulled her hard against him. "What did you hope for?" His voice was low and husky. "Tell me, Desire."

"Let me go," she said, but even as she spoke she felt the familiar, sweet-hot need stirring within her. It was as if she had been sleepwalking through the days since he had left her; now all at once she was coming alive again, her body awakening to his touch.

She looked up at him and her pride fell away . There was a fire within him that would set her ablaze, only to leave her again, alone in the cold and darkness. But it did not matter. Willingly, eagerly, she reached up and locked her arms about his neck.

He buried his face in her hair and gave a groan that came from the depths of his being.

Her breathing quickened so that she could scarcely speak. But she had to know, and now. "Morgan, you said in the letter that you needed to see me. Why?"

At first he did not answer. Then he lifted his face from the dark masses of her hair. He drew back slightly, his eyes guarded.

"Tell me, Morgan."

His mouth curved in a wry smile. "I had to be sure that you were safe and cared for. With a man like Warrington for your lover, I'll have no need to be concerned for your future."

"Believe what you please," she told him. "If the thought that Geoffrey and I are lovers will make you sleep more soundly, then by all means—"

"What else am I to think? You stayed with him at the Golden Anchor. You are living in his home now . . ."

"What, indeed? Since I yielded to you so willingly, no doubt you believe I am equally free and easy with any man who comes my way."

"Desire, don't make sport of me." For the first time since she had known him, she saw how vulnerable he could be. She had never thought to see Morgan looking at her this way, his eyes pleading for the answer he longed to hear. She was shaken to the very depths of her being. "Can't you see what it does to me, to think of you in the arms of another man? I never meant to fall in love with you—with any woman."

She was caught in a fiery tide of pure joy such as she had never known before. Her eyes meshed with his.

"You were the first man who possessed me, and there has been none other. I would rather sleep on a straw pallet with your arms around me than to share the royal bedchamber with the king, himself."

"Desire, my love!"

"No, it is best that you say nothing you will regret later. I gave myself to you willingly, and I shall let you go now, if that is what you want."

"But it isn't. Not now, not ever." He lifted her in his arms and she closed her eyes, giving herself up to the wonder of the moment. He carried her to the curtained bed and set her down upon it.

Chapter Eighteen

The storm was moving closer now, and Desire lay back on the wide bed, listening to the rising wind and the roll of thunder as they became one with the upsurge of her tumultuous feelings. Now the first heavy raindrops began to pelt against the windowpane, weaving a shimmering silver curtain to enclose her with Morgan in their own private world.

She raised her lids, and her senses were stirred by the sight of him standing beside the bed. He had stripped off his clothes, and his naked body, tall and splendid in its male beauty, glowed in the brief flash of lightning that cut across the sky.

And then he sat on the edge of the wide bed, his fingers dealing skillfully with the many buttons and ribbons that fastened her gown. She began to tremble as she felt him setting her free from the constraining folds of silk. He unlaced her tight busk, and she filled her lungs with the rain-scented air that blew in through the half-open window.

But even the breeze that stirred the heavy velvet bedcurtains could not cool her burning flesh beneath her thin, transparent shift. She heard his voice, deep and slightly unsteady.

"Take down your hair for me, love," he was saying. She smiled, remembering how long it had taken Tilda to arrange the thick, lustrous strands into this fashionable coiffure. Swiftly, Desire drew out the gold and tortoise-shell pins and placed them in a dainty porcelain tray on the small bedside table.

The room was furnished in a somewhat frivolous style, all

gilt, lacquer-work, velvet, and brocade. The bed was curtained in pale blue and silver; blue ostrich plumes stood atop the elaborately carved bedposts, at each corner of the taffeta-lined canopy.

Desire sighed with pleasure as she slid off her high-heeled satin slippers with their diamond buckles and let them fall to the thick carpet. Morgan drew the long, heavy strands of her hair through his hands, and she shivered with pure delight.

He stripped off her garters. His fingers lingered on her thighs, his touch tantalizing. Now he rolled down one of her silk stockings, then the other.

He bent his head and his mouth touched the sensitive flesh of her inner thighs. The brushing of his lips along her skin set her nerves aflame. Her shift was disarranged by his movements, so that it slid upward. He raised his eyes to the soft, dark triangle, and she heard him catch his breath at the sight.

He raised the shift still higher. "You'll have no need of this, my love. I want nothing between us . . ." She lifted herself from the bed long enough for him to take off the brief garment and toss it aside.

Deep within her loins warmth stirred, then blazed into white-hot passion. For only the fraction of a moment she hesitated. Then, driven by her own hunger, she reached out to him. Pressing her fingers against the sides of his head, she moaned softly.

"Tell me how you want me to pleasure you, my love." His voice, muffled against her flesh, teased her, challenged her to cast aside all shame.

"Morgan, please . . ."

"Say it."

But she could not force her lips to form the words. Instead, her hands tightened on his thick hair, and she guided him down to the moist peak of her womanhood.

He parted her with his fingers, then began to explore, to stroke and tease her with his touch. One fingertip moved deeper than the others, and her softness clenched around it, her body reacting with a will of its own.

When he withdrew his hand, she had to force back a cry of protest. A moment later he slipped his hands beneath her buttocks, raising her up, holding her against his questing mouth. She bucked under him as she felt the first rhythmic throbbing deep inside.

But even in her need, she longed to give as well as to receive the ultimate ecstasy. "Not yet," she whispered shamelessly. He raised his face and she saw his eyes, hazy with passion. He moved up over her, positioning his body so that the hardness of him brushed against her tingling bud of rapture.

Her fingers closed around his hot male shaft, and she guided him to the center of her need. She moved her hips in a slow, tantalizing rhythm. Morgan held back, delaying the moment of entry, stroking his hardness along the moist cleft of her femininity. Her hands slipped down the length of his back, lingering at the base of his spine, teasing him with light, feathering caresses.

She raised her legs and wrapped them around his hips, opening herself to him. He entered her with a single thrust, burying himself in her soft flesh. For a timeless moment he stayed quite still, and she felt the overpowering pleasure of enclosing him within her.

Her fingers pressed into the muscles of his back as he began to move with long, lingering strokes that set her aflame. Now she was moving with him, possessed with the sweet-hot urgency that must be satisfied.

Her soft, velvet sheath began to contract around him. He surged into her with the full strength and power of his manhood. When she felt she could wait no longer, she gave voice to her urgency in a wordless cry.

He exploded within her, and she was one with him now. Her whole being answered his, sharing the glorious moment of climax. She was joined with him in an exultant release that sent them soaring to the heights together.

* * *

Desire lay with her head pillowed on Morgan's shoulder. She heard the steady beating of the rain against the windows and saw the bedcurtains rippling in the breeze. He stroked her damp skin, then reached out and pulled the light silk coverlet over her.

She reached up and touched his cheek. "This is the first time we've made love in a real bed."

"I wish I could have offered you a different bed, one that was ours alone, and not in such a room as this." Never before had she heard that touch of apology in his voice.

"Then I guessed aright," she said. "This is a . . . a house of assignation."

"And what do you know of such places?" he demanded.

"Lady Mirabelle, Geoffrey's mother, chanced to mention one of them. No wonder the footman thought he had brought me to the wrong place."

"I did not mean that you should be exposed to such embarrassment—" he began, but she put her fingers over his mouth and silenced him.

"Have you forgotten what I told you?" she chided. "So long as we are together, nothing else matters."

She raised herself and searched his face, her eyes troubled. "Your letter . . . you said you were leaving London soon."

He cupped her breast in his hand, but although she felt her senses stirred anew, she would not surrender to the sweet sensation just yet. "Tell me," she insisted. "You've not changed your mind? You still mean to go away?"

"I must, my sweet," he said. "I would have left sooner, had it not been that I needed to see you first."

"But where will you go?"

"Hush, love," he soothed, stroking her hair. "It's better if you don't know."

"Then you are going to take to the highways again." The drowsy peace that had enfolded her only moments ago was slipping away now. She threw her arms around him, as if she could keep him beside her by sheer force. "Morgan, you can't, you mustn't."

"I have no choice," he told her.

"And what about me? Am I to leave you, not knowing when we'll see each other again?"

"It has to be that way," he told her. "I risked both our lives by sending for you today. Next time we meet, it must be far away from here."

"In Cornwall?" Try as she would, she could not keep the bitterness from her voice.

"It's the only way, for now. I'll come to you at Ravenscliff when I can."

She released him from her clinging embrace and sat up quickly. How could she give up all her carefully laid plans for a better future for them both?

"Morgan, no! I can't go to Ravenscliff, not yet, I must stay here in London."

His eyes narrowed, and she saw the first stirring of suspicion in their dark depths. "Because of Geoffrey Warrington?" he demanded.

She drew back as if he had struck her. "How can you possibly think that even now?"

"What am I to think? You say it doesn't matter where we meet, and now you're telling me you must remain in London. If it's not Warrington, then who is to keep you here?"

For a moment she felt an iron band contract within her throat, so that she could not speak.

"Answer me." His voice shook with jealous rage.

"King Charles."

The words came unplanned, and she saw him staring at her in disbelief. "Sweet Jesú, woman, do you know what you're saying? What has His Majesty to do with you?" He paused, searching her face. Then he said slowly, "You did tell me that you danced with him . . ."

"At the earl of Sedgewick's ball. I went there hoping to meet the king and get him to promise me a private audience." The words came in a half-incoherent rush. "I can scarcely believe my good luck now. He gave me his word to see me again and—"

"No wonder you won't leave London. A meeting with His Majesty. That's luck, indeed, for you."

"For us. If you'll be silent and listen, you'll understand why there is no question of my running off to Cornwall."

Quickly, she told him of the king's promise to grant her a private audience.

"He has many demands upon his time," she said, "but he won't forget. I'm sure he won't. And when I've told him about how you spoke up for his father's cause and were driven from Pendarren, and all the rest of it—"

"You have taken leave of your senses."

"Because I want to help you—to win a pardon for us both?" Her voice shook with indignation.

"If you mean to go through with this idiotic scheme, you'll win a hangman's noose for me, and another for yourself, more than likely."

"What other chance do we have? Morgan, let me try. His Majesty is a man as well as a king. He knows what it is to live in exile, like you. Why should he wish to punish you for your brother's treachery to the Crown? He will understand—I'll make him understand—"

He caught her by the shoulders, his fingers gripping her bare flesh. "I've listened long enough," he told her harshly. "Either you are hopelessly naive or you have lost your wits."

She gave a cry of pain, and he relaxed his hold. "Desire, give up this ridiculous scheme of yours right now."

Tears stung her eyes and spilled over onto her cheeks. He drew her against him. "If we are ever to be together, it must be my way. Don't cry, sweet." He held her gently, his hand stroking her back. "Even now, you are ignorant of the sort of world you live in. Maybe that's not so surprising after all. Less than a year ago you were a child, sheltered in your father's house, protected from any knowledge of evil."

"I'm no longer a child," she reminded him, her green eyes

fixed on his. "You should know that better than anyone else. You carried me off to your hiding place, you forced me to take up your lawless way of life, and now you're getting ready to leave me again—"

"Do you think I *want* to leave you? When I said I needed you, I spoke the truth. I'll come to you in Cornwall, as often as it's safe for us to be together." He held her away, and looking up at him, she saw the determination in his set face. "You will leave London for Ravenscliff as soon as you can make the journey safely."

"Safely? We tried that once. Enoch got himself shot, and as for me, it was a miracle the dragoons didn't capture me."

Morgan dismissed her protest with an impatient gesture. "This time you won't be traveling by public coach. You will go there in Warrington's own carriage, with his crest on the door and his footmen to guard you."

"Now it is you who've lost your wits. What possible excuse could I give Geoffrey for making such a journey?"

"Tell him you must visit your aunt."

"He'll want to come with me."

"You've said you refused to marry him. Now you may tell him you will reconsider his offer. But you wish to go alone, and take your time before making so important a decision. And since your great-aunt is your only remaining relative . . ."

"She's your great-aunt, not mine."

"He doesn't know that. You wish to seek her advice on this delicate matter. And should you decide to marry him, you want her blessing on the match."

"Morgan, I can't—"

"Why the devil not?"

"It would be heartless to go on encouraging Geoffrey when I have no intention of marrying him. He's been kind to me, and so has his mother."

"I'm sure you have endeared yourself to the whole Warrington family," Morgan interrupted impatiently.

"His sister, Rowena, was cold and suspicious when I first

came to the house, and though she pretends to like me now, I don't believe—"

"Spare me the details. Get hold of the coach as soon as you can and start for Ravenscliff."

"And if His Majesty sends for me in the meantime? Morgan, please let me speak to him. I am sure I can move him to—"

"You won't win a pardon for a highwayman, believe me. Although it's possible you can persuade him to show *you* clemency. If he were to see you as I do now . . ." Morgan gave a short, mirthless laugh. "King Charles is also a man— you said that yourself—and it would be difficult for any man to resist such beauty."

"Morgan, you fool! The king's pardon would mean nothing to me unless he granted one to you, too. Don't you know that?"

She threw herself against him, clinging to him. She looked up into his face, her eyes warm and glowing with love. "You are a part of me," she said softly. "When you sent me away before, and told me to use the earrings as a dowry . . ." Her throat constricted with pain at the memory. "You say you love me. How could you have hurt me so?"

His arms tightened around her, crushing the breath from her body. Then he lay stretched out on his back, holding her against him. His face was pressed against the soft swell of her breast.

"Maybe I wanted to make you hate me, so that it would be easier for you make a new start without me. Or maybe at that moment I believed what I said." His voice was low and hoarse now. "I only know you were scarcely out of sight when I started thinking about you married to another man. Lying with him like this. Opening your sweet body to his touch. And I couldn't stand it."

Moved by his admission of his own vulnerability, she stroked a lock of his dark hair back from his face. His lips closed on the nipple of one satiny breast, and she protested softly. "We shouldn't. It's getting late."

But even as she spoke, she felt the hot tide of sensation moving from her breast downward.

She tried to hold back, telling herself that she could not yield to him, not yet. If she surrendered now, wouldn't she be letting him believe that she was prepared to accept his terms? That she was willing to settle for a future of furtive meetings, sweet, stolen hours?

He grasped her hips, and somehow she found herself kneeling astride him.

"Morgan, no."

He took his lips from her breast, and she felt the ache of frustration. Then he shifted his attentions to the other nipple, and it too swiftly peaked under the caresses of his questing tongue. His fingers moved to the exquisitely sensitive flesh at the base of her spine.

Her lips parted and her green eyes went hazy with pleasure as she gave herself up to the delicious touch. She let her head drop forward, so that her long dark hair was like a rippling curtain around her face.

His strong hands lifted her, positioned her over him. She saw the tenderness in his eyes, and the overpowering need. With one movement of her body she lowered herself, taking him deep inside. He filled her, and she began to arch her hips, raising them up then lowering them in a series of long, voluptuous motions.

His fingers pressed into the roundness of her buttocks, communicating his growing urgency to her. She quickened her own pace, and now they moved as one, her throbbing mingled with the contractions of his manhood. Together they reached the moment of release, of ecstasy.

The sighing of the wind had died away when Morgan, now dressed again, pulled aside the heavy drapes. She saw that the rain had stopped. The half-open window overlooked the back of Paternoster Row. The damp air was filled with the smell of grass from the small square garden attached to the house.

"It's time I was getting back," she said softly, adjusting one of the pins in her hair. "Morgan, promise you won't leave London without seeing me again."

"How can I promise? It wouldn't be safe to meet here a second time, and I'll be damned if I allow you to come to Lena Yarrow's den in Southwark."

"But I can't let you go, not knowing when I'll see you again," she protested.

"You think I want it this way?" he demanded. With one swift, powerful movement he drew her into his arms and kissed her, his mouth lingering on hers as if he could not tear himself away. When he released her, he cupped her face in his hands. "Maybe I'll find a way to see you once more before I leave London. If I can, I'll get word to you."

She forced back the protest that sprang to her lips. She could not give him up, not now, not after he had confessed his love for her. Better to live in constant danger from one stolen meeting to the next than to spend the rest of her life in safety with any other man.

He lifted her cloak and started to place it around her shoulders. "Don't you find this too warm for spring?" he asked.

"You gave it to me," she told him. Then she stopped, and her eyes brightened for a moment. "And those earrings—I still have them in the pocket."

"You haven't worn them?"

She shook her head.

"Put them on for me now," he said softly.

She obeyed, her fingers trembling a little in her eagerness to please him. "The color suits you well," he said when she had fastened on the glittered, deep-green jewels.

"I'll wear them for you again next time. They'll bring you back to me . . ."

"Are you a sorceress, using the gems to cast a spell?" He smiled down at her, his eyes teasing. "You need no spells to draw me to your side."

203

He touched his lips to hers, then turned and strode from the room as if he could not trust himself to linger. She heard the door close behind him, and the sound of his booted tread moving down the whole length of the hall. The door of their room was only a few steps from the top of the front stairs. But perhaps he thought it safer to leave by the back way.

Swiftly she hurried to the window and pulled aside the heavy drape. After a brief wait, she caught sight of Morgan walking down the short path through the garden and out the gate. If only he would look up for a moment. But he kept going, and she was about to turn away when her eye was caught by a flurry of movement at one end of the alley. That bright flash of red reminded her of . . . what?

Then she remembered and her heart began to thud against her chest as she saw a soldier on horseback come charging into the alley.

Heedless of her own safety, she leaned from the window. "Morgan!" She cried out his name, but she did not know if he heard her, for he too had seen the redcoat bearing down on him.

He wheeled about, seeking another escape route, but at that same instant a large, heavy cart rolled into place at the other end of the alley. Although the two men on the seat wore no uniforms, it was plain that they had acted on a prearranged signal.

Morgan turned back, his pistol in his hand, as he tried to stand off the attack of the mounted dragoon. But a foot soldier who had concealed himself behind the garden wall came charging out. He raised the heavy oak stock of his musket and brought it down full force on the back of Morgan's head. He fell face down, the pistol skittering from his hand. More foot soldiers came swarming into the alley at either end.

Desire pressed her hand to her lips to stifle a scream. Morgan stirred, then raised himself to his feet. Two of the soldiers caught him by the arms and dragged him back against the gate. They held him, while another redcoat drove a musket stock into his midsection. He sagged forward, but his captors pulled him upright again. He kicked out with a booted foot, and the musket descended again, catching him on the side of the head.

Then the two men who had been holding him let him fall, and she could no longer see him, for he was concealed from her view by soldiers who swarmed around him. She felt a surge of anguish. The dragoons would surely beat him to death, while she was forced to stand there, helpless.

The mounted officer was shouting a command. "Hold off, damn you! You know your orders. His High and Mighty Lordship wants the whoreson taken alive."

She felt a tide of hope rising within her at his words. Morgan was alive.

Then she heard footsteps pounding up the stairs, and she turned swiftly, realizing for the first time that she, too, was in danger. She turned from the window and stood frozen, her green eyes enormous. There was only one door, and before she could make a run for it, she saw it flung open. A huge soldier stood looking at her, his eyes shining with unholy triumph.

"There she is—Trenchard's woman."

Other redcoats crowded in behind him. One of them leered at the disordered bed, its sheets rumpled, its silken coverlet hanging halfway to the floor. "The bastard enjoyed his freedom, at any rate."

Desire cringed before the brutal laughter that followed the man's words. Now they were advancing on her, their eyes filled with an animal hunger that turned her cold inside. She began to retreat step by step, then gasped as her legs struck the side of the bed. A moment later, one of the men, bolder than the others, pounced on her. He threw aside his musket, gripped both her wrists, and forced her arms down to her sides.

Instinctively, she began to writhe, and a scream tore itself from her throat. She heard his hoarse breathing and realized that her frantic movements could only serve to inflame his lust; she was helpless against the greater strength of his huge, heavy body.

She forced herself to lie still and allowed her lids to drop. The soldiers clustered around the bed.

"Jesú, what a beauty!"

"And see her finery. Trenchard was generous with his strumpet."

"Who wouldn't pay freely for a taste of this sweet morsel?"

The man who held her loosened his grip. Her eyes flew open to see him fumbling with the front of his white breeches. "I'll have more than a taste. And I'll pay nothing . . ."

His breath was hot on her face, and he tossed back her skirts. She managed to free one hand. As he straddled her, she raked her nails across his face.

He cried out in pain. "Bridle cull! I'll give you cause to regret that—"

"Attention! You there—on your feet!" Desire felt the man lift himself from her. Raising herself, she saw a tall, young lieutenant standing in the doorway. "Your orders were to bind the woman securely and place her in the constable's cart," he said, his eyes steely. "Twenty lashes for disobedience, Hatchard!"

"She was resistin' arrest, sir—"

"*Silence!* I want her bound and carried out of here at once."

The men sprang to obey. One of them turned Desire on her face and tied her wrists behind her. Another seized her ankles.

"That won't be necessary," said the lieutenant. "Unless you fear that the lot of you are no match for the girl, should she try to outrun you. She's a small one, at that," he added.

A moment later, Desire felt herself lifted and thrown, head down, across a powerful shoulder. The man gripped her firmly behind the knees. The room went reeling before her eyes, and she was jounced up and down as he carried her downstairs.

She heard the smashing of glass and the shrill protests of the owner. "Such a dreadful thing to happen in my shop! My trade will be ruined!"

Desire felt her insides lurch as she was assailed by the overpowering mixture of fragrances that filled the room. Then she was being carried outside into the street. The soldier set her down in a rough, open cart. Two men sat on the high seat behind the swayback horse.

A small crowd had already gathered to stare at her and ask one another why she was being taken away. "Don't often see a constable's cart here in Paternoster Row," said one.

"Mayhap she was tryin' to steal from the shop."

"Not her. Heard somebody say she was upstairs in one of the private rooms, bedding with the highwayman . . ."

The cart lurched forward, and Desire was nearly jolted off her feet. She grasped the tall board at the back of the cart, and as she did so, she caught sight of the Warringtons' coach.

A pale face was pressed against one of its windows. Rowena Warrington stared out, her eyes shining with triumphant malice.

The magistrate's office was small and dingy, with a low ceiling and two mud-spattered windows. Desire stood before him, looking up into his pale, fat face; she was flanked by the same two constables who had brought her here.

She looked around wondering if Morgan might be in the room, but instead she saw Rowena with two well-dressed gentlemen. Phillip Sinclair and Lord Bodine.

Weak and shaken as she was, and filled with fear for Morgan, she had to force herself to concentrate on the proceedings. She managed to hold herself erect, somehow.

"This shameless female—" Rowena began.

"Desire Guilford?" the magistrate asked. He spoke with the courtesy due a lady of Rowena's rank.

"The prisoner. She called herself Desire Guilford when she came into our home. But no doubt she has had many names, like all her sort. When she stayed at the Golden Anchor, she was bold enough to claim she was related to my brother, Sir Geoffrey Warrington."

"He was badly hurt. I cared for him. If you will send for him, he will tell you—"

The magistrate glared at Desire. "You'll remain silent until you are questioned."

"There's no need to trouble Lord Warrington," said Rowena quickly. "Should you want additional proof of what I say, no doubt Dr. Lucas Munroe will come here to support my statements. He attended upon my brother at the inn, and she—the prisoner—managed to deceive the doctor with her shameless lies."

"Your word is more than sufficient on that score, my lady," the magistrate assured her with an obsequious smile.

The air was close and heavy with the stench of oil lamps, and Desire's head began to throb. For a moment the magistrate's face, the high bench, the whole room began to waver before her eyes. She swayed slightly as she struggled to keep on her feet.

"Can't Mistress Guilford be permitted to sit?" She recognized Phillip Sinclair's voice, and she turned to give him a look of thanks. At a nod from the magistrate, the constables led her to a hard bench. She sank down gratefully. Her mouth was dry, but she hesitated to ask for water.

Now the magistrate was questioning Sinclair. Desire thought she saw a tinge of regret in his face as he testified against her.

"Yes, I do recognize her now. I am certain she is the girl who helped rob Lord Bodine's coach that night on Hampstead Heath."

"And yet you hesitated to identify her until now. Even though you saw her and danced with her at the earl of Sedgewick's ball. Why didn't you speak out then?" the magistrate demanded.

"There's nothing surprising in that," said Sinclair. He spoke with quiet dignity. "The lady—"

"You mean the prisoner."

"Mistress Guilford was dressed in the height of fashion," Sinclair went on imperturbably. "Even then, I thought I saw a resemblance between her and the girl out there on the Heath. The color of her eyes is most unusual. But I could scarcely suppose that a young lady who had been introduced to me by Lady Mirabelle Warrington could have been involved in highway robbery."

"Yet now you have no difficulty in swearing that she is the accomplice of the highwayman, Morgan Trenchard."

"She is now in a state of . . . disarry . . . as she was that night."

Only when he spoke did Desire realize what she must look like after having been manhandled by the trooper back in the room over the shop. She had lost most of her hairpins, so that her hair hung down in a tangle. Her dress was torn at one shoulder.

But it was Lord Bodine who gave the most damning testimony. "Those earrings the prisoner is wearing," he said. "Might I examine them?"

Desire went cold all over. Only now did she realize that she had forgotten to take off the emerald earrings. At a harsh order from the magistrate, she removed the glittering jewels and handed them to one of the constables.

Lord Bodine received the earrings and studied them for a moment. "These are most assuredly the property of Lady Isobel Killegrew who was traveling in my coach that night," he said with conviction. "Yes, indeed. Lady Killegrew was desolate at the loss." He glared at Desire and his voice boomed out. "I shall never forget a single detail of the robbery. I swore that I would bring every one of these miscreants to justice. They must be hanged at Tyburn, as a warning to others of their kind." His face was red, his forehead gleaming with perspiration.

"Pardon me, Your Lordship," said the magistrate. "You

may be sure that justice will be done. As for the jewels—"

"I, myself, saw the prisoner reach down and seize her La-dyship's jewelcase containing these earrings and a great many more valuables. She handed it over to one of her con-federates. Then she sat astride her horse, dressed in male attire, gloating over her evil deed. And now she is brought here, flaunting her loot—"

"Male attire!" the magistrate repeated. "She was wearing a man's breeches? And riding astride, on the king's high-way?" It was obvious that he found this description almost as damning as the accusation of thievery. He turned a bale-ful eye on Desire. "Your next ride will be to Newgate prison, where you will, no doubt, receive the punishment you deserve."

She sagged forward slightly as she took in the meaning of his words. Surely she would be allowed to speak out in her own defense. But the magistrate was already leaving his seat.

"On your feet, doxy," one of the constables said. She tried to obey, but her legs refused to support her. He swore as he and his companion hauled her from the bench.

Phillip Sinclair came over to her. She saw him reach into his purse and hold out a few coins. Then, realizing that her hands were bound, he wrapped the coins in his own hand-kerchief. He slipped the small packet into the bodice of her dress. "You will need a bit of money where you're going," he told her.

What could he mean? What need would she have for money in Newgate?

Before she could speak, she saw Rowena close beside him, glaring at him with her pale-lashed eyes. "Master Sin-clair, how can you feel the slightest compassion for her now that you know what she is?"

Sinclair turned to Rowena Warrington with a look of cold distaste. He bowed to her without speaking and walked out of the room. Desire stared after him, wishing he had waited long enough for her to thank him. But the constables were already leading her away.

Slowly, gradually she became aware of a strange rushing sound. It was inside her head. She felt as if she stood on a high precipice above a night-black sea. Too exhausted to struggle, she allowed herself to go plunging down into enveloping darkness . . .

Chapter Nineteen

When Desire began to regain consciousness, the rain had started falling again. She felt the chilly drops on her up-turned face and her hair. She was lying in the back of an open cart, swaying and jouncing along the narrow streets. Her muscles ached, but when she tried to shift her position, she realized that her wrists and ankles were bound; it was all she could do to roll over on her side and draw up her knees to try to shield herself from the pounding of the rain on her face.

"Drive careful, Jimmy," she heard a rough masculine voice saying. "That's a real fine lady we're carryin'."

A harsh burst of laughter greeted the remark. "Lady, is it? An' I thought it was Trenchard's fancy piece we were car-tin' off to Newgate."

Newgate!

The icy sensation that flooded over Desire had nothing to do with the rain. Ever since the night in Whitefriars when she had set out to steal in a desperate effort to survive, she had lived in terror of being caught and sent to Newgate prison. And now, just when she knew that Morgan loved her, when she had begun to hope that they might make a new start, here she was on her way to a cell behind those grim, stone walls.

Would she ever see Morgan again? The officer who had led his capture had said that Lord Bodine — "His High and Mighty Lordship" — wanted the highwayman taken alive. But only so that he might be tried and hanged at Tyburn, as an example to others.

Or perhaps Morgan would not live through the night, she thought. For a moment she shut her eyes tightly in a useless attempt to blot out the image of the soldier swinging the musket, smashing the heavy butt into Morgan's body. Had he survived the brutal beating, or had the officer's command come too late?

No, she would not allow herself to give way to such thoughts. She had to keep her wits about her, if she were to be of any help to the man she loved — and to herself.

But what could she do once they had her locked up in a cell, cut off from the outside world? She tugged at the ropes that bound her wrists. They were tied so tightly that she winced with pain. Her ankles, then. Perhaps if she could reach her ankles, she could undo the knots that held them. If only her feet were free, she could try to drop or roll from the cart as it moved through one of the unlighted streets. And then she could . . .

"Look, Thad, the wench is comin' around. Nothing like a good dousing with water to revive 'em." Then, to Desire, he said: "No good your wrigglin' that way, girl. I tied them knots meself, and I'm good at it, if I do say so."

"The iron fetters you'll be wearin' soon will be heavier than those ropes," said Thad.

"Now, don't be scarin' the wench," said Jimmy, with mock concern. "No doubt she'll be able to pay the turnkey's fee for easement of irons."

"An' if not, she can peddle her wares to get the money."

It was as if the two constables spoke a foreign tongue. What was "easement," she wondered. And as for "peddling her wares" . . . She shrank from examining the meaning of that phrase too closely.

"Wonder if she's to have a meeting with the floggin' cull," Jimmy remarked. "Be a pity to mark that fair white skin, an' that's a fact."

The flogging cull. She recognized the term, for one of the girls in Old Sally's house had been whipped through the streets.

". . . tied to a frame behind a cart, half naked, I was. The

213

streets were lined with people, all lookin' on . . ."

Desire felt her insides begin to churn. She would sooner die than to face such unspeakable humiliation, she thought. But she couldn't die, not while there was even the smallest hope left that she might be with Morgan again.

It was nearly dark when the cart drew to a stop. "Here we are," said Jimmy. Desire raised her head and saw the towering stone walls of the prison.

Newgate had once served London as a city gatehouse, but over the years it had been enlarged, and its walls reinforced, so that now it was a huge dumping ground for criminals of every sort. Its dark, disease-ridden corridors and filthy cells housed murderers, debtors, whores, forgers, religious dissidents, such as the Quakers, as well as children who had committed petty theft.

Desire's body tensed as she heard the great, heavy gates creak open, and then she lay back again, numb with despair. The cart went rolling into the yard, and one of the constables shouted, "Got somethin' special for you tonight, turnkey."

He pulled out a knife, and she shrank back, but he only cut through the rope that had been tied around her ankles. Then rough hands were hauling her down from the cart and she was being dragged along over the wet cobblestones and up a long flight of steps. Her feet had gone numb from the tightness of the ropes, so that she could never had made it under her own power.

The two constables thrust her forward, and a tall, rawboned man caught her by the arm. "Name's Guilford. *Mistress* Guilford."

"We get our share of fancy strumpets here," growled the turnkey.

"She's more'n that," Jimmy said. He spoke as if he had been personally responsible for her capture. "She was taken by the dragoons for the crime of robbery on the king's highway."

The turnkey stared down at her. She could not see him clearly in the dimly lit entranceway. She caught a glimpse of a long, narrow face topped by a shock of matted hair. "Are ye tryin' t' gull me, Jimmy?"

"I am not," the constable said, sounding outraged at the suggestion. "An' that ain't all. There was a power of high-born witnesses at the magistrate's office to make the complaint. Lord this an' Her Ladyship that. *An'* she was wearin' a pair of earrings that must've been worth a royal ransom. Stolen they were."

All at once the turnkey's grip tightened and he was staring down at Desire with great interest. "You've done your part of the job," he told the constables. "She's in my charge now."

"She ain't got the earrings now," said Thad with a short bark of laughter.

"She'd better have a few valuables about her, if she expects to pay her way here."

Desire stared from one to the other, wondering if she had heard aright. Surely she would not be expected to pay for the right to stay in Newgate prison.

"I have nothing—" she began.

The turnkey raised his hand and before she knew what was about to happen, he cuffed her sharply on one side of the head. "Hold your tongue 'till you're asked to speak."

He pushed her up against the stone wall on one side of the passage, then whipped aside the heavy folds of her velvet cloak. Her hood fell back, so that her face was fully revealed in the light of a candle, set in a lantern. Holding her by one arm, he ran his other hand roughly over her body. She tried to shrink away from the indignity of his search, but she was trapped between him and the wall.

With one swift motion, he thrust his hand into her bodice, his callused fingers groping between her breasts. She cried out in protest.

"One more sound out o' you, bitch . . ." He bared his jagged yellow teeth in a grin of triumph. "What have we here?"

She remembered how Phillip Sinclair had given her the coins, wrapping them in his handkerchief.

You will need a bit of money where you're going.

His words had meant nothing to her at the time. Now she understood.

"We could've searched her before we brought her in," Thad reminded the turnkey. "If we wasn't a couple of honest subjects, bent on doin' our duty."

The turnkey hesitated, shrugged, and handed him a coin. "A single shilling for the two of us?"

"That's a deal more than you buzzards make in a week of ordinary work," said the turnkey. He spoke with a firmness that brooked no further discussion.

Thad pocketed the coin. "We'll drink to yer health with this tonight, my fine lady."

"She'd better be stronger than she looks if she's to keep her health in this pesthole."

Desire shuddered as she heard Jimmy's remark to his partner. Then the pair were gone, and she was left alone with the turnkey.

"Lying jade," he said. "Tellin' me you had no valuables about you."

"I didn't remember—"

He shoved his hand into her bodice again. When he found nothing more, he drove his hard fingers into one of her breasts, so that she cried out with pain.

"Now, start rememberin'," he told her.

"You've taken all my money."

"It's not near enough to cover your expenses for the week, slut. The entrance fee is three shillings, for a start."

Entrance fee! She opened her lips to protest. The man must surely be jesting. But there was no trace of merriment in his cold eyes.

"What of them that don't have nothin'—that what you're wonderin'?"

Afraid to speak, she could only nod.

"They go down below. We got cells underground here, where there's not a bit o' light and the air's that foul, it ain't fit to breathe. They're stripped of every stitch they got on and left to stretch out naked on the stones. Even the strongest don't last long down there."

He was trying to frighten her, she told herself.

"That fine cloak you're wearin'." He fingered the fur trimming of the hood and nodded. Then he opened the fastenings and pulled it from her shoulders.

She felt the air strike chill and damp through her silk dress. But her physical discomfort did not trouble her as much as the thought that the cloak had been a gift from Morgan. He had put it over her shoulders only that afternoon, and had held her against him . . .

Tears stung her eyelids, but she blinked them back. "Now the shoes," the turnkey was saying. "Wouldn't want to get them dirty wearin' them in here."

She raised one foot, then the other, and in a moment she stood with nothing except her thin silk stockings between her and the damp floor.

"I'll have those, too."

When she hesitated, he grinned. "You goin' to take them off, or shall I do it for you?"

Hastily she dragged off her satin garters and rolled down her stockings.

"That'll do—for now," he said. He put away his loot in a wooden chest, folding each item carefully. "Not a bad haul," he said. He nodded with satisfaction as he added Phillip Sinclair's handkerchief to the pile. "Real linen," he said, like a canny shopkeeper.

Then he locked the chest and shouted into the darkness of the long passage. A short, hulking man emerged from the shadows.

"Take this one to Lady Felon's side, second level. She's to share a mattress with one of the other beauties."

"What about chains? The smith's at his supper."

"No chains," the turnkey said. "She's paid her easement fee."

The hulking man grunted and seized her by the arm. Numb with exhaustion, she struggled to keep up with him as he led the way into the dimly-lit passage.

Desire was surprised and confused as she made out the shapes of the prisoners milling about in the passageway. The sound of their voices echoed off the walls; some laughed, others cursed, a few wept, and someone was singing a bawdy ballad.

She had always supposed that the prisoners were kept chained and locked in their cells, but although she wanted to question the hulking guard about this, she thought it better to remain silent. She remembered how the turnkey had cuffed her for speaking out of turn. With each step, her bare feet grew colder. If only the turnkey had allowed her to keep her shoes. Her whole body began to shake with a clammy chill.

Outside it was late spring, but in these walls it was still winter. Only yesterday she had strolled with Geoffrey among the carefully tended flowerbeds of his garden; she had felt the sunlight warm upon her face.

Geoffrey. She hadn't thought of him since she'd returned to consciousness on the way to prison. What would he think when she did not return to Warrington House tonight? He wouldn't be kept in doubt long, she told herself. Rowena would be only too eager to expose her for what she was: a wanted criminal who had wormed her way into their home. A thoroughly unscrupulous creature who had trapped him in her spell, kept him at arm's length with her pretense of innocence, only to be captured after a tryst with her high-wayman lover in a notorious house of assignation.

If she could see Geoffrey, try to explain . . . But no doubt he would never want to set eyes on her again.

Her thoughts were interrupted by the sounds of uproarious shouting and laughter coming from one of the side passages. "They're lively enough in the taproom tonight," the jailer remarked. "They usually are, when the liquor starts workin'."

"Taproom?" Desire repeated.

The jailer nodded. "New prisoners are supposed to stop an' pay garnish."

"What's that?"

"Don't you know nothin'?" The jailer shrugged. "You got plenty of time to learn." He laughed as if he had made a

218

clever joke. "Garnish is the cost of buyin' a round of spirits for them in the taproom."

"The turnkey took all I had." Desire could not keep the bitterness from her voice.

"Not all, slut." His eyes moved over her, lingering on her breasts, then moving the length of her body. "You got somethin' under those fancy skirts that'll bring you a few shillings any time."

For a moment she went rigid with fear and tried to pull away. He laughed sourly and jerked her arm to drag her along again. "Wait till them others have had their fill . . . You'll be only too thankful to spread your legs for me."

She tried to shut out the vile images that went flashing through her mind. "Hurry up," he growled. "I ain't had my supper yet."

Exhaustion crept over Desire, and she had to force herself to put one foot before the other. When she thought she could not take another step, her jailer pulled her up short. The heavy iron door was ajar, and she heard women's voices. "Got another lodger to share these fine quarters." He gave Desire a hard shove that sent her stumbling through the door.

She tried to keep her footing for a moment, reaching out instinctively to steady herself. But she could find nothing to hold onto, and she went down on the hard stone floor with a force that jarred every bone in her body. She wanted to lie there, to close her eyes and shut out everything.

"She's paid the turnkey for her meals an' half a mattress."

The jailer turned and went on his way, leaving Desire to deal with her new surroundings as best she could.

Chapter Twenty

Geoffrey Warrington joined the crowd of bewigged, velvet-clad gentlemen who had drunk their fill and were now jostling their way into the cockpit at Whitehall Palace. Although he had never been particularly fond of the sport, he was restless tonight and ready to sample any diversion. He had dined out at the fashionable Black Bull tavern, had gone on to the Theatre Royale, but had left early, unable to keep his attention on the stage.

He had hired a barge and come upriver to the palace to join the crowd that thronged its splendid galleries and gardens. Tomorrow evening, he and Desire would attend the ball here, along with his mother and Rowena, but tonight, since he was on his own, he sought to distract himself in the masculine atmosphere of the cockpit.

Cockfighting had been a favorite sport of royalty since the time of Henry VIII, who had added the cockpit to his palace at Whitehall. To the Stuarts, it was the "royal diversion," and although Cromwell had tried to abolish the sport, King Charles had restored it to popularity.

Geoffrey did not see His Majesty in the cockpit tonight — no doubt the king was sampling more intimate diversions with Lady Castlemaine in the luxurious private apartment set aside for her in the palace. But the absence of the monarch did not dampen the enthusiasm of the spectators, who pressed as closely as possible about the pit.

"Fifty guineas on the gray!"

"I'll put my money on Albemarle's black! As fine a fighter as ever I've seen!"

Cocks were fought from the age of one year. Their

wings were cut and their tails reduced by a third. Their hackle and rump feathers were shortened, and their combs were cut down so as to present a lesser target.

Geoffrey watched as the setters unbagged the birds and stepped back quickly. The gray cock rose into the air, then swooped like a bolt of lightning to slash at the throat of the other bird. Blood spurted out, spraying the white lace ruffles of a few of those closest to the pit. The black cock struck back, making good use of the two-inch heel spurs with which both birds had been fitted out.

As Geoffrey took a quick step back, he felt a hand on his arm. "Not leaving already, are you, Warrington? The fun's scarcely begun."

He turned and saw the round, ruddy face of Lord Bodine through the haze of tobacco smoke. Bodine's stout figure was splendidly arrayed in a cinnamon velvet coat, a gold embroidered vest, and wide-legged brown taffeta breeches fastened with ribbons. His lordship held a large, half-empty wine goblet, and Geoffrey guessed from the man's flushed cheeks, overbright eyes, and slightly slurred speech that he was already the worse for wine.

"One of my own birds—Old Brassywing—is to fight in the next match. He's a sure winner, if I do say so. There's my trainer over there; he'll tell you." He poked Geoffrey in the chest to emphasize his words. "You put your money on that bird of mine. Can't lose!"

Geoffrey drew back, almost overcome by the fumes of brandy exuded by the older man. "I've no doubt your bird's a rare fighter," he said politely. "But I must be on my way."

"Take it from me, my boy. Nothing like a good match to raise your spirits. Then a couple of bottles and a plump young charmer to share them with. That'll help you to forget."

"Forget?" Geoffrey repeated.

"That business this afternoon. Most unfortunate, I grant you, but you're not the first to be taken in by a pair

221

of bright eyes and a fine shape."

What the devil was he talking about? "If you will excuse me, Bodine—"

But the heavy, red-faced man gripped his arm more firmly. "Nothing to be ashamed of," he said insistently. "She was a clever little strumpet. Might've deceived a far more experienced man than you, Warrington."

"I fear you have the advantage of me," Geoffrey began. But he felt gripped by an uneasy sensation. A shout went up as the grey struck again, opening the other bird's throat. "He's done for! No, not yet!"

"Go in!" Bodine shouted encouragement to the grey. "Go in and finish him off!"

Geoffrey hoped that he might be able to take his leave unnoticed, but when he started to draw his arm away, Bodine put a hand on his shoulder. "No female's worth losing a night's sleep over, my boy. Your green-eyed trollop got what she deserved."

Geoffrey jerked his arm away so suddenly that Bodine nearly lost his balance. Desire! This foul-mouthed bastard dared to speak of Desire that way? "If you are referring to Mistress Guilford, sir, I demand that you explain yourself."

Bodine stared at him in surprise. "What's to explain? There she stood, bold as you please, and wearing Lady Killegrew's emeralds, no less. I was called on to identify them for the magistrate, and so I did."

Geoffrey stared at the older man, trying to make sense of his words. "What the devil are you talking about?" he demanded, too shaken to care whether or not he offended Bodine.

"Good Lord, boy. You don't know, do you?" He blinked owlishly at Geoffrey, as if trying to clear his head. "Should've thought your sister would lose no time in telling you all about it. No love lost between her and the Guilford wench—"

"My sister?" Was the man so far gone in drink that he

had lost his wits completely? "Step outside, sir, if you please, and explain yourself at once."

"Can't leave now, my boy. There's my trainer looking for me. My bird fights next."

"To hell with your bird!" Never would Geoffrey have spoken to His Lordship this way under ordinary circumstances, but the mention of Desire's name, coupled with Bodine's insulting remarks about her, drove him beyond the bounds of reason, let alone common courtesy. "I'll have an explanation at once, sir."

"Go find Master Sinclair, then," Bodine said, swaying slightly on thick, unsteady legs. "Left him out in the gallery with a yellow-haired charmer. He was there at the magistrate's office this afternoon. He'll tell you all about it."

Geoffrey shouldered his way through the crowd of spectators and strode out into the gallery. Tonight, as usual, the palace at Whitehall presented a dazzling spectacle. Since the Restoration, it had become a great promenade for all who were able to gain admission. The wide galleries were hung with magnificent tapestries, the chambers richly furnished and crowded with courtiers clad in silks, velvets, and taffetas and decked out with glittering jewels.

They had come to to seek a new lover, to gamble, to gain a more imposing title, a lucrative position in the royal household, or another great estate to add to those they already owned.

Meanwhile, they enlivened their time by sharing the latest gossip—the bawdier, the better. Even the king, himself, was not spared.

"You've not heard Rochester's newest lampoon?" said a fop, glancing about to make sure His Majesty was nowhere nearby.

"Do tell us," a heavily painted lady urged with a giggle.

"Really, I should not. Considering the earl's own habits, it's a case of the pot calling the kettle black."

He lowered his voice only slightly, and his listeners

drew closer, their eyes shining with anticipation.

> Restless he rolls about from whore to whore
> A merry monarch scandalous and poor.
> Nor are his high desires above his strength
> His sceptre and his pizzle are of a length.

A burst of laughter greeted the scurrilous verse.

"Rochester will go too far one day," said one of the listeners.

"It's said he employs a footman to stand outside the door of every lady who's enjoying an amorous intrigue, then goes off to the country to write his libels . . ."

Geoffrey moved about in a state of mounting tension, stopping one acquaintance after another to ask the whereabouts of Phillip Sinclair. At last he caught a glimpse of the man through the half-open door of one of the chambers off the gallery. He was seated on a tapestry-covered settle beside an ornate fireplace with a blonde, rosy-cheeked girl who was singing a ballad and accompanying herself on a lute.

Geoffrey paused for a moment on the threshold, reluctant to walk in on a private tryst. But just then Sinclair raised his head and motioned Geoffrey inside. The girl, whose large white breasts were half bared by her pale yellow satin gown, paused in her song and pouted at the interruption. Then, recognizing the handsome young Lord Warrington, she gave him a dazzling smile. "Perhaps you are fonder of music than Master Sinclair," she said. "Your pardon, madam," Geoffrey said with a bow. He could barely contain his impatience. "May I speak with you alone, Master Sinclair?"

The other man nodded. "Amuse yourself at the gaming tables, my dear," he told his companion. "I'll join you presently."

The girl rose and favored Geoffrey with another smile; when she got no response, she tossed her head and went flouncing out in a flurry of yellow satin and ribbons.

"I was speaking with Lord Bodine," Geoffrey began.

"You know, then."

"I could get no sense out of him. He was flown with wine." All at once Geoffrey hesitated, gripped by a sense of foreboding.

"You have not spoken with Lady Rowena since her visit to the magistrate's office?"

Rowena again!

"I dined at the Black Bull and went on to the Theatre Royale."

Sinclair gestured to a chair on the opposite side of the fireplace. He took a long breath, looking like a man faced with an unpleasant but inescapable duty. Geoffrey seated himself, his slender body tense with apprehension.

"Yesterday morning I received a message from Bodine, asking me to come to his home," Sinclair began. "He's my patron, you see. I manage his estate in Norfolk."

Then, catching the grim look in Warrington's eyes, he went on to tell the man what had what he wanted to know.

"It gave me no satisfaction to identify Mistress Guilford as Trenchard's companion. But as a loyal subject of His Majesty, I had no choice." He sighed deeply. "A curious affair. A young girl with the face of an angel and the manners of a gentlewoman, allowing herself to be seduced by a highwayman."

"It isn't true!" Geoffrey was on his feet, his blue eyes hot with rage.

"I'm sorry, Warrington, but there can be no doubt. They were taken together this afternoon. She was still in one of the upstairs rooms at the shop of a certain Mrs. Latimer in Paternoster Row, while Trenchard was slipping out by way of the alley."

Sinclair was lying. They were all lying. Desire had gone out that afternoon on a charitable errand. She was to visit an old woman who had served her family.

But he had only her word for that. A feeling of cold nausea began to rise up inside him.

"Your sister saw Desire Guilford being dragged from the shop."

"My sister? What was she doing there?"

"It would appear she was the one who told Lord Bodine where Mistress Guilford and her paramour could be found."

"That's not possible! How could Rowena have known that Desire would be meeting Trenchard that afternoon?" Geoffrey demanded.

"Perhaps you should ask your sister that."

The pale, early morning sunlight slanted through the espaliered fruit trees in the garden at Warrington House. Rowena paused beside one of the ornamental flowerbed parterres where the dwarf boxwood enclosed a brilliantly-colored display of tulips.

Hearing footsteps on the path behind her, she turned and found herself facing her brother. His face was white and drawn, and he looked as if he had slept little the night before.

He had learned about Desire. She took a deep, steadying breath. "The tulips look splendid this year, don't they?" She spoke quickly. "I had hoped we might get more of those with the red and yellow petals, but that must wait until the war with Holland is over, I suppose."

Geoffrey made no response.

"I have planned an addition to the herb garden, instead. Perhaps you would like to see the sketches."

"You may stop your little farce right now," he said. "I haven't come out here to talk about the garden — or the war with Holland."

"You've heard, then. I am so sorry, my dear. I'd hoped to tell you myself. I waited up for you as long as I could, but I was exhausted after my ordeal in the magistrate's office. Such a dreadful place." She touched his arm lightly. "No matter. Desire is locked away by now in Newgate where she belongs. She will pay for her crimes against the law. As for the suffering she has given you —"

"How did the soldiers know where to find her?"

"Why, Lord Bodine had obtained a warrant from the chief justice," Rowena said. "He was determined to punish the highwaymen who stopped his coach that night on the heath and—"

"That was months ago," Geoffrey interrupted. "The hue and cry must have died down long since."

"His Lordship's a man of influence at court," she said uneasily. "No doubt the soldiers were under orders to go on with their search until they had captured Desire and Trenchard—"

"And yesterday, out of the blue, they discovered exactly where to look for her."

"And her lover," said Rowena, unable to suppress a tight little smile of satisfaction. She noticed that Geoffrey was not able to bring himself to speak Trenchard's name. "My poor Geoffrey. I know what you must be suffering, but it is better that you discovered the truth before you were foolish enough to offer marriage to that creature. Perhaps another time you will listen to my advice."

"I don't want your advice or your sympathy!" His voice was low, his blue eyes bitter. "You resented Desire from the first day she came here. You were jealous of her because she was young and lovely."

His words stung her, and she felt her hard-won control begin to slip away. "That's not true. I was afraid for you, because it was plain enough that she'd already trapped you with her pretense of kindness. A sweet little thing, she was, caring for a stranger so tenderly." Her pale-lashed eyes narrowed, and he saw the cold malice that glittered in their depths. "I knew her for what she was, a deceitful little slut. That day she went on about meeting an old family servant . . . said she was going on a charitable errand, to visit the poor creature and bring her a few comforts. And I had to sit and watch you and mother praising her kindness while all the time I knew she was going to that disreputable place to give herself to her highwayman." Rowena clapped her hand to her mouth.

"You knew? How did you know?"

She had said too much. How could she have let herself be carried away by her emotions? A dull pain gripped the back of her neck.

"Answer me, Rowena!"

Geoffrey seized her by the upper arms and started to shake her. The pain moved up into her head, and she began to feel dizzy.

"I . . . she wasn't here when the letter came, and I took it for her. It hadn't been properly sealed."

"What letter?"

"The letter from Morgan Trenchard. A boy brought it to the gate, the same day she made up that ridiculous lie about going to visit that old woman."

"And you played the spy! You read the letter. You knew. You were the only one who could have known when and where she was to meet . . . him."

"I had to do it, for your sake! Can't you understand that? I was trying to protect you, as I have since you were a little boy. I love you too much to stand by and allow you to ruin yourself with a common strumpet."

His blue eyes were dark with a killing rage. She cried out in pain and fear as his fingers bit deep into her arms.

"Geoffrey, stop!

Lady Mirabelle had approached, unnoticed by either of her children; she caught at Geoffrey's sleeve. "Turn her loose!" She tugged at her son's arm. He fought his way back to sanity and obeyed, pushing Rowena from him.

"My poor boy," his mother said. Her eyes were pink and swollen with weeping. "How dreadful this is for you, for all of us. Who could have imagined that Desire was capable of such wickedness?"

She turned to Rowena and put a comforting arm around about her shoulders. "Your brother is quite beside himself, and no wonder. You must not blame him—"

But Rowena drew away impatiently. She cared nothing for her mother's consolation. It was only Geoffrey who mattered. She had to make him understand, to forgive her. If only her head would stop its relentless throbbing.

"When you have had time to think," Rowena said, "you will realize that I only did what I had to. Can you imagine what you would have suffered, married to a debased woman, a harlot as well as a thief? She would surely have gone on lying, sneaking off to spread herself for any man who caught her fancy . . . or lain with a lusty handsome footman under your own roof whenever the craving seized her . . ."

Her voice trailed off as she slowly became aware of the terrible look in her brother's eyes. He was staring at her with deep-seated revulsion.

"I suppose I've known for a long time that there was this . . . this sickness in you," he said slowly. "I don't understand it, or perhaps I don't wish to." He spoke in a distant, unemotional way that frightened her far more than his rage had done.

"Run this house as you will, Rowena, for I will bring home no bride to interfere with your routine. Plant your herb garden, or have the tulip beds plowed under. I shall not be here to see it—or you."

A muscle twitched at one corner of her mouth. This was a stranger who spoke to her. It could not be her brother, her beloved Geoffrey, the only human being she had ever loved.

He took his mother's arm, and they turned away. Rowena stood in the watery spring sunlight, watching the two of them walking back to the house together.

Chapter Twenty-one

Desire lay on the floor of her cell, reluctant to rise and look at her new surroundings. It was easier to remain stretched out on the stones and give herself up to the feeling of despair that weighed on her. She heard the footsteps of the apelike guard moving away down the corridor, and then a woman's cackling laugh.

"Welcome to the Lady Felon's side, dearie. Stand up and let's have a look at you."

Slowly she raised herself to her knees. Her elbow throbbed, for it had been bruised by her fall. She shook her tangled hair back from her face and looked up. In the dim light she caught sight of a tall, heavyset harridan standing over her, a shawl wrapped about her shoulders.

"No use sleepin' on the floor after you paid garnish for a mattress," the woman said. "You can bed down next to Winnie, there in the corner."

She jerked her head in the direction of a small, thin figure who sat on a mattress with her bare feet curled under her. Silently Desire got to her feet and moved across the cell to drop down on the thin, straw-filled mattress beside Winnie. Still dazed, she began to look about her to try to get her bearings. She saw a rat peering at her from between two stones in the wall, and her stomach lurched with fear and disgust.

The only light in the cell came from a couple of tallow candles and a small sea-coal fire that flickered on the crude hearth; it was scarcely more than a hole set in the rear wall. As her eyes began to adjust to the dimly lit cell,

Desire was surprised to see that Winnie was scarcely out of childhood; the girl couldn't be more than fourteen, with pale straggling hair that hung in limp, greasy strands around her thin face, and round, frightened blue eyes.

"There's no blanket," Winnie murmured apologetically. "Maybe, if you got any money, Alf'll bring you one."

Desire shook her head. "The turnkey took everything he could get his hands on," she said.

"I can believe that," said a girl who came sauntering into the cell. "He's a greedy bastard." There was an air of tough vitality about the new arrival, who appeared to be a few years older than Desire. Her auburn hair hung in a thick, untidy tangle over her shoulders. Although her red woolen shawl and her dress were worn and faded, and she wore a pair of clumsy wooden clogs on her feet, she carried herself with jaunty self-assurance.

"I see we got company," she said, looking Desire up and down, her hazel eyes alight with interest. "You ain't a common kinchin mort, are you? How'd you get yourself scragged?"

Although Desire had not lived in Whitefriars for more than a few months, she had learned a little of its cant—the peculiar language used by the thieves and prostitutes who frequented the district. But she could not bring herself to answer.

This was a nightmare, she told herself in desperation, it had to be. If she remained silent, she would wake to find herself in Morgan's arms . . .

The tall heavy woman who had directed her to the mattress was seated on a heap of straw in front of the the sea-coal fire.

"The new one don't want nothin' to do with the likes of us, Bess, my girl. She's a high-priced strumpet. Look at that fancy silk dress she's wearin'. Real ladylike, she is. I could've got fifty guineas from the keeper of any bawdy house in Drury Lane for the likes of her."

"I'm not a strumpet," Desire started to protest, then

231

clamped her lips together. As long as she did not speak, all this wouldn't be real.

But it was real, she thought. There was nothing dreamlike about the sickening stench that filled the cell, or the penetrating dampness that struck at her, chilling her from head to foot. She glanced longingly at the fire. It had burned to a dull glow, but it was better than nothing.

She got to her feet and approached the crude hearth. As she stretched out her numb fingers, the tall harridan gave her a shove that almost knocked her over. There was solid muscle under the woman's pale flesh.

"Hand over your garnish or get back to your mattress."

"I paid the turnkey," Desire protested. For the first time since she had been pushed into the cell, she felt her weary indifference swept aside by her sense of outrage.

The woman drew back a huge, meaty arm in a menacing gesture. "You paid the turnkey for the coals. You want a place by the fire, you pay Hulda. That's me."

Desire hesitated. The woman looked capable of knocking her down with a single blow. But somehow she knew that if she did not assert herself now, she would be giving this unspeakable creature complete domination over her.

"You'll get nothing from me," Desire cried, her green eyes glittering. "Even if I had anything left, I wouldn't hand it over to you."

Hulda took a step nearer. Then she reached out and touched Desire's tangled hair. "What have we here? A couple o' fancy hairpins—tortoise shell and gold. Wouldn't be real gold, would it?"

Desire pushed her hand away. "Leave them alone. They're mine!"

"You're a fine lookin' piece, you are," Hulda said with an evil smile. "Skin like satin. Be a pity to scar it so that no man would ever pay tuppence to lie with you again."

Although Desire forced herself to stand her ground, she felt a surge of pure terror. She had no idea why Hulda had been sent to Newgate. Why, the woman might be a murderess, for all she knew. She looked about her, searching for a weapon with which to defend herself, but there was nothing. She threw a desperate look in Bess's direction. "The guard—call him," she cried, and was startled at the quavering sound of her own voice.

"He won't mix in," said Hulda. "This is between you and me. Now hand over those pins, and be quick about it."

Desire pulled one of the pins from her hair, but instead of giving it to Hulda she raised in in her clenched fist. "Get back. Don't touch me!"

Hulda's powerful hand closed about her wrist, twisting it viciously. Pain shot up Desire's arm and she screamed. She kicked out, forgetting for the moment that she no longer wore shoes. Her foot struck Hulda's ankle but inflicted no damage. Moved by some primitive instinct she scarcely recognized, Desire bent her head and sank her teeth into Hulda's hand.

The woman yelled and loosened her grip. Desire wrenched her arm away and braced herself for the next assault. Hulda swore and lunged at her, but Desire moved out of the way and put out her foot. A moment later, Hulda came crashing down on the stone floor.

But she was on her feet with astonishing speed, and now Desire retreated as the big woman came toward her, eyes narrow with fury, hair hanging down over her heavy shoulders. "You little slut, you'll pay for that."

She swung and caught Desire a heavy blow across the cheek, so that she staggered backward. The woman twisted her thick fingers in Desire's hair and closed the other hand into a fist, ready to strike again and finish the unequal battle with a single blow.

"Let her go, you stinking cow."

Bess had come up behind Hulda. She threw her shawl over Hulda's head. Then, as the huge harridan tried to free herself from its thick folds, Bess kicked her hard. Her heavy wooden clog found its ample target and Hulda

233

screeched with pain and indignation. Releasing her grip on Desire's hair, she looked from Bess to Desire and back again, as if trying to gauge her chances of taking them both on at once. She shrugged and rubbed her bruised buttocks. Muttering some of the foulest language Desire had ever heard, she left the cell.

"Go over and get warm," Bess said.

Desire stared at her for a moment, then quickly obeyed. She saw Winnie watching, her blue eyes wistful. "What about her?" Desire asked.

"You put up a good fight," Bess said. "She never did."

"I'm stronger than Winnie. She's a child. She shouldn't be here."

"There's plenty of them, younger than Winnie, in this hellhole," said Bess calmly. Desire was too exhausted to start a quarrel with Bess, and besides, she realized that she wanted the girl for a friend. She drew the remaining pins from her hair.

"Here, you can have these, if you want them. Let Winnie share the fire. She looks half frozen."

Bess stared at Desire for a moment, then took the hairpins, and motioned to Winnie. The child looked as if she could not believe her good luck, but then she scuttled over to the fire like a small, timid animal.

"What is she in here for?" Desire asked.

Bess shrugged. "Stealing, that's all I know. Doesn't talk much. How about you? Hulda took you for a fancy strumpet, and she should know. She used to get hold of girls fresh from the country. Told them she could get work for them as servants to good families. Then she sold them into whorehouses.

"I'm not a whore," Desire said, too exhausted to mince words. She sighed wearily. "I suppose you might say that I'm no different from Winnie. I'm here for stealing too."

"You don't talk like a common cutpurse."

"I tried my hand at it, but I lacked the skill." All at once, Desire realized that her eyes stung with tears. She was remembering her first meeting with Morgan, and it was as if she could hear his mocking words once more, and see his face, the strong planes and angles shaded by his wide plumed hat, his dark eyes gleaming in the moonlight.

"No need to bawl about it," Bess said roughly. "Purse-cutting's a knack not everybody can learn. Did they catch you with the loot?"

Desire shook her head. She knew she had to control her tears or risk the loss of Bess's respect.

"I'm not here for picking pockets," she said. "I'm charged with highway robbery."

Bess stared at her in disbelief. "You makin' sport of me?"

Desire shook her head. "I robbed a coach on Hampstead Heath."

"That's a heap o' gammon if I ever heard it. A little thing like you, riding out by herself with a pistol in each hand!"

"I never said that. I wasn't alone, and I didn't go willingly. Morgan Trenchard forced me to ride out with him and his men."

The girl's hazel eyes widened. "Morgan Trenchard!" She gave a long, low whistle. "You tellin' me you're his doxy?"

Bess stared at her, deeply impressed. But Desire scarcely noticed, for she was seized again with her fear for the man she loved. What had happened to him since she had watched him being beaten by the soldiers in the alley behind Paternoster Row? Where had they taken him, bleeding and unconscious?

"You lay with Morgan Trenchard," Bess said slowly, "and you rode the highways with him." If Desire had announced that she was Lady Castlemaine herself, Bess could scarcely have stared at her with greater awe.

"Why didn't you speak up for yourself sooner? Trenchard's girl! Hulda wouldn't have touched you if she'd known that," Bess said. "Wait till I tell her."

235

"Please don't say anything about it to Hulda," she said. "There's nothing Morgan can do for me now. He was taken by the dragoons the same time I was. They beat him with their musket stocks. Two soldiers held him while another . . ." Desire could control herself no longer. She buried her face in her hands, and her body shook with the force of her sobbing.

"Stop that," Bess told her brusquely. "That won't do any good. Where is he now?"

"I don't know. He wasn't in the magistrate's office when they brought me there."

"Maybe they dragged him off an' locked him up someplace to try to make him tell where they could find you and the others that rode with him."

"Oh, no! Bess, they wouldn't! They'd have no reason to, once they'd taken me." Then, belatedly, she remembered that Enoch was still at large. She must be careful not to implicate him by a careless word.

Bess shrugged.

"Morgan wouldn't inform on a friend, no matter what they did to him." But the thought only filled her with greater anguish.

"Don't start your caterwaulin' again. Won't do you any good, nor him neither." The cell door creaked on its hinges. "Here's Alf with our supper."

The apelike guard came in and set down a wooden trencher with four slices of bread and a pitcher of water. Behind him came a wizened little man carrying a heavy iron pot.

"Stew tonight—a proper banquet," Alf said. The other man reached into his loose, ragged jacket and handed Desire a wooden bowl and spoon, while Bess hurried to get her own utensils from a bundle at the foot of her mattress.

"Settlin' in, I see, Mistress Guilford," he said with a grin. "Bess, my girl, you see she learns her way about."

Winnie held out a flat piece of wood, and the wizened

man piled a portion of the stew on it. The child began to eat with her hands.

Alf departed, followed by his helper.

"Guilford," Bess repeated. "What's your other name?"

"Desire."

"I ain't never heard that for a name before. Sounds kind of special-like." She grinned. "It suits you."

She had already started eating her stew, and when she had finished, she carefully wiped the remaining morsels with her piece of bread.

Desire tasted the thin soupy mixture and gagged. It was rancid and lukewarm and tasted of spoiled fish. She put the bowl aside.

"I can't eat this," she began.

"You'd better eat what they give you if you want to keep alive."

"I'm not sure I do," she said. "Morgan's gone and without him—"

"Don't be a fool," Bess said. "You ain't the first girl to go soft over a man. But there'll be others."

"I don't want any other man. Ever."

"You will. You're goin' to be in here until they take you to the quarter-session at Old Bailey to stand trial. That won't be for a couple of months yet."

"And when they do try me . . . Bess, I know the punishment for highway robbery as well as you do."

"You got a chance," Bess told her. "You may not end up wearing a Tyburn tippet after all. You may get sent to the Indies as a bondservant. You might even earn your freedom after a few years."

When Desire made no reply, Bess took her by the shoulders and shook her.

"Listen to me! You got to keep going as long as you can," she said fiercely. "Now go ahead and finish your stew before the rats get at it."

Desire shuddered, but she forced herself to pick up her spoon. Somehow she had to find the strength to survive.

She had to keep on believing that Morgan was alive, and that there was still a chance for them to be together. Slowly she began to eat the rancid-tasting mixture that was her supper.

Following Bess's example, she wiped her bowl with her bread and chewed it. She felt a heavy drowsiness creeping over her. Winnie had already crept off to her mattress, and Desire followed.

"Take your bowl and spoon," Bess warned. "Otherwise, somebody'll nick them, like they did with Winnie's."

Bess stood up, stretched, and tossed back her mane of auburn hair. "Me, I'm off to the taproom. The ale there's better than this horse-piddle they call water." She went strolling out.

Wearily Desire stretched herself on her mattress. The noise from the other cells went on unabated. Somewhere a woman sang in a shrill, off-key voice; men wrangled and fought; and drunken laughter echoed through the crowded passageways.

Only that afternoon she had lain in a canopied bed with smooth linen sheets and a silk coverlet. She had felt Morgan's arms about her. His hands had caressed her body, lingering on her breasts, stroking the smooth flesh of her belly and thighs, then invading the moist, hidden places . . . She had felt the full force of his surging masculinity thrust into her, and she had given herself up wholly, completely, to the wonder of their shared fulfillment . . .

For a brief time she had dared to dream of a bright new future that awaited both of them. Perhaps Morgan had been right to make a mockery of those dreams. Perhaps there had never been a chance for the life she had hoped to share with him.

But she couldn't give up that hope, not as long as she was young and strong. And alive.

She rolled over and buried her face in the sour-smelling mattress and sank into a heavy sleep.

"How long are you going to stay in this dreary hole?" Bess demanded. "It's been near onto a fortnight since Alf dragged you in, and here you sit like an old crone by the fire. Come down to the taproom with me."

But Desire shook her head. In the two weeks since she had come to Newgate she had not stirred from her cell. She had not even ventured out into the dark passageways.

Hulda had glared at her from time to time but had not attacked her again. Perhaps Bess had told the tall harridan that Desire had ridden the highways with Morgan Trenchard. Or maybe Hulda did not want to risk having to take on both Desire and Bess at one time. In any case, she gave Desire a wide berth. As for Winnie, she took no interest in her cellmates. She moved like a small, pale ghost, saying little, staring dully at the walls.

"Come along," Bess said impatiently. "At least you'll be able to get a decent meal and a mug of ale. Now summer's comin', that water'll be more foul than ever."

Desire shook her head. "I have no money left, you know that."

"I told you before, you don't need to pay—not a girl who looks like you do. There's plenty of men who'll be glad to pay your reckoning."

"Only if I were willing to offer myself in return," Desire said.

Bess grinned. "An' what's wrong with that?" You've done it before. I'll wager your highwayman had you on your back often enough."

"Bess, please!"

"Please, my arse. Don't start puttin' on airs with me. That man of yours didn't do all his ridin' on the highways, I warrant."

"You don't understand. I love Morgan. I think I did from the beginning, though I didn't know it until—"

"An' the others?" Bess interrupted.

"There weren't any others," Desire told her indignantly. "He was the only one."

Bess stared at her and shook her head. "Ain't easy forgettin' your first," she said. "Maybe you never do, really. Sometimes I still find myself thinkin' about the good-lookin' devil who started me off.

"I'd come here from Sussex to work as a milliner's helper when I met him. He was all honey-sweet talk, and the presents he gave me . . . Even a gold ring. Least, he *said* it was gold." She gave a self-deprecating little laugh. "An' then, when he had his way with me, he put me on the buttock and twang game fast enough."

"The what?"

"Still have somethin' to learn, don't you? Buttock and twang takes two, a good-lookin' girl an' her bully. He'd find me a rich young fool, visitin' the City and lookin' for a bit o' pleasure before settlin' down. After the bumpkin had his fun, he'd be ripe for plucking. It was easy enough to get him to give me money to lease fancy rooms or to settle up the debts I claimed to owe. Then we disappeared, me and my friend. And the poor noddy was too ashamed to make a complaint to the law." Bess gave a scornful little laugh.

"Or maybe it'd be an old cove with a vinegar-faced wife who'd only let him fumble her under the covers with the candles out. I gave him plenty more than that, let me tell you. Made him feel twenty again. And afterwards he'd pay, handsomely to keep his wife from findin' out."

Once, Desire would have been shocked by these revelations, but now she reminded herself that she was in no position to look down on Bess. Hadn't she already turned to thieving the night she met Morgan in Whitefriars?

"I loved that man something fierce," Bess went on. "Thought there wasn't nothin' I wouldn't do for him, until I found out he had a few others like me, all workin' on their backs and handin' him their earnings."

"I'm sorry, Bess," Desire said softly.

"Don't you go feelin' sorry for me, my girl." She glared at Desire, her hazel eyes shooting angry sparks. Desire should have learned by now not to show pity for Bess, who had a fierce kind of pride about her.

"And don't think I'll waste my time beggin' you to go along to the taproom with me. You stay here until you get as daft as little Winnie, if that's what you want."

"No, wait!" Desire's thoughts were moving swiftly, shaping a plan. "Those men in the taproom—do you suppose any of them will be getting out of Newgate soon?"

"If you're thinkin' about escapin', you can forget it," Bess told her vehemently. "Them that succeed—I could count them on the fingers of one hand. Most of them get caught before they're into the courtyard, and when they do . . ." Her hazel eyes were shadowed with fear. "The floggin' cull strips the skin off their backs, and they get branded on the cheek, as well. Don't you get notions about talkin' some fool into helpin' you escape."

Desire shook her head. "I wan't thinking of that," she assured Bess. "But if a prisoner had committed a lesser crime—if he was going to be released soon—perhaps I could persuade him to take a letter with him."

"A letter? Who do you want to write to?"

At that moment the door creaked open and Alf stood waiting, holding a candle with which to light Bess's way along the dark passages to the taproom. "If I could get a letter to Lord Warrington, Sir Geoffrey Warrington of—"

Alf gave a harsh bark of laughter. "The wench's lost her wits," he crowed. "Lord Warrington, is it? Friend of yours, my lady?"

"That doesn't concern you," Desire told him.

But the apelike guard was enjoying his own humor too much to stop now. "Mayhap you're the duchess of Newcastle in disguise, doin' us the honor of lodging here."

Even Hulda, who had guarded her tongue around Desire since that first night, joined in bating her. "Why don't you take her letter round to His Lordship, Alf? No doubt

241

he'll send a coach and horses to fetch her away."

Desire knew how unlikely it was that Geoffrey would want to help her. Rowena had surely lost no time in telling him everything that had happened at the magistrate's office, and had probably embellished the account to put Desire in the worst possible light. By now, he might have left London to travel to his estate in Yorkshire or visit the Continent. But however slight her chances, she must at least try to get word to him. Perhaps he would be moved to use his influence on her behalf.

She glanced anxiously at Alf, wondering if it was against the rules to smuggle out a letter. But the guard only said, "While you're about it, why not write to His Majesty? Always best to go straight to the top." He was laughing so hard his thick arm shook and the candle cast huge, weird shadows on the wall.

"Shut that big mouth of yours, and light our way to the taproom," Bess said boldly. She lifted her ragged skirt and tossed her head. "Come along, Desire."

Bess and Desire followed the guard through the dark maze of corridors, where prisoners roamed at will. Now and then, Bess called a greeting to an acquaintance.

When they reached the open door of the taproom, Bess handed Alf a coin. Desire could guess how her friend had earned it. She hesitated, knowing she could never bring herself to lie with any of the male prisoners, no matter how desperately she needed the money.

Maybe she should have stayed in her cell after all. But Bess was tugging at her arm impatiently.

"Come on," she urged, and Desire followed her into the large, low-ceilinged room, dimly lit by candles and thick with tobacco smoke. Both men and women smoked pipes, in the belief that tobacco fumes were effective in warding off infection.

Bess led Desire to a long table where men and women sat drinking together. One of the women was singing a bawdy ballad in a loud, off-key voice, while the men beat

242

time with their tin mugs.

The ballad had many verses, but the refrain was always the same:

Then he laid me down and made me do it again . . .

Desire perched herself on the end of the bench, next to Bess. "So you finally got your friend to join us," said a big, heavyset man with greasy hair that hung to his shoulders. "What's your pleasure, ladies?" he asked, with an appreciative look at Desire.

"Beer for me, Hawkins," said Bess, and Desire nodded, saying she would have the same.

The man called to one of the prisoners who served as a waiter. The taproom was not so different from a tavern on the outside, Desire thought.

"Drink up," Hawkins said loudly. He sat down next to Desire and pushed his body against hers. The bench was already crowded, and although she shifted, she could not avoid the unwelcome contact.

When she left her drink untouched, Hawkins grinned at her. "If you'd rather have brandy, say the word," he told her. He reached for his bottle, brushing his hand against her breast. She felt his fingers cupping the soft, round globe. Then he twined his other hand in her hair and tilted back her head to get a better look.

"Young and fresh, you are. A fine bit of goods, like Bess said."

Then he laid me down, and made me do it again, came the drunken voice from the other end of the table.

"How much d'you want to let me lay *you* down?" he asked. "I swear you got me hard as iron right now. Here, feel that." He kept his grip on her hair and released her breast, only to force her hand down to the front of his breeches. She tried to pull her hand away, but he began rubbing her fingers up and down against his hardness, grunting with animal satisfaction at her unwilling touch.

"Wait until I get that inside you. I'll have you all hot and yowlin' for more."

243

Desire gave a cry of protest, and Hawkins grinned. "I can see you're no common trull," he said. "I got my own private quarters where we can enjoy ourselves without nobody lookin' on."

Hawkins bent and pushed his broad face against Desire's. She tried to pull away, but he kept his grip on her hair. Forcing her lips apart, he thrust his tongue so far into her mouth that she started to gag.

Somehow she managed to turn her face away. "Let me go!"

"Never fear, I pay well for what I want."

Desire twisted her head, and pain shot to the roots of her hair. "Bess, help me!"

But Bess was no longer beside her. She must have slipped away on business of her own.

She clawed at Hawkin's broad face, her fingernails tearing at his skin. He seized her wrist and twisted it behind her. "None o' that. Two shillings for the night, an' that's it."

"Can't you see the wench don't fancy you, Hawkins?" she heard a man saying. "You're too rough-like. Let me have a go at her an' I'll get her purrin' like a kitten."

But Hawkins only swore and pulled her from the bench, swinging her up into his arms. Shouldering his way through the crowd, he carried her toward a dark corner. "Let me go! Bess! Bess, where are you?"

She bucked and twisted, but it was useless. She heard the other prisoners shouting encouragement, offering obscene suggestions as to what they would do in Hawkins's place.

He set her down, pushing her against the wall, his body pressing on hers. "Could've had a soft bed. Now you'll get it standin' up, doxy."

He pushed closer, so that she felt her breasts crushed against him, and she cried out, half-fainting with revulsion and terror.

Then he was jerked back, letting go of her so suddenly

244

that she would have lost her footing had it not been for the wall behind her. "What the hell—"

"Let her go. She's mine."

Desire, dazed and shaken, heard the words as if from a long way off. "Morgan." Her lips shaped his name but she could make no sound.

A moment later she saw him take hold of Hawkins by the arm, spinning him around. Morgan drove his fist into the other man's face. Hawkins grabbed a bottle from the nearest table and smashed the bottom off. He pulled back his arm, and the jagged edges glinted in the dim candlelight.

She drew in her breath, her eyes wide with fear for Morgan. But a moment later he sprang, swift and lithe as a panther. He came in low under Hawkins's arm and struck the man in the midsection with his shoulder, putting all the force of his body behind it.

Hawkins made a choking sound and fought for breath, but he was a powerful man, and he recovered himself, still keeping his grip on the bottle. He lunged at Morgan, who swiftly raised one arm to shield his face. Morgan crouched, then thrust his knee between Hawkins's spraddled legs, throwing him off balance. Hawkins fell to his knees. Morgan's booted foot shot out and caught the other man on the side of the jaw. He fell face downward, twitched like a landed fish, then lay still.

Then Desire caught sight of a guard shouldering his way through the crowd, a heavy wooden truncheon in his hand. A thin, pale-faced slattern quickly nudged the broken bottle with her foot, rolling it under the table.

"What's all this?" the guard demanded, looking down at Hawkins, then glaring suspiciously at Morgan.

The slattern gave him an impudent smile. "Hawkins guzzled too much brandy even for him. Passed out, he did."

The guard, not satisfied by her explanation, looked around at the crowd. Desire pressed her teeth into her lower lip and tried to keep silent. She was tense with fear for Morgan, but she was not yet experienced enough in the ways of prison to know how to save him from punishment.

"That's right," a grizzled old man said. "Too drunk, he was, to give the green-eyed wench a good time."

"He'll be mighty disappointed when he comes round," said a fat, blowsy woman. "Mayhap I'll be able to console him."

"That ain't likely, you cow," said a voice from the crowd. The prisoners started to laugh and exchange bawdy remarks, then slowly moved back to their tables.

The guard hesitated a moment longer. "You're not out riding the highways anymore, Trenchard. Better remember that or it'll be the floggin' cull for you."

He strode off, satisfied that he had asserted the importance of his position. For a moment Desire could only stand there, looking at Morgan, her eyes locked with his.

Then Morgan reached out and drew her into his arms, cradling her against him, stroking her hair. She buried her face in his shoulder and clung to him, pressing her fingers into the muscles of his back as if to reassure herself that this was not one of those dreams that came to her at night in her cell. The hardness of his body, the warmth of him, told her he was real.

"Are you all right?" he asked at last. "If that bastard harmed you . . ."

He held her away and looked down into her face. "He had no chance," she said shakily. "But if you hadn't come when you did . . ." She shuddered at the thought.

"You shouldn't be here in this foul place," he said, his dark eyes filled with self-recrimination. "If I hadn't sent for you to meet me that day . . ."

She managed a smile. "You couldn't have known we'd be walking into a trap," she began.

Then she broke off, noticing that other prisoners at nearby tables were watching them. She was not surprised.

Morgan was famous for his exploits on the highways. To them, he was a heroic figure. Hadn't they closed ranks to save him from punishment only moments ago? But she longed to be alone with him to savor the full joy of their reunion.

No doubt he guessed what she was feeling, for he held out his arm to her as if they had been promenading in St. James's Park. She put her hand on his sleeve, and he led her through the smoky, crowded taproom. She noticed that more than one female prisoner stared after them, eyeing her with envy. A man raised a glass to them, and Morgan gave him a friendly nod.

Then he picked up a candle from one of the tables, and they went out into the dark passageway. She did not know where he was taking her, and she did not care. He was alive and they were together again. For now, that was all that mattered . . .

Chapter Twenty-two

"How did you manage to get these quarters?" Desire asked.

The room to which Morgan had brought her, after leading her through a maze of passages and up a long, narrow flight of stairs, was far from luxurious. But it was larger and more comfortably furnished than the cell she shared with Bess, Hulda, and Winnie.

A bed with a pillow and blanket stood in one corner; the battered table beside it held a tin basin and pitcher and a couple of tallow candles. There was even a high-backed chair with a frayed cushion. Morgan did not have to eat his meals crouching on the floor, as she and her cellmates did. "You have this place all to yourself?"

"Money will buy special privileges in here, as it does outside," he told her. "I have Enoch to thank for all this." He made a sweeping gesture. "He's been sending me what he can."

"The dragoons haven't found him—he's still free," she said with a deep sigh of relief. She had come to be fond of Enoch Hodges, not only for his kindness to her but for his unwavering devotion to Morgan. "But how did he know you were in here?"

"Gossip travels fast in the taverns and alleys of Southwark," he said. "A week after I arrived here, Polly Yarrow, my landlady's sister, brought me money for garnish."

"Thank heaven for that." She put a hand on his arm, still not quite able to believe that she had found him. She could not take her eyes from him, as if she feared that he might vanish at any moment.

"But you, my darling," he said, his face shadowed, his voice filled with remorse. "I'd fall asleep thinking about you. And then when I'd wake at night in a cold sweat, imagining you weighed down with chains and thrown in one of those foul underground cells, half starved . . ." His eyes darkened with anger. "I wanted to tear this place apart, stone by stone." He drew a long breath, and she saw that he was fighting to regain his self-control.

"I was never chained at all," she reassured him quickly, her hand closing around his. "And as for my cell, it's not too bad. I was able to use the money Phillip Sinclair gave me for garnish."

"Phillip Sinclair? Who's he?" Morgan demanded. "One of the prisoners here?" She caught the swift flash of jealousy in his eyes.

"Hardly." She forced a smile. "Master Sinclair is the gentleman who was traveling in the coach with Lord Bodine on Hampstead Heath. You remember him, don't you?"

Morgan nodded, and his features relaxed slightly. "How did he know you'd been arrested?"

"He was summoned to the magistrate's office with Lord Bodine and Rowena Warrington. He identified me as the girl he'd seen with you that night. He had to, I suppose, but he didn't gloat over my sentence, as Lord Bodine and Rowena did. Then, before the constables took me out, he gave me a few coins. But the turnkey wanted more." A sob caught at her throat. "He made me hand over the cloak you'd given me."

He glanced down at her bare feet. "And your shoes, your stockings . . . It's a wonder he didn't strip you to your shift." His voice shook, and his dark eyes were filled with pain. "Desire, what have I done to you?"

He lifted her into his arms and carried her to the bed, where he set her down gently. Then he was beside her, his arm around her. He cradled her against him. "When I think how frightened you must have been here all this time — alone, friendless . . ."

"But I do have a friend," she said quickly. "Her name's Bess."

"I suppose she was the one who introduced you to the gentry in the taproom," he said. A ridge of muscle stood out hard against the line of his jaw, and his face went dark with anger. She knew he was remembering how he'd found her, backed against the wall with Hawkins pawing at her like a savage animal.

"Bess wasn't to blame for what happened," she assured him quickly. "I went to the taproom of my own free will, and . . ." She sought for a way to soothe him, to erase the harsh frown from his face. "And if I hadn't been there today, we wouldn't have found each other." She pressed closer to him, resting her head against his chest. Then she reached up and stroked his cheek, as if to reassure herself that she had really found him again.

And now that he was with her, now that she felt his body, warm and solid against hers, she yielded to the overpowering need for release. The rigid self-control that had made it possible for her to get through her first weeks behind these grim walls gave way like a rushing spring torrent, breaking through winter's icy grip. Her words came swiftly, tumbling from her lips, easing the tightness inside her.

"After you'd left me in that room over the shop, I stood watching from the window. I tried to call out a warning but you didn't hear me, and then I saw the soldiers beat you unconscious in the alley. I was so afraid for you, and afterward, when I was brought before the magistrate and you weren't there, I thought they'd killed you."

"That would have been against their orders," he told her. "The bastards dragged me to their barracks and kept me there for the night." His lips closed in a hard, tight

250

line, his eyes bleak, the skin drawn taut over his angular cheekbones.

What had they done to Morgan before sending him on to Newgate? She tried to push away the ugly pictures that formed in her mind. Lord Bodine had wanted him alive so that he might be brought to trial and made to pay the price for his crimes in full view of the London crowd.

But she had seen with her own eyes the cruelty the soldiers were capable of. She could not allow herself to imagine what violence such men might have inflicted on Morgan, all the while making sure he stayed alive . . .

One thing, at least, was certain. He hadn't betrayed Enoch's whereabouts. Whatever brutal tactics they had used on Morgan, they had not broken him. He was still the man she knew and loved.

She drew him closer, pressing his face against her breasts. "Morgan," she whispered. "I've wanted you so. I longed to have you with me like this."

"We're together now, love." A sweet warmth went coursing through her as she caught his meaning. No matter what they had suffered or what dangers still lay ahead, this brief time belonged to them. His mouth covered hers in a tender, lingering kiss. His tongue explored the moist sweetness within, sending flickers of heat shimmering through her body.

Her fingers went to the buttons on his shirt, and she opened them quickly, then slid her hand inside and stroked his chest, stirred by the friction of the dark crisp hair against her palm.

"Forward wench, aren't you?" He laughed softly, and she took comfort in the sound. Her fingers moving lightly, tracing circles on his flat nipples. She heard him catch his breath and felt the tightening of his muscles. Her other hand went to his belt, and she started to unfasten the buckle.

"Have you no shame at all?" She caught the familiar,

teasing tone and saw the swift, hot light of passion that glinted in his eyes. A shiver of anticipation ran along her nerves and set them tingling. Morgan released her and pulled off his boots.

She lay back against the pillow, and for the first time she noticed a patch of light high in the wall. Unlike her own cell, his had a window. It was no more than a foot square at most, but it framed a glimpse of blue sky, a few rays of pale sunlight.

She tensed, filled with a brief, soaring hope. But a moment's observation told her that no creature larger than a cat could have slipped out through such a space, and it was far too high up to reach without a ladder. Still, she felt reassured as she thought of the bustling, crowded city outside these walls.

In those streets and gardens, men and women walked together, sharing the delights of spring. And at night they could hold each other in the warm darkness, their love unshadowed by fear. Somehow she and Morgan would find their way to freedom. Stubbornly, against all reason, she clung to her hope.

Morgan had shed all his clothes, and she began to unfasten her bodice. "Let me do that," he said. He helped her off with her dress and her few undergarments. Then she was lying back once more, with nothing to conceal the curves and hollows he had come to know so intimately. A ray of sunlight touched her, lingering softly on the whiteness of her breasts, her flat belly, and the dark, downy triangle at the apex of her long, curving thighs.

Fierce hunger rose up in him at the sight of her, but he told himself that he would not take her in haste. Although she was playing the bold hoyden for his benefit, he could guess how she had suffered these past weeks. He would deal with her gently, considerately. Together they would savor each moment to the fullest.

She held out her arms, and he went into their soft embrace. He felt like a man sinking into the depths of a mountain stream, cool and sweet . . . He was stirred by the memories of that afternoon when he had come upon her bathing in the pool near the blacksmith's forge. Her black hair had spread out on the water like a shining fan. He had carried her to the sloping bank and set her down under the trees . . .

"Morgan!" He started, brought back to the present by her cry of distress. Her hand, softly caressing, had found a raised welt on his heavily muscled thigh. It was nearly healed now, but her body tensed and she drew away, her green eyes filled with dismay. "The soldiers. They did that to you!"

"Don't, my love," he said. He cursed silently as he saw her soft lips tighten with distress. They must not let time slip away in useless regrets. "Desire, you're here with me and nothing else matters. My love, I need you — now . . ."

For a moment she did not respond. And then he felt her satin softness moving against him, her body slipping downward. She bent her head, her mouth brushed lightly over the his skin. Her lips parted and he felt the moist warmth of her tongue.

But the touch that was meant to soothe and comfort him set his senses on fire. His loins tightened and hard urgency caught him in an inexorable grip. It spun itself out into almost unbearable tension as she shifted her position and began to flick at his hardness with the tip of her tongue. He fought back the scalding tide of need that threatened to break down his hard-held control. Reaching out, he stroked the night-black waves of her hair.

His passionate, loving Desire. Generous, free-spirited, utterly female.

Raising himself, he took her face between his hands, and his eyes held hers. Then, with one swift movement he rolled her beneath him. She parted her legs, opening herself to him.

253

He slid his hands under her, cupping her soft roundness, raising her, sheathing himself in her with one swift thrust. Her breasts rose and fell with her breathing, and her green eyes were open wide, burning with the hot glow of her long-denied need.

She began to move under him, but he whispered, "Not yet, love."

It wasn't easy for her to lie quiescent while he kissed her mouth, her throat, the soft curves of her breasts. When he took first one nipple, then the other, between his lips, they hardened and a shiver ran down the length of her. Her loins burned and ached with her need for release. Then he felt the first tremulous pulsations deep within her, and he began to move in long, slow thrusts.

She tightened her hands on his shoulders and closed her legs around him, arching her hips, her whole body demanding fulfillment. They were moving together now, more and more quickly. His hands cupped her buttocks, drawing them taut so that she might feel the full pleasure from the hard friction against the center of her femininity.

He was taking her with him, drawing her to the farthest limits of sensation. Only when she cried out, her body exploding in the ultimate moment of fulfillment, did he give way to his own overpowering need. Together they touched the glorious heights of their shared ecstasy.

She lay with her head on his shoulder, his arm heavy across her breasts. Then slowly she opened her eyes and saw that the square of blue high in the wall had changed color. It glowed with the reddish light of approaching sunset. She longed to look away, to pretend that their time together would go on and on, but it was no use.

Morgan shifted and raised himself on one arm to look down at her. He stroked her hair back from her face, his touch infinitely tender.

"It's time to for me to leave now, isn't it?" She kept her voice steady, for she was determined not to reveal the aching sadness that engulfed her at the thought of their parting.

"In a little while," he said. Then he caught her to him, holding her tightly, crushing the breath from her body. "Dear God, how can I—let you go?" He sounded like a man in torment.

"Morgan! You speak as if you thought we won't see each other again."

She searched his face anxiously, alarm stirring within her.

"I can come down to the taproom as often as I please," she went on. "I'll wait for you there."

"You're not to set foot in that place again," he told her, his voice harsh with concern. "And I don't want you roaming around the hallways, either. When I think of what might happen to you . . . Promise me you will stay inside your cell."

Shaken by his intensity, she said: "I promise. But we've got to find a way to be together again."

He released her, got out of bed, and reached for his clothes. He began to dress quickly, his eyes brooding, his mouth set in a hard, thin line.

She drew on her shift and slipped into her dress. When she could bear his silence no longer, she went to him and put a hand on his arm. "Why can't I stay here with you? If Enoch can find a way to raise enough money for garnish, surely it can be arranged."

He spoke reluctantly. "It might be possible . . . if there's enough time."

Black terror shot through her. "You're keeping something from me," she said. "What is it?"

He drew her to him, holding her by the shoulders, looking down into her face. "The quarter-session assizes are to be held earlier than usual. In a fortnight, perhaps less, I'll be brought to trial."

"So soon? But I thought we'd have until autumn."

His lips curved in a faint, sardonic smile. "The judges are anxious to leave the city before the summer heat brings the danger of another plague."

She moistened her lips and forced herself to speak calmly. "Aren't we to be tried together?"

"I don't know. Either way, I'm going to convince the court that you did not take part in the robbery willingly. I'll say I forced you to go."

"But you can't. You mustn't!"

"I made you ride with us that night," he reminded her. "And if I can make them believe me, you may get off with a lighter sentence. But remember, when you are brought to trial, your account of the robbery has got to be the same as mine." He went on quickly. "Say I kidnapped you at pistol point, took you from London by force, raped you in a ditch . . . Tell the judge whatever you must to convince him that you were an innocent victim."

"You think I would speak out against you?" she demanded, her eyes burning with indignation.

"It's the only way. Perhaps you'll be sentenced to servitude in the West Indies."

"But what about you? I can't allow you to take all the blame, to face the worst kind of punishment."

His lips curved in a sardonic smile. She stared at him in disbelief for a moment, and then she understood. He was already convinced that he would not escape the gallows. Resigned to his own fate, he was determined to protect her in any way he could.

He held her against him, and she heard the strong, steady beat of his heart. Her arms went around him, and she gave herself up to the deep, overwhelming love that filled every part of her being.

Then she realized that he was speaking to her, his voice quiet and controlled. "Maybe you are frightened at the prospect of penal servitude in the New World. God knows, you deserve a far different future. But it isn't as terrible as it sounds. Remember, I spent some years in the Indies. Female servants there are not treated any worse than many in England. If you are fortunate enough to be bought by a decent master . . ."

She made a sound of protest, but he went on in the same even tone. "It is possible for an indentured servant to buy her freedom. You are young and lovely, you have your whole life ahead of you."

With a swift movement she pulled herself away from him. Her eyes burned with emerald flame. "What future can there be for me without you? If we can't be together, I don't care what happens to me."

He looked down at her and his throat tightened. For the first time since boyhood he felt an aching tenderness stir within him, the sting of tears prickling his eyelids.

How could he have guessed that the dark-haired girl he carried off with him that night in Whitefriars would change him so completely? Why had it taken him so long to realize what she meant to him? He pressed his lips together, forcing himself to hold a tight rein on his emotions. She needed his strength to hold onto. He could not bring himself to crush every vestige of hope in that determined spirit of hers.

"Prisoners have managed to escape from here," he said. "It's possible, with Enoch on the outside to help, we might be able to find a way."

"There is nothing he wouldn't do, no risk he wouldn't take to help us." But even as she spoke, terror gripped her. She remembered Bess's grim warnings. How could they hope to escape when so many others had tried and failed. And they had so little time to make plans.

Even now, the sky outside the small window was darkening with the coming of evening.

"I'll take you back to your cell," he said, but she shook

her head. She knew she was perilously close to tears, and she did not want to give way until she was out of his sight.

"One of the guards can light my way," she told him quickly.

"As you wish," he said. He went to a shelf near the bed and reached up. "I want you to take this," he told her. She caught her breath as she saw him holding out a knife to her. "Keep it hidden in your garter."

"I don't have them anymore. The turnkey . . ."

He nodded, and then, with a slight smile, he rummaged around until he found a shirred bit of red satin.

"Morgan, who gave you this garter?"

"It's a keepsake from Polly Yarrow," he said. She gave him a searching look, but this was no time for a display of petty jealousy. He was thinking of her safety, and she must reassure him as best she could. She put the garter on and tried to repress a shudder as she slid the knife inside.

"Don't let anyone know about the knife . . . they're not easily come by in here."

Before she could reply, he opened the door and summoned a guard who was loitering outside. She longed to cling to him, to plead with him to keep her with him a little longer. Then she looked at his face, and saw the fierce tension in every plane and angle. And she did not know how long she would be able to keep her own anguish under control. Better to part this way, she told herself.

She took his hand and pressed it to her cheek. "This isn't the end for us, my love. I won't let it be."

And even after she had left him, to follow the guard down the long, narrow flight of steps and through the maze of passages leading back to her cell, she kept saying the words to herself over and over again. There had to be a way for her and Morgan to gain their freedom.

"He's going to do that for you?" Bess said as they sat on the floor in front of the hearth. "He'll take all the blame on himself to try to save you from the gallows?" She sighed a little wistfully. "No man ever felt that way about me."

"There must be a way," Desire said stubbornly. "We've got to be together . . . somehow." She stared at the dead coals in the hearth. The cell was bearable without a fire now that summer was almost here. But the thought gave her little comfort, for she remembered that the quarter-session was to be held before the warm weather arrived.

"If only the king had sent for me sooner," she said, half to herself. "At least I'd have had a chance to plead for a pardon for Morgan, and for me."

"So now it's the king, no less!" Bess stared at her in dismay. "You listen to me, my girl. There's some who go daft locked up in here. You want to be one of them?"

"I did have His Majesty's promise of a private audience. I swear it, Bess," Her eyes were half closed, as if to shut out her surroundings, and she conjured up the memory of the great ballroom, the candles reflected in the glittering mirrors, the music of the lute and the brilliant satins and velvets of the guests. "I danced with the king at a ball in Lord Sedgewick's house. He came there with Lady Castlemaine. She hurried him off, but he gave me his promise first . . ."

Bess seized her by the shoulders and shook her so violently that she feared her neck would snap. "Stop that talk! Stop it right now! First it was some fine lord you were dreamin' about and now—"

"Lord Warrington," Desire said, wrenching herself free from Bess's hands. "And it was no dream. Bess, I don't blame you for not believing me, but it's true. The only reason I went down to the taproom was to find someone who'd be getting out soon."

"You thinkin' about goin' down there again? Because if you are, remember how you took on when Hawkins tried to get you to lie with him."

"As if I could forget," she said with a shiver of disgust. "And besides, I promised Morgan I wouldn't leave my cell." She put a hand on Bess's arm. "Surely you know of someone who can deliver a letter for me. But it must be soon."

Bess started to rise, but Desire's hand tightened. "Please. Geoffrey—Lord Warrington—will pay you back handsomely."

"Maybe I'm gettin' unhinged listenin' to you," Bess said. But there *is* a man—one o' those Quakers. A strange lot, they are. He was whipped at a cart's tail and locked up for nearly a year, but he's gettin' out soon. Alf says his family's got money. They're payin' his fine."

Desire had heard her father speak of the Quakers, who were persecuted and imprisoned like criminals because they would not renounce their beliefs. "I've always found them to be decent and honest in their business dealings," he had said. "As for their faith, I believe each man should be permitted to seek salvation in his own way."

She felt a swift stir of hope. "I'll need a scrap of paper and a quill," she began. "And money to pay the Quaker, if he'll agree to do the errand"

"Mayhap he'd do it out of kindness. They're like that. But what do you hope you'll gain with your letter? Even if you really know His Lordship, if he bedded you one night, you think that'd bring him runnin' to Newgate to help you now? Once a man's had his fill of a girl he—"

"I never lay with anyone except Morgan," Desire said. "But Geoffrey wanted to marry me." She clutched at Bess's arm, her green eyes pleading. "You don't have to believe me. I can't blame you for thinking I've lost my senses. But do it to humor me. I can't pay you for the quill and paper now, but you'll get your money back."

Bess sighed. "I doubt it," she said with a cynical smile. She stood up and smoothed her shawl around her shoulders.

"Then you'll help me." Desire embraced her friend, who looked embarassed at this display of gratitude.

"Now don't go gettin' your hopes up," Bess warned, freeing herself and heading for the door.

Chapter Twenty-three

Desire sat curled up on her mattress, her long, slender legs tucked under her. Now, in the late afternoon, Winnie was the only other occupant of the cell, for Bess had gone down to the taproom and Hulda was bustling about the maze of crowded passages, engaged in her business dealings.

The tall, hulking harridan had taken up her former trade, acting as a bawd here behind the walls of Newgate. Bess had explained to Desire that Hulda was making a substantial profit working as a go-between, bringing together the younger, prettier female prisoners and the men who had the means to pay for their services.

"That bitch'd play the bawd for the devil himself if he made it worth her while," Bess said.

"At least her business keeps her out of here most of the day."

Although Hulda made a point of ignoring Desire, she still felt uneasy around the hard-faced woman. The account of Morgan's fight with Hawkins had spread through the prison, and no doubt even Hulda was wary of arousing the highwayman's anger by mistreating his woman. But what might happen to her after Morgan had been tried and sentenced?

Desire could not allow herself to think about that. Although she had not seen him since their afternoon together in his private quarters, she still clung fiercely to the hope that he would send for her again. Tenderness and passion stirred inside her as she remembered their last meeting —

the hard strength of his body, the reassurance of feeling his arms about her, cradling her against him . . .

If only Morgan would speak out in his own defense when he came before the judge, perhaps he might be given a measure of clemency. But she remembered the look of cynical acceptance she had seen in his face at their last meeting. He knew the punishment for his crime, and he expected no mercy at the hands of the court; his only concern had been for her, his only hope was that she might be given a lighter sentence.

She glanced over at Winnie, who sat picking at a loose thread in the ragged hem of her skirt. After much patient questioning she had learned that the girl was indeed guilty of stealing a beef and kidney pie. "I wanted to share with it with my mum an' the others when I went home to see 'em," Winnie had said.

How would Winnie fare when she came to trial? Surely no judge would sentence her to a flogging, or the pillory, for such a petty crime. But when she had said this to Bess, the girl had answered only with a shrug. Like Morgan, Bess obviously expected little mercy from an English court.

Now Desire turned her head, hearing the door creak open. She sprang up from her mattress. "Bess, what have you heard? Have the trials begun yet?"

She had asked the same question of her friend for nearly a fortnight, and each time she had gone weak with relief when Bess had said no. If only her letter might reach Geoffrey before she and Morgan were brought to trial, perhaps they still had a chance.

Bess took off her shawl and tossed it onto her own mattress. She wiped her forehead with the back of her hand. "What I wouldn't give for a breath of fresh air. Once summer's here this air in here'll be thick enough to cut with a knife."

But Desire interrupted impatiently. "Bess, please. Surely you've heard something about the quarter-session by now."

Bess gave her a look of compassion, then sighed. "They

started takin' prisoners out of their cells this mornin'. The judges are sittin' tomorrow. But that don't mean we'll be called right away. Could be a few weeks, or maybe they won't get to hearin' our cases until September."

"But what about Morgan? Has he been taken away?"

Bess's hazel eyes flashed with impatience. "It's time you started thinkin' about your own neck."

"Bess, for the love of heaven, if you know anything about Morgan, you've got to tell me!"

"There's nothin' to tell. Nobody I talked to knew if your precious Morgan Trenchard went with the first batch, an' that's the truth."

Then perhaps he hasn't been called yet, Desire thought, clinging avidly to her hope. With so many here in Newgate awaiting trial . . .

"Why don't you go over what you'll say when it's your turn to stand there in front of the judge?" Bess gave Desire a reassuring grin. "I'll wager you got a fair chance if you keep your wits about you. Why, with your genteel way of talkin' an' those fine manners, you might be able to get even some cold-hearted bastard of a judge to feel sorry for you. Desire, are you listenin' to me?"

"I'm trying to, but I can't help thinking about—"

"Think about yourself, unless you want to be wearin' a Tyburn tippet," Bess told her. "If you can manage a few tears when you start tellin' the judge all that about Morgan Trenchard kidnappin' you . . . throwin' you down an' rapin' you while you begged for mercy . . ."

"But it wasn't that way at all." Desire looked at her friend indignantly. "I've told you, Morgan saved me from a gang of ruffians after I'd picked his pocket—"

"An' then he rode off with you to that farmhouse where him an' his thievin' friends was hidin' out," Bess reminded her.

"He carried me off, yes. But if he hadn't, I'd have had to go back to Old Sally. Or roam the alleys of Whitefriars on my own until I was forced to steal again, or starve . . ."

"Forget all that, for pity's sake! You got to make the judge believe you were an innocent little virgin when Trenchard got hold of you. A respectable servant girl. Or a lady's maid. Tell him your mistress sent you on an errand an' you lost your way. Morgan Trenchard got hold of you an' took you with him —"

"Mistress Guilford!" Alf called to Desire from the doorway. Why was he addressing her so politely when he usually called her "slut," or worse?

Then the apelike guard stepped aside and behind him was Geoffrey Warrington.

Desire stood still for a moment, unable to move or speak. She felt a surge of relief and gratitude at the sight of him, for until now she had not been at all sure that, even if he did receive her letter, he would come.

He dismissed Alf with a wave of his hand and walked slowly into the cell. She wanted to run to him, to throw her arms around him and tell him how thankful she was that he had answered her plea for help. But now she held back, startled and bewildered by the change in his appearance.

He was not wearing one of his fashionable velvet suits with an embroidered vest and wide-legged breeches. His lean wiry body looked taller and broader of chest and shoulders, and he wore a red tunic with gold epaulets glittering on the shoulders and gold braid at the cuffs. Tight blue breeches and polished cavalry boots completed his uniform.

"Geoffrey, what have you done?" Desire cried.

But he did not answer at once, and she realized that the differences in him went far deeper than his change of clothes. She flinched inwardly as she studied his firm, unsmiling mouth, his blue eyes, shadowed with an expression of disillusionment. He looked older, harder, and she knew that she was to blame.

How shocked and humiliated he must have been when he had learned the truth — that he had offered his love, his proud name and title, to a highwayman's mistress. Had Rowena been the first to tell him, gloating as she did so? Desire felt her throat constrict with pity.

"You . . . got my letter," was all she could say. He nodded but remained where he was, regarding her in frozen silence. Then she realized that she, too, had changed. Perhaps he was repelled by her appearance. Her bare feet were grimy, her hair disheveled, her green silk dress torn and stained. She was no longer the fashionable, elegant young girl with whom he had fallen in love.

"Your uniform," she said in an attempt to break the unbearable tension between them. "It is . . . most impressive."

"I've purchased a commission in His Majesty's cavalry." His tone was brisk and impersonal. He glanced over at Bess, who was staring at him, her lips parted, her hazel eyes round with surprise. When she had managed to recover herself, she gave Desire a slanting smile of encouragement. She grasped Winnie by the wrist, hauled her to her feet, and led her from the cell. The younger girl made no protest as the two of them disappeared into the gloom of the passageway outside. No doubt she would remain close to the door, straining to catch every word from inside the cell.

Geoffrey looked about him, his nostrils quivering with distaste. "A barbarous hole," he said. "The air's foul in here, and it will be worse in a month or two."

Desire sensed that he was keeping his conversation impersonal because, even with the other two girls gone, he could not bring himself to speak freely of his feelings. It would be up to her to bridge the gap between them.

"If you'd chosen to ignore my letter, I would not have blamed you," she said, forcing herself to look at him squarely.

"I wasn't going to come. Lord knows, I didn't want to see you ever again. Even after your Quaker friend managed to find me. I'm no longer living at the house with mother and Rowena. But these Quakers are a persistent lot. He tracked me to regimental headquarters. The guards tried to drive him away, cursing and threatening him, but he wouldn't stir

266

until he'd carried out his errand, and finally it was the guards who gave in."

"You are living in a . . . a barracks?"

"I share quarters with one of the other bachelor officers in my regiment," Geoffrey said.

"But you never said anything to me about wanting a military career. Why did you purchase a commission?"

Swiftly he came to her side, unable to maintain his remote manner any longer. "I had to get away from the house, from everything that reminded me of you."

"Geoffrey, how did you find out about . . ."

"Bodine was the first to tell me. I met him by chance at the Royal Cockpit in Whitehall. I wanted to believe that he was drunk or out of his mind. But afterward, when Phillip Sinclair told me all that had happened in the magistrate's office that afternoon, I was convinced." He drew in his breath, and Desire could see how hard he was fighting for control.

"I'm sorry. I never meant to hurt you, Geoffrey. Whatever you may think of me, you must believe that."

His eyes glinted steely blue. "Why should I believe anything you tell me? You lied to me from the beginning, pretending that you cared what happened to me when I lay unconscious at the Golden Anchor. Feigning concern for a stranger, hovering there beside my bed, so gentle and angelic. And all the time you were using me to put the dragoons off the track. But that wasn't enough. You came into my home, you traded on my mother's gratitude, you went on deceiving me . . ."

"I didn't want to come to London with you. Surely you remember that. I meant to go on to Cornwall as soon as it was safe for me to travel."

"Why Cornwall? Do you really have relatives there?"

"No, but Morgan does."

"Morgan," he repeated, and she saw how difficult it was for him even to speak the name. "It was always Morgan Trenchard, wasn't it? You allowed me to believe you were a

267

virgin — gentle, innocent, everything I wanted in a wife. Did it amuse you to make a fool of me?"

"No! Geoffrey, no, it wasn't like that at all, I swear it! That night at Lord Sedgewick's ball, it would have been easy for me to accept your offer of marriage."

"Why didn't you?"

"Because I cared for you too much to behave so dishonorably, to shield myself with your name, your position, when I knew that I could never love you."

She put a hand on his arm, half expecting him to draw away; but instead he stood still, looking down at her. "Think what it would have meant to me if I had married you. I'd have been safe from the past forever. No one would have dared to accuse Lady Warrington of having committed highway robbery. The mere notion would have been unthinkable. And I had more to gain, so much more. You would have given me whatever I asked for. I might have made a place for myself at court. I'd have been admired, flattered, sought-after."

Her voice was unsteady, but she forced herself to go on. "If you remember that I might have taken advantage of you that night, and chose not to, perhaps you'll be able to think less harshly of me."

Her green eyes searched his for some sign of forgiveness, of compassion.

"Is that why you sent for me, to tell me you were sorry? To ask my pardon?"

Desire tried to remember what Bess had told her, that she must think only of herself, that she must do whatever she could to survive. Her heart speeded up and she ran the tip of her tongue over her dry lips as she sought the words that would win Geoffrey over.

"Why did you send the letter. The truth, Desire. You owe me that much."

"I did want to see you, to tell you how sorry I am," she began. He said nothing, and the silence stretched between them again. From the passageways came the now-familiar uproar: the laughter, the shouted curses, a woman's hysterical screaming, the clanking of iron fetters.

"You wanted to say you were sorry, and that's all? No, don't turn away from me. Look at me." He caught her chin in his hand and tilted her head back.

Her eyes locked with his. "The quarter-session of the assizes is being held early this year. The first of the prisoners will go on trial tomorrow."

"I see," he said quietly. "You sent for me, hoping to entice me into using my influence on your behalf. With so much evidence against you, how do you expect to convince me of your innocence? Surely you don't think me such a fool that I will believe Bodine to be mistaken . . . or lying? And what about Sinclair? He saw your face in the light of the carriage lamp that night on the Heath. Those green eyes, like no others, and those soft red lips . . ."

She shrank before the force of his anger. She tried to turn away, but his fingers tightened on her chin.

"And then there are the emerald earrings, let us not forget those. You were wearing them when you were brought before the magistrate. But perhaps they were only copies of the jewels stolen from Lady Killegrew."

Her face flushed under the lash of his icy sarcasm. "I *was* out on Hampstead Heath that night. I rode with Morgan and the others. He gave me the earrings."

Geoffrey's face went white, but he went on. "Stolen jewels for a highwayman's mistress. That was fitting, I suppose. But how careless of you not to have removed them. Or were you so carried away by your lover's embraces that you forgot such a trivial detail?"

Desire flinched at his stinging words and the look that accompanied them. How could she have believed, even for a moment, that Geoffrey would want to help her? Perhaps he might have forgiven her for helping to rob a coach, but how could a young man, in love for the first time, face the truth: that the girl he worshiped had refused his honorable offer of marriage, only to seek an illicit passion in the arms of a notorious criminal?

He released his grasp on her chin, as if he could no longer bear to touch her. She looked away, unwilling to let him see the despair in her face.

"No doubt you think I deserve to hang for what I've done," she said quietly. "Lord Bodine believes that the sight of a depraved female like me riding through the streets to Tyburn in an open cart will serve as a warning to others. At least it should provide a lively spectacle for the crowd—"

"No!" Desire raised her eyes at his cry of denial. She saw a shudder run through his lean body, and the pain that shadowed his face. "Don't go on this way. I can't bear it. If you could make me understand why you did these terrible things, what drove you . . . Surely you must have had some reason."

"What can it matter now?"

"If you were forced to break the law, if you acted against your will, any judge would have to take that into account."

"Then you will try to help me, even now?" Desire asked, her green eyes filled with renewed hope.

"It won't be easy. My regiment's been ordered to the Continent. We sail within the week."

His words struck her like a blow. It had not occurred to her that his military duties would take him abroad so soon. Once he was out of England, she would have no one to turn to for help.

The courage that had sustained her for so long now began to falter. But she would not give way until she was alone. Her chin went up, and she squared her slender shoulders under the torn green silk of her gown.

"You will wish to spend your remaining time in London with your family and friends," she said. Although every muscle in her face was stiff, she even managed a smile. "Forgive me for bringing you here on a useless errand."

He regarded her in silence, but she saw the change in his expression, the faint gleam of admiration in his blue eyes. He put his hands on her shoulders. "I trusted you once, Desire," he said. "I still want to believe that at least a part of what you told me was true. Your account of your family . . . you told me they were respectable people. That your mother and father died in the plague last year."

"I wasn't lying about that, Geoffrey. I was shut up in my own house, hearing the sounds of the dead carts rumbling along the street. I cared for my parents as best I could, but there was so little I could do. I listened to their delirious ravings until sometimes I thought I might lose my own reason. And then, after they passed away, after those dreadful men came and carried them off, I was left alone."

"The servants?"

"They fled, all but one. And she was the first to die."

"And then, what happened afterward?"

"When the danger of infection had past, the house was besieged by creditors. Maybe I shouldn't have run away, but with no one to advise me I gave way to panic. I fled from the house and wandered through the city, and when I got to Whitefriars . . ."

She stopped speaking abruptly. Geoffrey's eyes were filled with sympathy, and she dared not risk telling him about Old Sally. And of her own brief career as a pickpocket.

"Was that where Morgan Trenchard first saw you, in Whitefriars?" She nodded, and Geoffrey went on, "You must have been easy prey for such a man."

It hadn't been like that, but she knew the futility of trying to make Geoffrey understand the circumstances of her meeting with Morgan. Later, perhaps, she would explain.

"He was drawn by your beauty and your helplessness. And he carried you off. He threatened you, he forced you to submit to his lust."

Geoffrey wanted to believe that she had been the innocent victim of a violent, lawless brute. She saw it in his eyes, heard it in his voice. Once he had loved her. Surely a little of that love must still remain. If he cared for her enough to use his position, his influence, in her behalf, perhaps she still had a chance.

What was it Morgan had said? "Tell them I kidnapped you, raped you in a ditch . . ."

Say it, then, she told herself. It's what Morgan wants you to do, what you *must* do to save yourself. Now, while you still have a chance, tell Geoffrey what he needs to hear.

"Trenchard took you against your will, didn't he?"

It was the only possible answer if she was to restore Geoffrey self-respect, his male pride.

"And once he possessed you, he had to degrade you even more. That was why he forced you to come along the night he robbed Bodine's coach. He had to make you a part of his own lawless way of life so that you could never get free of him. And even when he discovered that you had found shelter under my roof, he tried to get you back. Why did you go to meet him at that house of assignation? Did he use threats, blackmail?"

"No! Morgan didn't . . . it's not true, any of it! He's not like that!"

She clutched at Geoffrey's arm, but he wrenched himself free. His blue eyes hardened and his muscles went rigid under the scarlet and gold tunic.

"You know nothing about Morgan Trenchard. He was a victim of a terrible injustice. He was forced to flee England when he was no more than a boy. And he returned to find that he had been unlawfully deprived of his estate. He hadn't the means to plead his case and so he —"

"That's enough, damn it! You must think me a lovesick fool to try to persuade me, even now, that your highwayman is a blameless victim of injustice."

"Not blameless, perhaps." Driven by her fierce need to save the man she loved, she went on in desperation. "Once I thought that I might win a royal pardon for him but now it's too late for that. But if he were transported — to the New World, to the Indies —"

"And you along with him?"

"That doesn't matter. Even if I never saw him again I could go on, knowing that he was alive somewhere."

The tears rose in her eyes, and she could say no more. She heard Geoffrey speaking, his voice harsh with pain and frustration.

"You love Morgan Trenchard. You always have. He didn't need to force you. You gave yourself to him willingly."

"Geoffrey, don't look that way, as if you hate me."

He shook his head. "I don't hate you, Desire. It would be better for me if I could."

He turned on his heel and started for the cell door. She stood motionless for a moment, then hurried after him. Her fingers closed on his sleeve.

"I never thought you a fool for loving me," she said softly. He turned and looked down at her. "I was honored that you wanted me for your wife. Believe that, at least. And one day you will find a girl who will give you the love you deserve. Perhaps then you will be able to forget."

"I'll marry in time, no doubt. The last male Warrington must produce an heir to carry on the name. But I'll never forget you, Desire—never."

He reached into his tunic and pulled out a leather purse. When he tried to give it to her, she pushed his hand away. A black apathy had begun to rise within her.

"It may be some time before you're brought to trial," he said. "You'll need this to provide yourself with the common necessities."

She shook her head.

"As you wish," he said, but before he could put the purse away, Bess came through the cell door. "She don't know what she's saying. If you please, Your Lordship, I'll keep the money for her."

Geoffrey hesitated, then shrugged and dropped the purse into Bess's outstretched hand. Desire stood watching in silence as he disappeared into the shadows of the passage.

Then she heard Bess berating her. "You've ruined your chances. You almost had him believin' you, ready to go out and move heaven and earth to save you, the silly young fool."

273

"Don't, Bess. You mustn't speak of him that way. I was the first girl he ever loved. He created an ideal in his imagination, and when he discovered the truth about me, that I was a common thief—"

"I don't know about ideals," Bess interrupted. "But I do know most all there is to know about men. He wouldn't have blamed you for helpin' to rob that coach. An' he might have been able to forgive you for layin' with another man, as long as you made him believe it wasn't your fault—that Trenchard took you by force."

"You heard all that we said?"

"Much as I could," Bess said without the least shame. "He'd have tried to get you a pardon, and like as not, he'd have done it, too. Not much he couldn't do—a man like that."

"And afterward?"

Bess stared at her in bewilderment.

"Suppose Geoffrey did succeed in getting me released. What would become of me then?"

"Why, he . . . I guess he wouldn't want to marry you. Him with his high title, an' all. But you could've gone to join him after he was settled. An officer's mistress lives high, with fine lodgings, gowns, a coach and pair . . ."

Bess stopped speaking, moved by the dull, indifferent look in Desire's eyes. "Morgan's the only man I've ever wanted."

Bess sighed, took her by the arm, and led her to her mattress. Desire sank down and Bess seated herself close by. Then she opened Geoffrey's leather purse.

"Holy God!" Her hazel eyes widened and her lips were parted in awe. "Desire, look at this! I never saw so much money before, not all at one time. Your Lord Warrington must be as rich as His Majesty."

She plunged her fingers into the purse and smiled with pleasure as she let the bright coins slide through her fingers. "Mayhap he's even richer, for they say His Majesty's squanderin' a fortune on that Castlemaine slut, to say nothin' of all his other women."

She shook Desire's arm impatiently. "Now aren't you glad that I was right there outside the door? You'd have let him go off with all this in his pocket. An' it don't mean that much to him, I'll wager. The way he handed it over to me, free an' easy."

Desire still said nothing. She stared across the room, her eyes fixed on the fireless hearth.

"An' you needn't worry," Bess went on. "I won't part with a single guinea without askin' you first. But we got to keep it hidden." She thought for a moment, then slipped the purse into a space inside the wide waistband of her skirt.

"I don't wear drawers, and the men in the taproom are forever shovin' their big paws between my tits. But they can flip my skirts up all they please, an' the money'll be safe enough where I got it."

Although Desire heard Bess speaking, the words meant little to her. Geoffrey was gone. He would not come back. In a few days he would sail away from England, leaving her to her fate.

She had lost her only chance to win Morgan's freedom, and her own.

Chapter Twenty-four

As summer drew closer, London lay dry and dusty under the cloudless blue sky. In the gardens of Whitehall Palace, and the great mansions along the Thames, the grass yellowed and the flowers wilted for lack of rain. Gilded coaches rolled over London Bridge, carrying the wealthy, bound for their country estates.

Within Newgate, the dampness lingered along the slimy stone walls, and the air, although warmer, was heavy with the stench of close-confined humanity. Bess went on visiting the taproom, but she seldom returned to the cell without mentioning another prisoner who had succumbed to jail fever.

On an evening late in June, she walked in carrying a bottle of Rhenish. "You can drink it with your supper," she told Desire.

"Not all of it, surely. Bess, I've told you, I don't have your head for wine."

"I'll share it with you," Bess offered, but although she smiled, there was a certain uneasiness in her hazel eyes.

"You'd better, or I'll get tipsy."

"It'll be a damn good thing if you do." Her voice was harsh, and Desire stared at her in surprise. "What need have you to stay sober in this hellhole?" Bess added quickly.

That was not like Bess, who rarely wasted her time in complaining. Indeed, they were a little better off since Geoffrey's visit; during the past two weeks, Bess had busied herself with striking a few shrewd bargains in the passages and the taproom. Desire now wore a pair of high-heeled leather shoes, slightly scuffed but serviceable. Using only a small amount of the money concealed in her skirtband, Bess had also bought Desire a comb, a needle and thread, a cake of soap, and a tin washbasin.

Winnie, who had been eating all her meals off the same flat bit of board, had been bewildered at first by Desire's gift of a proper wooden bowl and spoon.

"That's a waste of a few farthings," Bess protested. "The poor addled creature won't know the difference. But Bess had been wrong, for when Desire, who had learned only fine embroidery work, took off her gown and tried to mend it, Winnie said, "I can do that."

Surprised, Desire handed over the torn green silk and watched in surprise. Winnie worked quickly, the needle flashing in and out of the material with practiced skill. When Desire praised her, the pale-haired girl said, "I did all the mending for my mistress, and she was terrible strict. Rapped my knuckles if one stitch was bigger than the rest, or a bit crooked." Then she lapsed into her usual silence.

She now kept her bowl and spoon carefully wrapped in a bit of ragged cloth and tucked under her mattress. When Alf came in with a pot of thin, greasy soup, the girl proudly undid her bundle and held out her new possessions.

But Alf ignored her, for his eyes were fixed on the bottle. "I could do with a swig of that," he said. Bess shrugged and handed it over. He tilted it to his lips and took a long, gurgling swallow.

"Mind you leave enough for us." Bess grabbed for the bottle and he handed it over.

"Nothin' but the best," he said. "That young officer must've paid handsome for his pleasure." Desire felt revolted by his words, and the leer that accompanied them, but she had learned the folly of showing any response.

"Mayhap he'll be comin' back one of these days," Alf went on.

"No, he won't," Bess snapped. "He's sailed off to fight the Dutch. An' we've spent most of the money he left."

Hulda came strolling into the cell for her supper. She

277

gave Desire a flattering smile. "There's plenty of other men who'll pay for your favors, my dear," she told Desire. "Ever since they got a look at you in the taproom, they've been waitin' for you to drop round again. Why, I could get you a pound, maybe more, anytime you're ready."

Desire flinched at the woman's suggestion. She turned away, remembering how Morgan had led her from the taproom to his quarters. Her green eyes glowed softly as she started to recall each precious moment, each sweet sensation: the touch of his hands as they stroked her, arousing every inch of her; the warmth of his lips on her breasts; the wonder of their shared ecstasy . . .

Hulda's coarse voice brought her back to the present. "Name your price then, for an hour or a night . . ."

"I'll have no dealings with you or your customers, you hag." Desire could not restrain her fierce dislike for this woman a moment longer.

"Mind your tongue, my girl." Hulda's eyes narrowed at the insult. "No doubt you'll be thankful for my help soon enough, now you don't have Trenchard to protect you."

Desire, who had been holding out her bowl for Alf to fill, let it drop from her hand. She felt a band of iron tightening around her chest. "Morgan! What's happened to him?"

"Why, Bess," said Hulda with mock reproach. "Ain't you told your little friend yet?"

"You rotten old bawd!" Bess moved quickly, placing herself between Desire and Hulda, as if her body might serve as a shield. But Desire took her by the shoulder and thrust her aside.

She confronted Hulda with a look of such terrifying intensity that the older woman moved backward. "What about Morgan? Tell me."

Alf broke in. "Your highwayman's had his trial. He's goin' to meet the toppin' cove at the next Tyburn Fair."

Desire began to tremble violently, as if she stood naked in an icy gale. The topping cove. That was the hangman. And execution day was aptly named Tyburn Fair.

"Bess, you knew . . ."

"I would've told you, after I'd got you drunk enough."

Hulda ran her tongue over her lips and moved farther from Desire. "Gone barmy, she has."

Desire pressed her fingertips to the sides of her head, as if trying to get a grip on her whirling thoughts. "The king," she heard herself saying. "I danced with him that night at the Lord Sedgewick's ball. I wore Lady Mirabelle's pearls and—His Majesty said he'd grant me a private audience. I must see him at once, while there is still time."

"Lost her wits, an' no mistake. Seen it before with her genteel kind," Hulda said.

"Long as she's quiet, like that one over there." Alf spoke with indifference, jerking his head in Winnie's direction. "Quiet loonies are no bother. Otherwise it's off to Bedlam for our fine lady."

Under other circumstances, Desire would have been terrified at the mere mention of Bedlam. Like all Londoners, she had heard nightmarish accounts of the conditions in the home for the insane, south of the Thames in Lambert. The inmates suffered the torments of the damned there at the hands of their brutal caretakers. Not even the most hardened Newgate felon would wish to change places with a Bedlamite. But right now, Desire was too shaken to feel any fear at Alf's threat.

Bess, who had her wits about her, intervened quickly. "She didn't mean all that foolishness about His Majesty." Her hand closed firmly on Desire's arm. She half-led, half-dragged her friend across the cell and pushed her down on her mattress. "She was only jokin' like."

"She don't have much to joke about, now," Hulda said. "Though it's not likely she'll end up in Bedlam, neither, Alf. Not with her own trial comin' along. Chances are, she'll be ridin' off to Tyburn Fair with her highwayman."

"That's all you know," Alf retorted as he ladled soup into Hulda's bowl. "Trenchard spoke up for her at the trial. Said she was a proper young girl 'fore he clapped eyes on her one night. He dragged her into an alley and pushed her up against the nearest wall, with her screamin' for mercy. He flung up her skirts an' . . ." Alf made an obscene gesture. "Then he carried her off with him."

"But she helped to rob the coach," Bess said. "Them two at the magistrate's office recognized her, didn't they?"

"Trenchard forced her to go along, that's what he told the judge. Even said he tore the kerchief off her face himself so them in the coach'd get a good look at her."

"Quite the gallant gentleman," Hulda said. "Takin' all the blame on himself."

"Happens like that sometime," said Alf, flaunting his superior experience. "Even the worst of 'em, when they know they're headin' for Tyburn, they try to make amends. One I remember, he kept repentin' out loud 'til his cellmates threatened to strangle him an' save the toppin' cove the job."

Later that night, after the others were asleep, Bess and Desire talked in hushed tones. "If I offer Alf a large enough bribe, would he get me in to see Morgan?" Desire asked.

"If you're thinkin' of escapin' with him, it can't be done."

"I only want to be with him for as long as I can." Desire whispered.

"Not a chance. Once a man's been condemned, he's kept locked in his cell day and night under heavy guard."

Desire sat up with a cry of anguish, but Bess quickly silenced her, putting a hand over her mouth. "Don't start takin' on again. Want to wake Hulda, that poxy old bawd?"

She reached for Desire's untouched cup of wine. "Drink this now. It'll give you a night's rest."

"How can I sleep when I know that Morgan's in his cell, that he'll be kept there all alone until they come to take him to Tyburn?"

"He could be a lot worse off," Bess said brusquely. "They might have tossed him into one of those filthy ratholes in the Press Yard, with a dozen condemned men. Down there they chain 'em to the walls an' feed 'em on bread and water."

"But they haven't taken Morgan there. Why not?"

"He's got friends on the outside, payin' handsome for his

board an' lodgin'. That's what I heard in the taproom." Bess held out the cup, but Desire pushed it away.

"How's it goin' to help him if you stay awake cryin' all night?" Bess demanded in her practical way. "He's done all he can for you. He gave you a chance. You think he'd want you to throw it away?"

The words penetrated Desire's grief-numbed mind. Morgan loved her. He wouldn't want her to fall apart now. Somehow she must find the strength to go on as he would want her to.

She took the cup, swallowed, coughed, and made herself keep on drinking until she'd emptied it. She had eaten only a little bread and cheese that day, and the wine started taking effect almost at once. "That's enough," she protested. Bess ignored her and poured a second drink. She held the cup to Desire's lips. "Finish it off," she ordered.

Desire obeyed. She felt a warm glow spreading through her, melting away the icy knot in the pit of her stomach. Her taut muscles began to relax. "You got to keep hold of yourself till you're brought to trial," Bess was saying.

The words sounded blurred, as if they came from far away. Desire lay back on the mattress, the empty cup slipping from her limp fingers. She had felt this way once before . . . when had it been?

"The night I met Morgan . . . he carried me off to the farmhouse . . . gave me brandy . . ."

Her eyes closed and she let herself drift back to the past. She had tried to run away from the farmhouse but the brandy had made her tipsy. Morgan had lifted her and carried her back into the firelit kitchen . . .

His caresses had stirred her senses, unawakened until then. His mouth on hers . . . his lips at her breast, his fingers stroking her thighs . . .

Now her lips moved, shaping the words that came from the depth of her being.

Morgan . . . Morgan . . . my love . . . don't leave me . . .

A soft blackness enveloped her and she drifted off to sleep.

* * *

The summer was slipping away, and Desire dared not count the passing days. The wind, blowing over London from the east, brought no rain. Concerned citizens began to worry over the threat of a water shortage.

At Warrington House, on an afternoon late in August, Rowena stood on the terrace. Still no sign of a coming summer storm, she thought with a sigh. The sun was a glowing scarlet ball hazed over with blue-grey mist. With diligent care, she had managed to keep her flowers from withering on their stems.

She had lost her enthusiasm for planting the herb garden. It would be wiser to wait until the drought passed. And even then, why should she make the effort? Why take any interest in the running of the great house with Geoffrey gone?

If only he had not rushed to buy a commission now, of all times, with England actively engaged in a war with the Dutch. In July, when Monck had defeated de Ruyter, and again in August, when British forces had landed on the islands of Vlie and Terschelling to burn a town and sink one hundred and sixty ships in the harbor, Lady Mirabelle had given way to hysterics. Even Rowena's assurances that Geoffrey's regiment had taken part in neither engagement failed to calm her mother.

"We don't know what those wretched Dutchmen may do next," Lady Mirabelle lamented. "My poor boy. I'd rather have seen him married to Desire than lying wounded on a foreign battlefield."

She ignored her daughter's look of fierce disapproval. "I mean it," she said, her small rouged lips quivering. "At least he'd be safe here in London."

Stifling an urge to shake her mother, Rowena said: "There's talk the Dutch may retaliate by sending a fleet right up the Thames. Perhaps it would be best if you went to Yorkshire for awhile."

"For shame! To think I would go running off from a lot of

Dutchmen when my dear boy's away defending his country!"

In the filthy, narrow streets of Whitefriars and Southwark, the hard-pressed inhabitants were more concerned with their own endless battle against poverty, fever, and starvation. When the news of Morgan's trial and sentence reached Lena Yarrow's lodginghouse, Barney crowed with anticipation. "I mean to be there early! Get me a place right close to the gallows, so I can see it all. He'll stay game to the end, see if he don't!"

"Heartless little toad!" Polly had been clearing away the remains of Enoch's supper. She turned swiftly and struck Barney a stinging blow on the cheek. Then she burst into tears. Enoch patted her shoulder absently. "If he hadn't gone to lie with that fancy piece, the soldiers wouldn't have caught him," she sobbed.

"The Guilford wench won't be comin' to trial till next quarter-session," Barney said, rubbing his sore face. "Too bad—she might've hung along with Trenchard. That would've been somethin' to see."

Polly, still crying, aimed another blow at him, but he ducked under her arm and disappeared into the alley. She wiped her eyes on her sleeve. "Think there's a chance of gettin' him out, Enoch? If he's still got that knife I brought him . . ."

Enoch's ruddy face was drawn, his eyes bleak. "It'd take a sight more than a knife to get a condemned man out of Newgate, Polly."

Desire woke with a violent start, roused by the clanging of the bells from St. Sepulchre's, the parish church of Newgate. For a moment she lay rigid with fear. Bess had said that these bells rang on the morning of an execution day. Then, remembering that it was Sunday morning, with church bells chiming all across London, her terror ebbed away. She sat up slowly and smoothed back her dark hair.

But it was already the second of September. The execution day could not be far off. And soon after that she would stand trial at the next quarter-session.

Bess, already awake, was drinking from a small cask of ale. Because no rain had fallen for weeks, the prisoners' water supply was even more foul than usual. Desire paid for wine or ale for herself and her cellmates. She disliked even washing with the scummy water, but she put aside her distaste, using her bit of soap carefully to make it last.

Bess spoke often of a generous gentleman who rewarded her lavishly for her favors. With her hard-won shrewdness, she cautioned Desire that no one must know of Geoffrey's money, concealed in her skirt. "Let them think I'm payin' for the ale an' such."

Hulda had already gone out into the passageway in search of business, and Winnie slept curled up like a cat, when Alf appeared, holding a thin, sharp-featured woman by the arm.

"Here's company for you. Be sure'n make her feel at home," he said. The woman tried to jerk free, and he gave her a shove that sent her sprawling. Desire, who remembered her own rough handling on the day of her arrest, quickly came to help the woman to her feet.

"You needn't think to get any garnish from me," the woman snarled. "That stinking turnkey—"

"I want no garnish," Desire assured her. "We have ale if you're thirsty."

The newcomer's sharp features relaxed when Desire pointed to the cask. She took a battered cup from her pocket. "I had to trade a silver candlestick for this," she said in disgust. After she had drunk, she wiped her mouth on the back of her hand. "Peg's the name." She sat down in the corner, her back against the wall. "I traded the other candlestick for a mattress. That guard said he'd bring it."

"Where'd you get hold of a pair of silver candlesticks?" Bess demanded skeptically. "Smash an' grab?"

"Not today," Peg retorted. "Not with all that household

goods fallin' off carts an' left behind. Why, there's shops with the doors open, because the owners hadn't time to lock them."

"It's not the plague again, is it?" Desire asked.

The woman shook her head. "It's fire—spreadin' somethin' fierce."

Bess shrugged. "There always fires this time of year," she said.

"Not like this one! You can't know, locked up in here without even a window. It started sometime durin' the night, an' what with this wind, it's movin' fast. Plenty of people are loadin' carts with all they'll hold. An' merchants are bringin' their goods out of the warehouses on the river an' loadin' them onto boats."

Winnie scurried over and clutched at Desire's arm, her eyes round with fear. "What's goin' to happen to us?" she whimpered.

"Don't be frightened," Desire soothed her. "We're safe enough in here."

Chapter Twenty-five

Although Desire's words reassured Winnie, they drew a harsh laugh from Peg. "Much you know about it," the woman said. "You haven't seen what I saw. If you'd been out there since dawn, you'd be singin' a different tune."

"Stop your bellow-weatherin'," Bess interrupted, her hazel eyes scornful. "I was born close by this place. Grew up lookin' at it, I did. I'd be out stealin' offal from the butchers' market in Blow-Bladder Lane an' I'd see the cutpurses an' whores bein' dragged in by the constables. An' I'll wager that old Newgate'll be standin' here, come plague or fire, long after we're gone."

Desire tried to share Bess's conviction, but she felt a growing uneasiness stirring inside her.

"How far had the fire spread when they brought you here?" she asked Peg.

"Don't get her started again," Bess began, but Peg was eager to share what she knew.

"Pudding Lane's gone. That's where the fire started, in a baker's shop, so they say. An' then it moved to the river front. The timber warehouses, the sheds, they were flamin' soon as the hot cinders reached 'em. They're nothin' but a heap of ashes now. An' Fishmongers' Hall was burnin' too. It's this damn wind, keeps it spreadin'. It's blowin' west, and it hasn't stopped for days. An' the drought's made it worse. All them houses, dry as tinder, and the gardens, parched for want of rain." She glanced at the ale cask. "I could do with another cup o' that, after breathin' all the smoke."

"Go ahead. Maybe it'll shut up your croakin'," Bess said.

But Peg proved herself capable of drinking and talking at the same time. "St. Martin Orgar an' St. Michael Crooked Lane—I heard tell they'd burned, too. There's some folk out there runnin' about an' cryin' that it's a judgment on the wickedness in the city, with all its whores an' fornicators, but that don't' make sense, cause the churches are burnin' along with the bawdyhouses."

As Desire listened, her fear grew swiftly. Cold sweat sprang out on her body, and an icy trickle moved down between her breasts. If only she could go to Morgan. All at once she was overwhelmed with longing to be close to him, to feel the comforting strength of his arms around her. She could face anything with Morgan beside her.

"Bess, do you think if I were to ask Alf now, he might find a way to get me into Morgan's cell?

"Don't you start takin' on about Morgan Trenchard," Bess said impatiently. "Like I told you, they've got rules. A condemned man can't have any visitors. He can't talk to anybody but the guards."

"It wouldn't do any harm to ask."

"It wouldn't do no good, neither. Your highwayman's lucky he's not in chains, with an iron collar 'round his neck, layin' on a heap of dirty straw, like them poor bastards in the condemned hold."

Enoch still must be sending money regularly, she thought. But how was he managing to get it to the turnkey? That girl Morgan had spoken of—Polly Yarrow—might be acting as courier.

Desire still wore Polly's red satin garter around her thigh, with the knife tucked inside. She had become so used to the cold touch of the metal against her skin that she was scarcely aware of it any longer. She was thankful that she'd had no need for the knife. She wasn't at all sure she would be able to use it against another human being.

She wondered about Polly Yarrow. Why was she going to all that trouble, carrying garnish to Newgate? Perhaps she was Enoch's mistress. But if so, why had she given Morgan her garter as a keepsake?

Desire felt a brief pang of jealousy, but she thrust it aside. If the girl was helping to keep Morgan in some degree of comfort, nothing else was important.

As the morning wore on, and the guards brought in more prisoners, panic began to spread through the dark hallways and cells.

"It's them Dutchmen!" one of the new arrivals kept saying as the guard led him to his cell. "They're out there right now, settin' more fires. Dutchmen's revenge, that's what it is, because we burned their fleet."

"No, not the Dutch. It's the cursed Frenchies," a woman cried from the dark corridor outside. "Everyone's sayin' there's an army of French Papists, thousands of 'em—all movin' on the City."

Bess dashed out and seized the woman by the arm; her fat face was black with soot, and the heavy smell of smoke clung to her ragged clothes and grey-streaked hair.

"Has the lord mayor called out the soldiers yet?"

"That fool. Much good he is! They had to drag him from his bed in the early hours, an' even then he took a look at the fire an' said it didn't amount to nothin'. 'A woman might piss it out,' that's what he said, an' then he went back home to bed. He's the one should've been brought here, not me—"

"Come along, you old crow," said a guard, "an' don't be insultin' your betters."

He hauled her away into the darkness, but Desire could hear her, loudly berating the French, the lord mayor, the parish constables, the magistrates, and the baker in whose shop the fire was supposed to have started.

Desire heard the bells of St. Sepulchre's still clanging away, but now the peals were being rung backwards. She remembered that this was the recognized fire alarm in the City, and the sound strained her nerves closer to the breaking point.

The guards, confronted with the task of keeping order in this mounting chaos, had not found time to bring around the usual breakfast of bread and cheese. Hunger pangs made the prisoners even more restless and uneasy. Fights broke out in the corridors, and guards swore and laid about them with their heavy wooden truncheons.

Desire set her jaw. She mustn't give way to the rising dread that threatened to engulf her. Determined to keep to her routine, she forced herself to wash with what little was left of yesterday's water, and to comb her hair. Bess began to pace the width of the cell, a frown of concentration between her brows.

Shortly after midday, Alf opened the door. "An' about time," said Hulda, who had returned from one of her forays into the corridors. "Where's our breakfast? Mean to starve us?"

But the guard carried no food. Ignoring Hulda's questions, he took his keys from his belt. "What are you goin' to do?" she demanded.

"Lockin' you in. Turnkey's orders," Alf said.

"But it's not evening yet," Desire protested. Then she understood. The prison authorities, faced with a horde of milling, terrified inmates, many of them violent criminals, feared a riot. Under ordinary conditions the guards could keep order, using force when necessary, but the threat of encroaching fire had changed all that.

"We'll be shut up an' left to burn alive," Peg wailed. Winnie's blue eyes went round with fear, and even Hulda looked uneasy.

Bess ran across the cell and grabbed Alf's arm. "Don't lock that door," she said.

"I take my orders from the turnkey," he said, trying to free himself, but she hung on.

"You can forget one cell in all this uproar, can't you?" She spoke softly, her eyes fixed on his. "If we make it worth your while?"

"What've you got to offer—a few shillings?" he asked scornfully. But she had caught his interest, and he made no move to lock the door.

"I could pay more than that."

"Don't try to cozen me with your lies. You been spendin'

your money as fast as you earn it — like all trollops."

She stiffened for a moment, then reined in her temper and said calmly, "When you've locked the rest of the cells in this passage, come back here. I'll show you what I've got."

He hesitated, shrugged, and moved on to the next cell. Desire's blood froze when she heard him slamming the doors all along the passageway, while the women in those cells screamed and pleaded.

"Lord help us, we'll burn alive!

"Let us out, you whoreson! Give us a chance to save ourselves!"

Alf shouted for help, and another guard came pounding along the passage, lantern in hand. Desire heard the sound of blows from the wooden truncheons, followed by a scream of pain that ended in a whimper.

She started to tremble uncontrollably, touched by the frenzy that moved through this section of the prison like a tangible force, but Bess seized her arm firmly. "Hold on," she said. "If we can get him to leave the door unlocked, we can make it into the passage."

"But there's no way to escape to the outside. You've told me so, often enough."

"That was before the fire. They're afraid of a riot now, that's why they're locking us in early. If the guards can't keep control, or go running off themselves . . ."

Her hand darted under her waistband, and she pulled out the purse. "Ten guineas should be enough to tempt Alf. Say the word an' I'll offer him that much." The other women were moving closer, exchanging glances, torn between hope and desperation.

"Do it," Desire said quickly. Bess counted out the coins, then closed the purse and pushed it into Desire's bodice.

Tension flickered through the small, huddled group of women. "Listen," said Peg. "He's comin' back."

"Keep still, all of you," Desire ordered. "Let Bess handle him."

The guard stood in the doorway. "Let's see your money," he demanded of Bess.

"Not until you let us into the passage."

"I haven't said I'd do it."

But his small eyes glittered with greed. He stood aside and allowed Bess and Desire to go out into the dark passageway.

"What about us?" Hulda's voice was a pleading whine. "You ain't goin' to leave us behind?"

Although she had no reason to care what happened to Hulda, and she scarcely knew Peg, she could not bring herself to leave them trapped inside the cell. As for Winnie, she had come to feel a certain responsibility toward the small, timid girl. "We all go together, Alf," she said quietly, her green eyes fixed on his.

Bess shrugged. "It's your money," she said, handing over the coins. Alf grinned as he pocketed the bribe.

Outside the cell, Bess seized Desire's arm. "Come on," she said. "We'll find us a corner to hide in, an' soon as we see our chance, we'll make a break for it."

But Desire shook her head. She took Winnie by the shoulder and shoved her gently in Bess's direction. "Take care of her," she said.

"But you're comin' along. Why do you want me to . . ." Bess sounded uneasy. "What're you up to?"

Desire did not answer. She embraced Bess quickly and kissed her on the cheek. "Don't forget Winnie," she said. Then she turned to Alf.

"Take me to Morgan Trenchard's cell."

"You never said a word about that," Alf protested in a hoarse whisper. "He's a condemned felon. His cell's guarded day an' night. If you think I'm goin' to risk my own skin tryin' to get him out—"

"I haven't asked you to, have I?" Desire interrupted. "I only want to get in to his cell, to be with him."

"You're plain looney," he told her. "I've said so all along an' now I'm sure of it."

"How much do you want to get me into Morgan Trenchard's cell?"

"Desire, you can't!" Bess pleaded. "Stay here with me. It's

291

your only chance."

A burst of shrill, demented laughter echoed down the passageway. In the thick shadows, Desire saw darker shapes moving, like figures in a nightmare. She and her cellmates were not the only ones still in the corridors. Murderers, madmen, might be prowling about like so many jungle beasts. She fought down her fear.

"How much?" Alf repeated.

"Another ten guineas."

"Twenty," Alf bargained.

"After you get me into his cell." A plan was taking shape in her mind. Vague as yet, and surely dangerous, but it might possibly succeed.

"I could get drawn an' quartered for this."

"I'll go alone if I have to," Desire told him, trying to sound more confident than she felt. She turned away from Alf and the others. "Desire, wait!" Bess's voice came to her from the darkness, but she went on, keeping one hand against the damp wall, groping her way.

Alf overtook her and seized her wrist. "You'll never find Trenchard's cell without me."

Until now, Desire had seen only a small part of the prison. Endless corridors branched out in all directions. A lantern burned at the foot of a long flight of stone steps. Alf lifted it from the wall and held it before him to light their way. They climbed in silence, Alf's hand closed tightly on her wrist.

On the landing, she started at the sound of shouts and curses. Guards and male prisoners were locked in a fierce battle. One of the prisoners, a giant of a man, used his chains as a weapon, swinging them from side to side. A guard went down, clutching his smashed face and howling with pain. Other prisoners, who had managed to arm themselves with knives and clubs, closed in around the guards, fighting with violence and skill learned in the streets and alleys of London's slums.

Alf dragged at Desire's arm and they moved up to the next level. He pulled her into a niche in the wall and shut the iron flap on the lantern, cutting off the light. Two guards went stumbling by, one supporting the other, who was bawling a song in a loud, slurred voice.

A moment later she caught a glimpse of flickering candle-light and heard a burst of drunken laughter. "It's the tap-room," Alf said. "Some of the guards are drinking up whatever they can lay hands on."

They moved on, and in the darkness she saw the flitting shapes of those who had managed to get out of their cells. As they climbed another flight of stairs, she caught the faint smell of smoke.

"The cells got windows up here," he told her. "Smoke's comin' from outside."

A narrow corridor led to the right from the stairway landing. Alf stopped, then pushed her against the wall. "Trenchard's cell is around the next turn," he said softly. "Got to get rid of the guards. You wait here."

He went on, leaving her in the darkness alone, her heart pounding. Alf had believed her when she said she only wanted to get in to see Morgan. Now it was up to her to help set him free.

She heard Alf's voice from around the corner of the passage. "There's a riot in the Press Yard," he told the guards. "They need help down there. Come on!"

Desire flattened herself closer against the wall as two guards hurried past. Alf followed them a short distance, then fell behind and made his way back to her.

"That'll give us time," he said.

"The key to Morgan's cell—do you have one?"

"I do now," he said with a grin. He flipped open the lantern shutter, and she saw the dull glint of metal in his palm.

"Take me to him. Hurry!"

"Let's have the money first."

"Not until you open the cell." If she could delay him in the open door, fumbling with her purse, counting out the money slowly, Morgan would manage to overpower him.

293

"I've taken all the orders I'm goin' to from you," he said. He set down the lantern, then thrust his heavy body against her, pinning her to the wall. She started to cry out in protest, but he struck her across the face, then thrust his hand into her bodice and seized the purse. Stunned by the force of the blow, she could not even try to fight back.

He took a quick look inside. "A king's ransom, that's what it is. An' you were only goin' to pay me a paltry twenty guineas."

"It's yours, all the rest of it . . ." Fear flooded through her, turning her voice to a shaky whisper.

He fondled the purse. "Nice an' warm," he said, and she felt sickness stirring inside her at the change in his voice. He pawed at her breasts. "You been keepin' it warm right here . . ."

His thick fingers groped inside her bodice, and she gagged at the reek of his breath. She tried to scream, but no sound would come.

He pulled up her skirt and she caught at his hand, trying to push it away. Her fingers brushed the knife, thrust into her garter. Moving with swift, instinctive fury, she gripped the handle and drew the weapon free.

He thrust his leg between hers, forcing them apart. She struck out, but the knife only grazed his arm. Roaring an oath, he seized her wrist and twisted it with brutal force. The knife slipped from her fingers. "You're all hot an' ready for your highwayman, but Alf's not good enough for you!"

She prayed that she would faint before he took her, but suddenly he was no longer pressing against her. Bewildered, she watched him step away. "All you sluts are alike in the dark," he said. "With what's in that purse, I can buy myself a dozen plump whores, all ready an' eager."

Was it possible he did not mean to rape her after all? She caught her breath as she heard him saying, "Come on." He seized her arm and she stumbled after him. He stopped outside a heavy iron door and thrust the key in the lock. He opened the door and pushed her inside.

Only then did she remember that he already had her

purse. She had to delay him somehow. "Alf, wait! There's more—"

But he had already slammed the door shut, and even now she heard the key grating in the lock. She and Morgan were trapped in the cell together.

Chapter Twenty-six

Desire, thrown off balance by the force with which Alf had pushed her, struggled to keep her footing, but Morgan moved swiftly, and a moment later she was in his arms. She clung to him with all her strength, her hands clutching at his shoulders, her body pressed to his.

"You got your highwayman now." She heard Alf's voice harsh and vindictive through the grill in the door. "Pleasure yourself with him while you still can, strumpet!" His retreating steps echoed along the corridor.

For a timeless moment she and Morgan held each other, and she gave herself up to the overwhelming solace of being with him, feeling his body strong and protective against her own. Then Morgan released her and held her away, looking down into her face. "That man. Who was he?"

"A guard in charge of my cell. He brought me here." A sob caught at her throat as reality came flooding back again, stark and terrifying. Alf was gone, leaving her and Morgan caged and powerless.

Morgan cupped her face between his palms. "Desire, did that swine harm you?"

"He tried, but I cut him with the knife . . ."

His features relaxed slightly. "You did what you had to do," he reassured her. "When I gave you the knife, I wasn't sure you'd be able to use it." His lips brushed her forehead. "There's nothing to cry about. He deserved a lot worse."

Although she was moved by Morgan's solicitude, she had to explain the real reason for her distress. "You don't understand. I came to get you out. I had it all planned, and when Alf agreed to bring me here, I was so sure—but he outsmarted me."

"Easy, love," he said softly. He kept his arm around her as he led her to the bed and seated himself, drawing her down beside him.

A pair of candles burned on the table nearby, their light flickering over the stone walls. She recognized the cell, for it was the same one he'd been confined in before his trial. He pressed her head against his chest, and her hands moved over the hard muscles of his shoulders as if she needed to reassure herself that she was really with him again. She felt him stroking her hair, his touch gentle and soothing.

"Can you tell me about it now?"

She rested against him and began to speak quickly, somewhat incoherently at first. Gradually, as she grew calmer, she told him what had happened from the time Peg had brought word of the fire. He listened in silence as she explained about the bribe Bess had offered to keep them from being locked in their cell.

"After Alf let us out of our cell, I said I'd give him more money to bring me up here. I let him think I only wanted to see you again. And he believed me. I'm sure he did."

His shoulder muscles tightened and his chest went rock hard. "Go on," he said, and she caught the change in his voice. He had stopped stroking her hair, his hand still, fingers tensed.

"I knew he wouldn't want to share the bribe with your guards, that he'd find a way to get rid of them. And when he opened your cell, I meant to distract him, to keep him there."

She paused, waiting for Morgan to say something, anything. The silence stretched between them until she went on, her voice growing unsteady. "I wasn't clever enough after all. Alf took the purse from me by force back there in the passage—and then he tried to—"

Morgan thrust her away. He grasped her by the shoulders, startling her with his violence. An unearthly red glow from the small window shifted over his high, angular cheekbones and hard jawline. She shrank away as if she found herself confronting a cold-eyed stranger.

"You fool!" His fingers tightened on her shoulders with cruel force. "You crackbrained little fool! You were out of your cell — you'd managed that far. What with the uproar over the fire, you might have found a way to slip into the courtyard. And then —"

"Don't you think I know that?" Unable to restrain her pent-up tension any longer, she lashed out at him with a fury that matched his own. "Bess wanted me to stay with her, to wait for the right moment and try to get away."

"But you didn't listen to her." He gave her a shake. "What possessed you to go off with that bastard, to believe you could trust him?"

"I didn't want to go. I was frightened out of my wits every step of the way, if you must know. But I couldn't leave you behind. I couldn't!"

Morgan stared at her, the anger draining from his face. He released her and turned away, but not before she saw the naked torment in his eyes.

She waited a moment, sensing his need to get himself under control. Then she touched him lightly on the arm. "Morgan, whatever you're feeling, let me share it. Don't shut me out, not now."

He went rigid for an instant. Had she gone too far? But he drew a long breath and released it slowly. His arm encircled her, lifting her onto his lap, cradling her against his chest. She felt the warmth radiating from him, enveloping her, renewing her.

"You couldn't leave me behind," he said, and she heard the wonder in his voice. "You were willing to risk everything for me. Why?"

She did not speak. There was no need. He saw the answer in her upturned face, her wide green eyes, brimming with tenderness.

"You should never have let yourself fall in love with a man like me," he told her. "You should have chosen more sensibly."

"I couldn't help myself," she said with a tremulous smile. "Love's not like that, not for me. You came to me out of the

298

darkness that night and took me away with you. Maybe I began to love you even then."

"You gave no hint of it," he said softly. "You held me off as long as you could."

"Only because I was sure that if I gave myself to you, nothing could ever be the same again." She reached up and stroked a lock of dark hair back from his forehead. "I think perhaps you knew, too."

"How was I to know anything about that kind of love?" He spoke softly, his voice husky.

"There were other women . . . And you needn't glare at me. Enoch told me all about them."

"Enoch talks too much."

She ignored the interruption. "But those others—beautiful, some of them, skilled in the arts of loving, no doubt, and—"

"Not one like you—not ever."

"Not even Polly Yarrow?"

His dark brows shot up, and he stared at her in surprise.

"Polly? What do you know of her?"

"You told me that she brought you the knife. And the money for garnish. And she—"

His mouth curved in the hint of a smile, and she saw the teasing light in his eyes, challenging her to go on.

"She gave you that red satin garter. As a keepsake, you said."

"No doubt she's given such little gifts to half a dozen men who've lodged in her sister's house. A generous girl—free and easy in her ways," he countered warily.

"And the other women you've . . . known? Were they all like Polly?"

He was silent for a moment, his eyes thoughtful. "I suppose they were," he said slowly. "I wanted it that way. There was no room in my life for the sort of love you're talking about."

"You were a boy when you were forced into exile. Enoch told me that, too. But later, during those years in the West Indies, did you never want to settle down?"

He shook his head. "I never stayed in one place long enough. Enoch and I kept on the move."

He had taken to highway robbery after his return to England, driven by resentment at finding his estate in the hands of a stranger. Lacking the means to redress the injustice, he had shown his contempt for the law. She understood his actions, even though she did not condone them.

Maybe it would be better not to question him too closely about his years of exile in the Indies. But there could be no secrets between them, not now.

"How did you manage to get along in the islands?"

"I worked as overseer on a sugar plantation in Barbados for awhile. But I couldn't drive men as if they were animals, to whip them until they dropped . . . Enoch felt the same, so we left before the harvest was over.

"We hunted boar in Hispaniola, and sold the hides and dried meat. We cut timber — mahogany trees, and satinwood, too. We served as mercenaries with the French forces in Martinique."

"And the women there in the islands?"

"Tavern girls," he said. "And camp followers. Rich, pampered Creole ladies, too — neglected by their husbands, seeking the spice of an illicit adventure."

His arm tightened around her. "But I knew nothing about love — until now." His voice was low and bitter. "Now, when it's too late. When I can give you nothing, nothing except useless talk and —"

She covered his lips with her hand. "No, my darling. Never believe that. There's more. We have this time together. It's ours . . ."

She lay back against his chest and listened to the slow, steady beating of his heart. "I belong to you, Morgan. I always will . . ."

"We belong to each other," he said, his arm tightening around her. "Now and for eternity."

It came to her that they had exchanged a pledge of lasting love, as tender and solemn as any they might have spoken in a cathedral. Tears swam in her eyes, blurring the points of candlelight so that they might have been not two but a hundred. She felt a brief pang of regret, thinking of all they might have shared. But it passed swiftly, and now she was caught up in the wonder of the moment.

She lay back across Morgan's thighs and felt the stirring of tension in him. He supported her with his arm as he began to undo the buttons of her dress. She let her head fall back and as her gaze moved upward, she caught sight of the dark, reddish glare, framed by the small square window high overheard. From far off she heard a heavy, rumbling noise. London was aflame, its buildings cracking, timbers burning through and crashing to the ground.

Back in her own cell she had been afraid. And perhaps she would know fear again. But now she was filled with a need so strong, so overpowering, that nothing else mattered. Somehow she would weave a spell to shut out the encroaching destruction. She would draw him with her into their own special haven.

She was happy that this was not the first time for her. Morgan had taught her all the ways of loving, and now she would share the sweet fruits of her womanly wisdom. She would be bride and mistress, angel and wanton . . . for him . . . only for him . . .

He drew her gown from her shoulders, his movements slow and sensuous. The gown slid to the floor, and she lay stretched across his knees. His eyes ravished the white mounds of her breasts, lingering on her nipples, firm and pink beneath the shift that was their only covering.

He brushed his lips against the hardening peaks, flicking at them with his tongue, sending wave after wave of tingling sensation through her.

Then he tugged gently at her shift, so worn that it was almost transparent. "I don't want anything between us," he whispered.

His voice, his look, sent a spreading warmth coursing through her. She moved one way, then the other, to make it easier for him to draw off her one remaining garment. Her firm, round buttocks rubbed against his thighs, and she heard him groan deep in his throat.

"Do you know what that does to a man?" he asked in mock reprimand.

"I think so," she teased. How could she not know, when she was already feeling the iron-hard pressure of his manhood beneath her? She rotated her bottom in a slow, sensuous motion, while keeping her eyes fixed on his.

"That's a game two can play, my sweet," he warned. He stripped off her shift and tossed it aside. Then, parting her thighs, he began to probe her satiny cleft, invading and withdrawing. The sweet torment began to grow inside her, until she was caught up in a wave of unbearable need. She arched upward, her body pleading for fulfillment.

He rolled her over onto the bed, and she lay there while he sat up and pulled off his boots. He started to unbutton his shirt. She raised herself, reached inside his shirt and moved her hand over his chest, stroking the crisp curls with slow, tantalizing movements. Her fingertips traced the arc of his ribs, then reached down to his belt.

"Patience, my love," he told her.

He stood up, took off his shirt and tossed it aside, then unfastened his belt.

"You helped me to undress," she reminded him. "Now it's my turn . . ."

Kneeling on the bed, she undid the front of his breeches, then tugged them down slowly, inch by inch. Her green eyes flickered with her growing need. She pressed her face to his flat abdomen, rubbing her cheek against the hard ridges of muscle. Her arms encircled his waist and her fingers found the sensitive place at the base of his spine.

She stroked him there with little feathering movements. Raising her eyes, she saw the fierce hunger in his face. Swiftly he drew away from her embrace, to pull off his breeches.

She lay back on the bed and held out her arms to him. And now he came to her, kneeling above her, kissing her lips, her throat, her breasts. She parted her thighs and he positioned himself between them. His hardness was cradled by her moist, hidden cleft. He moved against the tingling peak of her womanhoood, and her need grew to an unbearable aching hunger.

Her hands went down the length of him until they reached

his lean hips. She could wait no longer. She wanted him inside her now, filling her completely. Her body spoke for her, her legs raised to encircle him, to drawn him into her silken sheath.

He entered her with a thrust that went deep, and deeper yet, and then he held himself motionless, waiting. She tightened around him, asking for release, demanding it, her head thrown back, her hair spread out in a dark fan, her green eyes glowing under half-closed lids.

He answered her need, thrusting again and again, plunging into the burning core of her, taking her with him, upward in the spiraling ascent to a place of wonder undreamed of until now. Together they touched the heights and shared the timeless glory of their ecstasy.

Resting her head against him, she felt the rise and fall of his chest as his breathing became slow and even once more. She reached up and stroked his cheek.

He raised himself and looked at her, his dark eyes filled with tenderness. Gradually she grew aware of the stillness around them. She took comfort in the quiet that was enfolding her with Morgan, as if they were in a world of their own.

They might have been back at the forge in the hills, only the two of them, savoring the warm fulfillment that came after their loving. The breeze had been sweet and fresh with the scent of new grass. Spring sunlight had flickered down through the trees as they lay on the bank beside the pool.

Desire felt a vague uneasiness touching the edge of her consciousness. She tried to push it away, to linger in the aftermath of their joy. With a little movement, she burrowed closer, pressing herself against Morgan's body. His arm tightened around her, and his hand stroked along her spine.

For a brief time she was able to give herself over to the delicious sensation of his fingers moving on her damp skin. Then he drew the coarse blanket over her. "The guards will be coming back," he began.

"Maybe not," she said quickly, trying to recapture the illusion of being with him in some perfect haven of peace.

"How did you manage to get them away from the door? They've been out there day and night since I was brought here after my trial."

"It doesn't matter. I think maybe they won't return at all."

Desire hoped to distract him. She did not want him to think about where they were, what might be happening outside, in the maze of corridors around them. She pressed herself against him, as if she could shut out everything else with the touch of her body, the power of her love. She began to push away the blanket, to bare herself to his gaze.

"Desire, not yet. Why don't you think the guards will come back?"

She sighed, knowing she could not put him off. "Alf sent them off to help quell a riot in the Press Yard."

"He only said that to get rid of them," Morgan reminded her. "But by now they know there's no riot."

"Not in the Press Yard, maybe, but the prisoners are rioting." She shuddered slightly. "I saw them myself as I was coming here. One of them used the chains between his wrists to strike a guard. Others had knives and clubs. They'll stop at nothing to keep from being locked in their cells now."

"Don't, sweetheart," he said quickly, his arms tightening around her. "If the guards are kept busy, we'll have more time." He broke off and she felt his body tense for a moment. Looking at his face, she saw that he was holding himself under control, drawing on all his inner strength to conceal his feelings.

"Morgan, if only we could have found each other in another time . . . another place. When I think of all we've never shared—" She spoke with quiet tenderness. "The small, precious moments other lovers take for granted. Riding in the woods together on a spring morning. Walking along the cliffs in your Cornwall."

"Among the ruffians and smugglers of Ravenscliff?" He forced a smile, reminding her of what she had once said.

"How was I to know that you meant to send me to your great-aunt's home?" But she could not keep up the pretense of teasing any longer. "There's so much I might have given you."

304

"But you've given me everything," he told her, his voice husky. "You've taught me all I know of loving. . ." Desire lay enraptured by his voice. Never had she thought to hear Morgan Trenchard revealing his innermost feelings this way.

She lifted her face to his, parting her lips for his kiss—a long, lingering kiss that shut out the world again for a brief space.

But when he let her go, she saw that his eyes were thoughtful, his gaze fixed on the heavy iron door. "If we could get through to the passageway," he said slowly.

"Maybe the guards will return after all," she said. "They must bring you food and water."

"Must they?" The corner of his mouth slanted down with a touch of the familiar irony she had come to know so well.

She knew what he was thinking. If the fire reached the prison, the guards would think of nothing except saving their own skins.

"Are there other cells nearby?" she asked.

"Only one, and that's unoccupied. These splendid accommodations are beyond the means of most prisoners."

Her spirits plummeted still lower, for if Morgan's guards fled, or were overpowered, who would even remember that he was in here? But she must not speak her thoughts.

"I suppose Enoch's still sending money for garnish," she said. "I'd have thought he'd used up most of the loot from the robbery."

"Maybe he has." He spoke with indifference, his eyes bleak, and she guessed what he was thinking. There would be no need to pay garnish for Morgan's keep any longer. Frantically, she sought to distract him.

"Where is Enoch now?"

"Still lodging with Lena Yarrow at her den in Southwark. He'll be there now, unless the fire moves across river and drives him out."

"Surely it can't spread that far."

Morgan shrugged. "When one of my guards brought my breakfast he told me that the wind was carrying the sparks across the river and had already set fire to two of the houses on the other side."

"Then Southwark's going to be destroyed . . ."

"Maybe not. The firefighters on the other side of the bridge showed enough initiative to pull down a third house before the blaze could reach it. A desperate measure, but it's the only way to stop the spread of such a fire."

"Then there's a chance Enoch will get through this safely." She could not go on. The patch of sky looked darker now, much darker. She reached out and clutched Morgan's arm.

"It can't be going on toward evening, not yet." She looked up at him, seeking reassurance. He turned her away from the small square of window and pressed her face against his shoulder.

"It's the smoke," he said. His arms tightened about her. "I saw a fire in the canefields once, back in the Indies. They burn a field, sometimes, to clean it. The fire strips off the leaves so that the stalks go through the mill faster, you see."

She knew that he was talking to distract her, and she forced herself to try to listen. "We dug firebreaks, but the wind changed direction and the flames got out of control. By midday smoke had turned the sky black as night."

He broke off. "Sweet Jesú," he whispered. "I've got to get you out of here. Somehow—"

"Don't, Morgan," she said, her voice muffled against him. "Keep talking. Tell me about the Indies." And when he did not respond, she went on, saying whatever came into her mind. "One of the sea captains who used to visit my father said those islands are beautiful. He spoke of butterflies, much bigger than those in England, with shiny blue wings. And flocks of birds—parrots with red and green feathers. He said one of his sailors tamed a parrot and taught him to speak, but I didn't believe—"

He silenced her then, his mouth on hers, his tongue darting between her lips. Slowly he moved against her, glorying in the feel of her pliant white body, her firm rounded breasts against his chest. He lay on his side, his arm beneath her head, and began to stroke her back, trailing his hands down the length of her spine.

306

Her nearness aroused him once more, but he hesitated, fearing that she would not be able to give herself freely, joyously as before. How could she, when surely she must dread the hell that lay outside these walls?

"Don't stop," she whispered, her breath warm against his cheek. She bent her leg, resting her thigh on his, opening herself to him.

He felt the longing in her, and knew that she was eager to give herself once more. His hand moved around from her back to her belly in one sweeping caress. And when his fingers stroked the soft delicate triangle, dark against the whiteness of her skin, she moved closer, urging him to seek out the intimate core of her. The movement reassured him, for he knew her too well to be deceived by any pretense of passion.

He felt an aching hardness as he slid inside her. Now he was moving slowly, and she was moving with him. She did not close her eyes, but kept them fixed on his.

The need in him grew steadily, and now she answered it with her own. He felt her start to throb around him, contracting more and more quickly. And then came release, hot and overpowering.

He did not withdraw but lay still, lingering within her soft sheath. His heartbeat steadied, and he breathed deeply, evenly.

He was filled with a sense of wonder. She was his, and in all the world there were only these walls, this room — their own private place for whatever time remained to them.

Chapter Twenty-seven

West of the City, at Whitehall Palace, Lady Barbara Castlemaine sat up in bed and pushed away the satin coverlet. She leaned back against the headboard, which was shaped like a great shell, draped in blue velvet embroidered with silver. The canopy and bedcurtains were also of blue velvet, lined with pale azure satin. The four slender posts supporting the canopy were topped with vase-shaped finials holding ostrich plumes.

Barbara glanced at the pillow beside her own; it was rumpled after a night's pleasure with the king. Smiling at the memory of his lovemaking, she raised her arms and tilted back her head, stretching like a lazy, beautiful cat.

She held the pose for a moment, hoping to catch Charles's admiring gaze. His Majesty had been called away to the outer chamber of Barbara's private apartments a short time ago, but he was back now, standing beside the marble fireplace and leaning an arm on the mantelpiece. His dark brown eyes lingered appreciatively on the lush swell of her breasts, scarcely concealed by her sheer silk nightdress.

"I hope you sent that tiresome Mr. Pepys about his business," she said. Samuel Pepys, clerk of the Privy Seal and secretary of the Admiralty, was one of the king's most trusted civil servants. He had arrived at the palace a short while ago and had requested an immediate audience, refusing to speak with anyone but His Majesty. "Doesn't the man know better than to intrude at this hour?"

"It's nearly noon," Charles informed her. "And he was right

to come to me. He carries information of the greatest importance."

Barbara raised her eyebrows, surprised by the seriousness in the king's voice. His swarthy face had lost its customary look of easy good humor; she saw the grim lines etched about his mouth.

Without pausing to ring for one of his attendants, he took off his brocade dressing gown and tossed it aside. Under it, he wore tight breeches and a fine cambric shirt with wide, loose sleeves.

She felt a stirring of anticipation at the sight of his tall, muscular body. Even now, after their night of lovemaking, she was ready for his caresses again. He was a skilled lover, whose sensuality matched her own.

But he made no move to return to the bed.

"The news from the City is worse than I'd feared," he said. He reached for his waistcoat.

"A fire along the waterfront?" Barbara was not particularly concerned. She did not trouble herself with matters in which she was not directly involved. Thoroughly selfish, set on maintaining her own enviable position as the royal favorite, she cared little for the well-being of Charles's less fortunate subjects. Dull, hard-working shopkeepers, scriveners, bricklayers, fishmongers, and the drifting, unemployed rabble, criminals and whores, most of them, who lived and bred like rats in the dirty alleys and courts of Whitefriars and Houndsditch . . . Why should Charles give them a thought?

"The blaze has already spread much more swiftly than I'd feared," he said, buttoning his waistcoat with quick, impatient movements.

Barbara's blue-violet eyes widened beneath her long, dark lashes. "We're in no danger here at the palace, are we?"

A cynical smile touched the king's mouth. Barbara's reaction did not surprise him, for he understood her self-centered, calculating disposition well enough. He appreciated her for what she was—a white-limbed, full-breasted beauty, eager and responsive in bed, skilled in the arts of satisfying his own

309

lusty passions. He demanded no more of a mistress.

But although Charles shared Barbara's pursuit of pleasure, there was another side to him that she would never understand. He was truly concerned with the welfare of all his people, not merely the courtiers who fluttered about him here at the palace like so many brilliantly colored butterflies.

He had not forgotten his own lean years of exile in Europe, moving from one capital to the next, always short of funds and forced to live on the charity of foreign rulers. Now that he had come home and regained his rightful heritage, he was determined to serve his subjects to the best of his ability.

Blessed with boundless energy, he enjoyed his favorite sports—tennis, racing, cockfighting. He took a lively interest in the latest scientific developments, made his own experiments, and was generous with his gifts to the Royal Society.

He could carry on a brief affair with a highborn lady or an orange girl at the theater, while keeping Barbara thoroughly satisfied in bed. But his zest for pleasure was balanced by a strong sense of duty.

Barbara tossed back her thick mane of shining red hair, her lips pursed in a pouting little frown. "The way those people live, crowded together in timber houses, their streets piled with litter, it's a wonder there aren't more fires." Occasionally, when she rode in her gilt carriage to visit her favorite astrologer, she peeped through the curtains for a glimpse of the less savory sections of the City. "Surely the lord mayor can cope with this."

"I'm afraid he can't," Charles told her. "Tom Bludworth's been running about since dawn, but now that he's faced with the responsibility of ordering houses blown up to create firebreaks, he's dithering about, losing valuable time."

"Then send Clarendon, or Mr. Pepys, that officious little man. No need for you to go."

She gave Charles a slow, inviting smile, leaning forward to offer an even more enticing view of her breasts. The neckline of her nightdress slipped lower, so that her large, deep pink nipples were half bared. "We can find more pleasant ways to spend a Sunday morning, surely . . ."

Charles adjusted his carefully curled black periwig and picked up his plumed hat. "You might go to the chapel and spend your time in prayer for the unfortunate people there in the City."

"I'll leave that to your Papist queen," she snapped. She had hoped that he would marry her, and she had never gotten over his firm refusal. She enjoyed every luxury she asked for: jewels, gowns, servants, this magnificently furnished apartment in the palace. But she wanted more . . .

She, and not the shy, devoted Catherine of Braganza, should be queen of England. Hadn't she already proved that she could give him the sons he wanted so much? Surely he could find a pretext for divorcing his frail, barren wife. It never occured to her that Charles, in spite of his flagrant infidelities, was devoted to Catherine in his own peculiar way.

Even now, Charles's eyes narrowed briefly at her slighting reference to his queen. "I'm sure you'll be able to find some way to amuse yourself until my return," he told her.

She swung her long, elegantly shaped legs over the side of the bed and reached for the dark blue velvet robe she had discarded the night before. Sliding her arms into the wide, fur-trimmed sleeves, she tied the robe about her, thrust her small feet into her high-heeled slippers, and hurried to the king's side.

"You're sure the fire won't move this far west along the river?" she asked with a touch of concern.

"Since my talk with Mr. Pepys, I can't be sure what may happen next. That's why I've given orders for the royal barge to be prepared. I'm going to the City with James, to see what may be done."

"Surely you and your brother don't mean to work among the common firefighters?" She spoke with lazy amusement, looking up at him from beneath her long curving lashes.

"We'll do what's necessary to save London."

"That should be an interesting sight — you and James, standing in a line with those common fellows, handing along the water buckets. Perhaps I shall come too. We could make a party of it. I'll arrange for hampers of jellies and pastries. And music — we must have musicians aboard the barge to —"

His face hardened. "It's obvious you don't understand how serious this could be."

He turned on his heel. She ran to his side and grasped him by the sleeve. "There's real danger then?"

"Danger! 'Ods' fish, why else would I be going to help fight the fire?"

For the first time, she felt a touch of fear for Charles, but even more for herself. When she had left her husband, she had turned to the king for protection and had lived in splendor here at court. But her ruthless disposition and explosive temper had made her many enemies. Without Charles at her side, she knew how quickly her so-called friends would desert her.

"You must be careful," she urged. She slid her arms about his neck and pressed herself against him. "Promise me you'll take no risks."

He smiled down at her. "Don't concern yourself, my dear." His kiss was warm and sensuous. Then he glanced at the wide bed. "I intend to share your company for many nights to come."

Leaving the bedchamber, he strode through the outer room, where his brother, James, duke of York, came to join him. James was tall and well built, with curling blond hair and blue eyes and a slight cleft to his chin. He was already wearing his cloak and boots.

An attendant hurried forward, carrying the king's cloak. While the man was helping him to finish dressing, a favorite spaniel awoke, leaped down, and began yapping. Charles picked up the small dog and stroked its long, silky ears. Other spaniels came dashing forward to paw at his boots, filling the room with their shrill commotion.

They pranced about the king and waved their plumelike

tails as he and James strode down the long passageway leading to the great banqueting hall. The high-ceilinged room was crowded with courtiers as usual. Like Barbara, they were obviously indifferent to the news of the fire.

Some played cards at the round oak gaming tables; others lingered at the huge buffet on one side of the hall, choosing from an elaborate assortment of delicacies. A young boy dressed in a white satin doublet trimmed with silver lace sang a love song in a true soprano voice, accompanied by the music of a dulcimer.

Catching sight of the king, the courtiers paused in their merrymaking, but he waved them off and went on into the Privy Garden.

"Belasyse has already gone down to the barge, along with Craven," James told his brother. A few members of the court were concerned with the danger to London. Lord Belasyse, Lord Harrison, Lord Ashley, the earl of Craven, and the earl of Manchester — all had volunteered their services in battling the fire.

The spaniels were still yapping and prancing around Charles, running between his legs. His Majesty gestured to an attendant, who hurried to take charge of the pampered beasts.

"Tom Bludworth complains that the citizens won't cooperate when he asks them to help with the firebreaks," James went on.

"I don't know that I can blame the poor devils," the king said. "Not when it means destroying their own homes and shops. But I'll see that it's done as quickly as possible."

No citizen of London would question the king's authority or hesitate in carrying out his commands. Pepys knew that, and had lost no time in taking a boat to the palace to ask His Majesty's help.

But more important than any practical aid he might offer, Charles knew that his subjects, seeing him in their midst, would take heart and go on battling the fire with renewed vigor. No monarch since Elizabeth had been so popular with the citizens of London.

Aboard the velvet-hung barge, emblazoned with the royal crest, the noblemen moved about the deck, talking among themselves. Charles gave them a smile of gratitude for their loyalty in this crisis. He had inherited the Stuart charm in full measure, and he knew how to use it. The crew cast off, and as the vessel moved eastward along the Thames, he began to lay a plan of campaign.

"The flames must not reach the Tower," he said.

"We'll see to that, sire," said Belasyse gravely. The others nodded, recognizing the danger. The rooms inside the Tower of London were made of timber, dry and flammable.

"The archives stored in the Chapel of St. John—they've got to be saved," Manchester said.

The king nodded. "But above all, we've got to protect the White Tower."

Now that England was at war with the Dutch again, the White Tower was being used as an arsenal. "All those tons of gunpowder," James said. "If the fire reaches them . . ."

"It won't," Charles said, his deep voice ringing out. "I'll see to that myself, if I must."

The men exchanged glances, reassured by the king's words. He made no idle boast, and they knew it. They remembered his daring escape from England following the execution of his father. Not one of them questioned their monarch's physical courage, his ability to act quickly, decisively, under pressure.

As the barge approached the City, Charles caught the heavy acrid smell of smoke. Up ahead, the sky was growing darker, and the wind carried cinders over the surface of the river.

Samuel Pepys stood to one side on the deck. He had accepted the offer of a return trip on the royal barge and had maintained a respectful silence in the presence of his king. He was only a civil servant, after all. The son of a tailor, he had worked his way up to his present position through his own diligence and and attention to detail. Now Charles gestured him to approach. "The landing at Queenhythe, is it still accessible?"

"It was when I left for the palace, sire."

"That's where we'll try to go ashore. Then we'll set up central headquarters."

"Ely Place might do, sire. We should have fire posts, too. With Your Majesty's permission, they might be set apart all around the edge of the City. Aldersgate, Coleman Street, Cripplegate, perhaps."

Charles clapped him on the shoulder. "An excellent beginning," he said. "But what of yourself, Master Pepys — your own home, your goods?"

"My wife must manage as best she can, with the help of the servants, Your Majesty." But he was moved that the king should concern himself with the welfare of a single subject at such a time. No wonder the people were so devoted to him.

"When I left the city, nearly half of Upper Thames Street was ablaze," he went on. "Those shops and warehouses are filled with tallow, oil, pitch, and tar. The bridge was still standing, but the flames were spreading to the houses nearest the north shore."

"If the fire crosses the bridge to Southwark, Lord knows how far it'll spread," James said.

"Where the devil are the firefighters?" Manchester demanded. "Is there nothing they can do?"

No one answered. The firefighting equipment was woefully inadequate in such an emergency. What good were small brass hand-squirts, ladders, or leather buckets in fighting against so terrible a blaze? As for the fire wagons — great barrels mounted on wheels — these often broke down or got stuck in the narrow streets and alleys where they were needed most.

The barge was passing the great mansions lining the river now. Charles, squinting through the yellow-grey pall of smoke, caught a brief glimpse of Warrington House. For a moment he remembered the green-eyed young girl, a guest of the Warringtons. He had danced with her at Sedgewick's ball, and she had pleaded for a private audience.

But she had not attended the banquet at the palace, and

Lady Warrington had explained that the girl had been called away to her family's home in the country. Charles had not pursued the matter. No doubt the girl's need for an audience had not been so urgent after all.

". . . the debtors in the Fleet prison." Charles realized that Belasyse was speaking to him, and he turned his full attention on the man. "Can we leave them there to burn or suffocate from the smoke?"

"We'll consider that after we've set up our fire posts," Charles said. "Surely, other quarters can be found for the debtors."

"What about Newgate?" Lord Harrison asked.

"We can't turn loose a horde of vicious criminals to prey upon helpless citizens at such a time," James protested. "Debtors are victims of misfortune — perhaps some provision might be made for them, but as for Newgate . . ."

The barge, moving against the wind all this time, now drew up to the Queenhythe Dock, which was still untouched by the flames. But Charles stared in dismay at the terrible devastation that raged beyond the dock. The air vibrated with a deep thunderous roar. "God's terrible voice is in the City this day," one of the crew said with quiet awe.

The king, never deeply religious, heard him. He stiffened, shocked by the sight of the devouring flames that spread in all directions, lashing their great, scarlet tongues at the smoke-filled sky as far as he could see. He remembered descriptions of hellfire he'd heard as a child.

How could any man, even a king, hope to deal with such elemental fury?

But he recovered himself quickly. He had come to help his people, to give them the will to go on fighting.

"Master Pepys, to the Naval Office with you." A thought struck him. "Our English sailors are strong and fearless — and experienced in fighting fires aboard ships. Round up those who are ashore now. I want them put to work at once, wherever they're needed."

Someone laid a plank between the barge and the dock.

Without further hesitation, Charles led the others ashore. On every side he heard the cries of terrified women and children, the shouts and curses of men, fleeing before the fire. Some pushed handcarts laden with their possessions. Merchants bargained with laborers to help them load their goods on wagons or into boats. Others carried their sick and injured in improvised litters.

The king raised his head, confronting the searing heat, the whirling sparks and wind-driven cinders, the din of crashing timbers and falling masonry. Squaring his shoulders, he strode forward into the inferno that was London.

Chapter Twenty-eight

Morgan opened his eyes and looked over at Desire as she lay sleeping in his arms, her dark hair spread across his chest. Her softly curved body was pressed against his, and one slender hand rested on his shoulder.

He did not know how long they had slept, bathed in the peace that came after their loving. Time had ceased to have any meaning here in their cell. The two candle stubs had guttered out and no guards had brought new ones. The only light came from the window, a smoky sulfurous glare.

Best to let Desire go on sleeping, he thought. The corridor outside the cell was silent, and it was unlikely that any guards would come back to check on them. Fortunately, there was still a supply of bread and cheese on the shelf, and half a bottle of brandy. More than enough to last them for whatever time they had left.

He drew Desire closer and looked at the delicate curve of her cheek, the dark crescents of her lashes, her soft, red lips, slightly parted. Under her shift, her breasts rose and fell with her even breathing.

Abruptly he lifted his head. Was it his imagination, or had he heard footsteps mounting the stairs? He got out of bed, swiftly pulled on his breeches and boots and ran to the door.

"Nobody's up here," he heard a man grumbling. "You might've saved us climbing those stairs."

"Got to carry out our orders," said another voice. "We're to search every cell in this part of the prison."

"There's only a couple of cells down this way, and no light

318

coming from either of them."

"In here!" Morgan shouted. "We're in here!" He pounded his fists against the heavy iron door.

"Morgan, what is it?" Desire was awake now, and sitting up in bed, her hair falling around her face in loose waves, her shift slipping from one shoulder.

Morgan called out again, his powerful voice reverberating off the stone walls. The sound of booted feet grew louder. Desire heard it now. She pulled the blanket around her, and reached for her dress.

A key grated in the lock and the door swung open. Morgan tensed, his muscles tightening; he was ready to fight his way out. Once he and Desire were outside the cell, he would manage the rest.

But now he saw that the two men confronting him were not prison guards; they wore the uniforms of the City militia and carried pistols in their belts. One held a lantern.

"Fine quarters for a prisoner," said the older of the two, raising his lantern high and looking around the cell. He stared at Desire. "By Jesu, he's got a woman in here with him."

"Finish dressing, and be quick about it, girl," said the other. He was a big, strapping young man, his face black with soot. He averted his eyes as Desire pulled her dress on over her shift.

"Damn lucky you hollered out when you did," said the older man. He held the lantern steady, resting his other hand firmly on his pistol grip. "Else we'd have left without you."

Desire thrust her feet into her shoes and ran to Morgan, who finished buttoning his shirt. He put a protective arm around her and gave her a reassuring smile. The militiamen hustled them out of the cell, moving along close behind them.

"Where are you taking us?" Morgan demanded.

"We've got orders to clear the place before the fire gets any closer."

"Orders?" Desire echoed. She was still dazed at the unexpected turn of events.

"His Majesty's orders, girl. The Fleet prison's being emptied as well."

"The fire's spread that far?" Morgan asked.

"It's out of control. Lord knows where it'll stop," the younger militiaman said. "His Majesty's been going back and forth between the palace and the city these past two days—him and the duke of York. They've been workin' along with the firefighters."

As they approached the foot of the stairs, Desire heard a babel of voices. Prisoners who only a short while ago, had been terrified at the prospect of facing an agonizing death by fire were shouting or sobbing with relief at their unexpected release. Guards rapped out commands as they tried to keep order.

"Hold it right here, you two," said the man with the lantern. A line of ragged men, chained together with heavy manacles on wrists and ankles, moved across their path, guarded by soldiers carrying muskets with bayonets at the ready.

"Condemned felons, they are. His Majesty's even letting them out. Burning's worse than hanging, I guess," said the younger militiaman.

"I've heard the smoke strangles a man before he can feel the flames," the other remarked.

"Where are they being taken?" Morgan asked. The question sounded casual enough, but Desire knew better. Looking up, she saw his eyes narrow and alert in the lantern light. He was making plans even now.

The man with the lantern gave a short, harsh laugh. "They'll be put into their own special wagon—it's closed and barred, like them that carry bears to the fair grounds."

"Only they won't be going to a fair grounds," the other said. "They're to be locked up in jails on the other side of the river," he said. "All they got to look forward to is next execution day."

"And what about the rest of us?"

The man shrugged. "We got you out, like they told us to.

320

It'll be up to the keeper of Newgate to arrange for space in those other jails."

The militiamen obviously had no idea who Morgan was; they did not know that he, like those chained men, had been sentenced to hang at Tyburn. Silently Desire blessed Enoch for keeping Morgan out of the condemned hold.

Now the militiamen were pushing Morgan and Desire along into the milling crowd of prisoners, all surging in the direction of the great open doors at the end of the passage.

"The wagons are lined up right out there in the courtyard," the younger man said.

For the first time since her arrest, Desire found herself outside the walls of Newgate. But she stepped back as the searing heat enveloped her. Heavy smoke hung over the courtyard, obscuring her view of the wagons. Horses stamped and whinnied in terror, and a few of the female prisoners succumbed to hysterics, shrieking to be let back inside. Morgan's arm tightened around her, and she made herself go on.

She caught a glimpse of the two squat, uneven towers of the prison, shrouded in the smoke. Thick and grey, it came swirling in through the great semicircular archway at the far end of the courtyard. The heavy, acrid fumes seared Desire's throat, making her cough and gasp for air.

Somehow, the militiamen and those guards who had not already fled managed to form the milling prisoners into a semblance of a line. She heard the first of the wagons starting to roll out under the portcullis, whips cracking, drivers shouting encouragement to their teams, the wheels rumbling over the cobblestones. Soldiers stood on either side of the courtyard, their muskets at the ready.

Walking in line, Morgan and Desire reached the back of one of the wagons. A guard jumped down to help with the loading of his group of prisoners. He lifted Desire into the wagon and motioned to Morgan to follow. Then the guard froze, peering into Morgan's face.

"What's *he* doin' with this lot?" The guard raised his voice in outrage. He had recognized Morgan. Desire felt as if her heart had stopped for a moment, before starting to thud against her chest.

The two militiamen exchanged bewildered glances. "We brought him and the girl down from their cells . . ." one of them began.

The guard gripped Morgan's shoulder with a huge, powerful paw. "This here's Trenchard—Morgan Trenchard, the highwayman!"

Desire managed to stay on her feet, but her legs began to tremble so that she had to clutch at the side of the wagon to steady herself.

"Get him over there with the other felons!"

"Chains, bring chains!"

"Call the blacksmith, somebody!"

"Trenchard—it's Trenchard!"

Desire heard Morgan's name coming from all sides. They mustn't be separated, not now, when they were outside the prison walls at last. She wouldn't let them take Morgan from her.

Morgan shook off the guard's grip, drew back his arm, and slammed his fist into the man's face, sending him sprawling on the cobblestones. But the two militiamen closed in, grabbing Morgan's arms, pushing him against the wagon. Again he broke free, and now he was fighting with the ferocity of a lion at bay. He fought with his fists, his head, his knees, his booted feet.

A musket shot cracked out, and Desire felt her insides knot with terror. She was too frightened to scream.

"Hold your fire, dammit!" came an officer's hoarse command. Thick black smoke filled the crowded courtyard. If the soldiers started firing blindly into the crowd, the prisoners would surely riot.

Desire struggled for breath. She leaned forward trying to see into the smoky darkness. She caught a glimpse of Morgan; he was still on his feet and moving toward her. A guard swung at him with his heavy wooden truncheon, but Morgan seized the man's wrist, forced it down, then smashed it against the iron wagon wheel. The truncheon fell to the cobblestones.

The horses, already terrified by the fire and the crowd, plunged forward. The driver lost control of the reins, and the wagon gave a sickening lurch. Desire felt it tilting far to one side, and the prisoners around her shrieked and cursed as they were thrown to the floor.

Somehow she kept on her feet, her fingers locked on the side of the wagon. Her eyes were fixed on Morgan's face.

"Now!" he shouted, holding out his arms and she jumped. He caught her a moment before the wagon toppled over. He set her on her feet and circled around the wagon, holding her arm, half-pulling, half-carrying her with him.

A guard hurled himself into their path, only to be shoved aside by a powerfully-built female prisoner. The woman yelled in triumph. "Go on, Trenchard!" Other prisoners shouted encouragement as Morgan and Desire made for the open archway.

Morgan lifted her off her feet and shouldered his way through the crowd, swerving to avoid the flailing hooves of the horses. A gust of wind blew the smoke aside for a moment. A soldier leaped at them with fixed bayonet.

Morgan moved swiftly to one side, twisted his body to protect Desire, and took a cut on his upper arm. And kept going . . .

She buried her face against Morgan's shoulder, as he carried her out of the courtyard and into the hot, smoke-filled street beyond. Here they were caught up and submerged in the tide of humanity surging forward, some on foot, others in carts or coaches, bent on saving themselves from the fire.

Down the length of Newmarket Street they went, borne along by the crowd. The half-timbered houses on either side of the wide, straight thoroughfare were already ablaze.

At the east end, the way was blocked by the little church of St. Nicholas-le-Quern. Carts and wagons slowed to a crawl, and those on foot kept moving around the obstruction. Morgan set Desire on her feet.

"This way," he said, his voice hoarse from the smoke. He led her through the Newgate Market, with its butcher shops and shambles. She gagged at the sickening stench of charred offal, but she kept moving along beside him.

At the entrance to a narrow alley she was forced to stop, unable to catch her breath. Morgan supported her against him until she recovered herself. His sleeve was torn and bloodied from the soldier's bayonet, but the wound was not a deep one.

"We've got to keep moving," he told her.

"But where—"

"We'll go east. If the bridge is still standing, we'll get across to Southwark. We'll join Enoch at Lena Yarrow's house."

In all this burning hell, he could speak as if making plans for an ordinary excursion across the river. "And if the bridge is afire, what then?"

"I'll find a way," he told her. "Can you go on now?"

She nodded and they started off again. Jostled by the crowd, they made their way up Paternoster Row toward Cheapside. The noise of the fire came to them from all sides—crashing timbers, toppling walls, crackling flames blended into one unceasing roar.

She caught sight of a man coming out the ruins of a building. He was shouting to the passersby, clutching at one, then another. "Help me! Someone's got to help me. For the love of God! My wife's trapped back there."

But the crowd kept going, too terrified or numb to respond.

The man plucked at Morgan's arm. "Please, won't you help? She's under that beam. I can't lift it off her."

He was crying, his thin, slight body shaking, the tears making runnels down along his soot-blackened cheeks. "My bookshop . . . we went back to try to save some of the stock."

Morgan looked at the man, then at Desire. For an instant he hesitated. Then he led her to one side and pushed her into the shelter of a brick archway.

"Wait for me here," he said.

The bookseller grasped Morgan's arm and tugged him

324

away. Desire heard his broken words of gratitude. Her eyes stung, and not only from the smoke, but she kept them fixed on Morgan. She saw him a short distance away. He was trying to raise one end of a heavy beam, but it would not budge.

She flattened her body against the side of the archway, scarcely aware of the heat of the bricks. A man pushing a heavily laden handcart moved past, and she managed to get out of his way in time to keep from being knocked down. Behind him, a woman, her satin cloak blackened with soot, her wig askew, moved along, her eyes like those of a sleep-walker. She carried a painting under one arm. The canvas was hopelessly charred, but she kept a grip on the elaborate gilded frame.

Desire gave a violent start as a deafening explosion rent the air. She cried out, and heard other voices raised in panic. A crowd of people came plunging through the narrow archway, jostling one another in their desperation to escape. A pair of liveried footmen set down the velvet-curtained sedan chair they had been carrying and took to their heels.

A woman shrieked in terror throwing her apron over her head. "It's the Dutch—they're here in the City!

"They've captured the Tower!"

"They're shooting the cannon! They'll kill us all!"

Other voices took up the chorus, adding to the already widespread fears of the crowd. Desire was pushed out of the protection of the archway and carried along with the rest. Handcarts overturned, blocking the street, forcing the stream of people to go off in different directions. And all the while they cried out their groundless accusations, seeking a scapegoat to blame for their plight.

"Them French Papists, they're the ones who're to blame!"

"Set the fire, they did. One of 'em got caught throwing fireballs into a shop on Pudding Lane!"

Another explosion split the air. The mob went surging first one way, then the other. Desire tried to break free. She grasped a railing, but it was no use. She lost her hold and was carried along like a leaf on the surface of a raging river.

"Morgan!" Her cry was swallowed up in the roar around her. Burning timbers fell from overhead, and she had to keep going, choking on the smoke, heat searing her throat and lungs.

A line of wagons and carts went rattling by, and a bundle dropped from one of them. Desire tripped over it and fell to her knees. As she tried to rise, she saw a team of horses rearing up almost on top of her.

She screamed with all her strength. The driver pulled on the reins, the heavy muscles standing out in his arms and shoulders. He brought the team to a stop, and at his command, a sturdy boy clambered down from the wagon.

"Lift her up here with us, Obadiah," a woman's voice cried.

The boy slid one arm under Desire's knees, the other around her waist, and heaved her onto the back of the wagon as if she had been a sack of flour, then clambered up after her. The driver cracked his whip and the team lurched forward.

Desire started to cry out in protest, but she realized it would be useless to try to get back to Morgan on foot. Her head was swimming, and motes of light danced before her eyes.

As the first shock wore off, she saw that the wagon was loaded with large wooden crates and an assortment of household goods: a teapot, a pair of andirons, a brass clock, and a spice chest. Besides the woman, who still wore the once-white cap and apron of a respectable housewife, and Obadiah, the boy who had saved her, three younger children were clustered together, wide-eyed and silent.

Desire managed to murmur her thanks, but her words were cut short by another deafening explosion.

"Those people in the crowd—some said the Dutch were firing on the city . . ." Desire began.

"There are always a passel of fools running about making trouble." The driver spoke without turning his head.

"A Dutch baker in Westminster nearly got himself killed

by the crowd," the woman told Desire. "They said he was helping to spread the fire, when all he was doing was lighting his own oven."

"They'd have finished him off," said young Obadiah, "if it wasn't for the duke."

"James, duke of York," his mother explained. "He's here in the City, helping them fight the fire."

"But those terrible explosions," Desire began.

"That's our own folk, blowing up houses, trying to make clearings to stop the fire from spreading any further."

Desire remembered what Morgan had told her about the necessity for firebreaks. Her heart lurched and she forgot everything else. How was she to find Morgan again?

She turned to the woman, clutching at her arm. "Where are we heading?"

"Be easy, now," the woman told her. "You're a deal safer here with us than down there in the mob—a little slip of a girl like you."

"But I have to know which way we're going," Desire insisted. "My husband's going to try to get us across the river. But what with the crowd and the other wagons breaking down and blocking the way, who knows how long it'll take us? We'd have done better to hire boats," she went on. "I said so from the first."

"And I told you, there's not a lighter to be had for hire at any price," her husband shouted over his shoulder.

"He's right, Mother," the boy said. "And besides, the river's not safe. It's afire with burning timbers off the docks."

Desire could scarcely take in their words. All she could think of was Morgan. She had to find him again, but how?

She forced herself to collect her thoughts and plan ahead. She must stay in the wagon. If they were lucky enough to get across the river, she could get out on the other side and go in search of Enoch.

But Southwark, like Whitefriars, was a maze of alleys and courtyards, many of them swarming with criminals. If only Morgan had told her how to get to Lena Yarrow's house. She would have to go about on foot, asking directions, until she found it. Morgan would get through to her somehow. They would be together again . . . soon.

Morgan tugged at the beam, sweat streaking his face, his shoulders straining. The woman lay face down, and he could see only her hair, the thick blonde locks tarnished by soot. She might well be dead, but he could not bring himself to say that to her distraught husband. Nor could he give up, until he had freed her.

The man tried to help him, but he lacked the sheer physical strength to be of much use. He could only wring his hands and repeat his wife's name over and over. "Emily . . . my dear Emily—if only I hadn't let her go back inside to help . . ."

Morgan turned to the man. "Drag that board over here." The man stared at him blankly. "Drag it," Morgan shouted through clenched teeth. "When I raise this timber, try to wedge it underneath."

The man obeyed, struggling with the board. Morgan threw all his weight into his task. The beam was heavy, and the heat seared his hands unmercifully, but he bent his knees and heaved upward. It was lifting now, an inch at a time.

"Push that board. No, not that way—to your left, man! That's it."

Carefully he let the beam down. With less than a foot of clearance between the underside of the beam and the woman's body, he released his grip. Closing his hands around the woman's shoulders, he began to ease her out as gently as possible.

"Emily," her husband groaned.

Slowly Morgan turned her over.

Her eyes were closed, her body limp.

"My dearest love, don't leave me!"

Morgan saw her eyelids flutter. "She's alive," he told the man beside him. He tugged her further from under the beam until she was completely free. Her skirt was torn to

328

shreds. He ran his hands over her legs, which were covered with cuts and bruises. "I don't think there are any broken bones."

Then he got to his feet and turned to the archway. "Desire!" he shouted. But there was no answer.

With the man's fervent thanks following him, he ran through the heavy smoke. The archway was deserted. He went numb, gripped by a fear like no other he had ever known.

Afterward, he could never quite remember how long he had searched around the archway, heedless of the burning rubble that fell from overhead. He peered into smoke-black alleys and courtyards, calling Desire's name. His voice was swallowed up in the noise of the crowd, the unending rumble of the fire.

Then he was walking aimlessly, his hands hanging at his sides. Sweat ran down his face, mingling with the blood from a cut on his face. Absently, he wiped his forehead and winced at the searing pain in his hand. He stared at his palms as if they belonged to a stranger.

He heard someone shouting. "Back—get back!"

A tall, fair-haired man on horseback rode up and down, surrounded by troopers of the Life Guard. James, duke of York, drew his sword and raised it as if leading an army into battle. He had already given the orders for the laying of gunpowder. A seaman, pressed into service as a firefighter, lit the fuse. The crowd surged back.

Morgan heard the shattering roar of the explosion. He saw a row of houses rise a few feet in the air, as if in defiance of gravity. Then they settled into a smouldering heap, and the rest of the seamen surged forward with leather buckets.

Morgan turned away and kept walking, heading east, in the direction of the bridge.

Desire sat on a sack in the back of the wagon, her legs drawn up under her. One of the younger children began to whimper, and the woman opened a hamper of food.

"Help me feed the little ones," she told Obadiah. "And have some bread and ale for yourself and your father."

"Just the ale," her husband shouted back to her.

She turned to Desire. "You must have a bite to eat too," she said.

Desire shook her head, but the woman insisted. "We don't want you going into a swoon, poor little thing," the woman said. "The bread's stale. It's from last week's baking. When I get back home, I'll have to start another batch."

She stopped abruptly, her face furrowing. Desire guessed that the woman tried to cope with the fear that her house was no longer standing. What was to become of her and her family, stripped of their home and their possessions, everything except what they carried in the wagon? The woman sighed, and pulled herself together with a visible effort.

She handed Desire a piece of bread and poured the ale into a wooden cup. "Dip the bread into the ale. That'll soften it."

Desire obeyed, then chewed and swallowed without tasting. "You've been so kind," she said. But she wanted to thank the woman in a more practical way.

Remembering how Geoffrey's gift had helped her in her own time of need, her hand went to her bodice. Then she remembered that her purse was gone. How many days had passed since Alf had taken it from her in the dark passageway? She glanced at the respectable woman beside her and wondered what she would say if she knew she was helping a fugitive from Newgate.

The wagon had been moving slowly, one of a line of heavily laden vehicles. Now the driver jerked on the reins, bringing the wagon to a halt and narrowly avoiding a collision with a cart that had stopped in front of him.

"What's wrong?" he called out. "Broken wheel?"

The man ahead stood up and shouted back. "Nothing is moving all down the line."

For a moment Desire felt a surge of fear. Then she recovered herself. Surely they would not be hunting her or Morgan in the midst of such an overwhelming disaster.

"Obadiah, take the reins," said his father, and the boy obeyed. The man swung down and went ahead to try to discover the cause of their unexpected stop. They had already been forced to make several detours to avoid burning buildings or heaps of smouldering ruins.

To Desire, intent in getting over the bridge to Southwark, every delay was agonizing, but she reminded herself that she had been fortunate to have a ride at all. Now the driver returned. He clambered back on the seat. "We'll be here for awhile," he said. "There's Tower Street, up ahead." He pointed and Desire raised herself to peer into the haze. She saw the Tower of London, half veiled in smoke.

"Nobody can get through," the man shouted to his wife. "Got to blow up all the houses round the Tower to make a firebreak."

"A fine bit of work that is," a man called out indignantly. "Poor folk losin' their goods and now their homes. They got no right to do it. No right at all!"

He spoke with the vehemence of any Londoner, whatever his station, when his rights were ignored.

But a voice challenged him loudly. "His Majesty's giving the orders. An' he's the one who'll save us, wait an' see."

"That's right. He'll protect us from anything—"

A tall, buxom girl in the cheap, gaudy finery of a streetwalker, added her praises. "He's been out fightin' the fire himself, more'n two days now. Saw him with my own eyes when I was camped over in Moorfield. Ridin' about on his horse, calmin' folks down."

Desire gripped the side of the wagon and raised herself up.

"The king—where is he now?"

"Why right up ahead there, by the Tower," the girl told her. "He's overseein' the firebreaks himself, him an' his soldiers." She grinned up at Desire. "There's them as talks against him 'cause he's got an eye for a good-lookin' female. What's wrong with that, I'd like to know?" Several of the men around her laughed.

But Desire's thoughts went back the night of the ball, when she had danced with the king. His brown eyes had shone with open sensuality, lingering over her shoulders, her throat, and the place where the strands of pearls fell into the shadowed cleft between her high, rounded breasts.

And before Lady Castlemaine had come to take him off with her, he had made a promise. He would give her a private audience at the earliest opportunity. How different the future would be for her and Morgan if only she had been able to speak to the king alone, to plead for a pardon.

Her mind, dulled by the shock of all she had gone through that day, began to race. She raised her head, and her eyes shone with emerald brillance. Her fingers closed around the side of the wagon.

She cried out to the nearest man in the crowd. "Help me down, please!"

"You don't want to get into this mob," he told her.

"I've got to!" She insisted. At any other time she might have hesitated, but she was not thinking calmly now. The whole world was going up in flames around her, and somehow, in the midst of terror, she felt a stir of hope.

The urgency in her face, the green glow of her eyes, moved the man. He reached up and swung her to the ground.

"Wait, come back here!" She heard the voice of the woman in the wagon calling after her.

She plunged into the crowd and made her way forward. Filled with an unnatural strength that verged on hysteria, she pushed along, wriggling between closely pressed bodies. No one tried to stop her. Every gaze was fixed on the Tower, standing like a sentinel, guarding the City.

Only when she reached a line of soldiers, in the uniform of His Majesty's Life Guards, was she forced to stop.

She caught one of them by the arm. "Let me through! I've got to get through to the king!"

He turned and looked down at her. "No one gets through," he told her firmly. "Stay where you are."

She tried to slip between him and the man next in the line, but he blocked her way.

"They're getting ready to set off a charge of gunpowder," he told her. "The king's orders—"

Looking up, she caught sight of the tall, muscular figure, seated on his horse. King Charles kept control of the bucking, rearing animal with some difficulty while he relayed his commands to the officer beside him. His velvet doublet was stained with soot and water. The wind tossed the plumes on his hat, and his lean face was streaked with sweat.

"The king gave me his word!" she screamed, her whole body shaking with fierce determination. "A Stuart doesn't break his promise!"

"Mind your tongue," the soldier began.

"Who said that?" A commanding voice rang out, and the soldier stiffened to attention.

"It's a woman, sire. She says she must speak with you."

"Bring her here." The soldier stared at the king, then took Desire by the arm and led her forward. She tilted her head back, and her eyes met those of the king.

"Who are you?" he demanded.

The ground was swaying under her feet, but the soldier's arm supported her.

"Mistress Guilford. Desire Guilford, Your Majesty."

"I heard you speak of a Stuart's promise, and you spoke the truth. What promise did I give you?"

"At Lord Sedgewick's ball . . . you said I might have a private audience, sire."

The noblemen around the king exchanged glances, surprised by the woman's daring. Surely he would order her away.

Instead, Charles held his horse steady, controlling the animal with his powerful thighs. He gripped the reins and leaned down.

"I'll not break my word, Mistress Guilford. But right now, my first duty is to London and all its people—"

A burly seaman came forward, cutting off her view of the king. He spoke to Lord Belasyse, who relayed his words to

His Majesty. "They're ready to light the fuse, sire. That house near the moat is already ablaze. No time to be lost!"

Desire felt hope draining from her. What had possessed her to confront the king at such a time? Her head began to swim, and an overpowering weakness gripped her body. She sagged against the soldier's arm, and he caught her a moment before she lost consciousness.

Chapter Twenty-nine

It was evening when Morgan reached the open space on Tower Hill, but the sky still glowed with the reflected glare of the fire. The homeless were settling down for the night here in the open field, surrounded by whatever possessions they had been able to salvage from their ruined houses. Some were finishing their supper, seated in front of tents provided by the army, while others arranged their makeshift bedding in back of their wagons. Mothers soothed their frightened, wailing children and tried to get them to sleep.

Here and there, small groups knelt in prayer. Others played at dice, and a few enterprising whores already had begun plying their trade. But most of the refugees were exhausted and shaken, wanting only to rest.

Morgan walked about looking for Desire, stopping from time to time, asking the same question over and over. "Have you seen a dark-haired girl with green eyes? She was wearing a green silk dress."

A few of them looked at him with pity, but most were too stunned by their own losses to do more than shake their heads. No one remembered having seen a girl who answered Desire's description.

Doggedly he kept going, ignoring his own need for food or rest. He paused at last beside a small, garishly painted wagon. A bony, swayback horse stood tethered nearby, and the owner, a wiry, grey-haired man, sat munching on a meat pie and drinking wine from a bottle. Once more Morgan asked his question.

"I don't remember seeing such a girl," the man said. Morgan started to walk away.

"Wait a bit," the man called. "Are you hungry?"

Morgan paused. When had he eaten last? Not since the night before, when he and Desire had supped on bread and cheese in their cell.

"I have enough for two. You're welcome to join me," the grey-haired man offered.

"Thanks," Morgan said, sitting down beside him and resting his back against the side of the wagon.

"Caleb's my name," he said. "Caleb the Juggler, that's what they call me."

"Mine's Tom," said Morgan.

"I've been on the road all spring and summer." The juggler shook his head. "It looks like I picked a bad time to come back to London."

Morgan gave him a nod of sympathy. He was in no mood to talk, but he soon realized that his companion, a garrulous fellow, was perfectly content at having found a good listener.

"It's all well enough to go roaming about the roads in warm weather, but when it gets to autumn, I head for London," he went on. "Sleeping in the wagon during the cold weather, the ague strikes me something fierce. And a juggler needs nimble fingers, see?"

He took a swig from the bottle, wiped the top with his sleeve, then passed it to Morgan. "You won't taste no better port than this, and it didn't cost me a penny," he said with a smile. "I came upon a whole crate down by the waterfront. Most of the bottles were smashed—but not all."

Morgan winced as his hand closed around the bottle. For the first time he felt the pain of his scorched palms. He held the bottle awkwardly as he raised it to his lips.

"Careful, there," the juggler cautioned. "Hurt your hands?"

"I burned them lifting a smouldering beam," Morgan

336

said.

Caleb shook his head. "Lucky you don't make your living as a juggler," he said. "Never seen a fire as bad as this. Lord knows when they'll get it under control." He shrugged. "No matter. I'll find myself a place to hole up, until I can start performing again. London's best for my kind—jugglers, acrobats, bear-leaders, strolling players."

Morgan nodded and kept on drinking. The port was excellent. It slaked his thirst and cleared away the acrid taste of the smoke.

The juggler pushed the large basket in his direction. "Try one of these pies. Got pork, eel, beef and kidney—a regular feast. Helped myself at the food stalls in Eastcheap. The fire was getting close by then, and there's no sense letting good food burn to cinders."

Morgan bit into a pork pie, realizing how hungry he was.

"I always do well in London," Caleb went on. "Folks here are a free-spending lot. But come spring, I get restless and take to the road again. I've done my turn at fairs from here to Land's End."

"I hope you've had a profitable summer," Morgan said.

"That I did. I'm skilled at my trade, if I say so myself. But back when Cromwell was in the saddle, it was hard going for my sort."

"So I've heard."

"You weren't here in England during those times, then?"

"I went off to the Indies," Morgan told him. He had finished his pie.

"Have another," Caleb said. Morgan nodded his thanks and helped himself.

"They treated us something fierce, those Roundheads did. Jugglers like me, strolling players, acrobats . . . And for what? We gave folks a little pleasure, to take their minds off their troubles. That's no crime, is it?"

"I've heard of worse ones." Morgan said with a wry smile.

"All the same, I was locked up in Salisbury jail, set in the pillory to be pelted with rotten fruit and dead cats. Flogged

337

more than once."

"Why didn't you find a safer line of work?" Morgan passed the bottle back to the juggler, who took a long swig.

"Juggling's my trade, and the road's my home." He spoke with pride.

"Were your parents jugglers, then?"

"I should say not. My father kept a snug little inn, and we did a good business. A hard taskmaster he was, with a heavy hand, but if I'd stayed there, I'd own the place by now, no doubt."

He shrugged. "A juggler slept in our stable one night. He showed off his skills and talked about his roving life. It sounded a lot better than scrubbing the taproom and carrying food from the kitchen. So when he said he needed a likely young fellow to bang the drum and gather a crowd, off I went."

The juggler laughed ruefully. "I soon found it wasn't all play. Plenty of nights when I slept under a hedge with my belly empty, I wished I was home. My father would've beaten me black and blue, but he'd have taken me back."

"But you never returned?"

Caleb shook his head. "Once the road becomes a man's way of life, there's no going back. You don't fit in with ordinary, respectable folk no more."

"A man can change," Morgan said abruptly.

"Maybe so, if he's got a good enough reason."

Desire, he thought, and it was as if he saw her there before him, her green eyes warm and soft, her lips parted in a smile. His love for her had given him reason to make a new beginning. He would build her a home, comfortable and secure. There he would care for her and protect her, so that she need never know danger or privation again.

But first he had to find her.

"You ain't leaving yet, are you?" the juggler asked as Morgan got to his feet. "Those hands need bandaging."

"I'll take care of them when I get across the bridge. Is it still possible to cross, do you know?"

338

"Last I heard, the fire hadn't reached it, which is more than you can say for St. Paul's."

Caleb's words stopped him for a moment. "The cathedral's gone?" The great dome, shining in the sunlight, had dominated the London skyline for as long as Morgan could remember.

The juggler nodded. "The dome's still ablaze, they say. And the rest of the place is in ruins."

But Morgan had lingered too long, and now he shifted impatiently, anxious to be off.

"Can't wait to find that girl, I suppose. Is she your wife?"

"She's going to be."

"Good luck to you, then," said the juggler taking another drink.

Morgan thanked the man for his generosity and moved on into the crowd. Wherever Desire might be, she couldn't have forgotten that they'd been heading for Lena Yarrow's house when they'd become separated. She was probably on her way to Southwark right now. But how was she to find Lena's house?

The question brought him up short. He didn't want to think of Desire wandering about the streets and alleys of the outer borough, where a shifting population of actors, bearleaders, acrobats, and jugglers like Caleb shared the narrow tenements with thieves, whores, and receivers of stolen goods. Perhaps he would be able to find her before she reached Southwark, and take her on to Lena's place himself.

He moved through the night, finding his way only by the reflected glare of the flames against the pall of smoke hanging low over the city. At last he saw the outline of the bridge looming up ahead, jammed with people also heading for safety across the river.

"You got away!" Polly Yarrow cried, throwing herself into Morgan's arms with a shrill cry of welcome. "I knew you were too clever for them!" She looked past his shoulder for a

339

moment, then, seeing that he was alone, she kissed him, her mouth moist and clinging. "You look a proper sight, black as a chimney sweep—but you made it here. How'd you manage it?"

Before she gave him time to speak, Enoch was standing in the kitchen doorway. "Morgan," he said quietly, but there was no mistaking the intense relief in his eyes.

"Desire . . . have you seen her?"

Enoch shook his head. "How'd she know to come here?"

Morgan lips tightened as he fought down his bitter disappointment, his fear for Desire's safety. But he gave Polly a friendly hug and a pat on the bottom before he and Enoch went up the stairs.

Once inside, Enoch took his hand and gripped it in both his own. Morgan drew in his breath. Enoch let go and stared at his his friend's burned palms. "How'd that happen?"

"I took hold of a smouldering beam. I didn't even feel the heat."

Then he sat down on the bed and, while Enoch bandaged his hands, he explained what had happened from the time the militiamen had released him and Desire from the cell.

"Since she knows about this place," Morgan said, "this is where she'll be heading."

But his heart sank, and he tried to blot out a host of frightening pictures from his mind. Desire, lying unconscious on some burning street back in the City. Or lost in the alleys of Southwark, at the mercy of a gang of lustful ruffians. Or perhaps she had fallen into the hands of a bullyboy who had dragged her off to one of the many brothels in Maypole Alley.

"I'm going out to find her," he said.

"The fire's addled your wits," Enoch told him, gripping his arm firmly and shoving him back on the bed. "Have you forgotten you're a condemned felon? They've been bringing over wagons full of prisoners from Newgate. Word of your escape is bound to spread—if it hasn't already."

340

"You expect me to sit here waiting for Desire to find the place herself?" He glared at Enoch, but he knew he couldn't ignore the warning. As an escaped felon, sentenced to hang, he dared not take unnecessary risks.

"It's nearly daylight," Enoch said. "You can't show your face out there now. I'll look for Desire. I know my way around Southwark as well as you do."

Without giving Morgan a chance to argue, Enoch bent down and pulled off his boots. "Get some sleep," he advised. "You look like you could use it."

Morgan lay back and closed his eyes. But although he was tired, he could not fall asleep. Images formed and shifted behind his lids.

Desire's face close to his, her dark hair spread across the pillow as they lay side by side on the bed in his cell. Her softly curved breasts rising and falling as she slept. Her eyes, steady and trusting, as she jumped from the wagon into his outstretched arms. And again and again he was tormented by the memory of his last glimpse of her, standing in the archway as he went off to rescue the woman trapped beneath the fallen beam.

If they had kept going along with the crowd they would be here together. She would be lying in his arms now. But loving Desire as he did, he had not been able to ignore another man's frantic need to save his wife.

Morgan shifted restlessly, but at last he turned over on his side and fell into a heavy sleep.

It was not until late afternoon that he awoke with a start. He saw Enoch standing beside the bed. Desire was not with him. Morgan sprang to his feet, a driving fear in his eyes.

"I tried every place I could think of," Enoch said. He put a hand on Morgan's shoulder. "Easy, now."

"Where is she? What's happened to her?"

"It'll be slow going for a woman on foot," Enoch said. "There's a great crowd swarming over the bridge. And more coming ashore at the landings. She'll find the house. You wait and see."

"It isn't easy to find, hidden by those others. Why else do you think Lena chose it for her sort of business?" Morgan's voice was hoarse with tension.

He broke off, hearing a knock at the door. But it was only Barney, carrying a tray of food.

"Polly fixed this for you." He grinned at Morgan and set down his burden. If he was not to see the highwayman hanged, he could still enjoy a sense of vicarious importance. Morgan Trenchard, who had escaped from Newgate at the height of the fire, was right here under his mother's roof.

"I was over in the City myself," he said. "Running an errand, I was, and almost got roasted to cinders in White-friars. Most of it's gone now. What wasn't burned was blowed up by the gunpowder."

Enoch shook his head. In a few short days, the fire had altered the face of the City forever.

"That's nothin'," Barney went on with relish. "St. Paul's went, too. An' I saw it close up. That was a sight!"

"I heard they were bringing the fire under control at last," Enoch interrupted. "The Tower's still standing, and the bridge. And it hasn't reached as far west as the palace."

"So they say, but I was tellin' you about St. Paul's," Barney went on. "Good as a show, it was. The workmen left their scaffolding around the dome. They was making repairs, see. An' the cinders blew over onto the wood, and up it went. Then the timbers under the roof, they caught afire, and the next thing I see, the lead dome's meltin' an' runnin' down the walls. An' then the stones started flyin' right out, fallin' from overhead. Wonder I wasn't brained."

"God save us," Enoch said quietly.

St. Paul's, although defaced by the Puritan soldiers during the days of the Commonwealth, had still been standing, strong and proud, when Charles II had come back to claim the Stuart throne. The merchants of London were so sure that the catheral would remain invulnerable that they brought their goods there for safekeeping at the start of the fire, and stored them in the crypt.

Barney, encouraged by Enoch's response, went on with enthusiasm. "Meltin' lead went runnin' along the streets, so nobody could get near. Heard somebody say the dead folk were burned to ashes inside their tombs."

"That's enough," Morgan said, cutting him short. "I've got an errand for you myself."

"I'm not goin' back into the City," the boy interrupted.

"You don't have to," Morgan told him. He reached into his pocket automatically, only to remember that he hadn't a coin.

"Give the brat a few farthings," he said to Enoch.

His friend hesitated for a moment, then counted a couple of coins into the boy's outstretched palm. Then Morgan sent him off to ask if anyone had seen a girl answering Desire's description.

"We running low on funds?"

"I'm afraid so," Enoch told him. "That private cell cost more than you'd believe. And so did the food, candles, easement of irons. Then, after you were sentenced, Polly had to bring garnish to the keeper of Newgate himself, along with the turnkey and half a dozen guards, to keep you out of the condemned hold."

"If it hadn't been for you, Desire and I wouldn't have had a chance," Morgan assured him. "I owe you my life. And not for the first time." He gripped Enoch by the shoulder, heedless of the pain in his hand.

Enoch looked embarrassed, and he spoke quickly. "Now we've got to look ahead," he told Morgan. "We're not going to be able to stay here much longer."

"We must stay until we find Desire."

"Lena doesn't run this place as a charity," Enoch reminded him. "Once our money's gone, we'll have to get as far from London as we can go. Out of England, maybe."

"Not without Desire," Morgan told him. He spoke quietly, but Enoch knew that tone, and the look that went with it. There was no reasoning with Morgan at such a time.

"You wait here in case she arrives, and I'll go looking for

her," Morgan said.

"It's not safe for you out there, even after dark," Enoch protested. "There's plenty of informers hanging about the stews and taverns. They'd lay evidence against their mothers for a shilling, and besides—"

But Morgan was already out the door.

Chapter Thirty

"Morgan . . . ."

Desire stirred, and her lips shaped his name. She reached out her hand, seeking him beside her. But he wasn't there. When she opened her eyes she found that she was lying alone in the middle of the largest bed she had ever seen. Overhead, she saw a canopy lined with white silk.

Instead of the ceaseless roar of the fire, the crash of timbers, and the crackling of flames, she heard only a soft, rhythmic sound. Now, at last, the rain had come.

Slowly she raised her head and stared about her in growing bewilderment. The raindrops were beating against two tall, mullioned windows, framed with drapes of rose-colored velvet. Beyond the windows, she saw the leafy branches of elms and oaks.

One wall of the room was hung with a large tapestry. In a corner stood a marquetry dressing table with a gold-framed mirror above it. A smaller table of rosewood held a silver pitcher and basin.

Desire sat up and realized that she felt a little dizzy. She called out Morgan's name again, half expecting him to come through one of the doors leading into the room. Instead, a woman entered. she wore a dress of heavy grey silk, covered by an embroidered white apron. Her brown hair was parted in the center and pulled back into a neat chignon.

"You're awake at last, Mistress Guilford," she said with satisfaction. "The physician told me you would sleep the clock around after he gave you that draught. And so you have."

"Physician? Have I been ill?"

The dizziness was receding, and except for a somewhat bitter taste in her mouth, Desire felt well enough. The woman reassured her quickly. "You were exhausted, and a touch feverish. And no wonder, coming from London at the height of the fire."

Bending over the bed, the woman plumped up the pillows and smoothed the coverlet with the deft efficiency of a well-trained upper servant.

"I'm not in London?" Desire asked.

"No, indeed. And a good thing, too. The fire is under control, but the City's in ruins. Even as far away as this, we saw bits of charred wood and paper, carried by the wind."

"But where . . . what is this place?" Desire asked.

The woman gave her a reassuring smile. "Why, you are in Whitehall Palace. Now don't excite yourself, Mistress Guilford. I'm here to care for you. My name is Abigail Frobisher."

Whitehall Palace. But she had been on her way to Southwark, to Lena Yarrow's house. To Morgan . . .

"When was I brought here, Mistress Frobisher?" She tried to get the whirling fragments of memory to fit into a coherent pattern. Perhaps this woman could help her.

"You arrived at the river landing aboard His Majesty's own barge early yesterday evening," said Mistress Frobisher. "Will Chiffinch carried you here to this apartment."

Desire looked at her, more bewildered than ever.

"Master Chiffinch is His Majesty's Page of the Back Stairs. A most discreet and valuable servant."

An odd, knowing look flickered for a moment in Mistress Frobisher's blue eyes. Then it was gone. But Desire's uneasiness lingered.

Exactly what services did the Page of the Back Stairs perform for the king? "Why was it necessary to carry me here?" she asked.

"You were unconscious, my dear. Overcome by smoke, perhaps."

Desire rested back against the pillows and closed her eyes

for a moment. She was starting to remember her flight from Newgate, not as a coherent whole, but in individual bits and pieces.

Morgan had carried her out of the prison courtyard into the flaming streets. Her brow wrinkled as she tried to concentrate. She recalled waiting for Morgan in an archway. The explosions, and then the crowd pushing her along, taking her farther and farther from him. Her journey in the wagon. And then Tower Hill and the king, mounted on his horse, looking down at her . . .

Mrs. Frobisher touched a light hand to Desire's forehead. "It's quite cool now," she said with satisfaction. "For a time last night, you were feverish."

"Did I . . . say anything?" Desire asked cautiously.

"You spoke a few words, but I could make little out of them," the woman told her. "Then the physician roused you for a moment, to administer his draught. You called out a name. Morgan—that was it. After that, you slept soundly enough."

Morgan. Thank goodness she had not said anything to betray him. But what had he thought when he had returned to the archway and found her gone? Maybe he had managed to get through to Southwark. If so, he'd be waiting for her there, half out of his mind with worry. If only she could get word to him.

With mounting agitation she pushed back the coverlet and started to rise.

"There's no need to get up, unless you're sure you're strong enough," said Mistress Frobisher.

But now Desire remembered why she had approached the king, back on Tower Hill. Until she carried out her purpose, Morgan would be in danger. She put her legs over the side of the bed, and the maid steadied her with a firm hand.

"Perhaps you would like a warm bath before supper," she suggested. "I washed your face and hands and got you into that nightdress. But I didn't want to disturb you anymore than I had to." She shook her head regretfully. "I had to dispose of the gown you were wearing. It was quite black with smoke."

And the grime of Newgate, Desire thought. How had she dared to speak to the king in a torn, dirty dress, her face streaked with soot, her hair in a tangle? But he had probably assumed that the fire alone was to blame for her disheveled appearance.

The next time she saw him, however, she must look her best.

"You are most thoughtful," she told Mistress Frobisher. "I could do with a bath."

"I'll have the maids fill the tub at once."

A short time later, in the adjoining bath chamber, Desire descended a few steps and settled herself in a huge tub of rose-colored marble. It was big enough to hold two people at once, she thought, as she stretched out and felt the warm water laving her body. For a moment she gave herself up to the sheer physical pleasure.

Then she realized that Libby, the pert young maid who had come to assist Mistress Frobisher, was asking her preference in bath oils from the bewildering array of bottles on the marble shelf nearby. "Carnation, perhaps? Or sandalwood? Lady Castlemaine prefers a blend of ambergris, musk, and damask roses. It's most favored here at court . . . for now."

Libby gave Desire a knowing little smile.

"Sandalwood will do," Desire said. She was puzzled by the girl's last remark, and even more by the smile that had accompanied it. But then she reminded herself that she knew little about the intrigues of the court.

Libby poured the exotically scented oil into the water, then began to wash Desire's back and arms with a soft cloth.

"And now, your hair, madame." She lathered Desire's tangled tresses thoroughly. "How soft and fine it is," she said with admiration. "After I've rinsed it with lemon juice and brushed it dry, it will shine like satin." She giggled. "I shouldn't like to be Lady Castlemaine's maid, not tonight. She'll be in a fierce temper. A proper Tartar she is, when she's roused."

"Libby, you forget yourself," Mistress Frobisher reproved her sternly. "Go and fetch Mistress Guilford's new clothes at once."

She rinsed Desire's hair with several pitchers of water, and finished with the juice of half a dozen lemons—a rare luxury.

"What did Libby mean about Lady Castlemaine being in a temper?" Desire asked. But Mistress Frobisher dismissed the question.

"These silly young maids. It takes such a time to train them, and even then they tend to forget themselves."

She glanced at a brass clock on the shelf and said: "I'd better go and see to your clothes myself. Libby may have stopped to gossip with one of the other girls. I hope you'll forget her nonsense about Lady Castlemaine."

But Desire wasn't quite reassured by Mistress Frobisher's explanation. She remembered meeting Lady Castlemaine at the Sedgewick's ball. The imperious red-haired beauty had stared at her with open hostility, and then had lost no time in dragging the king away.

Did she believe that Desire had been brought here to the palace to lie with His Majesty? Was it possible that Mistress Frobisher, and Libby, thought so too?

He was handsome enough, and according to gossip, he was a skilled and passionate lover. If a lady pleased him in bed, he was known to be most generous, rewarding her for her services not only with gold but with jewels and sometimes even a title and an estate. No doubt most of the ladies here at court would be delighted to share his bed for a night, or as long as he wished.

But I'm not one of them.

Desire had fought her way through the crowd on Tower Hill with one purpose only: to remind him that he had promised her a private audience. A chance to gain a pardon for herself. And for Morgan.

She lay back in the water and looked down at her body, smooth and white, with tiny drops of scented water glistening on her breasts. Thinking of Morgan, her longing came alive within her. She craved to feel the touch of his hands.

If only she could rise from the bath, her skin smooth and scented, go into the bedchamber, and find him waiting for her in the great canopied bed.

She laughed softly. If he were here right now she would not want him to wait. she would entice him into the tub with her. It was certainly large enough for the two of them. Closing her eyes, she gave herself up to the sweet sensuality of her imaginings.

She would turn on her side to face him and reach down into the water, trailing her fingers over the wet, curling hair on his chest. Then she would move her body against his, and at last she would reach for his hard manhood, and stroke and tease him, until he seized her in his arms and held her to him. He would slide into her with one swift stroke and the surface of the water would be churned by the movements of their joined bodies.

Her eyes flew open, and she wrenched her thoughts away from the delicious fantasy. Before she could be with Morgan again, she must speak to the king. If only she could find the right words.

What if she were unable to convince His Majesty to pardon Morgan? Before, he had only been sought for highway robbery, and that had been bad enough. But now he had been tried and sentence to hang. Even so, the king could still exercise the royal prerogative of mercy — if he chose to.

Now that she was in the palace, and so close to her goal, she felt the harsh grip of fear. It still wasn't too late to back out, she told herself. Once she was thoroughly rested, fed and dressed in her new clothes, what was to stop her from slipping out of Whitehall? She was a guest, not a prisoner here.

Surely she could find a way to travel back east along the river. With the fire under control, she could go to Southwark and set out in search of Lena Yarrow's house.

The notion was tempting, but she dismissed it, rebuking herself for her cowardice. Setting her jaw and pushed back her wet hair, she got out of the tub.

When Mistress Frobisher returned, Desire was already back in the bedchamber, a towel wrapped around her, ready to face whatever lay ahead.

"I trust the gown is to your liking," the woman said, taking it from its wrappings and holding it up for her approval.

"It's magnificent," Desire said, looking at the pale yellow satin with its overskirt of delicate, intricately draped black lace. Libby was arranging the accessories to be worn with the dress: long black gloves, a fan of black plumes, a pair of yellow satin shoes.

"But this is a ball gown," she began.

"You will find it suitable to wear to the banqueting hall tonight," said Mistress Frobisher. "All the other ladies —"

"I can't go there!"

Both maids stared at her in surprise. "Are you feeling ill?" asked Mistress Frobisher anxiously.

"No, not at all . . ." She stopped short. How could she explain her reason for not daring to go to supper in the great banqueting hall, crowded with courtiers and hangers-on?

"I would prefer to take supper here in my rooms," she said.

Mistress Frobisher and Libby exchanged glances.

"Your lovely gown," Libby began.

"I'll wear it to my audience with His Majesty," said Desire.

The banqueting hall would be crowded, and it was most unlikely that she would be recognized. But as long as there was the slightest chance of meeting Lady Mirabelle, Rowena, Phillip Sinclair, or Lord Bodine . . . No, she could not take such a risk.

And that was exactly why she could not run away from the palace, before she spoke privately with the king. Unless her name, and Morgan's, were cleared, there would always be this uncertainty, this fear of being recognized and arrested. Even if it never happened, she could not live her life that way, her most precious moments shadowed by fear.

"How long do you think it will be before the king has

time to see me?" she asked Mistress Frobisher.

But it was Libby who answered, with a pert smile. "I've no doubt His Majesty won't keep you waiting long."

Charles, wrapped in a brocade robe, stood beside the bed in Lady Castlemaine's chamber and looked down at her lush body with keen appreciation. She had greeted him warmly on his return from London that afternoon; and had responded to his lovemaking with even greater ardor than usual. Now she lay back, the candlelight flickering over the lush curves of her hips, the rounded breasts with their large, deep pink nipples. The coppery triangle at the apex of her thighs was a shade lighter than the mane of red hair that fell across her pillows.

"What shall I wear to supper tonight?" she asked with a slow, lazy smile. "The cinnamon velvet, perhaps? Or the purple and gold?"

"I prefer you exactly as you are now," the king said. He laughed softly, then reached down to take one of her nipples and roll it between thumb and forefinger; under his touch, it hardened swiftly. Barbara turned on her side. She slid one hand inside the opening of his robe and raked her nails lightly, seductively, over his muscular thigh. "You don't have to leave yet . . ."

He drew away with a sigh of regret. "I fear I must, my dear."

"We'll meet at supper in the banqueting hall, then," she said. "And in the meantime, you may try to guess which gown I've chosen." She looked up at him from under her long, curving lashes, teasing him with a smile.

"You will have to choose another companion tonight, Barbara. No doubt Craven or Buckingham would be honored to—"

"But you *must* escort me to supper tonight!" She caught herself in time. Even his favorite mistress did not tell Charles Stuart what he must or must not do. She rose from the bed with slow, feline grace, and spoke more softly.

"You've been away so much during the past week. I've missed you, sire."

"There'll be other nights," he reminded her.

"We needn't go to the banqueting hall," she said. "Now I think about it, I'd rather dine here with you."

He shook his head. "I have pressing affairs of state to attend to, my dear. I can't put them off."

Barbara could no longer restrain herself. Picking up her silk robe, she flung it about her shoulders. She put her hands on her hips and confronted him, her eyes darkening to stormy purple, as they did when she was angry. "You can't wait to visit that black-haired wench your panderer brought here, can you?"

"Master Chiffinch takes care of many important functions for me," Charles reminded her. "The man is one of my most trusted servants."

"Don't try to cozen me, sire! That little slut's not here at Whitehall on matters of state."

"You forget yourself, Barbara." He gave her a long, cold stare. "You're beginning to sound like a jealous wife."

His words, although spoken quietly, struck her like a dash of icy water. No, she was not his wife. And she never would be. She knew all too well that even the most pampered mistress could be replaced at the whim of her protector.

Always on the lookout for possible rivals, she had built up her own elaborate network of informers. They had lost no time in running to tell her about the dark-haired young beauty who had been carried into the palace the day before.

Whitehall was a large, sprawling group of red brick buildings, with many separate apartments, to house not only the royal family but also visiting noblemen, favored courtiers, and other hangers-on. But Charles had given the newcomer one of the finest suites in the palace.

"I've heard the girl was unconscious when your . . . when Chiffinch carried her from your barge. Surely it wasn't necessary for you to have her drugged and kidnapped in order to bring her here. Is it possible she's a virgin? I should think there'd be little pleasure in deflowering an innocent little

353

creature by force—"

"That's enough, Barbara."

Although Charles usually spoke with careless good humor, he was nearing the end of his patience. Barbara was a magnificent female, eager and lusty in bed. No man could have asked for a more passionate or willing mistress—or a more beautiful one.

But after nearly a week of helping to battle the fire, standing up to his ankles in water, riding from Moorfields to Tower Hill to calm the fears of the homeless and provide for their immediate needs, he was in no mood to cope with one of Barbara's tantrums. When she was aroused to fury, her voice grew shrill, and she could curse like any fishwife.

"John Evelyn's drawn up plans for rebuilding London," he began, hoping to distract her long enough to make his exit with as little fuss as possible. "He has suggested a straight street, to run from Temple Bar to St. Dunstan's. With five large squares along the way."

Barbara tossed her head, her eyes narrow with barely controlled fury. What the hell did she care about Evelyn or his plans? If that woman appeared in the banqueting hall with Charles as her escort, tongues would begin to wag. When it came to spreading gossip, the courtiers of Whitehall were no better than a lot of village crones.

True, she would be surrounded by a dozen handsome gallants, all vying for her favor. But that would not prevent the sidelong glances, the whispered remarks that perhaps Charles had grown tired of her and was about to replace her with another woman. She clenched her fists so tightly that her nails cut into her palms.

"Evelyn wants an enormous oval at the Fleet Conduit," the king went on. "And another oval around St. Paul's. He also has suggested a large piazza surrounded with colonnades, and a fountain in the center." He paused, his dark brown eyes thoughtful as he considered the suggestions. Then he shook his head. "Most impressive, but somewhat impractical, I fear."

But Barbara was not to be put off so easily. "Since you're

obviously too busy to dine with me, perhaps you will do me the honor of returning here later tonight." She strove to keep her temper in check, but she could not restrain the sarcasm that crept into her voice.

"I doubt it. I must show Evelyn the courtesy of going over his plans again. Perhaps some of the details will prove to be workable. But probably I'll go along with Christopher Wren's ideas. That man's extraordinary. He was already drawing up his own plans even before the fire was completely under control."

Barbara's fingers closed around a small silver patchbox on her dressing table. She felt a powerful impulse to hurl it straight at the king's head. But even in the worst temper, she was not so rash.

"And that girl," she asked with poisonous sweetness. "No doubt she has also been brought here to help you with your plans for rebuilding London."

Charles gave his mistress a sardonic smile. "She is far too young and lovely to concern herself with such matters," he said.

"And your plans for *her*—"

"Who can say, my dear?"

He turned on his heel and left her, relieved to have escaped the full force of her tirade.

Chapter Thirty-one

Desire followed Master Will Chiffinch down the stone gallery of the palace. She quickened her steps and tried to ignore the tension that gripped her. Now, after four days of anxious waiting, the king had sent for her at last.

Since her arrival at the palace, she had kept to the luxurious apartment provided for her and had spoken to no one except her two maids. Mistress Frobisher had managed to persuade her to emerge the night before, and had led her by a roundabout passage to the shelter, a small enclosure looking down on the banqueting hall.

"This used to be the minstrels' gallery during the reign of Henry VIII," the older woman explained. In these times, the hall had been redecorated and enlarged to accommodate the growing number of visitors; the court musicians who entertained the guests with lute, viol, and dulcimer performed on a flower-decked platform at one end of the hall.

The banqueting hall was like a public promenade. While the royal family and the courtiers dined there, throngs of hangers-on milled about, enjoying the music, listening to the latest gossip, and watching the king at his supper.

But last night, King Charles had not appeared in the hall. "No doubt he's too busy," Mistress Frobisher told Desire, adding that His Majesty had been meeting with a great number of public officials to tackle the overwhelming task of restoring order to the stricken city.

If the king could not take the time to dine in state, how long would it be before he would be able to see her? Unable to enjoy the colorful spectacle below, she left after less than an hour and went to bed early.

But sleep eluded her, and she tossed about on the wide bed, staring into the darkness. She caught the scent of damp earth and shrubs mingled with the fragrance of lavender and hollyhocks from the garden below her windows. Her body was stirred, and she longed for the touch of Morgan's hands.

She remembered every moment of their last night together, and it was as if she could feel his warm lips, caressing, exploring her in so many intimate ways. Turning, she pushed her face into her silk-covered pillow. Would they ever be together again?

Then today, when she had been working listlessly on a piece of embroidery, she had received word that the king would see her in two hours. Mistress Frobisher had helped her to put on the yellow satin gown with the black lace overskirt, while Libby had arranged her hair and helped her to apply a touch of lip rouge, a light dusting of powder. "And the sandalwood perfume," the girl reminded her. Desire touched the stopper of the scent bottle behind her ears.

Now, as she made her way down the stone gallery, she could not help but notice the avidly curious stares of the bejeweled ladies and the fops in their satin coats and beribboned breeches. She did not return their glances but held her head high. Nevertheless, she was relieved when Master Chiffinch led the way into a side passage and stopped at last before a door draped in scarlet velvet. The two yeomen of the guard, who had been standing at attention, moved aside.

A moment later Desire stood in an oak-paneled chamber with a marble-topped fireplace and narrow windows. A tall figure in a black periwig turned from one of the windows. She found herself face to face with King Charles, who welcomed her with a warm smile.

She tried to ignore the unsteadiness in her legs as she

managed to perform a graceful curtsy.

"Please be seated, Mistress Guilford," he said, indicating a velvet-padded chair on one side of the fireplace. Then, after dismissing Chiffinch with a wave of his hand, he took a seat opposite her.

His eyes rested appreciatively on her for a moment. The pale yellow satin was a most seductive garment, cut daringly low to reveal her shoulders. Her breasts were pushed up high by her tightly laced busk, and a gold and topaz necklace touched the shadowed cleavage between them.

Libby had brushed Desire's hair until it glowed with a blue-black luster, and arranged it in a most flattering style, with a mass of curls swept to one side to fall over her bare shoulder, and coquettish little ringlets at the temples.

"I trust you will forgive the delay in arranging this audience," King Charles was saying.

"It is I who should ask your pardon, sire, for forcing my way to you so boldly on Tower Hill."

His smile was reassuring. "It was a most unconventional approach," he agreed. "I've had little time for anything except the business of trying to restore order to the City. But I've found myself thinking of you often. I keep remembering those words. 'A Stuart doesn't break his promise.' "

"They were my father's words, Your Majesty," she told him. "During all the years of your exile, he never stopped believing you would return."

"Is your father in London now?"

"Both my parents died in the plague, sire."

"A bitter loss for one so young as you," he said with deep sincerity. He had been not much older when his own father had been executed by the Parliamentarian forces. Then he paused, his eyes thoughtful. "I don't believe I know the name of Guilford," he went on. "But you are related to the Warringtons, are you not?"

Desire was startled to realize that, with so many urgent affairs to occupy his attention, he remembered the circumstances of their meeting at the Sedgewick's ball. She looked at him more closely. The strain of the past few weeks had left their mark. She saw that the lines bracketing his full, sensual lips were deeper than she remembered. But his brown eyes were alert.

"I am no kin to Sir Geoffrey or any of his family," she said. "He took me into his home out of kindness, and his mother treated me most graciously." She gave him a long, straightforward look. "I soon caused them to regret their generosity."

Charles's thick eyebrows shot up. "You are unusually forthright — especially for a young lady," he said.

Her mouth went dry, but her eyes did not waver. She must speak the truth and take her chances. "I deceived the Warringtons," she began. Her voice was unsteady, but she made herself go on. "I said I was a respectable young lady who had found myself in unfortunate circumstances through no fault of my own. Lady Mirabelle took me at my word. She showed me only kindness. And as for Geoffrey . . ."

Charles nodded, a smile touching his lips. "The young man was swept away by your loveliness, as what man would not be?"

"Geoffrey was in love with me. That night of the ball he asked me to be his wife. But if he had known the truth about me he never would have. And now he's off fighting the Dutch and it's my fault. He never would have gone except for —"

The king held up his hand. "Compose yourself," he said. "And go back to the beginning."

The beginning. But where had it begun, the long, twisted path that had brought her here?

"I suppose it started with the plague," she said slowly. "I lost not only my parents but my home — everything except the clothes I was wearing when I ran away."

The king nodded, then sat back in silence. She sensed the keen mind behind those brown eyes, weighing every word. Without glossing over the truth, she told him about her

359

meeting with Morgan.

"He carried you off against your will and held you prisoner?"

Her cheeks flushed. "That's what I tried to tell myself at first. But now I know better. I love him, sire. I think I have from the beginning."

"You're so young, my dear. It would have been no great matter for a man like Trenchard—handsome, you tell me, and daring, to seduce a girl who had led such a sheltered life."

"Morgan Trenchard didn't seduce me, nor did he use force. I was not too young to know I had found the only man I'll ever love."

He looked past her for a moment, as if stirred by memories of his own. Then his eyes returned to her face. "Go on," he said quietly.

He did not interrupt again until she told him of Morgan's trial and sentence. "He took all the blame on himself," the king said.

"He did it to protect me, sire. He hoped perhaps in that way I might get off with a lighter sentence. That I'd be sent as a bondservant to one of the colonies in the New World."

"And was that your sentence?"

"I've not been brought to trial yet. My case would have been heard at the next quarter-session, but the fire—"

The king nodded. "I gather that you and Trenchard escaped from Newgate during the fire. How did you manage that?"

She told him the rest, driven now by a mounting sense of urgency. He looked at her curiously. "You asked me for a private audience when you were still living under the protection of the Warringtons. You were safe enough then. Had you married young Warrington, chances are you'd have had nothing to fear."

"But I could not have married him, loving Morgan as I did, sire. And I thought if I could clear Morgan's name, we would be free to marry, to live together in peace. I even

360

hoped there might be a chance that you'd have restored his estate."

"And Trenchard—did he know of your plan?"

"I told him, sire. He tried to talk me out of it. He said there was no chance. But I wouldn't believe that. I couldn't . . ."

For a long time the king was silent. She heard the ticking of the clock on the marble mantelpiece, the soft crackling of the logs in the fire. Clasping her hands in her lap, she watched his swarthy, inscrutable face.

At last, when she thought she could bear it no longer, he spoke quietly. "Trenchard forced you to take part in waylaying Lord Bodine's coach. And you escaped from Newgate under the most extraordinary circumstances." He gave her a faint smile. "I do not believe I am taking any great risk in granting you a full pardon, Mistress Guilford."

For a moment, she could not take in his meaning. Then she understood that she was free. Relief and gratitude welled up in her.

"But Morgan Trenchard's case is quite different," he went on. "The man's a habitual criminal. He's committed highway robbery many times. And he has already been condemned to hang."

Desire's short-lived joy ebbed away. What good was her freedom without Morgan to share it? Fighting back the despair that threatened to overwhelm her, she drew on every ounce of inner strength she possessed.

"Your Majesty, I beg you to consider. Morgan's father died defending the Stuart crown. Morgan was brutally treated by his half brother. He was forced to flee from his estate, from England, because he spoke out in the Royalist cause. He survived as best he could there in the Indies, but he committed no crime until he returned to find that he'd been stripped of his lawful inheritance."

"My dear Mistress Guilford, you have only Trenchard's word for all that. A woman in love will believe what she wishes to believe."

"Morgan wasn't lying, sire. I know it."

"Your loyalty does you credit," he interrupted gently. "But an English court has found him guilty and sentenced him to hang."

Desire felt her last hope slipping away. A moment later she was out of her chair, facing the king. She dropped to her knees before him, her full skirt billowing out around her, her green eyes raised to his.

"You can save him, sire." Her voice rang out, strong and passionate. "I ask the royal prerogative of mercy for Morgan Trenchard."

Charles stood up, took her hands in his, and raised her to her feet. He was no longer moved by a woman's tears or hysterical outbursts. Years of experience had taught him to distrust such feminine devices. But Desire Guilford had spoken with courageous strength, appealing to his sense of justice, asking pardon not for herself but for the man she loved.

He held her hands a moment longer before releasing them. "Mistress Guilford, I can offer you no promises. But if you wish me to consider your request, you must agree to my terms."

Desire took a step backward. Her eyes filled with consternation. She had known from their first meeting that the king was attracted to her. He had spoken of terms. Would he ask her to come to his bed? Was that the price of a pardon for Morgan?

"I want to know where Trenchard is now."

This was not what she had been expecting, and she was thrown off guard. "He might be anywhere. He could have left the country by now."

The king said nothing, but his features were set, his eyes implacable.

"There's a lodging house in Southwark, owned by a woman named Lena Yarrow. She provides shelter for hunted fugitives. Morgan and I were going there when we got separated in the fire."

She had put Morgan's life in danger without any assurance that he would be pardoned.

"Meanwhile," His Majesty went on, "You are to remain at the palace as my guest. You may feel free to enjoy the diversions here at Court." Although his words were pleasant enough, she recognized that this was another of his terms.

"I shall send for you again when I have made my decision," he told her. Then he walked to the door and summoned Will Chiffinch to escort her back to her apartment.

After she left, Charles did not turn to his other duties at once, for he could not get her out of his mind. A most unusual young girl — courageous, beautiful, and capable of great passion. Under other circumstances, he might well have asked her to share his bed. Surely she had expected him to.

He smiled, a little ruefully, as he remembered her instinctive retreat, the distress in her eyes at the mention of terms. He could have told her that her fears were groundless. He had never taken a woman against her will. There had been no need.

His thoughts went back to his first love, pretty, brownhaired Lucy Walter. He had been eighteen then, and had come back from Holland to fight for his father's cause. But he'd met Lucy and she had given herself to him with a youthful passion that matched his own. She'd given him a son, too, and though she'd made no claims on him, he had acknowledged his paternity, and given the boy a title, duke of Monmouth.

And all those other women who had shared his bed. Not one had been reluctant. What pleasure could a man find with a frightened, unwilling female in his bed?

He sighed, thinking again of Desire Guilford. She was one of those rare women who gave her love once, and for all time.

When Chiffinch returned alone to the audience chamber, the king gave him a list of instructions regarding Morgan Trenchard. Charles had told Barbara the truth when he had said that Master Chiffinch was a valuable servant in many ways.

True, he often escorted a lady to the king's chamber and then saw her safely home. But Chiffinch had also proved his worth in gathering information for the king, quickly and efficiently. He was capable of drinking most men under the table while keeping a clear head. With his giant stature, he he could fight his way out of any tavern brawl, but he also had the speech and manner that gained him admittance to more elegant surroundings.

Chiffinch, having received his orders, left the royal presence. Almost at once, the king turned his thoughts to the many other matters that demanded his attention.

He would have to take immediate measures for the relief of those left homeless by the fire. Close to fourteen thousand houses had been destroyed, and their former inhabitants could not be left without shelter when winter arrived. He would dispatch more army tents at once. He would also grant permission so that wooden shacks might be built in the artillery fields in Finsbury and on Moorfields and Smithfield, where so many of the refugees were now sleeping in the open.

He considered a petition from the lord mayor that the area at the north end of London Bridge should be cleared, the road railed off, and another settlement established there as soon as possible. Funds would have to be allotted and laborers brought in and put to work.

The king paused and allowed himself to think of more personal matters for a moment. Barbara's spies would be busier than ever, watching his comings and goings. Once she knew for certain that he had not visited the apartment set aside for Mistress Guilford, her volatile temper would cool. He must snatch a few moments to choose a valuable piece of jewelry, a diamond necklace or a sapphire brooch for his tempestuous mistress.

"If Desire was coming here, she'd have arrived by now," Enoch told Morgan in the upstairs room at Lena Yarrow's house.

A chill rain had been falling all that evening, and now Morgan, returning from another fruitless search of the taverns and bawdyhouses of Southwark, sat in brooding silence. "We've both searched high and low for her. Barney's been hunting for her too—though he won't go on much longer. Not unless we can make it worth his while."

"Tomorrow I'll go over to London. She may be in one of the refugee encampments. And there are the cellars and vaults under the ruins." He could not bring himself to go on, remembering what he'd heard of these abandoned shelters. Thieves and murderers had established themselves there after the fire had driven them from their dens in Whitefriars.

"Look here, Morgan, it's been more than a fortnight since you saw her. She may have left London and found work for herself in some little village."

Morgan turned on Enoch, his brows drawing together in an angry frown. "Go on, say what you're thinking."

"It could be she decided not to come here at all. Could anybody blame her for wanting to make a fresh start? It was bad enough for you, locked up in Newgate all that time. Think how it must have been for Desire."

"I know how it was for her. But she'll never find herself in such a place again. As soon as we're together, I'll take her away. Out of London. All the way to the Indies, if I have to."

Enoch's habitual calm was wearing thin. "How much longer do you think we'll be able to stay here?" he reminded Morgan. "Soon as we're out of money, Lena'll show us the door."

"We'll get the money somehow."

"You mean to take to the highway again." He looked at Morgan curiously. "There's plenty of good pickings right now. All those rich folk who fled the city will be coming back in their fine carriages. Barney told me he'd get word of a likely pigeon, ripe for the plucking. I'm ready to ride out whenever you give the word."

Morgan shook his head. "That's all over, Enoch."

"Then would you mind telling me how you mean to live from now on?"

"When I was making my way across London to the bridge, I stopped to share a meal with a man named Caleb," Morgan said. "He was a juggler."

"Are you going to take up juggling at fairs then, to earn your bread?"

But his smile faded before the serious look in Morgan's eyes. "Caleb said that once a man took to the road, there was no turning back. I've thought about that. It may be true for him, but not for me."

"Don't be too sure. You've lived a roving life all these years," Enoch reminded him. "Mayhap this juggler fellow knew what he was talking about."

"When we fled to the Indies, we had little choice," Morgan went on. "Roderick was master of Pendarren, and I was too young to fight for my rights against him. But it was different when we returned to England."

"What choice did you have then, with Pendarren given to Lord Wyndham—and him a friend of the king?"

"That was what I told myself. I was too ready to use that as an excuse for taking to the highways. Maybe I'd grown used to living without responsibilities, moving about as I pleased. It was an free and easy life, in its way.

"Not so easy, and damned dangerous," Enoch reminded him.

"Maybe I liked the danger, too. I risked my neck, and yours, a dozen times over."

"I went of my own free will," Enoch reminded him.

"Or out of loyalty to me and my family." He was silent for a moment.

Enoch looked faintly embarassed. "Whatever we did, there's no going back now. Don't waste precious time thinking about the past. Let's get out of England fast. They need soldiers to fight the Dutch, and they're not likely to ask too many questions. We can't stay here much longer, that's certain."

He spoke with hard common sense, and Morgan was forced to consider his words. Reluctantly he nodded. "Another fortnight," he said. "If I haven't found her by then, we'll move on."

Chapter Thirty-two

Lady Castlemaine sat before her dressing table, a smile touching her lips. Her blue-violet eyes glowed with pleasure as she lifted the necklace from its velvet box and moved it slowly from side to side so that the magnificent star sapphire, set in a circle of diamonds and suspended from a gold chain, caught the candlelight.

"It is magnificent, sire." She turned her head to smile up at the king. He had come to her apartment only a few moments earlier and had sent away her serving woman. It had been over a week since he had shared her bedchamber, and she had been growing more uneasy with each passing hour.

But now he was here at last, and had brought her this splendid gift. Her delight with the necklace was genuine enough, for no matter how many jewels she already owned, her acquisitive nature knew no bounds. This latest gift was particularly significant, and not only for its beauty—so valuable a peace offering assured her that Charles was still eager for her favors. She had not been supplanted by that dark-haired, green-eyed little upstart after all.

Only this evening, Barbara had been filled with resentment when Desire had appeared in the banqueting hall, accompanied by Mistress Frobisher. And this wasn't the first time. Two weeks ago the newcomer had ended her period of seclusion. After her audience with the king, she left her apartment each day and moved freely about Whitehall, dressed in the most becoming and expensive new gowns.

Although Desire was besieged by the attentions from the

368

court gallants, she did not respond to their flattery; a certain aloofness in her manner discouraged their advances. According to Barbara's most reliable informants, not even the most handsome and dashing of the courtiers had gained access to Desire Guilford's apartments. And neither had the king.

But this last piece of information was not particularly comforting to Barbara. Perhaps the clever little witch was keeping His Majesty at arm's length in the hope of impressing him with her virtue.

"Maybe she thinks His Majesty will be excited by a show of modesty," the duke of Buckingham had remarked to Barbara, over the card table only that evening. "When a man reaches a certain age, a reluctant virgin can present a certain challenge." He gave Barbara an insolent grin. "Most of the king's women have been such easy conquests."

King Charles had not appeared at the banqueting hall that evening. One of the Gentlemen of the Bedchamber had told Barbara that His Majesty was with John Evelyn and Dr. Christopher Wren again, going over their latest plans for the rebuilding of London. Barbara, in ill-humor, had retired early to vent her spleen on her long-suffering serving woman.

But now Barbara's spirits soared. Charles had come to her again. He took the necklace from her and fastened it about her smooth, white neck, while she sat admiring her reflection in the mirror over the dressing table. She leaned back and he pushed her dressing gown off one shoulder, then bent to brush his lips across her satin skin. A shiver of delicious anticipation went tingling through her. But even now, a small doubt kept nagging at her.

"Did you select the necklace yourself, sire?" she asked.

"Certainly, my dear. The London jewelers suffered devastating losses during the fire, but they managed to save some of their stock. Several of them came here this afternoon with their finest offerings. I take it you approve of my choice."

She gave him a brilliant smile. "You know my taste so well," she purred. "And how flattering to think that you took time from your many pressing affairs, to select a gift for me . . ."

He slipped his hands beneath the silk and lace of her dressing gown to cup the soft fullness of her breasts. "I cannot spend all my time with architects and city officials," he said. His fingers moved to her nipples, and he tugged at them gently.

But she could not let herself yield completely to the wave of sensuous delight that might otherwise have swept her away. Not yet. First, she must be sure of Charles's feelings for her.

"I wasn't thinking of architects and officials at the moment, sire."

He laughed softly. "Neither was I. That's why I am here, my love," he told her, his voice deep and husky.

She turned from the dressing table and looked up at him. He saw the shadow of uneasiness in the depths of her eyes. He sighed as he realized that his gift was not enough. Before he could enjoy his pleasure to the fullest with Barbara tonight, he must set her doubts at rest.

"Don't trouble yourself any longer, my sweet," he said with a trace of chagrin. "The lady is not willing."

"The lady?" Her blue-violet eyes looked at him in a pretense of innocent bewilderment. "I fear I don't understand your meaning, sire."

He pulled her to her feet and put his hands on her shoulders, towering over her. "I haven't bedded Desire Guilford, and I'm not going to. If I asked her to lie with me, she would refuse."

"But she's still here. You've given her one of the choicest apartments in the palace."

"And she'll continue to stay until I have studied her case carefully and made my decision."

Barbara's look of surprise was genuine now. "You speak as if she were a criminal and you were her judge, sire."

"She's no criminal. But her lover is. That's why she sought me out and asked a private audience. I was moved by her plea in defense of the man, I must confess—"

"She's in love with a . . . criminal? What's he done?"

"He's been found guilty of highway robbery."

"A highwayman! But surely any girl in her right mind would be only too willing to cast aside such a man. Especially if she thought she had a chance to . . . to . . ."

"To lie with the king?" He shook his head. "Not this girl." His voice was soft and touched with a kind of awe. "She loves this man completely. For her, there can be no one else."

Barbara was silent for a moment, but her selfish, practical mind moved swiftly. "Then you must grant her plea and restore her lover to her."

She moved closer to the king, so that her breasts brushed against his chest. "You have made me so happy, sire. Loving you as I do, having you here with me tonight . . . I can't bear to think of that poor girl pining away alone."

"You're a tenderhearted creature," he said. "But I fear that in this case I can't make my decision without more information." Seating himself on her bed, he drew her into his lap. Briefly he explained the reasons for his delay in deciding on the fate of Morgan Trenchard.

"No matter what he's done, you have it in your power to grant him a pardon." Her arms went around his neck. "You will, won't you, sire? To please me . . ."

"I wish to please you, my love," he said. "And I can't wait much longer to prove it." He opened her silk sash and slid her dressing gown from her smooth, white body. Lifting her from his lap, he eased her back across the bed. The silken garment slithered to the floor, and she lay before him, wearing only the star sapphire necklace. It glowed softly, invitingly between her breasts. Quickly he disrobed and stretched out beside her.

Calculating minx, feigning a tenderhearted concern for Desire. He knew well enough that she only wanted to get the girl back to her lover, and as far from Whitehall as possible.

On a rainy evening nearly two weeks later, Desire sat patiently while Libby helped prepare her for her appearance in the banqueting hall. Perfumed and powdered, her busk tightly laced, she was waiting for the maid to arrange her hair when Will Chiffinch presented himself at the outer door of the apartment. A Mistress Guilford was to accompany him to the royal audience chamber — at once.

Desire's heart speeded up, and her mouth went dry.

Mistress Frobisher left Chiffinch waiting while she hurried back and helped Desire into a new gown of honey-colored taffeta, trimmed with gold lace. Somehow she forced herself to stand still until the last button was fastened and the bell-shaped skirt was draped in smooth, graceful folds. But when Libby attempted to pin up her hair, she could restrain herself no longer. She snatched up a length of ribbon and tied back her hair with shaking fingers; then, lifting her full skirt, she ran from the bedchamber to confront the huge man in the brown periwig.

"I'm ready, Master Chiffinch," she said.

He escorted her into the Stone Gallery. After waiting so impatiently for the king to summon her, she now tried to compose herself, but it was no use. She heard the buzz of voices, and saw the courtiers turning to look at her. Their brilliant silks and velvets blurred before her eyes. Once more she followed Chiffinch into the side passage, and on to the scarlet-draped door.

"His Majesty's been detained," said one of the yeomen of the guard. Chiffinch opened the door and stood aside to let her pass, then followed her into the chamber.

She started slightly when she heard the clank of metal chains. Then she forgot everything else, for Morgan was standing before the fireplace. Her joy at seeing him blotted out everything else. But a moment later she gave a cry of dismay. A guard stood on either side of him, each armed with a long pike. Heavy manacles had been fastened around his wrists and joined by a thick iron chain.

His shirt and breeches were soaked through by the rain, and his black hair was plastered against his forehead. One side of his face was bruised.

Heedless of Chiffinch or the guards, she ran to Morgan, her arms outstretched, her whole body aching with the need to hold him again, to comfort him. But the two guards lowered their pikes and crossed them, blocking her way.

"Careful, my lady," said Chiffinch. "The rogue's dangerous."

Morgan's dark eyes raked over Desire, taking in her taffeta gown, the gold and topaz chain around her neck, the lustrous sweep of her hair.

"The lady's safe enough," he said. He was speaking to Chiffinch, but his eyes were fixed on Desire's. "I would not put a hand on her, even if I could." He glanced down at his fettered wrists.

After an instant of stunned bewilderment, Desire understood the reason for his icy glance and the contempt in his voice. He had been captured at Lena Yarrow's house after what must have been a violent struggle, and brought here in chains. He must have guessed that she had told the king of his whereabouts.

When he spoke again, his voice was drained of emotion.

"How well you're looking," he said. "A fine new gown and a jeweled necklace. And your own apartment here at the palace, so I've been told." He gave the king's page an ironic smile. "I did you an injustice, Master Chiffinch. You spoke no more than the truth, after all."

"Morgan, for the love of heaven, listen to me!"

"You told His Majesty where Enoch and I might be found, didn't you?"

"I had to. His Majesty insisted—I was in no position to refuse."

"You decided there was nothing you could refuse His

Majesty, isn't that right?" She flinched before the stinging lash of his words. "You've done well for yourself, my love. Once you'd managed to see the king in private, you knew exactly what to do. It wasn't difficult for you to gain a pardon for yourself, was it?"

She felt a brief flare of anger. It was unfair for him to condemn her without giving her the benefit of the doubt. "That's enough, Morgan. If you'll allow me to explain—"

"Spare me your explanations," he cut in. "You weren't light-fingered enough to earn your living as a pickpocket, my sweet. But you're quick-witted, I'll give you credit for that—you know how to talk your way out of a tight place."

Her eyes began to fill. "There no need for tears, Desire," he told her. "You're to be congratulated. Half the women in England would be happy to change places with you now."

"But I'm not . . . I haven't . . ."

"I can only wish you success in your new . . . occupation. No lovelier lady ever graced the royal bed, I'd stake my soul on that. And to prove I bear you no malice, I'll give you a word of advice. Guard youself against Mistress Castlemaine. I'm told she can be a ruthless enemy."

"Mind your tongue, Trenchard."

At the sound of the king's deep, commanding voice, the two guards stiffened to attention, and even Morgan fell silent in the presence of his sovereign.

Charles strode into the audience chamber. He cut an impressive figure in his coat of plum-colored velvet and his black knee breeches. His periwig was meticulously curled, and fell to his shoulders.

"Now, Trenchard, if you can manage to control that devilish temper of yours, we'll have those chains off," His Majesty said. "Chiffinch, release him."

Will Chiffinch unlocked the iron bands from Morgan's wrists, gathered up the chains, and stood awaiting further orders. "Wait outside," the king told him. Then he dismissed the two guards with a wave of his hand. When they were gone, he turned back to Morgan.

"You do Lady Castlemaine an injustice, Trenchard," he said, the corners of his mouth twitching slightly beneath the thin line of his mustache. "It might surprise you to know that the lady made a most touching plea for your release."

Morgan's icy control wavered for a moment. The king's words had thrown him off guard. He exchanged glances with Desire, but he saw that she, too, was baffled.

"And now, if you'll both seat yourselves, we've much to talk about." He indicated a sofa near the fireplace. Desire obeyed, and after a slight hesitation, Morgan sat beside her. The king drew up a chair opposite.

"You've caused me a good deal of trouble for one man, Trenchard—and at a time when I have more than my share already," the king began. "I don't condone your crimes, make no mistake about that. My subjects should have the right to travel the highways in safety, without fear of being set upon by 'gentlemen of the road.' "

He paused and stroked his thin black mustache thoughtfully. "Your friend, Enoch Hodges, says you have already decided to give up that trade. Is that correct?"

"Enoch! What've they done with him?"

"He's safe enough," the king assured Morgan. "He's been questioned for the past two days and nights—"

Morgan started up from the sofa, his eyes grim.

"Questioned!"

"He's unharmed," the king said. "What he told us did not contradict Mistress Guilford's account in any particular."

Morgan resumed his place, but Desire could feel the tension that surrounded him like a tangible force. He leaned forward, the heavy muscles taut beneath his torn shirt.

"But I haven't made my decision on his word alone, or that of Mistress Guilford, either," the king went on. He looked at her with a touch of compassion. "I know how difficult the waiting must have been for you, my dear. But it took some time for Master Chiffinch to make the journey to Cornwall and back."

"Cornwall!" Morgan's face darkened. "If your Master

Chiffinch went there to get the facts about the Trenchards from Lord Wyndham, he could have spared himself the journey."

"My orders to Chiffinch were to seek out those tenants who had lived at Pendarren and in the countryside nearby during the Civil War and to speak with them in private. He managed admirably, as usual.

"They confirmed all that you have told Mistress Guilford of your early life there. They said that your half brother, Roderick, was the only one of the Trenchards to take up arms in Cromwell's cause. That your father was loyal to the Stuarts, and died in battle, fighting for our cause. No doubt, had you been older, you too would have fought beneath our standards."

"He did fight—in the only way he could!" Desire sprang to Morgan's defense, her voice filled with indignation. "He spoke out for the Stuart cause in the presence of Roderick and his Parliamentarian friends. He was brutally beaten. He'd have died of the punishment they gave him had it not been for Enoch."

She put a hand on Morgan's arm, and he did not try to draw away. Instead, his fingers closed over hers.

"And then you fled from England," the king said. He was silent for a moment, lost in his own thoughts. "I had to run for my life, as you did. After the Battle of Worcester, it was," he continued. "I know what it feels like to be an exile, deprived of one's rightful heritage.

"For fifteen years I kept moving about the Continent, leading a rootless, wandering existence. Charles Lackland, that's what they called me. I don't like to look back on those years. They shaped my character and not entirely for the better, I fear."

"But you returned in triumph to claim your throne, Your Majesty," Desire said. "I stood in the crowd with my parents that day. I saw you ride into London with your followers. I remember the banners snapping in the breeze and the sound of the trumpets. I'd never seen so many people—the

376

streets and the balconies were crowded with your subjects. They were cheering, welcoming you home."

"It was a memorable day," Charles agreed. "But you, Trenchard. Your return was quite different, wasn't it?"

Morgan's dark eyes went bleak. "When I learned that I'd lost Pendarren, that another man held the estate, I was angry and bitter. I lacked the money and influence to fight Wyndham. After that, I tried to tell myself that I had no choice except to survive as best I could. If it meant breaking the laws of the land, why should that trouble me? The law had already deprived me of all that was rightfully mine."

"And if you had it to do over again," the king asked. "Would you take to highway robbery?"

Morgan was silent for a moment. Desire pressed his arm, trying to warn him to choose his words carefully. He must not allow his hot temper to get the better of him — not now, of all times.

"I don't know, sire," Morgan said. "Perhaps I would. None of us get that chance, though, do we?"

Charles smiled. "An honest answer, and I like you for it, Trenchard. Not many men in your place would dare speak out so plainly."

He turned to Desire. "You asked me to exercise the royal prerogative of mercy for Morgan Trenchard. Your request is granted, Mistress Guilford."

Desire longed to throw herself into Morgan's arms, to hold him close, her face against his chest, and give way at last to her emotions. But somehow she managed to control herself in the presence of the king.

"And Enoch Hodges, what of him?" Morgan asked.

"Hodges, too, is pardoned."

"Thank you, sire," Morgan said, with quiet dignity. He got to his feet and bowed to the king.

"Now, as for Pendarren," His Majesty went on, "that does present something of a problem. When I was restored to the throne, your estate, along with so many others, lay desolate, its fields fallow. No legal heirs had come forward to claim it.

I gave it to Lord Wyndham in recognition of his loyal service to my father."

"But Morgan wasn't even in England then to put forth his claim," Desire said.

"Nevertheless, I gave the estate to another. And a Stuart does not break his promise."

She fell silent, for she had cause to remember those words. But surely now that Morgan was pardoned he had a right to his property at last.

"With all respect, sire," he said to the king, "perhaps I would not wish to return as master of Pendarren, even if you offered it to me."

"And why not, Trenchard?"

"A roving life changes a man," he said. "I've begun to think that I might find the day-to-day routine of a country squire too tame. And besides—"

"Go on," the king urged.

"Gossip has a way of traveling, even as far as Cornwall. If my neighbors were to hear the rumor that I had been a highwayman, condemned to swing on Tyburn tree, it could prove embarrassing, to say the least."

The king looked at him in surprise. "I should not have thought you'd be the sort to shrink from the clacking of malicious tongues."

"It's my wife I'm thinking of," Morgan explained. "A shy, modest gentlewoman like her would suffer great distress, should her neighbors—"

"Your wife!" Desire sprang to her feet, her green eyes wide with shock. Even the imperturbable Charles was startled.

But Morgan took her hands and held them firmly so that she could not free herself without an unseemly scuffle. When he spoke, his voice was filled with a vibrant tenderness. "That night in our cell, with the fire all around us, we exchanged our vows, remember? You have been my wife since then, in all that matters." He smiled down at her. "We'll have a more formal ceremony as soon as it may be arranged."

Heedless of the king's presence, he drew her against him, holding her close to his side.

The king got to his feet. "That's all well enough," he reminded Morgan. "But you will need some means of supporting your wife. I agree that her future happiness should not be shadowed by the fear that your past may come to light. What would you say to a grant of land in one of the colonies across the sea?"

Morgan looked down at Desire, and she nodded her assent.

"I accept your generous gift—and most willingly, sire," said Morgan.

"Then we will arrange the formalities of the grant as soon as possible." The king relaxed and a smile touched his lips. "I've no doubt there'll be challenge enough in the New World, even for a man of your tempestuous nature, Trenchard."

He strode to the door, then paused for a moment. "It's growing late," he said. "And since there's been no opportunity to provide suitable quarters for you here at the palace, perhaps Mistress Guilford would be willing to share hers."

"Yes, indeed, sire!" Desire spoke without thinking, her answer coming from the heart. A moment later she blushed at the unseemly boldness of her words.

But His Majesty was already at the door, calling for Will Chiffinch.

When they reached her apartment, Libby was waiting up to help Desire prepare for bed. The maid stared round-eyed, and her lips parted in surprise at the sight of the tall, dark-haired man dressed in a torn, rain-splattered shirt and breeches. He kept an arm about Desire's waist as he stood looking about with complete self-assurance.

Eager to be alone with Morgan, Desire was about to dismiss Libby. Then all at once she smiled, her green eyes

379

dancing. She drew the startled Libby aside and spoke to her so softly that Morgan could not hear.

The maid stared at Morgan, curtseyed, and went quickly into the adjoining bath chamber, closing the door behind her. Desire unfastened her necklace and put it down on the dressing table.

"What's wrong with that girl? Why hasn't she stayed to help you disrobe?" Morgan asked.

"She has more important duties to attend to." She gave him an inviting half smile. "Perhaps you'll assist me—if you're not out of practice."

"My pleasure, madam," he said. His fingers moved swiftly, unbuttoning the bodice of Desire's elaborate gown. He paused to push aside her hair and touch his lips to the nape of her neck. She shivered at the delicious sensation. Then, wearing only her silk shift, she seated herself on the edge of the canopied bed. "Shoes and stockings next," she said.

Morgan knelt and took off her satin slippers and rolled down her stockings. He paused to press his mouth against the soft white flesh of her inner thigh. The warmth of his lips sent a tingling through her.

"How else may I serve you, my lady?"

Without giving her time to answer, he drew her shift higher and parted her legs. But she twined her fingers into his thick, dark hair and tugged hard. He made a sound of protest.

"Not yet," she said. He looked up at her, frustrated yet intrigued by the hint of laughter in her voice.

"You were eager enough to share your bedchamber with me," he reminded her.

She rose with one swift, fluid motion, and grasping his shoulders, turned him to face the mirror.

"Look at yourself," she said, with mock severity. "Shall I bed with such an uncouth creature? You must make your-self presentable first, and then perhaps . . ."

"You've been staying here at the palace too long. If you

think I'll start going about like one of these court fops, with ribbons on my breeches and perfumed gloves, you're much mistaken."

"Heaven forbid! I only thought that you might want to refresh yourself before coming to bed."

She encircled him with her arms and slid one hand inside his shirt. Her fingers tantalized him, moving from his chest to the arc of his ribs, then down along his flat belly.

Then she took his hand and he laughed softly as she led him into the bath chamber. Libby had filled the tub and left for the night.

"Surely you don't expect me to undress and bathe without the assistance of a few flunkeys," he said, his eyes challenging her.

"I'll serve you, my lord." She unbuttoned his shirt, trying to control her unsteady fingers. Then she unfastened his belt.

"I can still take off my own boots and breeches," he told her. He sat himself on a cushioned bench and proved it.

When she saw him standing there, with the candlelight playing over his broad-shouldered, narrow-hipped body, she was seized with a swift hunger. She was no longer sure she could go on with the game.

But Morgan was already striding toward the huge tub, and lowering himself into the water. He made a low sound of satisfaction as he submerged himself. Then he motioned to her with an imperious gesture.

"Come here, girl—if you're going to serve me, you may start by washing my back."

Barefooted, and wearing only her silk shift, she padded across the floor, to perch on the wide rim of the tub. She reached for a cloth, rubbed it with scented soap, then began to lave his muscled shoulders, then moved downward.

He nodded approval. "Not bad . . . for a start."

His voice sent a soft flurry of excitement through her. Under her shift her body started to tingle, and she felt a sensation like flowing warm honey moving in her loins.

381

Quickly she turned her attention to his chest, soaping the wet whorls of hair.

"Enough," he said, his tone low and husky. He took the cloth from her fingers dropped it into the tub. Then, encircling her waist with one arm, he held her firmly. His other hand went up under the hem of her shift and she gasped with pleasure as he began to stroke her thighs.

Her need grew as his wet fingers slid along her flesh. When he started his slow, sensuous exploration of her dark triangle, a quiver rippled through the length of her body.

His arm tightened around her, and she cried out as he began to ease her over the edge of the tub. She landed with a splash that sent the water running down the rose-colored marble in shining rivulets.

"My shift," she protested. The wet silk molded itself to her body, clinging to the curves of her breasts and hips.

Drawing up his knees, Morgan settled her on top of him with her back resting against his powerfully muscled thighs, while her legs straddled him. She looked down into the candlelit depths of the water and drew in her breath. He pulled her closer. She rocked her hips, savoring the friction of his hard manhood against the bud of her sensation.

When she could bear the tension no longer, she moved to take him inside her. She cried out softly as he thrust into her, filling her, overwhelming her senses with the delight of their joining.

He bent his head to nuzzle at her breasts through the wet silk of her shift. She rotated her loins, and now he was moving too. Ripples began to spread across the surface of the water in ever-widening circles.

Her sheath tightened around him and he quickened his thrusts, drawing her on to the edge of fulfillment. Together they shared the explosive release . . .

Long past midnight, Desire lay in Morgan's arms, drowsily contented after their loving. For the first time, she knew what it was to share the aftermath of passion without fear of what might lie ahead.

Morgan spoke softly, his cheek resting against the curve of her breast. "You know, I think His Majesty envied me when he saw us leave together."

"That was only your imagination," she said fondly, reaching up to stroke his hair. "With all those beautiful women vying for his favors?"

"There's not another like you, my love. And you belong to me — always."

He turned, and his lips found hers. The moonlight streaming in through the windows bathed the great bed in a silvery glow.

Soon they would be leaving England. They would set out across the sea to make a new beginning. But the thought did not trouble her. She gloried in the prospect of sharing a love no longer shadowed by the past. Morgan drew her closer, and she knew that whatever lay ahead, his arms would always be her home.